the MAGE'S MATCH

FINLEY FENN

This is a work of fiction. Names, characters, places, and incidents are the product of the author's imagination or are used fictitiously. Any resemblance to actual persons living or dead, business establishments, events, or locales is entirely coincidental.

The Mage's Match

Copyright © 2019 by Finley Fenn

info@finleyfenn.com

All rights reserved. No part of this book may be reproduced or transmitted in any form or by any means, electronic or mechanical, including photocopying, recording, or by any information storage and retrieval system without the written permission of the copyright owner, and where permitted by law.

No generative artificial intelligence (AI) was used in the writing of this work. The author expressly prohibits any entity from using this publication for purposes of training AI technologies to generate text, including without limitation technologies that are capable of generating works in the same style or genre as this publication. The author reserves all rights to license uses of this work for generative AI training and development of machine learning language models.

Cover design by Sylvia at The Book Brander

Sign up at www.finleyfenn.com for bonus stories and epilogues, delicious artwork, complete content guidance, news about upcoming books, and more!

ALSO BY FINLEY FENN

THE MAGES

The Mage's Maid

The Mage's Match

The Mage's Master

The Mage's Groom (Bonus Story)

ORC SWORN

The Lady and the Orc

The Heiress and the Orc

The Librarian and the Orc

The Duchess and the Orc

The Midwife and the Orc

The Maid and the Orcs

The Governess and the Orc

The Beauty and the Orcs

The Widow and the Orcs

The Artist and the Orc

Offered by the Orc

Tryggred by the Orc

Yuled by the Orcs

Tales of Orc Sworn

ORC FORGED

The Sins of the Orc

The Fall of the Orc

PROLOGUE

Regin Agmund's magic was, apparently, fucked.

"How unfortunate for him," Selby said politely, to the well-dressed, bespectacled customer who'd seemingly felt compelled to share the news. "Very upsetting."

"Indeed," the man replied, as he lifted a small statue of a bear, and inspected it. "His ability to serve our beloved Vakra has been severely impacted."

Selby bit back a snort, because said country of Vakra was probably only beloved to wealthy, well-placed men like him. Most certainly not to poor pedlar peons like herself, who could only hope to escape the scourge of overpowered, government-shill mages like Regin Agmund.

"Well, Agmund's supposed to be the strongest air-mage in the world, isn't he?" Selby said, taking care to keep her voice neutral. "I'm sure he'll come round. Will you take the bear? It's red soapstone, only three copper."

The man seemed to consider it, and turned the bear over in his fingers. Several of which were wearing heavy gold rings that—Selby's eyes narrowed—were likely worth more than the combined contents of her entire shop wagon.

"You are a mage yourself, are you not?" the man said, giving

Selby a long, measured look over his spectacles. "Earth, I hear?"

Selby's heartbeat stuttered, but she kept her eyes steady, her chin lifted. "You've heard where, sir?"

He didn't reply, just turned the bear over again, and Selby's heart pattered faster, stronger. People weren't supposed to hear about her magic. Not when it was at best suspicious and, at worst, quite possibly illegal. And most certainly not registered with the government, the way it was supposed to be.

They'd use you up and spit you out, her mother always said, and Selby shot a helpless glance over the man's shoulder, toward where their other wagon should have been. But her mother and Simon had taken it across the river, at Selby's urging, to try their luck in the next town over.

"I have connections, Ms. Seng," the man said, and Selby twitched at those words, that use of her name. "I belong to Vakra's esteemed Coven for Magical Advancement."

The Coven for Magical Advancement. Selby's mouth dropped open, her hands clenching on the wagon's little counter between them, because even she knew that was where the best mages in the country worked. Where Regin Agmund worked.

"And yes, I work with Mr. Agmund," the man continued, his words smooth, careful. "My name, in fact, is Klaus Ketill."

Selby gripped the counter harder, because the name Klaus Ketill was almost as well-known as that of the great Regin Agmund. Agmund was Klaus Ketill's protege, his greatest discovery, a rare true lightning-caster. And everyone knew that it was only thanks to Ketill and Agmund—and their terrifying lightning storms—that Vakra's entire government hadn't been overthrown by those brutal peasant uprisings, a few years back. They'd said Regin Agmund had walked in and electrocuted an entire army, with just a snap of his fingers.

"If you're truly Klaus Ketill," Selby said, her voice not quite steady, "what the hell are you doing here, at my shop?"

The corners of Ketill's mouth turned downwards—no doubt he was unused to being addressed with anything other than reverence—and he set the bear down on the counter. "I am here," he replied thinly, "because Regin's magic is weakening. Diminishing. Becoming unpredictable, unreliable, perhaps even dangerous."

Selby opened her mouth to ask, again, what the hell that had to do with her—but Ketill raised a hand, gave her a sharp, quelling look. "And," he continued, "every remedy attempted, every specialist consulted to date, has failed. Regin's magic, and therefore his usefulness, grows weaker by the day."

His usefulness. As though the great Regin Agmund could be reduced to a mere minion, rather than the most powerful air-mage in the world. And while Selby felt no warmth toward Agmund—gods knew, beyond the tales of his conquests, her only real exposure to him had been through his ubiquitous smug-faced portraits, and the atrocious prices people were willing to pay for them—she felt herself stiffening, her lip curling with a dislike that she couldn't quite hide.

"Yes, very unfortunate," she snapped, "as I've said. Remind me, Mr. Ketill, how this has anything whatsoever to do with me?"

Ketill drummed his fingers on the counter, making his gold rings clink together. "For the past year, our Coven has directed extensive research into solutions for Regin's—difficulties," he replied. "And our most recent conclusions have led us, Ms. Seng, to you."

To you. A shiver rippled up Selby's back, and she put her fingers to that soapstone bear, felt the solid, quiet substance of it, memories of an old woman who'd lived long ago. "With all due respect, Mr. Ketill," she said, "I'm a pedlar, and I have no magical training. I'm sure there's been some mistake."

Ketill's eyes were very cool, very calm. "Oh, we make no mistake, Ms. Seng. According to our extensive research, you have been clearly identified as having the closest affinity to Mr. Agmund of any other human on this continent."

Selby blinked at him, and her fingers gripped tighter on that bear, its images surging brighter in her thoughts. She knew of affinities, of course, everyone did, alignments of magic that led to better casting, better results. And yes, earth-magic was the usual corollary to air-magic, but—

"Affinities work through proximity, Mr. Ketill," Selby said, stupidly, because of course he'd be aware of that, wouldn't he? "And touch. You can't honestly be suggesting—"

She couldn't seem to finish, because no, that was absolutely ridiculous—but there was an unnerving, satisfied smile on Ketill's thin mouth. "I am making precisely this suggestion, Ms. Seng," he said. "I am here to offer you a temporary position—a three-month term, perhaps—on-site at the Coven's world-renowned research and training facility, Coven Manor, working with Regin Agmund."

That satisfaction deepened in his eyes, in his voice, like he was extending Selby some kind of—favour. Like she was supposed to be excited, or honoured, or something, but there was only a shocked, staring, unthinking disbelief.

"What?" Selby said blankly. "You mean—you want to ship me halfway across the entire *country*, just so I can follow this guy around? Hold his hand or something, while he casts his lightning spells?"

Ketill's smile twitched higher, into something condescending, almost mocking. "That wouldn't hurt, I'm sure. But for the full effect, the proximity required is of course rather more... intimate."

Intimate. Selby's hand clutched desperately at that bear, and somehow she laughed, the sound far too high-pitched, carrying across the clearing. "You can't honestly mean that," she said. "You want to offer me a job doing—going to *bed* with him? With *Regin Agmund*?"

Ketill nodded placidly, like such an appalling conclusion

were the most natural thing in the world. "Of course," he replied. "This is not an illegal transfer of magic—an activity our Coven would never condone—but rather a fundamental connection. A grounding and expansion of Regin's air-magic, via your earth-magic. A deep-seated intermixing of vital fluid and intimate bodily space."

The words were chaos in Selby's head, a ridiculous preposterous mess. Klaus Ketill wanted to hire *her*, at the *Coven for Magical Advancement*, so she could have a *deep-seated intermixing* with *Regin Agmund*?

"There's no way," Selby said, and thank the gods, the words came out crisp, clear, sure of themselves. "Absolutely not, Mr. Ketill. No."

"No?" Ketill repeated, white eyebrows rising over his spectacles, and Selby shook her head, hard enough that her thick black waves smacked her in the face. "Of course not," she snapped. "It's ridiculous. Why the hell would I abandon my family, my *life*, to move halfway across the country, and be some murdering air-mage's *harlot*?"

The frown etched deeper onto Ketill's face, his eyebrows furrowing hard together. "Regin does not *murder*, Ms. Seng," he said coldly. "And there are many excellent reasons to accept my offer. You will serve your country. You will receive fair compensation. And you will gain invaluable experience working for an *extremely* influential organization, doing *critically* important work!"

With the words, his eyes gave a swift, disdainful glance that encompassed both Selby's shop wagon, and her patchwork dress. As if to suggest that her current work—her current *existence*—was woefully inadequate when compared to the glowing alternative of fucking Regin Agmund.

And while Selby could admit—at least some days, and never to her mother—that the prospect of spending her life running the shop wagon wasn't exactly thrilling, at least it was honest work, for honest wages. And it didn't involve sacrificing herself—offering up her own *body*—so a smarmy, smug-faced, scourge-on-the-earth air-mage could get his poor lost magic back.

"No," Selby said, and even the word was a refuge, a relief. "I won't. Absolutely not."

Ketill looked dumbfounded, his mouth hanging comically open, and Selby took the chance to sweep the remaining items off her counter, and fold it back into the wagon.

"Now if you'll excuse me, I must be moving on," she added. "Best wishes to Mr. Agmund for a speedy recovery, and many more accolades, and portraits, and unjust murders, and so forth."

She closed the window's curtain without waiting for Ketill's reply, and noisily began packing away her things. Waiting, waiting, waiting for him to leave—but she could still see his silhouette out there, could still almost feel his cold, empty rage through the too-thin curtain.

"Farewell for now, Ms. Seng," Ketill said finally, though his tone set something prickling again, all down Selby's spine. "Please do let me know once you change your mind."

1

The Coven for Magical Advancement's principal facility was a huge old stone manor in the south, only two days' ride from Vakra's capital city.

It was a beautiful, isolated place, surrounded at first by broad swathes of dense forest, and then by rolling, manicured grounds. The main building itself was four stories high, looming grandly over its surrounding gates and outbuildings, and to Selby's untrained eyes, it looked far more like a lord's lofty country home than a facility for magical training and study.

And, also, it *reeked*.

The pedlar caravan had deposited Selby and her bags outside the manor's massive front gate, and she stood there staring at it, her hand clamped over her mouth. Buildings didn't *smell*. Did they?

"No soliciting," came a hard voice, and Selby blinked up at the gate's squat stone watchtower, and the grey-haired head of a man just visible inside it. "We don't tolerate pedlars here."

Selby shot a brief glance down toward her dress, which indeed clearly announced her as a pedlar, with its distinctive patchwork fabric and warm, practical layers. Pedlars came from many backgrounds—Selby's own parents had descended from separate countries across the sea—but this style of clothing had long ago become customary among them, and Selby certainly hadn't been about to bother with scrounging up new clothes, just for this.

But maybe she should have considered it, because while pedlars supplied much of Vakra's trade, they were still often viewed with mistrust, or even contempt. And it was already bad enough that Selby was even here, without the way this gatekeeper was looking at her, his beady eyes lingering on her voluminous skirts, and then on the large, heavy bags at her feet.

Selby pulled in a deep, shaky breath, and subsequently almost choked on it, because *gods*, this place smelled vile. "I'm not soliciting," she said, and shook her head, tried to think. "And look, can you smell that? *Feel* that?"

The frowning gatekeeper leaned out his little stone window, and pointed a stubby finger toward the nearby forest. "No," he snapped, "and we don't tolerate pedlars here. Get lost, girl."

Selby briefly considered it—was it valid grounds to run for the hills if the gatekeeper wouldn't let her in?—but now here was the vision, the still-curdling memory, of handing over that ten-page contract, and accepting that heavy, clinking bag in return.

Thank you, Ms. Seng, Klaus Ketill had said, with that awful smug smile on his thin mouth. *We will expect you at Coven Manor within a fortnight.*

He hadn't had to say *or else*, because that contract had said it all for him, and Selby pulled in another breath. "I'm here at the express invitation of Klaus Ketill," she said coldly. "And I expect he will be very displeased if I'm sent away."

The gatekeeper gave her another disbelieving once-over, as if to ask why in the gods' names Klaus Ketill would care about such an obvious inferior—but finally he trotted off toward the manor, leaving Selby still standing alone outside the gate, with her bags at her feet.

She frowned again at the building's massive stone bulk, and all its not-so-subtle hints of wealth and prestige. The windows were large and clear, the trim smart and freshly whitewashed, the grounds well-kept and impossibly green. There wasn't a single stone out of place, a single blemish to be seen.

Except. Selby eyed the gate again, and slowly, reluctantly reached a hand to touch at its smooth black iron. And then she yanked the hand away again, wringing it hard, sucking in air through her teeth. Gods *damn* it. She had to go in here? *Live* here?

She plunged her hand into her dress pocket, finding the small collection of stones she'd stashed there, and she gripped them tight, let herself sink into the steady ancient weight of them. She could do this. Three months, to attempt the impossible, and then walk away, and never come back.

"Ms. Seng!" came a voice, and with it was the grey-haired, flustered-looking form of a middle-aged woman, rushing toward the gate. "You're late. I'm Miss Oden, Coven Manor's second housekeeper."

Selby nodded politely, and pointedly ignored the gatekeeper as he finally cranked the iron gate up, barely high enough for her to scoot beneath. And there was no chance of him offering to carry her bags, of course, so Selby hoisted one over her shoulder, and dragged along the other behind her on the cobbled stone path.

"Mr. Ketill has asked me to give you a tour, and get you settled," Miss Oden said, as she hauled open the manor's heavy oak door. "Do come in."

Selby squared her shoulders, and followed Oden inside—but then she staggered backwards at the sudden, shocking wave of almost overpowering stink. Like someone had shoved her face into something rotten, and left her there to die in it.

"Uh, Miss Oden?" she managed, around her shallow breaths. "What's the smell?"

But Oden only gave Selby a wary, suspicious look over her shoulder. "The kitchens, you mean?" she asked. "Yes, Ms. Seng, our cooks make fresh bread every day. It's one of the many benefits of working in such a prestigious Coven facility."

She waved a hand at the admittedly prestigious entry hall, all vaulted ceilings and wood panelling and costly-looking paintings, but Selby shook her head, wrinkled her nose. "No, not bread," she replied. "It's something—off. Like something's—*died*."

Oden's expression was definitely contemptuous, now, and her hooked nose gave an audible sniff. "That's impossible," she said stiffly. "If there was a mess, or a dead rodent, making a smell, we would clean it immediately. We don't abide such things in a facility of this calibre."

The tone of those words suggested that they didn't only apply to dead rodents, and Selby sighed, and trudged after Oden around the manor's main floor. Which apparently had a dining hall, a meeting hall, a shared common room, a set of baths, and the department heads' offices—but Selby barely noticed any of it, beyond the ever-present stink, and now the curious, watching eyes of every single person they passed.

"Is that a *pedlar*?" came the too-audible murmurs as the clusters of well-dressed, pale-skinned strangers walked by. "What's a pedlar doing here?"

"Maybe it's for someone's research," one guy supplied, too loudly, with a snicker. "Or for charity."

But if she heard, Oden didn't let on, and escorted Selby up to the second floor, which was just as beautiful, and just as malodorous, as the first. "Here, Ms. Seng, you'll find the library, and our specialists' private workrooms," she said. "Most of our forty-odd specialists on site are self-directed young adults, usually already prodigies in their respective areas of study.

You'll have heard about several of them—Mr. Agmund, of course, is known all over the continent..."

Her voice kept droning on, but Selby had stopped listening, because her thoughts had caught on the *Mr. Agmund* part of all that. She'd been trying very, very hard not to think of Regin Agmund these past weeks—had been trying, in fact, to pretend he didn't exist at all—but suddenly here was the low, sinking dread of him, dragging deep in her gut.

Regin Agmund was *here*. The most powerful air-mage in the world—the destroyer of hundreds, maybe thousands, of human lives—was here, now, in this very building. And Selby's contract—Selby was here—because—

"Up here on the third and fourth floors," Oden chattered on, "are the bedrooms. Each mage has a private room, each with its own fully functional water closet, a true marvel of magical engineering..."

Selby's head was beginning to ache—the smell was so vile, like a constant assault on her nostrils, on any semblance of decency—and her bags had begun to feel very heavy. She'd packed way too much, and while that was such a pedlar thing to do, it had almost been a defense. Things of her own to cling to, to hold against this, three months, that was all...

It was all becoming a bit muddled in Selby's head, and she almost missed Oden's chattering about her new bedroom. And while part of Selby was busy rejoicing at the thought of a bedroom, a little spot to make her own, the other part of her followed Oden inside it, and came face to face with quite possibly the most appalling sight in the entire appalling place.

It was the unmistakable, highly unwelcome form of Mr. Regin Agmund himself.

2

Selby's first thought was that Regin Agmund was in her bedroom—why would Regin Agmund be in her bedroom?—and the second was that the artists who'd littered the landscape with overpriced Agmund portraits had perhaps been a bit too kind.

He looked every bit the powerful murdering air-mage—tall, striking, with cropped hair so blond it was almost white—but his nose was somewhat crooked, his jaw and cheekbones too sharp in his pale face. He looked too sharp all over, really, and it was only once Selby had decided this to her satisfaction that she realized Agmund was glaring at her, with obvious distaste in his deep blue eyes.

"*This* is the girl?" he demanded at Miss Oden, crossing his arms over his bony-looking chest. "Why didn't they tell me she was a—"

He stopped before he said it, thank the gods, because the room had already begun to spin slowly behind him, and Selby had to close her eyes, grip at those stones in her pocket. Feel the earth, feel the depth, shove back the pounding in her skull, plug the stench in her nostrils. This was a done deal. Three months.

"Yes, I'm a pedlar, you'll have noticed," Selby said, trying, and failing, for a smile. "And my family isn't originally from here, though we've lived in Vakra for generations now. My name's Selby Seng, by the way."

Agmund didn't smile, and if anything he looked even more displeased, more forbidding, than before. "Yeah, they told me the name, at least," he snapped, his blue eyes settling back on Oden. "And Oden, why've *you* brought her in, rather than Ketill? Or Morley, or Argusson?"

Oden looked distinctly ruffled, muttering excuses about various people's necessary absences, and there was the sobering, but unsurprising, realization that new recruits were probably supposed to get special treatment, or at least some kind of proper welcome from the higher-ups. Not a secret drop-off by a caravan, and a furtive backstairs tour by the second housekeeper.

Somebody was laughing—not Agmund, at least—and when Selby glanced toward the source of it, she nearly dropped her bags at the sight of the other people in the room. Gods, there had to be six—no, eight—of them, guys and girls both, all likely in their twenties. And all lurking around behind Agmund, and looking at Selby with unfriendly eyes.

"You can't see why they had Oden let her in?" asked one of the girls, as she tossed her long blonde hair over her shoulder, and stepped forward to put a light, familiar hand to Agmund's arm. "I mean, *really*, Regin."

Oh. *Oh*. Selby couldn't help a searching, darting look downwards, because damn it, even discounting her obvious pedlar ensemble, her full week of intensive travelling had done her no favours. Her bags were wet and stained, her dress and boots were smeared with mud, and her heavy patchwork cloak had ripped along the way, bitten by a cranky caravan donkey.

But it wasn't just that, Selby thought, with another swift glance at the rest of the room's occupants. Like everyone else she'd seen in this place so far, they were all tall and well-fed, and their clothes hung off their bodies like they'd been properly made for them, and not handed down like most of Selby's clothes had been. And none of them had anything like Selby's wavy black hair or light brown skin, either, and if her head came up to any of their noses, she'd be amazed, or elevated, or something.

The blonde girl leaned closer into Agmund, slipping an arm behind him to whisper something in his ear, and that was even more mess in Selby's head, more offal in her nostrils. Was this Agmund's—girlfriend? And why hadn't Selby considered the fact that Agmund would have a girlfriend, or perhaps even several of them? He was the most famous and deadly mage in the entire world, he could certainly take his pick of them, and why would she have ever thought otherwise?

Selby was beginning to feel truly nauseous, now, and she turned abruptly to Oden, whose cheeks had flushed a deep shade of pink. "Th-thank you for the tour, Miss Oden," she stammered, "but I thought you were going to show me to my room?"

Oden's face went even pinker, if that was possible, and one of Agmund's other hangers-on let out a snicker. Leaving Selby feeling entirely lost, not for the first time in this ongoing nightmare, and she fumbled desperately for the stones in her pocket, her hand shaky enough that three of the stones fell out, and bounced about on the smooth tiled floor.

She'd still been holding one of her bags, but she had to drop it to rush for the stones. And maybe she should have better considered what that might look like, because more than one of the hangers-on began giggling loudly, and not kindly.

"Look at her, on her knees for you already, Regin," a brown-haired guy said, with a snort. "Getting in some practice."

One of the stones had rolled dangerously close to Agmund's booted foot, and though Selby should have left it, at the moment those damned stones were the only thing keeping her together, and the thought of losing even one in this horrible place felt like a sacrilege. But once she'd finally clutched that last stone in her fingers, and stood up again, the rest of the room's occupants were all openly laughing at her. Even Oden, and even Agmund, though his eyes stilled a little when Selby stared at them.

"Look, the rest of you get on to supper," Agmund said, waving a hand toward the door. "I'll catch up in a minute."

The hangers-on glanced at each other, but then shuffled past Selby, and out the door behind her. Even Oden scuttled off, leaving Selby alone with Agmund, and also with the blonde girl, who hadn't gone on to anywhere.

"You go too, all right?" Agmund said, with an over-familiar brush of his hand against the girl's shoulder, while Selby belatedly looked down, and gripped at her stones. Regin Agmund's girlfriend, in the same building, no doubt straight across the damned corridor. Three months.

The girl strode out, shutting the door loudly behind her, and when Selby looked up again, it was only Agmund left. Standing there and looking at her, and she didn't miss the quick flick of those blue eyes all the way down her frame, and back up again.

"Listen, Seng," Agmund said abruptly, his voice curt. "I want you to know that this is a business deal, and that's *all*. I didn't choose you, I had nothing to do with bringing you here, and this sure as hell isn't your once-in-a-lifetime chance to get cozy with a celebrity. And if I *ever* catch you trying to profit off any of this"—he waved at him, her, the room—"you're out, for good. And I won't give a damn."

Well. If that wasn't just about the worst thing he could have possibly said, at this point, and Selby had to make her eyes keep looking at him. Needed to get through this, three months to attempt the impossible, and then…

"Yes, I understand quite well, thanks," she said, with as much composure as she could muster. "I'll do my best to stay out of your way, if that's your preference."

Agmund grimaced, his blue eyes glowering at the wall behind her. "Yeah, well, that's not going to be so easy, because they've shoved you in here with me," he snapped. "And there's only one bed"—his hand gave a sharp wave toward it—"and I'm not sleeping on the floor, so I hope to hell you're used to it."

Right. The floor was made of hard stone tiles, with no softening rugs to be seen, but Selby had slept on far worse this past week, and at least she still had her cloak. And maybe she could ask someone, somewhere, for a bedroll, though she couldn't seem to look up from the floor now, not even as Agmund stepped purposefully around her, and went for the door.

"Don't touch my stuff," his flat voice said over his shoulder, before he slammed the door shut behind him. Leaving Shelby standing alone in the middle of this room, this ongoing nightmare, with her hands over her face, her breath dragging in the foul smell with every gasp, her stomach roiling with the revolting taste of it.

And it was just in time that she saw the adjacent water closet, with its own latrine, thank the gods. And in two lurching steps she was there, on her knees, and vomiting up her guts into it.

3

Selby's stint in Agmund's water closet lasted longer than she would have liked to admit. Her entire body had seemed to rise up in revolt at this awful place, and when she finally staggered back into the main bedroom, it was with trembly feet, and a foul-feeling mouth, and swollen, scratchy eyes.

But her thoughts had come around again, at least. And the topmost of those, the most insistent, was that no matter what Agmund said, or did, her own options hadn't changed. She'd signed that contract. Spent the coin. And given the Coven enough exposure to her magic to be tracked all over the continent, no matter where she went.

And while there was still the faint, nagging hope that maybe Agmund would put a stop to the whole deal, there was also the truth that he'd clearly known, too. That Selby hadn't been a surprise—other than her pedlar clothes, and the shade of her skin—and that Agmund would have had plenty of time to lodge any number of complaints before she'd turned up in his bedroom.

The bedroom was still empty, thankfully, and Selby glanced around it in the rapidly dimming light from its large, clear window. Objectively, it was a lovely room, with its wood-panelled walls and flawless tiled floor. And its furnishings—a bookcase, a desk, a wardrobe, the bed—all appeared to be by the same skilled maker, all well crafted costly hardwood.

But the *smell*. It lingered here, in this lovely room, just as much as it had in the rest of the place. And while a vindictive part of Selby wanted to blame Agmund for that, she was certain that it went well beyond him. Whatever the smell was, it was part of the entire manor, burned deep into the bones of it.

She looked again around the room, this time letting her eyes linger on the smaller things, the personal effects that claimed this place as the great Regin Agmund's. There was less to see than she'd expected—though of course, her expectations on that front were probably rather skewed—and she stepped closer to the bookcase, which seemed to hold the bulk of it. There were a few books, a few knives. A comb. A leather purse. An amber pendant.

And even as Selby's memory darted back to Agmund—*don't touch my stuff*, he'd said—her fingers reached out, seemingly on their own, and brushed up against the pendant. Only briefly, but still more than enough to spark a flurry of smells and images and tastes in her thoughts.

First, and strongest, was the earth, far to the east in Sifjar, where the amber had lived for so long, raw and untouched. And then there was the miner who had hacked it out, briefly gripping it as he'd tossed it into a cart, and then the refiner, who'd pried it from its surrounding stone. And after that the craftsman, who'd painstakingly transformed it into the distinctive hammer shape of the pendant.

And then, many years past, was the man who'd worn it. A tall, burly man with white-blond hair, who'd spent his days hunting and trapping, often with his small blond son in tow. And during the man's final sickness, he'd put this pendant into his son's hand, and his son had sobbed over it for weeks, months, powerful enough to infect it all through with the strength of his grief.

Too late Selby snatched her hand away, squeezing her eyes shut, but the knowledge was still there, parading through her thoughts. Regin Agmund had loved his father. Regin Agmund had no mother. Regin Agmund had spent years being shuffled around from one relative to another, until the magical day when Klaus Ketill had come.

It didn't fit how it was supposed to, and Selby gave a hard shake of her head, and trailed her fingers over the rest of Agmund's possessions, one by one. The leather purse was an expensive gift, from Agmund's blonde girlfriend, and that *did* fit how it was supposed to, Agmund smiling lazily toward her beautiful face as he opened an expensively wrapped box. The books were all air magic spellbooks, rare, but with only the barest trace of Agmund on their pages. And the knives, like most weapons, made Selby flinch, and take several long, cleansing breaths—but they hadn't been recently used, at least, and any kills they'd made hadn't been at Agmund's hands.

Next Selby's fingers traced the bookcase itself, lingering on the blessed, uncomplicated vision of maple and woodcutter and craftsman. The wardrobe felt the same, but a quick, furtive touch inside it at Agmund's clothes sent another furious flurry of images through her thoughts. This time all smooth skin and lean muscle, singed hair and crackling heat. Deep, delicious magic and deft, deadly competence.

Selby's cheeks had gone strangely warm, and she snatched her hand back, opening and closing her fingers. Taking one look over her shoulder at the bed, and then a step toward it—but no, no, she did *not* need to go there, and instead she pressed her hand flat up against the nearest wall.

And even though she'd expected it, the odious, pungent taste behind that wall was still enough to immediately set the nausea roiling again. But there were no distinct images, or hints as to why this would be—and it was as Selby was considering that, frowning, that the door slammed open behind her.

She jumped and whirled around, and found herself once again faced with the disconcerting sight of Regin Agmund. He was alone, still tall and pale and sharp-looking, and Selby couldn't stop her cheeks from heating, couldn't pull her eyes away.

He wasn't looking back—his eyes were intently avoiding her—but in his clenched hand was something that looked blessedly like a bedroll. And as Selby stared, he tossed it toward her, where it bounced to a stop at her feet.

"Here," he said, voice curt. "I go to bed early, and I'll expect you to do the same. No moving around or making noise, or you'll be sleeping out in the hall."

Well. Selby was usually a sound sleeper, and as far as she knew, she never snored. And, Agmund had brought her a bedroll, and a decent-looking one at that, so this was somewhat promising, wasn't it?

"Would you mind if I unpacked a few of my things?" Selby asked, before she lost the nerve. "Could I keep them near my bed?"

Agmund's eyes had settled on Selby's overfull bags—they were still sitting in the middle of the room, where she'd left them—and his lip curled into an unmistakable sneer.

"A *few* things," he replied, with heavy emphasis on the *few*. "You're not cluttering up my room with your pedlar junk."

Oh. Selby's body stilled for an instant, and she had to reach into her pocket again, clutch for her stones. They were still there, still strong and deep and familiar, and she took a breath, met Agmund's eyes. He was a rich, arrogant, murdering airmage—he'd killed hundreds, *thousands*, of people—and the fact that he'd loved his father long ago didn't mean squat.

"Is there somewhere I can keep my clothes, at least?" she asked coldly. "And a place I can put my bags, to keep them out of your way?"

Agmund's hand came up to rub at his face, his eyes gone even more contemptuous. "You can pile your clothes in the bottom of the wardrobe, but the rest of it has to go," he snapped. "Leave it out for the servants, they'll put it down in the storage room."

Selby flinched, because was Agmund really asking—really telling—her to be away from her things? To put them in some distant storage room, where she couldn't feel them, and they could be tainted, or lost, or stolen?

But Agmund didn't care, that was clear, and he stalked past Selby into the water closet, and slammed the door. Leaving her to silently curse under her breath as she set up her new bedroll by the bookcase, as far from Agmund's bed as possible. And since Agmund's books and possessions weren't nearly enough to merit his having the bookcase in the first place, its entire two bottom shelves were empty, and therefore seemed as good a place as any for Selby's things.

But only a few things, Agmund had said, and what did that mean, anyway? Two? Four? Probably not more than five, that was certain, but even a precursory look through Selby's bags showed her well over five things that she couldn't bear to lose.

There was the beautiful carved chest, created and cared for by a woman in a far-off land, that held Selby's father's ashes. There were the delicate white shells, speaking their stories of the sea, of the funny little creatures that had once inhabited them. There was a small collection of hair and bones, remnants of people and animals Selby had loved. And of course, there were the stones. Mountain stones, sea stones, fire stones, sky stones...

In the end, Selby put away most of the stones, but kept out the chest, and the lock of her mother's thick black hair, along with the cleverly carved wooden whistle her brother Simon had given her before she'd left. And finally, despite her hesitations—Agmund wasn't likely to approve—she set out the precious little white dog-skull, that even now, years after

Scarper had died, still radiated his love and warmth and affection, simple and strong and whole.

It felt better, having it all out and visible again, and Selby could almost taste the tiny pocket of clear air it carved out in her little corner of the room. And when Agmund stalked out again, looking freshly scrubbed and still angry, Selby met his eyes, and held her head high as she walked past him into the water closet, sleeping-shift in hand.

When she came back out the room was dark, and the curtains closed, blocking out most of the dim evening light. And Agmund himself was in bed, barely visible in the shadows, with his back toward her, straight and silent and forbidding.

That was that, then, and Selby slid into her own makeshift bed on the floor. There was no pillow or blanket, but she pulled over her cloak, and despite its still-grimy state, it was warm and familiar too, whispering quietly of home and her mother and Simon. Soothing enough that Selby could almost think again, and she turned on the bedroll, and looked at the dim outline of Agmund's sharp shoulder under his blanket.

He wasn't asleep yet, judging by the too-rapid rise and fall of his breath. And for an instant, there was the jolting, almost irrepressible urge to speak, and say aloud the questions that had become almost too strong to be ignored.

Why does this place smell like it does? Selby wanted to ask. *What has happened in it? And why did you agree to have me come here, if you're clearly so opposed? Why are you even now sleeping here, with me on the floor, when your girlfriend most certainly wouldn't have refused you room with her?*

And then, deeper still: *Do you still think of your father? Do you still miss him? How did you change from that lonely boy into the most powerful air-mage in the world?*

But Agmund didn't move, and Selby lay quietly back, and stared at the ceiling, and didn't say anything at all.

4

Selby did not sleep well.

It was bad enough that the stink of the place seemed to rise in the night, growing more and more pungent with every passing hour. But making it even worse was Agmund, who, after finally falling asleep, proceeded to toss and turn and kick throughout the night, going so far as to throw all his blankets on the floor, and set off a series of lightning storms in the direct vicinity of Selby's head.

It had been shocking, the first time, and thoroughly terrifying, to feel the air above her crackle and shift and charge. And even more alarming had been the sparks, and flashes of light, slowly growing stronger with every twitch from Agmund in his bed. And the first time a spark had actually forked to the floor—lightning striking, in a *bedroom*, complete with a little crack of thunder—Selby had had to cover her mouth to keep from screaming, or sobbing, or hurling the few remaining contents of her stomach all over Agmund's floor.

The lightning finally receded, enough that Selby settled down again, and tried in vain to sleep—until it started up again, and again. And continued, throughout most of the night, and by morning Selby was grimly convinced that yes,

Agmund's magic was fucked, and also, that it was no wonder he hadn't slept in his girlfriend's damned bedroom.

When Agmund finally sat up in bed and yawned, Selby was tired enough, and irritable enough, to sit up too, and cross her arms over her chest. "You couldn't have warned me?" she demanded. "Not even a *Hey, by the way, my magic might kill you in your sleep*?"

The look Agmund gave her was distasteful, and a little bit revolted, like she was some kind of beetle that had inadvertently crawled into his room. "It won't kill you," he snapped. "At this range you'd get a shock, at worst. And besides, isn't this why you're supposed to be here?"

Isn't this why. So they were talking about this, then, and Selby blinked at him, distantly noting that wisps of his cropped blond hair were still standing on end, like the electricity hadn't quite yet gone away. "Um, right," she said, as her thoughts swarmed with the vision of that contract, and its ten pages of stipulations. "My, uh, proximity. Supposed to help. And all."

It came out sounding awkward, and also ridiculous, because so far, all Selby had done was annoy Agmund, and take up space in his bedroom, and almost get electrocuted while he slept. And Agmund obviously was in full agreement, because he gave a snort, and strode off to the water closet without saying another word.

Selby twitched at the sound of the door slamming, and put her hand back to Scarper's skull, thankfully still within easy reach of her bed. She had to do this. She would get through this. Three months.

But the smell was still there, and the exhaustion just made it worse. And by the time Selby had dressed, and rolled up her bed, and piled her clothes inside the bottom of Agmund's wardrobe, her head was aching again, and her stomach had resumed its protests, too. None of which was helped by Agmund, who came back out of the water closet wearing a fresh set of clothes, and stormed out of the room without looking back.

He'd left the door open, at least, and after a long moment's staring at it, Selby brushed off her wrinkled dress, and followed him out. And even though Agmund had gone out of her view, she was unsettled to discover that following him presented no challenge whatsoever, thanks to the sparking, crackling feeling he left trailing in the air behind him.

The wood-panelled corridor was empty, at least, and Selby trailed her fingers along the wall as she walked. It smelled just as bad here as in Agmund's bedroom—worse, even—and she was so preoccupied by the increasing stink that she barely noticed that she'd gone down three flights of stairs, and around yet another wood-panelled corner, and straight into the manor's main dining room.

Oden had pointed out the dining room during their tour—it had distinctive arched windows, and a smart black-and-white checkered floor—but it hadn't looked nearly so large before, or so intimidating. Because it had been empty then, and it was most certainly not empty now. And it seemed to have fallen entirely silent, as nearly every single one of the multiple heads inside it turned around to gape at her.

Damn it. Selby froze in place, and she could feel her face burning, her stomach roiling, while the entire room looked their fill. Staring at her pedlar clothes, no doubt, and probably her hair and skin too, and already there were the low gasps, the whispers. The eyes looking purposely across the room toward where Agmund was sitting, surrounded by his friends, with the blonde girl by his side.

Selby gritted her teeth and spun around, fully intending to walk straight out again, when at her shoulder appeared someone else. Someone who was entirely too familiar, and Selby flinched at the sight of his smug, bespectacled face.

"Ms. Seng," Klaus Ketill said, with a not-quite-genuine

smile in his grey eyes. "How delightful to see you again. Shall we?"

He waved toward the dining room as he spoke, and there seemed to be no choice but to sigh and nod, and follow him over to the counter where two women were dishing out plates of food. "Breakfast for Ms. Seng," Ketill said firmly. "Your best, ladies."

Both women curtsied, and Selby was soon presented with an overfilled plate of meat and eggs and rubbery green things. Some looking familiar, but some entirely new, and Selby warily eyed them as Ketill steered her toward an empty table, apart from the rest.

"How has your stay with us been so far, Ms. Seng?" he asked, once he'd seated himself across from her on one of the room's many long wooden benches, which, Selby distantly noted, tasted of many unfamiliar people, and many meals eaten. "I hope you've been made to feel welcome?"

Selby's brief glance upwards found that most of the room's occupants had returned to eating, with the notable exceptions of the blonde girl, watching them with cool eyes, and the guy who'd made the rude comments in Agmund's room the day before. And Agmund himself, sitting between them, his eyes narrow and stony on Ketill's back.

"Not exactly, sir," Selby said flatly, as she poked her fork at some of the green things on her plate. "You neglected to inform me that Agmund would not welcome my presence here."

Ketill's smile went fixed, and his hands folded carefully together on the table in front of him. He hadn't gotten any breakfast for himself, and it occurred to Selby that he'd come down here just to meet her, maybe just to make a point.

"Regin can be—difficult, at times," he replied smoothly. "But he realizes very well the importance of this. He'll do as he's told."

That didn't sound promising, and Selby surreptitiously touched a finger to one of the green things, which had apparently been grown in water. "But he already has a girlfriend," she countered. "And I have absolutely zero desire to—to get in the middle of that."

Ketill gave a dismissive wave of his hand, his gold rings glittering in the light of the room's tall windows. "Regin has agreed that this project is of prime importance," he said. "And therefore, he has agreed to take a full hiatus from intimate relations with all other parties during the length of your contract. You may be assured that he and Ms. Hendersson have severed their relationship."

Severed their relationship. And while that should probably have been a comforting thought—at least in terms of preventing Selby from catching some sort of air-mage infection—it almost seemed to make it worse. Far worse, in fact, because that meant Agmund had dumped his girlfriend just for her, and how the hell would his girlfriend feel about *that*?

But Ketill appeared entirely unconcerned, and before Selby could protest further, he'd glanced over his shoulder toward Agmund, and his finger crooked in a sharp, imperious gesture. Meaning, *come here*.

For an instant, based on the vicious flash in Agmund's eyes, Selby was certain he was going to refuse, and there'd be some kind of air-mage brawl in the dining hall over breakfast—but then he stood, his movements jerky and stiff, and came to sit on the bench next to Ketill. He didn't meet Selby's eyes, but he wasn't looking at Ketill, either.

"What," he snapped. "Sir."

Ketill smiled, though again it didn't reach his eyes. "Good morning to you too, Regin," he replied blandly. "Ms. Seng has just been telling me of the welcome she's received here so far."

Gods damn it. Selby should have been happy Ketill was taking her part—he had an obligation, really—but at the same time, Agmund was looking at her with even more distaste, more dislike, than before. And if she was going to get through this—she *had* to get through this—the last thing she needed was to make even more of an enemy out of Agmund than she somehow already had.

"I'm sure you recall our discussions on this subject, Regin," Ketill continued, his voice calm, remote. "Considerable resources have been expended on finding and recruiting Ms. Seng to support you. If you wish to retain your position with the Coven, you will accept her presence, and be grateful for it."

Selby's whole body stilled, and it felt like something cold, and then hot, had been poured down her back. *If you wish to retain your position.* So Agmund truly *hadn't* wanted this, then? And the only reason he was tolerating it was because he didn't want to lose his *job*?

"Wait, Mr. Ketill, sir," Selby's voice interjected, too loudly. "If Mr. Agmund is unwilling, I would far rather be dismissed. I don't want to be part of anything that isn't by choice."

The words were followed by silence, and then Ketill and Agmund looked at each other, with something Selby couldn't read passing between them. Something that left Ketill looking smug, and Agmund almost sulky, or defiant.

"I'm willing," Agmund said, voice flat. "I just expected something—different."

Something different. Something that wasn't a pedlar, surely, and Selby looked very intently at her plate, and clutched at the bench beneath her, so hard her fingers hurt.

"Well, this is where we are, Regin," came Ketill's clipped voice. "So I suggest you make the best of it. Have the two of you attempted copulation yet? Or any kind of physical contact?"

Selby's stomach lurched, but a glance up at Agmund showed him looking still sulky, eyes narrow and angry. "No, sir," he said. "I was waiting for Seng to get settled. Also, I thought you said you were going to have a healer look her over first."

The heat flooding Selby's face felt almost painful, made even worse by the cool, dispassionate way Ketill glanced toward her. "Yes, Holben is expecting her," he replied. "I assure you, Regin, she will be cleared of infections, and a reliable birth control spell applied."

Agmund didn't look reassured—quite the opposite, really—but he nodded, and that was another flicker of satisfaction across Ketill's grey eyes. "Excellent," he said. "I'll escort Ms. Seng there now, and the procedure should only take a few moments. Afterwards, I suggest you two meet back upstairs, and make a good effort of it. Report to me once you've finished, Regin, ideally by noon."

Agmund was actually nodding again—actually agreeing to this?—and he stood to his feet, scraping the bench out under him. "Sir," he said, and then he stalked away toward the door, as several of his friends jumped up to trail along behind him.

"Not to worry, Ms. Seng," said Ketill's smooth voice. "Regin may be difficult, but by all accounts, he's not a brute in the bedroom. If you tell him it's your first time, I'm certain he will make every attempt to be solicitous."

Oh, would he now? And that was probably supposed to be reassuring, but suddenly Selby was just flat-out furious, so angry she nearly spat straight into Ketill's smug, condescending air-mage face.

"This is *appalling*, Ketill," she hissed. "You didn't tell Agmund I was a pedlar? And you didn't tell *me* that he wants nothing to do with me, or that he sets off deadly lightning storms at night, or that you made him dump his girlfriend for me? And now you're ordering me to go up there and pretend like everything is just fine, and fuck his brains out anyway, and wait for his magic to miraculously come back again?!"

Ketill's eyebrows lifted, and there was a tight little set to his mouth. "We were very clear with you about our expectations, Ms. Seng," he coldly replied. "You accepted this position willingly, without coercion, and Regin approved it under the same circumstances. Are you suggesting that you wish to renege on your contract, and pay the subsequent penalties? Do you need me to remind you what those penalties are?"

Gods damn him, the bastard, and Selby dragged in one breath, and another. "No, I remember them very clearly. Full and immediate repayment of funds exchanged, to be paid with my own labour as required."

Ketill replied with a chilly, unnerving smile. "They were generous terms, Ms. Seng," he said. "And I'm sure you'll recall, as well, our discussions around discretion? Especially concerning certain controversial—*characteristics*—of your magic? Which *some* close-minded people may interpret as an unethical invasion of privacy, or perhaps even a dangerous violation of the law?"

His eyebrows went up again, as if challenging Selby to counter that, but there was no countering it, damn him. Not only was seeing other people's thoughts and memories a highly suspect—and officially nonexistent—branch of magic, but it was also one that could look a hell of a lot like transferring the magic itself between users. An activity that was *extremely* illegal, since it so often ended up with people dead—and though Selby had never done such a thing, a lot of people wouldn't be able to tell the difference. And this slimy bastard knew it.

"Indeed," Ketill said smugly. "Thank you, Ms. Seng. You are doing your country a great service."

There was no possible reply to that either, but Ketill clearly didn't expect one, and he swept grandly to his feet, and brushed off nonexistent dirt from his spotless white robe.

"Come along to the healer, now," he said. "And afterwards, please"—he once again gave that cold, terrifying smile—"do try and enjoy yourself."

5

Twenty minutes later, after a mercifully painless stint in Mr. Holben's office, Selby trudged back up the stairs to Agmund's bedroom, her thoughts jolting with every endless step.

Don't do this, they shouted. *Turn around. Run away. This place is vile. Agmund hates you. This is never going to work.*

Harlot.

Selby had to stop on a landing for an instant, fight that last one back down, because she'd already gone through this, already made up her mind. Sex workers were just people, making their way, just like everyone else. They didn't deserve her judgement, and she wasn't going to judge herself over this, either. She was just doing a job. Doing what she'd agreed to do. That was all.

But even so, she had to make herself keep climbing, her steps shuffling against the stairs. What was she supposed to say to Agmund? What was she supposed to do? What *did* people do, with this? What would it even—feel like?

She winced, squeezing her eyes shut, but the question was still there, too loud, too powerful. Because Ketill had been right, utter bastard that he was, and in all Selby's twenty-three years, she still didn't—know. She'd never actually gone all the way with someone in bed before. Which meant that yes, Regin Agmund was about to be the first.

It wasn't that there hadn't ever been anyone else, because there had been—but when even chaste touching set off a firestorm of images in one's head, and a highly concerning degree of obsessive-compulsive attachment to whoever was doing the touching, intimacy was dangerous. A potential catastrophe.

And Selby had told that to Ketill, the second time he'd made the offer. But he'd just kept asking, and she'd kept on refusing, again and again and again, until—

She shook her head, hard, and made herself reach for the closed door of Agmund's bedroom. He was already there waiting, she could taste it, and she gave a long, shaky exhale as she pushed the door open, and stepped inside.

The room was dimly lit—the curtain was closed again—and Agmund was indeed there. Here. Sitting on the edge of his bed, wearing all his clothes, and looking at her.

There was just as much dislike in his eyes as there'd been on every other occasion they'd met so far, and though Selby should have been accustomed to it by now, she still felt her steps hesitating, faltering in the middle of the room. Her face was hot, her hands clammy, and her heartbeat was pounding louder, her thoughts still shouting along with every beat of it. *No. Run. Harlot.*

Agmund didn't speak, didn't move, and now there was the grim, terrifying certainty that he wasn't going to make this easy for her. This was going to be all on her, no doubt every awful, humiliating moment of it, and Selby squared her shoulders, and dragged up the last, pathetic dregs of her courage.

"You're sure about this?" she managed, her voice wavering in the silence. "Really sure?"

But Agmund only shrugged, and his eyes gave a dismissive little roll that spoke very clearly for him. *Of course I'm sure*, he meant. *Why else do you think I'm sitting here on my bed in the dark, waiting for you.*

Selby had to make herself keep looking at him, and she pulled in another long, unsteady breath. "And you're sure," she made herself say, "that you and your girlfriend are over, for good? You're not—cheating on her, with me?"

Agmund's lip curled, his blue eyes gone dismissive, perhaps even contemptuous. "Yeah, she was completely thrilled with this," he replied, his voice flat, and laced with obvious sarcasm. "No. We're done. Obviously."

Well. Selby didn't know whether to be insulted, or relieved, and she pulled in a breath, let it out. "Well, should I get undressed, then?" she asked. "Or just—"

She gave a vague wave down at her dress, because living her entire life with almost-zero privacy, she'd long ago learned that one didn't need to be unclothed to manage these things. But Agmund's eyes frowned at Selby's patchwork dress, maybe not wanting such an obvious pedlar item to touch his pristine pale body, and he gave a telltale little wave of his hand. *Get rid of it*, it meant.

Right. Selby's heart pounded louder, and her jittery hands carefully went to the dress's long row of large, mismatched buttons. Undoing them one by one, all the way down her front, revealing the fine, too-thin linen of the white shift beneath.

The shift was knee-length, form-fitting, with thin straps over the shoulders, and Selby could feel Agmund's eyes on it as she let the dress fall to the floor. It wasn't the kind of thing a pedlar usually wore, far too fine and costly, but her shifts were the one thing Selby had insisted on having new, and specially made to fit, with her own careful choice of fabric. Because when you could feel your clothes whispering to you all day long, speaking of their fibres and makers and previous wearers every time you moved, you needed something decent to keep the worst of it off you, to keep from losing your damned mind.

Agmund was still looking at the shift, his eyes lingering

rather longer than Selby would have expected, and she kicked off her short leather boots—the last thing she'd been wearing, beyond the shift—and put a trembly finger to the thin strap on her shoulder.

"Should I?" she said, thickly. "Keep going, I mean?"

There was an instant's silence, during which Selby's heartbeat thudded ever louder in her ears—but then Agmund gave a quick, purposeful shake of his head. Saying, *No, don't, leave it.*

Selby wasn't sure if that made it better, or worse, but she was doing this now, and at this point she just wanted to get it the hell over with. "Do you want to do it on the bed, then?" she made herself ask. "Lying down, or—"

She couldn't seem to finish, because the vision of Agmund pulling up her shift, and perhaps bending her over that desk, was making her heart fight to escape up her throat—but Agmund only gave a jerky shrug, and then dropped himself down onto his back on the bed, and closed his eyes.

Oh. Selby stared at it, at him, and waited—but he didn't open his eyes, didn't move. Which meant, again, that this was on her, and she forced one bare foot to pad forward, and then the other. Until she was standing there, right next to the bed, looking down at the long, lean form of Regin Agmund on it. His mouth set, his eyelashes pale and thick against his skin, his white throat bobbing as he swallowed.

And it was that small movement, oddly enough, that seemed to shift something in Selby's thoughts. Darting back to that amber pendant on the shelf, and the truth that Regin Agmund had loved his father, if nothing else.

The hammering thud of her heartbeat had receded slightly, and after another long, bracing breath, she carefully put a knee onto the bed. Which—thank the gods—had recently been thoroughly changed and aired, and mostly whispered of Agmund the night before, sweaty and writhing, miserable flares of electricity in the dark...

Selby drew in yet another deep breath, and settled her

other knee beside the first on the bed. Leaving her perched there precariously beside him, not quite close enough to touch.

Agmund still didn't look at her, or make any move to touch her, and Selby's eyes lingered on the heavy fabric of his grey trousers, still safely fastened around his waist. And though maybe she should be dealing with that, or touching him—or something—she couldn't make her hand move, couldn't do anything but sit there and stare.

"Do you—" she began, but her voice broke, and she pulled in more air, tried again. "Do you want me to touch you?"

Agmund's chest under his fine tunic rose and fell, showing Selby the too-clear rows of his ribs, the low concave of his belly beneath them. He was so tall, and so damned thin, and again there was a strange lurch of—something, in Selby's thoughts.

And then, without warning, Agmund's hands moved. Fumbling a little as they went to the drawstring on his trousers, yanking out the knot. And then shoving the trousers downwards, just enough to expose—oh.

It was small, pale, soft-looking, surrounded by light brown curls. And as Selby stared, Agmund put his hand to it, lifting it, fisting his long fingers around it. Almost concealing it from view, but then—Selby's breath caught—he slid his hand up, and up, and up again.

He was coaxing himself to hardness, Selby's distant thoughts whispered, since she obviously hadn't been enough to manage that on her own. But there wasn't even space in her head to be insulted, because it was working, oh gods. Making him grow thicker and longer in his fingers, hard and ruddy and smooth.

And then Agmund's hand dropped, leaving that swollen length resting there against his tunic, against the glimpse of bare belly. While Selby kept kneeling there beside him, still staring, fighting to sort out the mess in her head, and not at all succeeding.

Because this—*that*—was way too much, in too many

ways. And though she'd done embarrassing amounts of preparation for this, hiding alone deep in the trees with certain similar-shaped objects in hand, she clearly should have found the time, or the courage, to properly bed at least one other man before getting here. Because she had to get that thing inside her, somehow, had to do this, somehow, and what the hell had she been thinking, why the *fuck* had she agreed to this...

Her breath was coming too heavy, her face feeling painfully hot, and when she shot a furtive, half-terrified look up at Agmund's face, it was to the awful realization that he was looking back. His eyes narrow, assessing, perhaps even suspicious.

"Are *you* sure?" he asked abruptly, his voice flat. "You don't have to, all right? No matter what Ketill's told you. You can still walk out of here, forever, no questions asked. I mean that."

Selby blinked back at him, at those narrow watching blue eyes, and felt something clench, deep in her groin. Regin Agmund had actually said that? Actually meant that? She could really still leave, no questions asked? No matter what Ketill had said?

But his eyes had gone flinty on hers, his mouth a thin line, and suddenly, somehow, Selby believed it. She didn't have to do this. She could turn around, and walk away, and never see Regin Agmund again.

But even the fact that he'd said that, offered that—it meant something. Changed something. And Selby felt herself relaxing, her shoulders sagging, the unease twisting away, into something else entirely.

"No, I do," Selby heard her voice say, quiet but sure of itself. "Want to, I mean."

An unmistakable relief flared in Agmund's eyes, and that meant something, too. And when his hand moved down again, circling around that hard length of him, Selby swallowed at the sight. At the image of that, of Regin Agmund raising himself up, aiming toward the ceiling, and giving a slow, deliberate stroke. Gentler this time, more careful, more subtle.

It was an invitation, Selby realized. A request, or maybe even another kindness. *I'm waiting, then*, it said. *Whenever you're ready.*

So Selby pulled in another breath, deep. And then she somehow managed to pull up her shift, and make her leg swing up and over Agmund's hips. So she was straddling him, her body dangerously close to that thick hardness, still poised upwards, held there with the light touch of his fingers. Waiting.

Selby could almost feel the heat of it, so close now, and her bare body spread open over him felt swollen and strange. Waiting too, maybe, and with another breath, another gust of courage, she lowered herself down, just enough to touch.

And it was—*everything*. A firing exploding screed of scents and smells and images, swarming and shouting in her head all at once. Lightning and sparks and magic, assignments and targets and battles and death. Hunger and exhaustion and cold, warm and bright and home, trees up north and the ocean, but *you can't swim you'll stop your heart*. Fame and fortune and girls and fucking, used to this but so damn tired of this, been there, trapped there, *where is my magic why is my magic, fuck Ketill, fuck the Coven, fuck you all*—

An odd sound choked out of Selby's mouth, and she jerked up and away, hovering on shaky legs over him, staring down at those watching blue eyes. Gods, she should have touched him somewhere else first, somewhere innocuous, what the hell had she been thinking, letting his first touch to her be *that*, for fuck's sakes—

But that single touch had left something in its wake, too. Something sharp and cool and fresh, something new and different and perhaps even welcome. And maybe—maybe that was worth doing it again, letting her body sink down again, letting that smooth blunt warmth nudge up against her own wet, quivering heat.

Gods. The images streamed again, swarming her again, but this time Selby leaned into them, into the impossible, overwhelming sensation of Regin Agmund's body brushing up against hers. Magic and lightning and sparks, bright and dark and *don't you know who I am*, the most powerful mage in the world gasping for magic, drained for magic, lying in the forest pleading with the gods for magic—

It was too much, again, and Selby had to pull up, away—but Agmund's hand was still holding himself there, his eyes still on hers. Not critical now, not angry, but waiting.

So Selby did it again, and again. Just touching her hungry wetness to the head of him, feeling him, learning him. Almost as though she was compelled to keep doing it, drinking her knowledge of him like this, in careful sips, rather than through any actual proper fucking. But Agmund's patience with this said something, meant something, made something twist and turn and hold on tight.

And when Selby finally lingered longer against him, feeling that smooth blunt head prod just up inside her, she heard herself groan, felt her body clench all over in the sudden lurching craving of it. And then—oh fuck oh gods oh mercy—Agmund *vibrated* up against her, almost as though in reply to her, and this time she did cry out, streams of firing pleasure from that beautiful hard pressing heat.

And it was pressing, now. Driving slow and careful up inside her, because Agmund's hips were pushing upwards, pushing himself deeper. Actually wanting to do this, her frantic thoughts shouted, even as her mouth cried out again with the impossible frenzied strange tautness of it. Of being invaded, pierced, *filled*.

It didn't stop until Agmund was buried all the way up inside her, their coarse hairs meshed together. And Selby's body seemed to have escaped her conscious mind entirely, because she was clenching and flaring tight around him, pressing her whole weight down on him, while her chest heaved and her breath gasped and her eyes drank in the sight of him under her, taking her, *hers*.

The images hadn't slowed down in the least, but the rest of it all had submerged them, somehow, to a distant part of Selby's mind, to be felt and studied later. Leaving only this, this glorious streaming wild wonder, and when Agmund's hips thrust up a little further, Selby was there. Meeting him, gasping, choking aloud at the impossible feeling of him filling even more, vibrating deep and hard inside her.

He let out a gasp too, quiet but unmistakable, and that only seemed to ramp up the fierce craving frenzy in Selby's head. Enough to make her quivering hands go to his chest, spreading flat over the bones of his ribs through his tunic, but he wasn't complaining, and this time he pulled out just slightly before sinking deep again.

Oh. Fuck, that was good, and maybe rather painful, now, but Selby was too caught in it to care. Too consumed in feeling him, meeting him, taking him again and again as he set up a slow, agonizing rhythm. But then going faster, and faster, making something coil up bright and tense and agonizing, Regin Agmund was fucking her, Regin Agmund was inside her, Regin Agmund was the most beautiful thing Selby had ever felt in her entire damned *life*—

His gasps were matching his thrusts, now, and there was no judgement in his eyes now, no distance, no anger. Just something that seemed to echo what Selby felt, needing this and craving this, wanting all of it and any of it and more and more and more of it—

He stopped the rhythm, suddenly, digging himself even deeper up inside. And it all wrenched even harder, fuller, stringing up tight—and then he fired something out of him, and into her, in pulse after beating glorious pulse. And while Selby couldn't quite feel what it was, she could still *taste* it, could smell and breathe and consume it—and there was the towering, thrilling understanding that she'd made part of Regin Agmund hers. For keeps. Holy hell *almighty*.

She was shaking all over, suddenly, and somehow the room had gone cold and hot and cold again. And something had seemed to change in Agmund, both still inside her and in her eyes, and she blinked as his twitchy hand came up to his face and rubbed it, hard. As his chest under her hands rose, and fell.

"Get off," his voice croaked. "Please."

The cold froze all at once, flashing bright and painful, and there was the sudden, shouting compulsion to refuse. To say, *No, please, I need to keep feeling you, you can't even imagine what that just felt like—*

"Please," Agmund said again, harder this time, and somehow, Selby did it. Pushed herself up and off him, wincing at the loss of it, the silence of it, the slowly radiating pain. And then again at the sudden, shocking feel of the wetness he'd left behind, now trickling down the inside of her thigh.

Agmund immediately sat up, tucking himself away with fumbling fingers, and then shot to his feet. Not looking at her, not touching her. Not saying or doing any of the kind, silly things that Selby would have thought—hoped—would follow her first time.

"Should go meet Ketill," he mumbled over his shoulder. "Later."

And then he walked away, out the door, leaving her staring and alone behind him.

6

Selby spent the rest of the morning alone in Agmund's room, trying and failing to convince herself that she wasn't completely fucked.

She should have known. She *had* known. Remembered, all too clearly, every single other person she'd ever touched or kissed, the way they'd smelled, how they'd tasted, the secrets their bodies had whispered in the dark.

It had always been far too heady, too powerful, too dangerous. And her mother had always said, shaking her head, that people needed their secrets. That learning the kinds of things Selby learned about people wasn't a blessing, but a curse.

Of course, Selby's repeated protests along those lines had done nothing to dissuade Ketill, who in the end had promised to personally inform Agmund what her magic was capable of. But Selby probably should have checked, or mentioned it, before she'd gone ahead and fucked Agmund, and filled her head full of his thoughts, and her belly full of his seed.

Even cleaning herself up afterwards presented a challenge, since the barest touch of her fingers to her own tender, stretched-out body dragged up whirling clouds of memories. Not to mention the fact that despite her best efforts to clean it away, Agmund's thick, silken wetness was still there, concealed deep inside her. Still a fundamental part of him, but now belonging to her, for good.

It was appalling, is what it was, and even more was the way Selby was already ruminating—or perhaps obsessing—over Agmund's images and impressions and memories. Seeing that he was proud, yes, and sure of himself, of his magic and his power and his appeal. But seeing, too, the desperation. The loneliness. The misery.

The unpredictability of Agmund's magic had started up maybe a year ago, and ever since then, it seemed to overshadow all the rest. There were so many glimpses of times the magic had failed him, and all the remedies he'd tried. Meditation. Prayer. Exercises. Seclusion. Abstaining from sex, having more sex. Eating this, that, or that. Being willing to do anything Ketill or the Coven said, anything anybody said, if it might possibly help.

And that included Selby, of course. And she was certain, now, that Agmund had most definitely agreed to her coming here—but that his agreement had been fraught, too. With his own doubts, his own reluctance, the empty years he'd already spent alternately fucking and loathing women who only wanted him for his fame.

And, perhaps the biggest complication of all, there was the girlfriend Agmund had already had. Greta Hendersson, her name was, and she was an air-mage too, and a friend. Someone to settle down with, maybe, and the older Agmund got—he was twenty-six, now—the more he'd considered it. The alluring, disconcerting idea of making his own family, his own home.

Greta and her family had openly endorsed such a plan, to the point where it had almost felt inevitable. Until the last six months, at least, which had been increasingly tainted by Agmund's ever-deepening misery, and Greta's rising impatience. And Ketill's latest proposal—for Agmund to repeatedly copulate with some random girl they'd found out east who complemented his magic—had been the final death knell to a relationship that had already been badly foundering.

He wants you to what? Greta had demanded at Agmund, once he'd told her. *Do you not realize what people will say about us? About me? How could you even consider something so selfish?*

And as Agmund had stared at her, he'd felt the realization, like a kick in the stomach, that Greta hadn't cared about his fidelity. Hadn't cared about him sharing his body, his bed, with someone else, breaking two whole years of freely given faithfulness. No, the real insult would be to Greta's standing, her reputation, her name. What other people would say.

Things had gone rapidly and irrevocably downhill from there, to the point where all that remained—for Agmund, at least—was relief that it was over, and a flattened, resigned guilt. Because he was still doing exactly what Greta had most feared, smearing her name and her reputation in public. And despite a recent, stilted conversation in which they'd agreed to remain friends—outwardly, at least—people were still gleefully gossiping about Greta, about how she'd lost the world's greatest air-mage to a pedlar. And perhaps that was why Agmund had been so rude to Selby, why he'd left the way he had, why he hadn't been kind…

But no, absolutely fucking *no*, because Agmund had, on almost all fronts, been rude to Selby, and cold, and inconsiderate. He'd made her sleep on the floor, he'd set off lightning storms without warning her, he'd referred to her most precious possessions as *pedlar junk*. He'd fucked her without otherwise once touching her, or saying more than the absolute bare minimum that any decent person should have said.

Selby groaned aloud, and glared at the suddenly too-close walls, and their awful stinking smell. She needed space. Needed to get the hell out of this godforsaken place, that was it, and she made herself lurch toward the door, and out into the corridor. Down the stairs, toward where she remembered Oden had showed her the entrance to the gardens.

She passed a few people on the way by—a maid, who pointedly ignored her, and then a few more of the Coven's resident mages. None of them met her eyes, though she could hear their murmurs and laughs after they passed, the too-loud mentions of *Agmund* and *pedlar* and *harlot*.

The small, attached hedged garden seemed empty, at least, and Selby walked slowly around its curved pathways, taking in long breaths of the cool morning air. It still reeked of that awful stench, but thankfully it wasn't quite as strong as inside, and she finally dropped herself onto a bench, closed her eyes, and breathed. She could do this. Three months to attempt the impossible, and then leave this cursed place forever. That was all.

She was still repeating the words to herself when she was confronted by the feel of someone new, striding into the garden. Someone blond, of course, but more on the portly side, and he was wearing overalls, and carrying a pair of shears in his gloved hand.

"Oh," he said, stopping up short, and frowning at her. "Who're you?"

Selby couldn't remember seeing him in the dining hall— maybe he was a gardener?—and she tried to smile as she reached out a hand. "I'm Selby Seng. I'm sure you've heard, I'm here to, uh, *work* with Regin Agmund."

The guy shook her hand, but quickly, sending only a few scattered images through his gloved fingers. Gardening, earth, work, darkness, a huge house in the country, *Is Agmund seriously fucking this pedlar—*

"I'm Kal Merton," the guy said, though the look on his face wasn't a particularly welcoming one. "And yeah, everybody's heard about you. Agmund's new sidepiece."

Selby probably should have been insulted, but at least he was talking to her, and that was more than could be said for anyone else here so far. "I suppose," she replied, without enthusiasm. "Does he, uh, have a lot of those?"

There was a deepening curl on Kal's mouth, but he shrugged, and reached over to clip something off a nearby shrub. "Not lately," he said. "Not since Hendersson got her claws into him, a year or two back. She was supposedly going to be the one to finally get him to settle down, or some such rot."

He shot Selby a swift, furtive look, like he wasn't supposed to be gossiping about Agmund to her—but curse her, Selby was clinging to every damned word. "So you've worked here with Agmund for a while, then?" she asked, sitting up straighter on her bench. "What's he like to work with?"

Kal snorted, and clipped off another piece of shrub. "I don't work *with* Agmund. I'm not a prissy perfect air-mage, who gets all the funding, all the glory, all the ridiculous fucking concessions—"

He gave Selby another look, hinting all too plainly that she was one of those concessions, and then cleared his throat. "I mean, Agmund doesn't work with earth-mages," he added. "He goes out, he casts some lightning, he comes back, everyone cheers. At least, they did, until he lost his magic."

He didn't exactly sound disappointed about that, and Selby watched as he kept clipping, as his plant pieces seemed to clump themselves together in midair behind him. "And does anyone here actually know why Agmund lost his magic?" she tentatively asked. "Or why it can't be fixed?"

Kal shrugged. "He's probably just worn himself out," he said flatly. "It happens. He needs to be put out to pasture, sooner rather than later. Not that the old Coven codgers like Ketill want to admit it."

Right. Selby's hand had gone to her pocket, searching for the stones that were no longer inside it, since Agmund had sent them all to storage. Agmund, who should be put out to pasture.

The thought was strangely unsettling, and Selby clamped

down on the next Agmund-related question she'd been about to ask. "Listen, Kal," she said instead. "You're an earth-mage, you know about buildings, right? Have you ever noticed anything off about this one? Like a smell?"

She waved up at the manor's bulk behind them, but Kal gave her another look, and shook his head. "Uh, no. Buildings don't *smell* like magic."

Well, they weren't supposed to, but that was the entire damned point, and Selby bit back a sigh. "Well, what about all the work you mages do around here?" she asked. "Would any of that leave a residue behind? Or something?"

Kal shrugged, but his eyes were definitely avoiding Selby now, like she was venturing into dangerous pedlar territory. "Runar Alariaq's might," he said curtly. "But even if it did, it's all been approved by the directors, *supposedly*."

There was another obvious twinge of bitterness there, and Selby eyed him, considering that. "Who's *Runar Alariaq*?" she asked. "And who are the directors?"

Kal explained, very briefly, how all Coven Manor's mages were broken into five departments—air, fire, earth, water, and healing—each led by a high-ranking, Coven-appointed director. "Alariaq's in healing," he said. "Supposedly. And us earth-mages, we report to Morley, though there's only a few of us on staff right now, and her budget's less than a *tenth* of Ketill's."

Selby opened her mouth to ask why healing might leave a residue, and also, where she could find this Alariaq—but Kal had started sidling away, his clippings bobbing along behind him. "I have to go," he said. "Morley needs me."

With that, he took off toward the manor, leaving Selby frowning at where he'd gone. And considering again what he'd said about Agmund, would they really put him out to pasture, he'd worked so hard to fix this, put so much of himself into it, and—

Her entire body stilled, listening past the rustling of the nearby leaves. Because she could—feel him. She could *feel*

Regin Agmund. Not here in the garden, but just stepping out of the manor's front door, around the other side of the building.

Her heartbeat picked up, because while she could usually feel people who were close by, there was no way she should be able to feel anyone at that distance—was there? But yes, there was Agmund, and with that certainty was the equally alarming awareness that he'd just come from a room on the ground floor, no doubt Ketill's office. And, even worse, that Selby could actually hear him *speaking*.

"Fuck, but Ketill's in a state today," Agmund was saying, even as his voice came closer, toward the garden. "Even worse than usual. Thinks he runs the entire damned realm."

There was a laugh in reply, and though Selby had only ever heard the guy speak once, she could immediately picture him, Agmund's brown-haired asshole friend. And she could see him, too, in the twinges of Agmund's memory, could even supply his first name. *Njall*.

"Yeah, his head's way too deep up his own arse," the guy—Njall—said. "Like bringing in that pedlar for you. What the hell was he thinking?"

There was silence, like Agmund might have shrugged, and Njall laughed again. "So you *did* actually take the hit and fuck her, eh?" he asked. "How'd it go, then?"

They were walking closer, around the outside of the garden, and Selby distantly remembered that Oden had said something about training grounds around back, and a greenhouse. And even though Selby knew Agmund couldn't possibly see her through the garden's thick hedge, she flattened herself against a tree, kept her breath shallow, fought to hear over the echoing thud of her heartbeat.

"Went just how you'd expect," Agmund replied, his voice easy and light, but it felt like it was made of knives, scraping inside Selby's head. "Got in there, did my duty, got the hell out."

Njall laughed again, sharper this time. "Did she look decent under all that kit, at least?"

"No idea," came Agmund's voice. "Didn't take it off. Don't plan to, either. Didn't even touch her, beyond the crucial bit."

Their voices were even nearer now, and still coming closer, and had Selby somehow *known* Agmund would come out here, that he would talk about her, oh gods she was so *completely* fucked—

"So you're really going to keep at it, then?" came Njall's next question. "For the whole three months? You think you can stomach it for that long?"

Agmund laughed—*laughed*—as they rounded the garden's corner. "All I can do is try," he replied. "I'll get Holben to look me over every week, and spend as much time as I can out in the woods. Bleach out my brain as much as fucking possible."

Njall laughed again, and said something else, but Selby had finally clapped her hands to her ears, shaking her head, trying to force those words out again. Agmund couldn't have said—he'd had sex with her, just this morning, her first time, he *couldn't*—

But the words were still there, true, alive, and almost shockingly painful. *Don't plan to*, he'd said. *All I can do is try. Get Holben to look me over every week. Bleach out my brain...*

And what the hell was Selby supposed to do with that? With Regin Agmund saying these awful things about her, even after she'd been inspected—he *knew* that—and approved for his use.

It meant that everything was tainted, now, even the things she'd thought had been good. The way Agmund had slid up into her. The way he'd twitched and gasped. The way he'd let her touch him...

And now Selby's head was full of him, her body even still full of him, the beautiful brilliant mage who'd been her first time, and thought she was a diseased hideous harlot. And yes, she was completely fucked, and she couldn't stop the sobs from lurching up, trying to strangle her with the awful choking truth of it.

7

Selby didn't leave the garden until nightfall.

It was only the chill that drove her in, in the end. Not someone coming to look for her, not Agmund or Ketill or Oden to ask where she'd been. No one had come, because no one had noticed or cared, and more than once Selby thought about slipping through the hedge, climbing over the gate, and never looking back.

But even if she could avoid capture by the Coven, it still wouldn't be easy, what with no funds or supplies, and the fact that the coin was all gone. She still had to do this, three months, and there had to be a way to keep her distance, do her duty, and then get the hell out. Just like Agmund had said.

Selby twitched as she stepped back inside the manor—gods, the *smell*—and risked a stop in the empty dining hall to ask the kitchen staff if they had any leftovers from supper. They did, though the woman who gave Selby a hunk of buttered bread flinched when she touched Selby's fingers, and furiously wiped her hand on her apron afterwards.

It was food, at least, and Selby grimly chewed it as she trudged up to Agmund's bedroom. Food usually presented the same obstacles for her as did most things—there was nothing quite as gut-churningly awful as reliving an animal's final agonies while you ate it—but the bread was fine, its grain grown in a distant, uncomplicated field, and ground and baked by the same woman who'd given it to her.

Selby was still chewing the last of it when she finished climbing the stairs, and reached the door of Agmund's bedroom. She could feel him there inside it, unmoving on his bed, maybe even asleep—but when she opened the door and stepped inside, he was awake. Sitting up on his bed in the candlelight, and looking at her.

Selby swiftly dropped her eyes, and walked past his watching form to her bedroll. It was standing neatly in the corner, right where she'd left it, and she knelt and pulled it out, spread it onto the floor. Making sure to put it in the same place as the night before, as far away from his bed as possible.

"Where've you been?" came Agmund's voice, sudden and alarming—and Selby flinched, and blinked up toward him. Seeing him for really the first time since he'd walked out that morning, and even now the memories were swirling up again, and she could actually *feel* the traces of him, sparking deep inside her.

"In the garden," she replied, as she spread out her cloak over the bedroll, smoothed it with a suddenly shaky hand. "I didn't want to interrupt your much-needed brain bleaching."

The words came out before she'd realized she'd spoken, and Selby's whole body tensed, her hands snapping tight and clammy into fists. "I mean," she continued, too quickly, "this whole place stinks, it's like something's rotting in it, I have no idea how the hell you all just keep on *living* here—"

And now Agmund was going to think she was deranged, as well as dirty and diseased, and Selby clamped her mouth shut, closed her eyes. And tried to keep the lurking sobs away from her throat, gods damn it, because she didn't want him to know that it mattered.

But he probably already knew anyway, judging from his

continued silence. And he would go tell Njall later, and they could laugh together about the diseased pedlar harlot—

"Look, I'm sorry," came Agmund's voice, unexpected enough that Selby froze, and frowned up at him through her wet eyelashes. And Agmund did look almost sorry in the candlelight, his eyes uneasy, maybe even grim. "You weren't supposed to hear that."

But those were coward's words, a pathetic excuse, and Selby's eyes narrowed, the fury jolting sudden and hot. "Yes, well, I did hear it," she snapped. "And I realize this is an unfortunate situation, and you don't actually want me, but the least you could do is be a decent human being about it. If I *ever* heard my brother talking like that about a girl, I would fucking *smack* him, and I'm just an unwanted harlot, not the so-called saviour of the entire damned *country*!"

The words rang out in the silence, far too loud and pointed, and Selby fixed her eyes on the light of Agmund's candle, tried to breathe. Gods, why was she yelling at him, what if he reported it to the Coven, she needed to get through this, three months...

"I *said*, I'm sorry," Agmund's clipped voice replied. "But you honestly don't think I'm going to tell them anything else, do you? Every single word I say about this is going to go straight back to Greta, and I'm *trying* to be decent to her about all this, all right?"

Gods, it was so much rubbish, and Selby barked out a hard, brittle laugh. "So you being decent to Greta means you're a total asshole to me," she shot back. "Got it, thanks."

There was more silence, and when Selby looked up again, Agmund's eyes had that distance in them, the dismissive cool dislike. "*She* didn't do anything to deserve this," he said. "*You're* the one who took Ketill's coin, and signed a ridiculous contract, and moved halfway across the continent, just so you could fuck me!"

Oh, *gods*. Selby was *not* going to reply to that, but the words were bubbling up anyway, escaping out her mouth. "Oh, don't flatter yourself, asshole. I had just about as much interest in fucking the great Regin Agmund as I did the drunken town mummer. And by the way, the artists littering your portraits all over the countryside have been *exceedingly* generous!"

Agmund's eyes blinked, like he hadn't quite followed that, but then the dislike sharpened again, settling back into the line of his mouth. "Oh, and *you're* the judge now, are you?" he demanded, giving a sharp wave down at her dress, her body, maybe her face. "Really?"

There was no reply to that, nothing, and Selby's hands were visibly shaking now. And Agmund could see that, of course he could, he would tell Njall, and they would laugh—

Selby desperately fumbled for her cloak, yanking it up around her shoulders, and staggered to her feet, toward the door. Just needing to get away from Agmund's voice, his body, his eyes—

But in an abrupt, lurching movement, he was here. With his arm above Selby's head, his hand pressed flat against the door, holding it shut. And when she whirled around to glare at him he was so *close*, so damned *tall*, and she could taste him, taste those remnants of him, still sparking low in her belly...

"Where are you going," he breathed, and there was something in it Selby couldn't quite identify. "Ketill said you're supposed to stay here."

"Yes, and you've made it very clear you don't want me here," Selby replied, her voice wavering. "So I'll sleep in the garden until you have need of me. I'm sure you'll rest easier without my hideous presence anyway, and this way you can bleach the floor where I've slept, too. Good night."

With that, she whirled around to yank at the door handle, and thank the gods, it opened. And Selby ran down the stairs as fast as she possibly could, covering her mouth with both hands, because she couldn't bear for Regin Agmund to hear her sobbing.

8

Sleeping in the garden should have been a good plan.

It had seemed like an excellent one at first, when Selby had been blessedly alone again in the darkness, beyond the reach of those awful stinking walls. And beyond the reach of Regin Agmund, who she could feel, even now, pacing back and forth across his bedroom, undoubtedly enraged that a lowly pedlar had dared to call him out on his bullshit.

And maybe it was Selby's irrational brain again, but the longer Agmund paced back and forth, the louder it all raged in her thoughts. The look on his white face, the images in his head, the feel of his seed still whispering inside her. The bleaching out his brain, *you're the judge now, where the fuck is my magic, I'll do anything*—

Sleep came only in spurts, if at all. And by sunrise Selby felt ill, and deeply exhausted, with an aching head, and a chill that went all the way to her bones.

She only sat up, her heartbeat lurching, when she heard the sound of approaching footsteps—but it wasn't Agmund, Agmund was still in his bedroom, finally sleeping. Instead, this was one of the blonde mages. A girl.

Selby froze at the sight, but at least it wasn't Greta, or any of Agmund's other friends that she recognized—though this one still had the requisite slim form, and long fair hair, and large blue eyes. Which were now studying Selby intently, the blonde head tilting, like she was trying to decide who Selby was, and what she was doing here.

"You're the new earth-mage, right?" the girl said, her voice softer than Selby would have expected. "Hi, I'm Thora."

She actually smiled as she spoke, and extended an elegant hand, and after blinking at it for an instant, Selby briefly took it. "Hi. Selby Seng."

As always, there was the spurt of images at the touch, enough to inform Selby that Thora wasn't your typical government-shill attack mage, and instead used her magic to develop some kind of predictive strategy. And that was interesting, and so was the awareness that Thora didn't like living here either, and spent most of her days holed up in a workroom with a handsome fellow whose skin was even darker than Selby's.

"They haven't actually been making you sleep out here, have they?" Thora asked, with a twist of a dimpled smile. "I know they keep saying we're at capacity, but that seems excessive, even for them."

Selby's mouth twitched up too, and she shrugged. "No, this is all my own stupid fault. I'm supposed to be bunking on Agmund's floor, and getting attacked by lightning storms while I sleep."

Thora chuckled at that, her blue eyes glancing up in the general direction of Agmund's room. "Yes, we've all heard about those," she said. "How's it all going, with him?"

Selby felt her eyes narrowing—was this just a ploy to gain some new gossip to spread around?—but then her exhaustion won out, or maybe it was the loneliness. "Horribly," she replied, with a sigh. "Agmund's really against this entire thing. Against me, I mean. And nobody told me he had to break up with his girlfriend for me, either."

Thora didn't pretend not to know what Selby was talking about, thankfully, because clearly everyone here already knew. But her eyes were undeniably sympathetic, so Selby just kept talking, spitting out the rest of it. "He sent my things to storage, too. And this place smells like something truly foul. Like"—her voice cracked—"I'm going to be sick every time I step inside it, or so much as touch the damned *walls*."

Thora's blonde eyebrows furrowed together, her white teeth chewing her lip. "Really?" she asked. "I've never smelled anything like that. And I don't think Runar has, either."

Runar was the brown-skinned guy, Selby's brain supplied, and—her thoughts leapt—the same guy Kal Merton had mentioned as possibly making the smell, right? "What kind of work does Runar do?" she asked, too eagerly. "Is it something that could make a smell?"

Thora shot Selby an uneasy look, and shook her head. "No, of course not. He's a healer, and he's very clean. Obsessively so."

Her mouth gave that twist of a smile again, and flitting back through those images, Selby could see that Thora clearly held this Runar in high regard, both for his deeply impressive magic skills, and—Selby felt a little flare of commiseration—for other reasons, too, that had so far gone unfulfilled.

"I can ask around, though," Thora continued. "If I find out anything that could be a reason for a smell, I'll let you know."

It was the kindest thing anyone had said since she'd arrived here, and Selby blinked, and attempted a real smile. "Thanks," she said. "I really appreciate it."

Thora smiled back and waved it away, with still too much understanding in her eyes, and then she turned and left, her head disappearing around the hedge. Leaving Selby shivering and alone—at least, until a few minutes later, when an uneasy-looking, middle-aged gardener showed up. Giving repeated side-eyed glances at Selby as he worked, enough to make her decide that she was fed up, and freezing, and curse them all, she was going to have a hot bath.

It took some wandering, and asking for directions, and tolerating even more comments and snickers. Mockery that was fully audible, now, things like *Agmund actually fucked that pedlar, he didn't even take her clothes off, they're saying he went to see Holben, after...*

Selby ignored it all, and held her head high until she finally found Oden, and half-cajoled, half-threatened her way into the manor's beautiful private baths. Which admittedly did wonders to take the edge off the cold, and also to soak the still-tender soreness between her legs.

Selby was trying very hard not to think about that, or about Agmund in general, but once she was safely back out in the blessedly empty garden, and attempting uselessly to distract herself by touching every last object inside it, she could no longer deny the unsettling, highly unnerving truth. No matter where Regin Agmund went in this damned manor, Selby now knew about it.

He'd begun his day in his bedroom—he'd slept late—and then he'd gone to the dining hall, and then to what had to be Ketill's office. And then out to the forest—bleaching out his brain, no doubt—and after that he'd gone back to the dining hall. Because it was suppertime already, and somehow Selby had spent almost the entire day alone, following the taste of Regin Agmund's magic. And gods, even her worst obsessions had never led to anything like this before, and yes, she was truly, completely fucked.

The nearby manor's awful stench had seemed to rise in her nostrils, and she dropped herself back onto the bench again, taking shallow breaths, and trying and failing to sleep. All the while feeling Agmund lurking in the dining hall, until—her whole body twitched—there was the unmistakable feeling of him walking out toward the garden. Toward her.

Selby fought back the sudden urge to run, escape, hide—and instead made herself sit up, and wait. Head down, knees pressed tightly together, fingers gripping hard against the solid comforting wood of the bench.

She could feel Agmund coming closer, could hear his footsteps on the dirt, could almost weep at the responding brightening heat in her belly. At the part of him that was even now still there, hidden and quiet and lingering.

Agmund came to a stop a short distance away, but Selby didn't look up. Just kept her eyes on the ground, and the scuffed black leather of Agmund's expensive-looking boots. The sun was just going down, and in the dimming light his boots almost blended with the dirt, almost like he wasn't there at all.

"Um," his voice said. "Hi."

Selby grimaced, but didn't look up. Just kept waiting for him to say this, whatever the hell it was. Maybe how she owed him, or she should apologize, or she should take her bags and get the hell out.

"Will you come back," he said. "Please."

It was enough to make Selby's eyes dart up, briefly, to his pale face. And it wasn't mocking, or angry, or even critical. Just—wary, maybe. Uneasy.

"Why?" she asked.

She fully expected something about the contract, or Ketill, or her obligations—but there was a long minute of silence, a scuff at the dirt with one of those black boots.

"Because it worked," Agmund finally replied. "With my magic."

Selby's head snapped back up, and a sudden chill jolted up her spine. "What?" she said, her voice blank, shrill. "It actually *worked*?"

Agmund gave a dry little chuckle, a shrug of his bony shoulder. But it meant yes, *yes*, and as Selby stared at him, it was almost as though a strange, reluctant understanding passed between them. Yes, it had worked, yes, he'd thought it had been rubbish too, and what the hell were they supposed to do now?

"How?" Selby demanded. "Did it work, I mean? Your magic's just—*back*? Just like that?"

Agmund hesitated, his pale fingers clenching at his side. "Not like that," he said slowly. "But like—something. Like the air is there, when it wasn't before. Like I can *breathe* again."

Oh. The unwilling understanding flared again, and Selby gripped harder at the bench, at the vague, long-ago image of its black-haired builder. She did *not* understand Regin Agmund, she did not care, she didn't...

"It's the only thing that's made even the slightest bit of difference in this endless hell," Agmund continued, quieter. "I want to try it again. Please."

Of course he did, and Selby almost laughed, but didn't. "So now that it properly benefits you, suddenly you can stomach me after all?" her voice said, with surprising coolness. "Even if I am diseased and downright hideous?"

There was more silence from Agmund, and he closed his eyes, pinched the bridge of his nose. "Look, I didn't actually mean that," he replied. "Especially the bleach thing, I should have realized how that would come across. It wasn't what I meant by it at all, I'm sorry, I was just—"

"Being a total asshole?" Selby finished, sharply, and to his credit, he didn't deny it. Just swallowed hard, his pale throat bobbing, making something flip low in Selby's gut.

"Look, if you want the truth," Agmund began, "what we did yesterday, it was"—he paused, took a breath—"it was fine, all right? You were fine. I've had way worse."

Selby did laugh this time, low and bitter. "Such a ringing endorsement from the great Regin Agmund," she snapped. "I suppose I should feel flattered. Are you this kind to all your bedmates, or just diseased hideous pedlars?"

Agmund groaned aloud, kicked at the dirt with his boot.

"Look, I said, I'm sorry, I fucked up, all right? What else do you want me to say? This is supposed to be a business deal, you signed that fucking contract, so can't we just do our duty and leave the personal bullshit out of it?"

Gods, that duty bit again, and Selby glared up at him, at his stupidly appealing bony face. "Don't you dare put this on me," she shot back. "You're the one who made this personal in the first place with all those horrible comments, when you *knew* full well that every single person in this entire building was going to hear about them!"

And maybe, if Selby was honest with herself, that was the part that had hurt the most. Bad enough that Agmund had thought it, said it, but worse that now, thanks to him, everyone else knew it, too.

"I know it was a shit thing to say," came Agmund's voice, almost wearily. "You're right, I was being an asshole. I'll watch what I say from now on. And I'll tell Njall to keep his mouth shut, too."

But the damage was already done, and Selby had probably just made it worse by hiding away alone in the garden for an entire day. And suddenly she just felt so damned tired, and the awful smell had only seemed to become stronger, curdling deep under her skin.

"Look, it's late, and cold," Agmund said now. "Will you give it a few minutes, get something to eat or whatever, and then come up to my room?"

Selby's breath caught—he was really asking, really wanting to do this again?—but then she followed the rest of it, and her eyes narrowed on his. "Why a few minutes?"

Agmund looked away, his sharp shoulders rising and falling. "Look, if you don't want people gossiping even more about this, then we definitely don't want to be seen going into my bedroom together. All right?"

Of course. How very damned convenient that he wanted to avoid gossip now, now that he'd said all those things to Njall, and everyone else knew it. And Selby should have called him out on that, but instead she took a breath, rubbed hard at her eyes. She had to get through this, three months, and that was all...

"Fine," she said, though her voice didn't sound like hers. "Fine. I'll come."

9

Walking into Agmund's room should have been easier this time. Selby knew what to expect, what it would feel like, what he would do.

But even so, she still stood outside Agmund's door for far too long, dragging in deep, shaky breaths. It was only the sound of other people coming up the stairs that finally sent her stumbling inside, into the presence of Regin Agmund. Who was once again sitting on his bed in the candlelight, waiting.

Selby's face already felt hot, and she rubbed at the back of her neck. "So," she made herself say, to the floor. "Same as yesterday, then?"

She glanced up in time to see Agmund give a half-shrug, and something that might have been a nod. *Sure*, it said. *Why not*.

Right. That meant it was all on Selby again, and she let out a shuddery exhale before once again unbuttoning her dress. It was a similar dress to yesterday's, with the usual voluminous, patchwork fabric and big buttons—but the shift underneath was different. It was Selby's most costly one, made of close-fitting, paper-thin black linen, and if she wasn't mistaken,

Agmund's eyes flicked downwards, first to where it hugged her breasts, and then to where it curved close over her hips.

It was enough to bring more heat to Selby's cheeks, especially once Agmund's eyes met hers, and then darted away again. Like he knew he wasn't supposed to be looking, which he definitely wasn't, because they both knew the things he'd said. *Didn't take it off. Bleach out my brain. You're the judge now, are you?*

Selby took another deep breath, and made herself step forward, closer. And again, Agmund moved over and dropped his body back onto the bed, looking up at her, his eyes shadowed in the candlelight.

Selby's heartbeat was pounding now, racing inside her ribs, and she inhaled another breath, took the final step to his bed—but then a thought lurched up, suddenly, and she hesitated, cleared her throat.

"Um," her voice said, and she swallowed, tried again. "I should have told you, yesterday. My magic, when I touch people, I—see things about them."

Agmund blinked, but otherwise didn't move, looking up at her under his blond eyelashes. "Yeah, I know. Ketill said."

Oh. Selby felt her eyes going narrow, suspicious, and she frowned down at him as she carefully knelt on the bed beside him. "You don't care?"

His shoulder gave another shrug against the blanket. "Why would I?"

He seemed to be completely missing the point, and Selby's frown deepened. "Um, because what's inside your head is supposed to be private? And most people don't like other people finding out all their secrets?"

Agmund's eyebrows lifted a little, but he shrugged again. "Look, as long as you can keep your mouth shut, and it doesn't stop you doing your job," he said, "I really don't care."

As if to make his point, his hands went to his trousers, and untied them. Most definitely with less hesitation than the day before, and when he pulled himself out—Selby swallowed, hard—he was already ruddy and thick and long, the head of him smooth and slick and hungry.

She knew she shouldn't take it as anything other than him wanting his magic back—gods knew, the prospect of that probably aroused him more than she ever would—but somehow it still made it easier to shift her body over him, to straddle his hips. To meet his eyes, maybe asking the silent question—and then, witnessing his silent answer as he once again reached down, took that swollen shaft in hand, and guided it up toward her.

Gods, that was a sight, and despite everything Agmund had done, Selby was still caught in it for an instant, her breath coming out in a shuddery sigh. And if she wasn't mistaken, Agmund's cock gave a visible little shudder in response—and suddenly the craving to feel that again, to have that again, was so overwhelming, so overpowering, that Selby could barely think, barely breathe.

Her body seemed to move on its own this time, rising up over him, in just the right place. And once again lowering down slow, careful, until that smooth hot skin just brushed up gentle against her.

Fuck. The images exploded again, firing out from Selby's groin to prickle all over her skin, and with them was the impossible wheeling feel of it, of him, there. Fucking her, actually wanting to fuck her, because his thoughts couldn't deny that anymore, not now, not after yesterday.

How do you feel? Ketill had asked, afterwards, once Agmund had left Selby in his bed, and to Agmund's vague surprise, he'd actually said, *Good.* And then he'd raised his hand, and the air had just—been there, just as it was supposed to be. Not as immediate as it had once been, but still *there*, and Agmund had stared, and felt it again and again and again—

He'd spent half the day doing simple exercises, breathing, feeling the air move, while Ketill had watched, barking out orders and taking notes. And after that Agmund had gone outside with Njall, and he'd said those things, had had to say things, to Njall, to his blond friend Tomik, and then everyone else who had asked. Things like *pedlar* and *payment* and *contract* and *I didn't touch her, didn't look at her, just doing my duty—*

Even so, Greta had still cornered him in the corridor, red-eyed and furious. *I heard what you did, I still can't believe you, I don't care if it's working, how could you break up with me and turn around and publicly do that—*

And if Selby had had any nagging doubts about whether Agmund's relationship with Greta had really been over, at least this put them to rest. Because Agmund's thoughts had been only weariness, a dragged-out exhausted loneliness built up over weeks, months, of him with no magic no *life*, gritting his teeth biting his tongue because it didn't matter, Greta didn't want to know, no one wanted to witness the world's greatest air-mage weeping over how he couldn't even taste the magic anymore. Especially not his future wife.

It had hurt more than Agmund had wanted to admit, more than he'd let on to anyone around him. It had been two years with Greta, and he'd thought it had been safe, thought it had been good, and parts of it *had* been good. Especially in bed, she'd liked him powerful and in charge, and that had been the last thing to sour between them, because dominating Greta, driving himself into Greta, had been the only thing keeping him sane—

No. *No.* Selby yanked herself up and away, and squeezed her eyes shut, shook her head. She didn't want to know. And why the hell did she know, why had that been so easy to see—

"What?" said a voice, and it took too long to realize that it was Agmund's voice. Agmund, talking to her, like this.

Selby blinked down at him, and found that her hands were shaking. "Can you not," she managed, "think about that right now? Please?"

Agmund grimaced, like he knew exactly what she was referring to, and she saw his throat convulse, felt the slow exhale of his breath. "Sorry," he said, quiet. "What should I think about?"

Well. Selby swallowed the obvious yet stupid answer that maybe he could think about the person he was currently fucking, and she gave a helpless shrug. "I don't know," she replied, voice thin. "Magic, maybe? Whatever you air-mages get off to? Standing deep in that forest of yours up north, maybe, and striking down lightning onto every single tree in it?"

There was an instant's stillness in Agmund's eyes—maybe she shouldn't have let on that she'd seen that—but then he raised his eyebrows, and gave a pointed glance downwards. *Get on with it, then*, it said.

So Selby did, carefully bringing her body back to meet his again—and this time, in the mess of images, the strongest of all was Agmund, standing in the middle of that forest. With dark clouds swirling above him, and dazzling bolts of lightning streaking down, one after another after another, exploding the trees around him with deafening, furious force.

Selby stared at him, caught in the vision of that easy breathtaking power swarming him, becoming part of him. And there was the awareness, too, that he'd actually done this, actually liked to do this, and exploding trees in his father's forest was how he'd spent half his damned childhood.

Gods, it felt good, looked good, tasted good. And this time Selby didn't resist it, and when she felt that hardness start to drive inside, felt the pressure from Agmund's hips, thrusting up under her, she gasped aloud, and took it. Took that slow, torturous slide of his cock, deep up into her, because Regin Agmund used lightning like a god, and he felt so good, holy mother of *fuck*—

He was all the way in, now, deep and still so strange, and setting off a low burn in Selby's belly. But he was waiting, letting her take the lead, and without thinking she put both her hands to his tunic, and settled herself a little deeper.

The sudden flare of his cock inside her made her gasp, so she did it again, and again. Just rubbing up against him, feeling the hard ridges of his bones under his skin, the way he moved and throbbed within her. And oh, she could do this all day, every day, especially if Agmund kept thinking of that magic, fuck—

This time his hips thrust up, as hers pressed down, and *yes* that was even better. And he did it again, and again, driving deep inside her, fucking her, spreading her open with that overlarge cock, making her his, oh—

And maybe it was the angle of his hips, how he was driving up in just the right way—or maybe it was those visions of the forest and magic and trees exploding in the dark. But it made something coil up in Selby's groin, winding tighter and higher and closer, oh gods oh gods oh *gods*—

And then it all crashed down again, shaky shuddery sparking pleasure all over, swarming her from the inside out. Making her mouth cry out, her body pulsing tight and uncontrollable around that beautiful invading cock, trees and air and lightning, bright and hard and glorious.

When it finally faded again, Selby's hands were clutching at Agmund's tunic, her eyes darting furtive and ashamed up to his face. But there was no judgement, no mockery, just an unfamiliar hazy strangeness, and those eyes held hers as his hips slammed up again and again and again.

It was rougher than before, perhaps approaching painful, but Selby clung to his tunic, and met him in it. Feeling how the visions of the forest were starting to scatter, how his own pleasure had risen too, now teetering on a knife-edge, and there was the sudden odd image of herself, lips parted and cheeks reddened and dark eyes fluttering, arching her back and riding him, her breasts bouncing and her nipples straining through her shift, her body around him tight and hot and *fuck*—

Suddenly it was there, spurting up deep inside her, and in that instant there was nothing but this, the magic and the visions and the soaring, screeching, impossible pleasure. And the unmistakable sound of Agmund gasping, the feel of his whole body curling up in the strength of it, of his hands coming, oh so briefly, up to grip against Selby's hips, and hold her there, while he emptied himself inside as deep as he could go.

Fuck, it was good. So good. And when Agmund finally sagged under her, his hands dropping back down to his sides, Selby very nearly spoke, and let out the truth of all the things she was absolutely not supposed to say...

But she clamped her mouth shut, and thank the gods for it, because Agmund had thrown an arm over his eyes, as if to block out the sight of her. And then he gave a jerky wave of his other hand, saying once again, *Get off*.

Right. Selby did, or tried, but she was still shaky enough that her hand had to push at his chest again to keep herself from falling over onto him. And the temptation to keep her hand there was all-consuming, suddenly, and she had to hurl herself off the bed, stumbling toward her dress. Try to find the sleeves, the buttons, oh gods what had she just done, just betrayed...

Agmund's hands were fumbling too, shoving himself back inside his trousers, and he abruptly sat up, as though aiming to leave—but then he sank back again, like he'd thought better of it. Which was probably wise, because his face was just as flushed as Selby's felt, and there was a highly noticeable splotch of wetness on the front of his trousers.

Selby stared at him again, at those deep blue eyes, at the way his white-blond hair was sticking all up on end. And it occurred to her, wild and irrational, that she would like to touch that hair, perhaps run her fingers through it, and gods, she was so completely and *entirely* fucked—

"Look, Seng," came Agmund's voice, sudden and a little

rough. "From now on, I don't talk about any of this. With anybody. And I know I don't deserve it, but"—he took a breath—"if you'd do the same, I'd really appreciate it."

His eyes were on the floor, his hand smoothing over that mess of his hair, and it occurred to Selby that maybe he'd betrayed too much, too. What with the touching, the thrusting of his hips, the way he'd gasped. With the way he was still here, looking like this, where no one else could see him.

"Who am I going to tell?" Selby replied, her voice sounding just as scratchy as his. "I wouldn't anyway. Just doing our jobs, is all. Just a—a business arrangement. Just about the magic."

Agmund's shoulders visibly relaxed, his eyes meeting hers, and glancing away again. "Yeah," he said, and then opened his hand, and gave a heavy, sharp exhale as a tiny, perfect bolt of lightning sparked from out of nowhere toward his palm.

It was beautiful, and impossible, and the look on Agmund's reddened face was sheer, staring relief. As if this were the first spell he'd cast in months, beyond that nighttime horror show, and perhaps it was. And it was here, with Selby. Because of her.

He flexed his fingers, easy and quick, and there it was again, a perfect little bolt of lightning, connecting to his palm. Making Selby gasp, whether with surprise or something else, and Agmund's eyes flicking to hers were wry, and warm. And maybe—Selby blinked—maybe almost—amused?

"You sure earth-mages don't get off to lightning, too?" he asked, and when Selby gaped at him, her face flooding with heat again, he actually—unbelievably—gave her a small, crooked smile. "You can't deny it's pretty fucking hot."

Oh, *gods*. Selby couldn't bite back her hoarse half-groan, which made Agmund's smile go wider, maybe a little smug. And then Selby chuckled out loud, without at all meaning to, because the relief was making her giddy, and because damn him, he was probably right.

"Doesn't mean you're still not an arrogant lying asshole,"

she managed, once she'd caught her breath again. "And that I still wouldn't rather have the drunken town mummer."

The grin Agmund flashed her was broad and almost breathtakingly stunning, and she could almost taste the sudden lightness on him, the way she'd just put him at ease. Making it clear that any pleasure she might find in this was all about the magic too, and not him, not in the least...

Agmund rose to his feet again, looking less flustered than before, and stepped around Selby, making for the water closet. But then he hesitated and turned, not quite meeting her eyes this time.

"Will you be around tomorrow night again?" he asked, his voice a little too casual. "After supper?"

It was all too clear what he was asking, and there was a lurch in Selby's stomach, more heat rising to her face. "Probably," she replied, before she could stop herself. "If you want."

He didn't speak, but his head gave a curt nod, his eyes briefly meeting hers. Saying, *Yeah, I do want,* and the truth of that was doing strange things to Selby's head, to the still-wet soreness between her legs.

"Right," she said. "Tomorrow."

10

Sleep came quickly that night, despite the fact that Selby and Agmund didn't speak another word to each other, not even a muttered good-night. But it had been an excessively long day, and Selby had to admit that sleeping on Agmund's floor was far superior to the garden, especially with her own comforting things nearby, and Agmund's stupidly comforting breath, coming from the bed.

That was, until the lightning storms started to go off. While Agmund once again tossed and turned in his bed, raising his right hand to the air, and conjuring jagged white forks of light that streaked from the ceiling to the floor.

They were even brighter and bigger than the first night, and this time one of the blinding bolts caught Selby on her foot, stinging sharp enough that she spat out a loud string of curses. Which went entirely unheeded by Agmund, who just kept sleeping and casting and being thoroughly, brutally terrifying.

Selby eventually ended up sleeping in the water closet, curled in the furthest corner away, with the door tightly shut. Where she awoke, frequently and groggily, to the continually booming sounds of thunder, and didn't properly sleep again until the light finally began filtering under the door, and Agmund's storms faded to silence.

She woke to the feeling of something shaking her shoulder, and when she blinked her bleary eyes open, there was Agmund. Crouching over her, wearing only his trousers, and if possible, looking almost—guilty.

"Sorry," he said, his voice raspy with sleep. "Go get in the bed, if you want."

Selby wasn't going to argue, and she staggered toward his bed, dragging her cloak behind her. And then she collapsed down into the warm, wonderful taste of Regin Agmund, the scent and memories of him—of *them*—all over the pillow and blankets, cocooning her in its lovely soft contentment.

Sleep did come easy, then, and Selby didn't wake again until the strong afternoon sunlight streamed through the window. And stretching in Regin Agmund's warm bed, revelling in those heated memories upon it, was so delicious that she dozed for gods knew how long, fading in and out of sleep, until she could hear her stomach grumbling, and finally dragged her arse out of bed.

She leisurely washed and dressed, feeling more chipper than she'd felt in weeks. Because this was—doable. She could do it. She *would* do it. Three months. That was all.

Of course, there was the unnerving fact that she could still feel Agmund, perhaps even stronger than yesterday, even though he was now much further away, gone out deep into that nearby forest. And—Selby stepped into the corridor, and almost gagged—there was also the vile smell. Somehow even stronger, even more pungent than before.

She frowned as she shut the door behind her—why was the smell so much worse out here?—and then she heard the distinct sound of another door closing down the corridor. And a glance over her shoulder made her freeze all over, because there, walking straight toward her, was Greta.

And Greta was tall and slim and breathtakingly beautiful,

even more than Selby remembered, and—Selby's eyes briefly closed—that was because the last time she'd seen Greta had been in Agmund's thoughts. And Agmund, of course, thought Greta was one of the most stunning women he'd ever seen.

Greta hadn't even hesitated, striding smoothly toward Selby, her head held high. Going for the stairs, and that had to be all—but Greta's blue eyes on Selby were unmistakably contemptuous, and she slowed as she approached, her lip curling in obvious distaste.

"Regin's not in there," she said, voice frosty. "Some people actually *work* during the day, you know."

That was a pedlar insult, Selby knew very well, based on the fact that much of what your average person saw of a pedlar was them sitting around on a wagon, selling things. Of course, those people didn't see the constant travelling, the scouting and haggling and scam artists and thieves, the sheer amount of work and cunning it took just to keep food in your family's mouths.

"Yes, I do know, thank you," Selby said, just as cool. "You certainly seem very busy."

Greta's eyes immediately narrowed, and Selby silently cursed herself. She wasn't supposed to be making an enemy of Agmund's ex, she'd seen the awful things people had been saying about Greta too, and she didn't deserve that, even if Agmund had loved her and touched her and—

No, *no*, Selby was *not* going there, and she dragged in a long breath. "Sorry," she said. "And listen, Greta, I'm sorry about all the rest of it too, all right? I really am. I had no idea Agmund was seeing someone."

But that was clearly the wrong thing to say too, because Greta tossed her hair over her shoulder, and came a step closer. "Yes, and if you *had* known," she countered, "you wouldn't have come? You'd have said no, you won't sleep with a guy who's already taken, because you're a better person than that?"

Selby had already opened her mouth to protest—of

course she was a better person than that—but then she winced, her eyes dropping to the floor. Gods knew what she would have done if she'd known, because it would have been just more mess in a situation that had already been full of it anyway...

"Yes, I thought so," came Greta's clipped voice. "We all know why you're here, pedlar. And it sure as *hell* isn't out of the goodness of your heart!"

Selby winced again, but the unfairness of that brought her eyes back up, her jaw clenched tight. "I'm doing this for the payment," she said, and though she hated the sound of those words, there was a strange, tilting relief in actually saying them. "And that's *all*."

Greta laughed, not kindly, and her eyes lingered purposefully, mockingly, on Selby's dress. "You know, I might almost believe you. If Regin wasn't gorgeous, and brilliant, and the most famous mage in the entire *country*!"

Gods damn it, this was going badly, and Selby rubbed at her mouth, searched for something, anything, to fix it. "Agmund doesn't actually want me, all right? He's only doing this for the magic. He's made that very, *very* clear."

There was a flash of something like triumph in Greta's eyes—but then it was gone just as quickly, leaving only bitterness behind. "Of course he doesn't want you," she said, her voice cracking, her eyes blinking hard. "You weren't actually *expecting* him to, were you?"

With that, she spun on her heel, and strode toward the stairs. Leaving Selby staring after her, at the square set of her shoulders, at the swinging blonde hair down her back. Damn it. *Damn* it.

Selby spent the next few minutes scrubbing at her face in Agmund's water closet, but it didn't help, and neither did the sight of herself in the water closet's small looking-glass. She'd never been a beauty, though she'd never seen herself as hideous, either—but damn, right now she looked awful, with the dark circles under her eyes, the reddened nose, the tired-looking skin.

And seeing herself again was just one more reminder how different she looked than the rest of them. Her face rounder and fuller, her nose flatter and wider, her skin several shades darker. Not to mention her hair, which rather than hanging neatly down her back, was a mass of thick black waves around her face.

But it was no use dwelling on what couldn't be changed, her mother always said, and also—Selby's mouth thinned in the looking-glass—why would she want to change it anyway? She didn't care what these rich entitled assholes thought of her. She *didn't*.

She repeated that thought in her head as she once again made for the corridor, and this time, thankfully, there was no sign of Greta, or anyone else. At least, until Selby reached the next landing down, where—her steps faltered—there was Njall, and the guy named Tomik, and two more of their air-mage buddies. Just standing there, looking at her. Waiting for her?

Selby made herself keep walking, and fought to ignore their staring eyes, their barely concealed snickers and whispers. *Look at that dress, it's like she nicked it out of a dump, Agmund's a braver man than I am...*

"Hey, pedlar," came Njall's voice behind her, once Selby had finally walked past them. "Think fast."

Selby turned, just in time to see Njall throw a handful of pebbles straight toward her. Not lightly or easily, but a hard overhand throw, and she barely had time to cover her face before the stones pelted her, bouncing off her hands and her dress onto the tiled floor.

The disbelief shouted through Selby's head, and she dropped her suddenly shaking hands, and glared at Njall, at the lot of them. "What the *hell*," she hissed. "You're actually throwing *rocks* at me? Aren't you all supposed to be brilliant mages, and not petty spoiled *brats*?!"

Njall replied with a saucy smile, a sidelong glance toward the air-mages at his back. "Well, I thought you're supposed to be an earth-mage," he said coolly. "You should be able to deal with a few rocks, shouldn't you?"

Oh, so it was some kind of fucked-up *test*, and Selby gripped for the nearby railing, felt the solid strength of the wood, the skilled cheerful carpenter who'd carved it. "I'm not that kind of earth-mage," she shot back. "I, um"—what had Ketill told her to say?—"I identify object properties."

"Like Regin's dick?" Tomik replied, sending the rest of them into gales of laughter. While Selby's face went hot, her throat tight, and she whirled around, and started back down the stairs. She wouldn't cry in front of them, she wouldn't...

"That's not real magic," called Njall's voice after her, carrying far too loudly through the open staircase. "We all know better, pedlar."

Selby was dangerously close to sobbing—she didn't care, she *didn't*—and she kept her head down, and moved as fast as she could. Until she nearly collided head-on with someone, another blonde-haired girl, in the second-floor corridor.

"Hey, Selby," said a vaguely familiar voice. "What's wrong?"

Selby blinked up through watery eyes, and found herself looking at a pale-faced, concerned-looking Thora. "Um," she gulped, around that lump in her throat. "Just some of Agmund's friends. Saying shit."

"Of *course* they were," Thora said, her soft voice gone steely. "Come this way, then. *Now*."

Selby didn't have it in her to argue, especially not with Thora, who had still been the kindest person here so far. So she let Thora steer her away, down the corridor toward a heavy steel door.

"Runar and I are working," Thora said, her voice still

surprisingly angry. "Come on, I'll introduce you. And you're welcome here whenever you like."

As she spoke, her fingers on Selby's elbow leaked of indignation, and a dark, angry satisfaction. *How dare those bastards make her cry in the hallway, just wait until they see what Agmund actually—*

That was a very strange thought, but Thora abruptly snatched her hand away, and yanked the heavy door open. Revealing a chilly, sterile-looking workroom, dominated by a large steel table, which currently held several unidentifiable grey items that looked unnervingly flesh-like.

One of the items was being pored over by a brown-skinned, white-smocked guy with a scalpel—the Runar Selby had seen previously in Thora's thoughts—and when Selby walked in he glanced up, a clear question in his brown eyes. "Who's this?" he asked Thora, in a low, pleasing voice. "Wait, don't tell me. A pedlar... wearing those *clothes*... reeking of a certain air-mage..."

Thora rolled her eyes, and shut the door behind them. "Selby, this is Runar Alariaq," she said. "He's one of the few healers on site right now, and one of the most brilliant scientists in the country. When he can shut his big mouth, that is."

Thora's face had noticeably flushed, and went even pinker when Runar shot her a teasing, stunning grin. "Thora likes my big mouth," he added lightly. "And she neglects to mention the part where she's doing most of the work. Welcome aboard, Selby. We need more women like you in these parts."

He winked at her as he spoke, in a way that could definitely be construed as flirtatious, and Selby shot a quick, careful look at Thora's pink face. "Thanks, that's very kind of you," she said politely. "So what kind of work do you two do in here?"

Her eyes angled toward the table, her thoughts flicking back to this manor's ever-present stench. *Runar Alariaq's work might leave a residue*, Kal had said. And this was absolutely the kind of work that would smell like death. Wasn't it?

Runar and Thora exchanged glances, and Runar gave a too-casual shrug. "Neural pathways, at the moment," he replied, "and the effects of reactivating them magically post-mortem. Thora does the projecting, I do the digging."

Selby's eyebrows went up, and Runar gave another smile, one that didn't reach his eyes. "Yep, it's exactly what it looks like," he continued, with a wave at whatever his scalpel had been doing. "I'm our resident cadaver-carver. If you ever see the bodies coming in or out—many of them courtesy of your current bedpartner—you'll know where they're going."

What? Selby stared at him, and the nausea roiled sudden and powerful in her stomach. Courtesy of her current *bedpartner?* They brought Agmund's kills back *here?* Cut them *up?* The *hell?*

"Wait, is Agmund really still killing people?" Selby asked, her voice shrill. "I haven't seen—I mean, I thought, with his magic situation—"

Runar shrugged, and spun the sharpened scalpel in his gloved fingers. "True, he hasn't been sent out lately," he replied. "But now that our magical pedlar is here to save the day, it'll only be a matter of time before the bodies start rolling in again. Not that I'm complaining, mind you—his kills are always pristine. Nothing keeps things intact like a clean old-fashioned shock."

He winked at Selby again, like it was all a good joke, but she was feeling truly ill, now. Agmund had said this was working, with his magic—gods knew she'd seen it working, too—and of course this meant she would be helping him kill people. Didn't it?

"Not funny, Runar," came Thora's voice, sharply. "Selby does *not* need to think about that right now. She's already got a hell of a lot to deal with as it is."

Runar grimaced, and shot an apologetic look in Selby's direction. "Sorry, sweetheart," he said. "I just think this whole drama is hilarious. What I would've given to see Agmund's face when he first met you."

Selby wasn't sure how to take that, but Runar gave her another saucy grin. "You better believe Agmund thought his one true magic affinity would be with yet another lily-white rich blonde heiress," he added. "I still can't decide if it's brilliant or pathetic that Ketill didn't warn him first. Likely thought he'd back out if he knew."

Selby tried to smile, but her thoughts were still full of corpses, of Regin-Agmund-induced death. "Well, I thought he might still back out, at first," she said, toward her feet. "But he hasn't."

The words were followed by an instant's silence, and when she glanced up again Thora's eyes were sympathetic, Runar's contemptuous. "Of course he hasn't," he replied. "Now the gods' gift to the country has a perfectly acceptable reason to trade in his previous hot girlfriend for an even hotter one, and get his magic back in the bargain. What's not to like?"

There was a twinge of bitterness in his voice, not unlike when Kal had talked about Agmund, and Selby made herself think. "Er, has this kind of thing ever been—arranged—before?" she asked. "For anyone else, I mean?"

Runar laughed again, not kindly. "Not a chance in hell. They're saying Ketill spent half his year's entire budget finding you. Only one mage here gets that kind of treatment."

Thora had drifted over closer to Runar as he'd spoken, and gave his shoulder a little bump with hers. "To be fair, though," she said, "it doesn't seem like Agmund asks for special treatment. And he's not usually a jerk about it, either."

"Maybe *he* isn't," Runar replied darkly. "The rest of those talentless hot-air hacks, though..."

Neither of them elaborated, and Selby looked between them, waiting. "Well, what's with the rest of them?" she asked. "I thought you had to be really brilliant to work for the Coven?"

"On paper, yes," Thora supplied, her eyebrows furrowing.

"But in reality, the Coven's ruling Council is full of rich nobles—lots of them without any magic themselves. And if you're a rich noble, and your child shows some magical skill, you're going to want to them to come here, right? Where they can work with Regin Agmund, and tell people they're friends with him?"

"But I thought the air-mages here did all the most important Coven missions and research," Selby countered. "Fulfilling the government's goals, and all that. So wouldn't they all *need* to be really top-tier?"

Runar snorted under his breath. "You'd think," he said. "But when you've got Regin Agmund making all your kills, does it really matter? Why do you think they're so desperate to fix him?"

Oh. That definitely added an even more horrible perspective to all this, and after a few more minutes' uneasy chit-chat, Selby plodded down to the dining hall, and then back to Agmund's room. Where she knelt by her little shelf, and took each of her things in hand, one by one.

She could do this. Three months. She'd known what she was signing up for. Hadn't she? Killing people was Regin Agmund's job. Carrying out the Coven's work—the government's work—was what he did. Regin Agmund was a scourge on the earth. Everyone knew.

But—Selby closed her eyes, stroked her fingers along Scarper's sharp little teeth—she'd never actually considered the possibility that any of this would work, either. She'd taken the coin and come here, sure, but who in their right mind would truly believe that a nobody pedlar could bring Regin Agmund's magic back? It was ridiculous, right?

She was still holding Scarper's skull when Agmund finally walked in, maybe an hour later. And though Selby hurriedly put the skull back on the shelf, she didn't miss the way Agmund's blue eyes lingered on it, narrowing with that already-familiar dislike.

"Could you wash your hands?" he asked, stiffly. "Before—?"

Before she touched him, he meant. And the unfairness of that suddenly curdled in Selby's already-miserable thoughts, and her whole body launched upwards, toward his looming hypocritical bony face.

"Truly?" she snapped, her voice cracking. "A clean little dog-skull is too disgusting for you? Meanwhile, you're the one off *killing* people, and bringing them back here so Runar can cut them into *pieces*?"

Agmund blinked at her, his lip giving a slow curl of contempt. "Yeah, well, I don't *touch* them," he replied flatly. "And I sure as hell don't bring them into somebody else's *bedroom!*"

Of course, the murderer was just so innocent and fucking *perfect*, and Selby threw up her apparently filthy hands, and stalked off to scrub them in the water closet, using far too much soap. She'd signed the contract, three months, people were going to *die*...

When she came back out again, with her teeth gritted and her hands impeccably clean, Agmund was sitting in his now-usual spot on the bed, and staring intently at the floor. He'd taken his boots off, and Selby's traitorous eyes flicked to the neck of his tunic, where the laces looked much looser than when he'd walked in.

"Look, another thing," Agmund said, still without looking at her. "Greta said you two talked today."

Oh. Selby felt her whole body go even stiffer, her eyes trapped on Agmund's bowed blond head. "Yes. And?"

There was an instant of awkward silence, as Agmund's grey sock traced a small crack in the tiled floor. "She said you were trying to get in my room when I wasn't here. And that you were rude to her."

What? That was so deeply unfair, and Selby made herself choke back the retort lurking on her tongue. The last thing she needed was to get into a who-said-what situation with Greta, and maybe she *had* been rude, but what about what Greta had said? Not to mention Agmund's *friends* and their *rock-throwing*?!

"I didn't realize I wasn't allowed in your room when you're not here," Selby said, finally, because that, at least, was truth. "I thought you said I could sleep here this morning. Did I misunderstand somehow?"

Agmund's eyes angled up, and he ran a hand against his hair. "No, it's fine," he replied, a little distractedly. "I'd just— look, I'd rather you didn't let people see you going in and out, all right?"

Selby blinked at him, because he couldn't possibly mean that—could he?—but he was talking again, frowning down at his foot. "And can you also not spread it around that you're fucking me for the coin?"

The *what*? Selby's body betrayed an involuntary twitch, her hands clenching at her sides. "What would you prefer me to say, then?" she asked, through the rushing in her ears. "That I'm doing it because you're famous? Or, maybe because I'm too wanton to keep my legs closed?"

Something jumped in Agmund's jaw, but he kept staring at the floor, his mouth set. And somehow, suddenly, Selby understood what he meant, and she let out a hard, bitter laugh. "Oh, of *course*," she said. "You want me to do it for the good of our beloved Vakra, don't you? To help the Coven and the government keep the peace? When that same government is all too often a *menace* to its own people—*especially* people like pedlars—and keeps us all in line with the constant threat of overpowered killing machines like *you*?"

Her voice had gone shrill at the end, daring Agmund to try and refute that, and when his eyes finally came up they were cold, hard, glittering. "Oh fuck off, Seng," he hissed. "I'm just doing my damned *job*. And if you honestly think the government or the Coven would stop *anything* they do without me, you're fucking delusional. At least when it's me on a job, it's quick, it's painless, there's no collateral damage. No wasted soldiers, no bloodbaths, no kids. All right?"

He said it like it was a chant, like he'd said it many times before, but that only wrung the disbelief higher in Selby's head. "No, it's *not* all right!" she shouted back. "You walking in and destroying everyone in your path is deeply and horribly unfair! People have *reasons* for what they do, you just—you just *silence* them, don't give them a chance to speak or fight back or run or even *surrender*, it's just Regin fucking Agmund, the *end*!"

In a sudden jerky movement Agmund leapt to his feet, coming far too close. "How dare you," he growled down at her. "How fucking *dare* you. You waltz in here and take that coin to fuck me, and then you turn around and rail at me about shit like this? News for you, witch, *you're* the one selling yourself to give me my magic back so I can work again! At least my reasons are valid, yours are just about the fucking *coin*!"

He was right, gods curse him, and suddenly the fight all seemed to leave Selby at once. Three months. How many people would Agmund kill in three months? She'd justified it, at least to herself, but maybe there was no justification at all.

"You're right," she said. "You're right. And I think that's why"—she took a breath, looked at his furious face—"I should quit."

11

The silence was almost overpowering, ringing through the room, and Selby should have taken it, and left. Walked out with her grand statement, her integrity, her dignity.

But instead she just kept standing there, staring down at Agmund's sock feet. She should quit. It shouldn't matter if there were penalties, if all the coin had to be paid back. It shouldn't. People were going to die, because of her.

"You want to *quit*?" Agmund demanded, too close, though his voice was quieter than before. "You mean that?"

Selby nodded, still staring at his feet, and her nose gave a ridiculous little sniff. Gods, why didn't she leave, she should leave...

"But I thought it was going fine," Agmund said, a little rushed. "Wasn't it? You're here, we're figuring it out, you're getting to know the place, doing your job, it's *fine*. Right?"

It was enough to snap Selby's gaze back up, to glare at the odd unease in his eyes. "No, it's *not* fine!" she shot back. "In fact, I'm pretty sure these past three days have been the worst of my entire *life*. This place smells like *death*, I have to sleep on the floor and get attacked by *lightning storms*, I have absolutely *nothing* productive to do with my time, the servants refuse to *look* at me, your ex-girlfriend *hates* me, and your horrible friends mock me and throw *rocks* at me in the corridors!"

Agmund's mouth hardened, his eyes gone narrow, suspicious. "They threw rocks at you," he repeated. "Who. *When.*"

"Njall, this afternoon," Selby replied flatly, and though that was snitching, at this point she couldn't make herself care. "While the rest of them laughed. Trying to prove I'm not a real earth-mage, apparently."

She had to close her eyes against the memory, and she could feel Agmund shuffling on his feet, so close—and without warning there was a strange, shaky touch of his hand to her shoulder. And behind it, Selby could see—images. Words. His thoughts.

And Regin Agmund's thoughts were a mess. All *those fucking fools*, and *you can't leave, please*, and *I need my magic, the best three days of my entire fucking year*. And *I told Njall you were a real mage, Greta wouldn't stop crying, said you rubbed it in her face, acted like you were better than her. I don't even want to be sent out again, five whole months since a kill, the only good thing in all this mess, except—*

Agmund's hand snatched away, just as abrupt, the thoughts snapping off with it, and Selby stared at him, at his uneasy guilty eyes. He'd just—had he just—he'd *spoken* to her? Through his *thoughts*?!

And yes, maybe he'd done it in bed, with the memories of him exploding those trees—but this felt different, more stream-of-consciousness. Like Regin Agmund really, truly wanted her to know what he was thinking, right now, this very moment. And Selby couldn't recall anyone else ever trying that before, and the fact that Regin Agmund had tried, of all people...

"Look, I'll deal with Njall, I swear," Agmund said now, out loud, voice flat. "And if it's really that important to you, I'll ask Ketill if I can put off any assignments for a while. It's not like I'm anywhere close to top form yet anyway. All right?"

Selby was still staring dumbfounded at him, digesting all that. He'd showed her his thoughts. He'd deal with Njall. He'd ask Ketill if he could put off his assignments...

"Do you promise?" Selby asked, her voice wavering. "That you won't use my magic to kill people?"

There was another instant's stillness, Agmund's weight shifting from foot to foot. "They don't even send me out that often," he said, quiet. "It's only when nothing else works. Or to make a point."

Selby's eyes narrowed—he was trying to get out of it, right?—and she shook her head. "And you think that makes it *fair*?" she demanded. "What about that peasant uprising two years ago?"

Agmund sighed, and there was a hint of that familiar curl on his lip. "You didn't honestly think that was a good idea, did you? A few hundred farmers marching on the capital? It would have been a *bloodbath*."

Selby glowered back at him, and poked her finger into his bony chest, ignoring the requisite swirl of images behind it. "You killed *hundreds* of innocent people."

Agmund frowned down at her finger, but didn't move, or shove it away. "No, I didn't," he snapped. "I gave hundreds of violent rebels a clean, painless way out, instead of what the army would have done to them."

Selby's thoughts faltered, and she had to search for a reply. "Well, it's still not your decision to make," she countered. "*You* shouldn't be the bringer of death!"

"I'm *not*," Agmund shot back. "It's the government's call, and the Coven's. I'm just following orders. Doing my *job*."

Selby's hand was still on his chest, inexplicably, and she belatedly dropped it, and glared at his too-appealing eyes. "Just because it's your job doesn't mean that following unjust orders is *acceptable*!"

Agmund raised his eyebrows, gave a dismissive shrug. "And who gets to decide if the orders are unjust or not? Me? You?"

"Better than a bunch of out-of-touch nobles, isn't it?" Selby demanded. "Why do *they* get all the power? Just because they're rich? You weren't always rich, you know what it's like to be at other people's mercy, why do you give *them* so much credit?"

For an instant Agmund just looked at her, his eyebrows still high on his forehead, and Selby belatedly realized she'd just made it clear how deep her covert knowledge of him went—but he didn't complain, or question it. Just kept standing there, looking at her.

"Look, it's pretty clear we're not going to agree on this," he said finally. "But can you at least accept that I'm not going to run off and start murdering innocent people for no reason?"

There was something almost pleading in his eyes, and Selby steeled herself against it. "No," she whispered. "I can't."

And maybe she was pleading with him too, and maybe he even saw it, because he exhaled, and ran a hand against his hair. "Right," he said. "Fine. How about this. I'll still ask Ketill about taking a break from jobs. And whatever he says, whatever happens—I'll tell you."

Selby hesitated, blinking at Agmund, and she could feel the intent behind his words, the truth in his eyes. But it still wasn't enough. Was it?

"I'll be honest with you," he continued, faster now. "No matter what. So you'll know what's going on, and you can make your choices from there. You can even search through my head if you want, I don't give a damn. But either way, you'll know. Total honesty from now on. All right?"

Selby kept studying his eyes, so intent and earnest and almost—afraid, somehow. Like he truly did mean it, and as if to confirm that, his hand reached and brushed against her shoulder again. Whispering, *I promise. Please don't go.*

And Selby shouldn't trust him—couldn't—but all the same, she felt herself relaxing, her shoulder sagging against his fingers. "I'm holding you to that, asshole," she said. "And, you still need to try to get out of any murdering. *Actually* try."

The smile on Agmund's mouth was swift, and startlingly stunning. "So we're good?" he asked lightly. "You'll stay? Do your duty, and all that?"

Selby rolled her eyes at him, but she couldn't deny that sudden thrill of heat, of anticipation. Regin Agmund wanted her, Regin Agmund had shown her his thoughts. Regin Agmund was going to try to put off doing his job, was going to be honest with her. *You can even search through my head, if you want.*

And it was probably naive, short-sighted, selfish to even consider it. But when Agmund spun and strode over to sit on the bed, and looked up at Selby under those pale eyelashes, somehow, it was enough. Enough to make her shaky hands go down to her dress's buttons, undoing them one by one.

She was wearing another white shift today, and she didn't miss Agmund's eyes lingering on it as the dress fell to the floor. But then he glanced away, and rubbed a hand at the back of his neck.

"Look, I was talking to Ketill today," he said abruptly. "And he said—if we want to see even better results with this, we should have more—contact."

More contact. Another thrill of heat—or maybe unease—shot up Selby's back, and she held her body still, her eyes on Agmund's face. "What kind of contact?"

Agmund gave a brief glance upwards, a vague wave of his hand toward her shift. "You know. The usual."

Selby couldn't breathe for an instant, and she put her hands to her hips, and fixed him with a glare that was almost genuine. "Really?" she demanded. "You come in here today and insult me, and make ridiculous accusations, and imply that I'm too much of a harlot for you. And now you want me to strip naked while I fuck you, so you can get more magic from me?"

Agmund crossed his arms over his bony chest, but the corner of his mouth gave an unmistakable little twitch. "And you're refusing?" he said back, matching her tone. "You're the one who volunteered for this job, you knew exactly what it was, did you really think you'd get to keep your fucking *clothes* on the whole time?"

Gods, he was such a bastard, because *he'd* been the one who'd wanted Selby to keep her clothes on in the first place. And she should call him out on that, but he was flashing her a crooked little smile, and he'd spoken to her through his *thoughts*, and did he really want to *see*—

Selby grabbed for her shift with fumbling hands, and yanked it up, and off over her head. Leaving herself entirely naked and exposed, standing there in the middle of Regin Agmund's bedroom, while his eyes swept down, and up, and down again.

The heat seemed to follow his gaze, lighting up under Selby's skin, and she had to hold herself still, keep from covering herself with her hands. She'd never been dissatisfied with her body—it had always served her well, and she liked its smooth, ample curves—but now, under Agmund's too-obvious scrutiny, she was suddenly far too aware of the potential inadequacies of it. Whether her full breasts might hang too low, the nipples of them too dark. Whether her hips might be too thick, her legs too short, her groin too covered in its wiry black hair.

It didn't help that Agmund wasn't speaking, or that now his eyes were lingering, first on her breasts, and then lower down. And when he finally looked at her face again, his cheeks were flushed, his lips pressed tight together.

"Well?" Selby asked, her voice sounding huskier, warmer, than it should have been. Making something shift in Agmund's eyes, and with a sudden, jerky movement, he reached for his own tunic, and yanked it off over his head.

His bare chest beneath it was pale, with pink nipples, and a smattering of white-blond hair. And though Selby could see those rows of ribs beneath his skin, he was still surprisingly, strangely beautiful. Setting something clenching hard between her legs, and she had to look away, bite her lip, work to keep her breaths steady.

But Agmund's hands were moving again, now at the ties of his trousers, and Selby's eyes darted back toward him as he thrust the trousers downwards. Not off all the way, since he was still sitting up, but maybe a little more than he'd done the previous times—and now there was his swollen pink cock, pointing out toward her, and giving an unmistakable, betraying twitch.

A furtive glance at Agmund's eyes found him looking almost defiant, but Selby's own body was clenching again in reply. And somehow, she seemed to find the courage, or maybe the brazenness, to walk forward, toward *that*, and there was a sheer, tilting relief as Agmund slid his long body backwards, lowering himself down onto the bed.

This part was familiar now, thank the gods, and Selby straddled him with something almost like eagerness. Drinking in the sight of that bare chest beneath her, the lovely contrast of her skin against his, the thrilling sight of his hand once again moving downwards, taking his ruddy length into his fingers, and guiding it up toward her.

Selby met it willingly, lowering herself against that wonderful smooth hardness, and even though she expected it now, braced herself for it, it still swarmed her in a flood. The feel of him, the invading silken heat of him, the shouting exploding visions, far less controlled this time. Regin Agmund and his lightning, Regin Agmund and his magic finally working again, Regin Agmund gritting his teeth as he tried to placate his disconsolate ex-girlfriend, *I'm trying to keep it quiet, I can't help that people are talking, I'm just doing my fucking job, there is* nothing *to it beyond that—*

Too late Selby jerked herself away, glowering down at his stupid handsome face. "Watch it," she hissed. "Asshole."

Agmund rolled his eyes, but then raised an eyebrow, and

thrust his hips upward, nudging back against her. And between the truth of that and the feel of that there was the glorious, breathtaking vision of Regin Agmund, just today, out in a clearing in the forest, drawing in his focus, careful, careful, and then bringing down a single, beautiful streak of blinding jagged lightning, oh *gods*—

Selby's mouth let out an audible, undeniable gasp, her eyes fluttering closed for an instant, and beneath her Agmund actually gave a choked chuckle. Laughing at her, even as he raised his hips a little further, nudged a little harder, and something like triumph and maybe contempt played in his eyes.

"Fuck you," Selby muttered, and then winced at the unfortunate truth of those words, at the replying sharp laugh from his mouth.

"I'm waiting," he said, with mockery on his eyes, his mouth. "Get on with it, wench."

Wench. Selby's fury soared up at once, but at the same time so did Agmund's hips, snapping upwards enough that he sank halfway into her waiting wet heat. And fuck, that was good, enough to make her gasp again, enough for her traitorous body to sink downwards, to take him the rest of the way inside.

Oh. Oh, this was good, the pleasure and the ache and the impossible feel of him so deep, so hard. Firing down that jagged fork of lightning again, and she ground herself deeper on him, felt her whole body arch backwards as another groan escaped her mouth. *Fuck*.

Agmund laughed again, breathless this time, and even as a distant part of Selby cursed herself for actually wanting this, and letting him see that she wanted this, the other part of her was putting her hands down to that smooth pale skin of his chest. Spreading her fingers wide, feeling the warmth of him, the rapid-fire pace of his heartbeat.

"This has nothing to do with you," she breathed, but then his hips snapped up again, sending a bolt of pleasure so deep that her mouth betrayed a choked little cry. And Agmund was smiling again, darkly, and then—oh fuck—setting up a punishing, shocking rhythm, driving up and up and up again. Fast and hard enough that Selby could only cling to him, her whole body jolting above him, her lips clamped tight to keep her mouth from screaming.

When Agmund finally slowed, his face was red, there was a sheen of sweat on his chest, and his gaze—Selby swallowed, hard—was lingering on her breasts. To where they were still heaving, maybe still jiggling a little from the movement, their nipples pointed and hard and hungry.

And maybe it was another way of saying *fuck you*, but Agmund was still looking, and he was the one who'd wanted more touching, the cursed hypocrite. And his hands were still by his sides—*I didn't even touch her*, he'd said—so Selby grabbed one of those hands, and lifted it, and put it to her bare breast.

Agmund didn't resist—if anything, his fingers curved slightly around it—and Selby's mouth went dry at the sight, at how her heavy breast just filled his hand, bulging out just a little between his long pale fingers.

He was looking too, not otherwise moving, and that same twisted part of Selby took his other hand, and did the same on the other side. And gods, it felt good, looked good, and now she was the one riding him, with his hands gripping her skin, his cock driving deep and powerful inside.

The tension was spiralling up again, pooling and tightening, and Selby let her body take over. Leaning forward over him, grinding up against just the right place, pushing her breasts even harder into those still-willing fingers—and there it was, oh fuck oh gods, the pleasure sinking and collapsing and exploding outward, as sharp and stunning and electrifying as the visions of lightning still filling her head—

Then it was Agmund's hips snapping up again, sinking again and again into Selby's still-quivering heat. And oh, she could feel it, feel him twitching fuller and harder, his entire body stiffening under her, his hands clutching so tight they were almost painful—

And with one deep, final thrust, he emptied himself inside, pulsing out long and hard, his eyes rolling back, his mouth letting out a harsh, betraying groan of its own. Telling Selby that he'd wanted this, gotten off from this, and suddenly she felt shaky all over, her fingers light and fluttery on his skin.

Agmund's hands pulled away from her breasts, suddenly, and the loss of that seemed to make Selby even shakier. And gods, she was going to collapse on him, and that wouldn't go over well, and she somehow pulled herself off, and sank down onto the bed beside him instead.

She was still breathing hard, and so was Agmund, and he'd brought his arm up over his face, covering his eyes. Saying he was done with her, maybe, or maybe that she should leave—but he didn't actually say either of those things. Just stayed there, his face hidden, his bare chest heaving with his breath.

At least the bed was still soft and comfortable, even if too small to avoid touching him, and Selby was suddenly acutely aware of how her body was still pressed close to his, their damp skin sticking together. But he still wasn't protesting, or moving, and it occurred to her that maybe what Ketill had said about touching could extend to afterwards, too.

It was enough to let her relax again, her eyes fluttering closed, her thoughts shifting and changing toward sleep. And when Agmund finally elbowed her, jolting her back awake, the sky out the window was almost black, and she could just make out his hands tying up his trousers.

"Hey," his voice said. "You're in my bed."

But at the moment, Selby was too tired, or maybe too contented, to care. "So?" she asked. "I thought you said Ketill wanted us touching each other?"

Agmund let out an irritated huff of breath, and abruptly leapt out of bed, and stalked off toward the water closet—probably in a temper again, but Selby still didn't care.

Not much, at least, though she couldn't deny that when he came back again, looking freshly washed, and slid back into bed beside her, something seemed to flip upside-down in her gut.

"If you kick in your sleep, you're getting the hell out," he snapped, before rolling over onto his side, facing away from her. But he was still in the bed, and Selby wasn't on the floor, and maybe that was a victory, or a truce, or something.

"I don't kick," she said, and she knew it was true, because she'd been cramped in small beds with various family members for years. "And you're one to talk, with your terrifying nighttime lightning storms."

Agmund harrumphed, and then reached down, yanked the blanket up over his shoulder. "Terrifying, my arse," he muttered. "I'll probably wake up to you humping my leg while I sleep."

He was such an absolute bastard, but an appalling part of Selby chuckled, enough that she made both their bodies shake. "Fuck you," she managed, but she'd turned over too, so her back was snug up against his. "Asshole."

He made a sound she couldn't quite decipher, and pulled the blanket up higher. "In the morning," he said. "Witch."

And with those bizarrely comforting words ringing in her ears, Selby closed her eyes, and slept.

12

It was maybe an hour later when Selby snapped awake to a blinding flash of lightning, streaking from the ceiling straight down to the bed.

She almost shouted, but stopped herself just in time, clapping her hand over her mouth. She was breathing hard, her heartbeat thundering in her chest, and as she watched, another streak of lightning shot from the ceiling to the post of the bed near her foot, reverberating with a low rumble of corresponding thunder.

At least it hadn't actually hit her this time—maybe being closer to Agmund was something of a safety feature—but it still looked deadly, and the air felt dangerous, too. Strange and crackling, like it would feel in a real storm, and Selby twitched as another bolt shot from the ceiling, and made contact with the floor this time.

It was still highly terrifying, despite whatever Agmund said, and despite whatever liking Selby seemed to have found for it in Agmund's thoughts. And in the next flash of light she caught sight of Agmund himself, lying on his back beside her, with his eyes squeezed shut, and his right hand raised up in the air.

It was the same hand position he used when he was awake

and casting, Selby now knew. And something about that seemed to help her heartbeat slow, her breath returning to normal again, and she frowned down at Agmund's face, his clenched-shut eyes. Everything about him looked clenched, actually, what with his forehead furrowed, his jaw taut, the cords standing out in his neck. And in the irregular flashing light, he looked almost... wrong. Like a wraith, maybe, or a desiccated corpse, the bones of his skull standing out gaunt and sharp and white.

It was enough that Selby risked a tentative touch to his bare shoulder—but then she yanked her hand away, hissing through her teeth. He *felt* wrong, too, like something charged and strung too tight, and with the touch there'd been snippets of images, of dreams. Agmund on a battlefield, Agmund tracking coordinates, and instead of trees it was people, men and women, *snap snap snap* as they dropped limp to the earth, one by one by one, a rising pile of bodies staring blankly at the sky—

It was horrifying to see, to experience, and Selby shook her head, tried to thrust the visions out. She knew this was Agmund's job, damn it, especially after that fight they'd had earlier—but to actually *see* it, to *feel* it, to know that *this* was what Regin Agmund dreamed about at nights—

She gritted her teeth, and in the next flash of light, she reached to grip Agmund's upheld hand. Feeling the electricity on it, jolting out of him, and into her—and beyond that, above that, how it wanted to keep working. Needed to fulfill the orders, this was his job, his calling, his gift, couldn't let them down—

Selby gripped harder, wrapping her fingers around Agmund's, and dragged his hand down, back toward the bed. Still feeling the current in it, the strength of it, but she could feel the images starting to scatter, too. Cutting in with trees and sky, with people who were friends rather than enemies. His father, an old friend named Mik, Greta...

Selby winced, but thankfully the lightning around them had slowed, and then stopped entirely. So she carefully let go of Agmund's hand, placing it onto his chest, and then rolled over, and tried to go back to sleep.

But she was jerked awake again, some time later, by yet another flash of blinding light. She groaned aloud, rubbing at her eyes, and then grabbed for Agmund's upheld hand again. The feeling of wrongness on him was back, so powerful that it set the nausea roiling in her stomach—and this time in the dream, he was duelling. Fighting furiously against enemies who didn't have faces, who had shields over their heads, his magic fading, they were going to kill him, they were backing him toward a cliff over a rushing, white-topped river—

Selby yanked his hand back down, making the visions scatter again, and this time she kept her fingers gripped on his as she fell back to sleep. And when he tried to raise the hand again—gods knew when, but it was still dark—Selby shoved his arm down flat to the bed, and this time flopped herself facedown on top of it.

It meant she was pressed up beside him, with his bare arm under her bare belly, almost as though it was embracing her. And gods, Selby was fucked with this, but she couldn't deny that it was a warm, lovely feeling, and she easily fell back to sleep, and this time, didn't wake again until dawn.

It was the awareness of Agmund stirring beside her that finally brought her fully awake in the dim light, and when she blinked toward him he was looking at her, and frowning, and tugging at his arm that was still trapped beneath her.

"Can you move?" he snapped. "You're making my hand go numb."

Selby shifted accordingly, enough to let him pull his arm out, and then sank back into the soft bed beside him, against the warm heat of his skin. "Sorry," she murmured. "Just stopped you casting. Only way I could sleep."

Agmund didn't reply, but another sleepy glance at his face

showed him still frowning, and clenching and unclenching his fingers. Like Selby had done some irreparable damage to his pristine air-mage body, and she pulled herself up onto her elbows, so she could roll her eyes at him. "Oh, settle down," she said. "It won't kill you."

He shot her another dark look, but he dropped his hand, and Selby gave him her sweetest smile. Making something twitch in his clenched jaw, but he still wasn't getting up, or pushing her away. Wasn't even resisting the fact that she was naked up against him, and his words from the night before rose in her thoughts. *In the morning*, he'd said.

Maybe the same thought had occurred to him, because he was looking intently away, a faint flush creeping up his neck. And even though Selby's body was still sore from yesterday, and feeling rather a sticky mess, she found that the idea of doing it again wasn't an unpleasant one, not in the least.

Agmund still wasn't looking at her, but a night spent sleeping in his bed, against his skin, was doing curious things to Selby's still-drowsy thoughts. Giving her compulsions that she'd never imagined herself feeling before, and she couldn't quite believe it when her hand under the blanket moved, seemingly on its own, toward him. Toward his crotch, in fact, and Selby let out a slow, shuddery breath at the feel of that hard, swollen cock, twitching up toward her fingers through his trousers.

It wasn't her first time touching a guy like this, at least, so it wasn't exactly a shock—but even so, there were more images swimming unbidden in her head, cloudy ones of magic and dreams, empty faces, that river. Not conscious thoughts this time, not trying to speak to her, just—there.

But Agmund didn't protest, and Selby let her eyes flutter closed, while her hand began to do as it willed. Sliding carefully up and down the length of him over his trousers, venturing a little further each time, until her fingers trailed down over his bollocks, and then up over that hard rounded head.

Gods, he was lovely, beautifully made, and he still didn't protest, didn't move. Not even when Selby's fingers went to untie his trousers under the blanket, and then—oh gods—reached in and pulled him out, all bare smooth willing heat.

Agmund still didn't move, so Selby let herself keep exploring, keep learning. Feeling how silken the skin of him was, how it slid so easily up and down, how her fingertips could barely touch when they circled around him. How—she gasped, and maybe he did, too—even the slightest pressure of her fingers like that made him twitch, and go just a shade harder, and how the balls at the base of him were full and soft and round, the perfect size to cup in her hand.

His hair was just as coarse as hers down there, though there seemed to be much more of it, and next Selby explored the smooth head of him, pulling the skin down, running her finger gently over the slit. Feeling the wetness there, and then letting herself linger on that, on the intoxicating, dizzying truth that he liked this, Regin Agmund was hard from this, he was letting her touch him, letting her do whatever the hell she wanted with him.

So her brazen, inexplicable fingers went even further. Exploring the creases of his bony hips, and where the hair spread down his thighs. And then even deeper between his legs, below those heavy bollocks to where it was warm and secret, clenching against the rub of her finger.

She knew some people liked being touched there—one guy back east had begged her to do certain unspeakable things to it—and a furtive glance up at Agmund's heated face showed that he didn't exactly seem to mind, either. But now he'd caught her looking at him, and then he swallowed, and gave a jerky wave of his hand.

"Get on with it, will you?" he said, his voice scratchy. "I don't have all day here."

It felt like a slap, and Selby had to close her eyes for an instant, find truth again. Regin Agmund was still an asshole, she knew that, and he probably thought her groping him like this was just part of the deal. And that was all it was, even if he'd let her caress him like that, touch him like that, if he—

There was an abrupt movement from his hand, thrusting down the blanket, exposing himself to her, making his point clear. And even now, Selby was caught in the sight of him, in matching what she'd just felt to what she now saw, and why did he have to be so damned appealing, and what would he say if she were to cup those balls again, just once—

But no, no, she was supposed to get on with it, and with a groan she shoved up to her knees, letting the blanket fall. Giving Agmund a good eyeful as she straddled him, and then—she gasped—she felt the remnants of last night's activities slipping out of her, dribbling down onto his bare belly.

Agmund stared down at it, with something entirely unreadable in his eyes, something not unlike disgust. While Selby's mortified face flooded with heat, her hands fluttering between her crotch and her mouth, looking for something, anything, to wipe the mess away.

"Oh, gods," she breathed. "Damn it, sorry—should I go—"

She flailed a frantic half-wave toward the water closet, and made to lurch up toward it—but then Agmund's hand clenched on her hip, holding her still. "No, I don't care," he muttered. "Just—finish it, all right?"

Finish it. Selby's face flushed even hotter, and she shot a chagrined glance downwards. Toward where Agmund hadn't moved to guide himself up this time, and instead his hand just kept waiting there, heavy on her hip.

That left her to do it, then, and Selby unsteadily reached down, took the hard heft of him in her fingers. And then lifted him up, even as she brought herself down, and this time rather than lingering, getting used to him, she made herself take him all the way, biting her lip to keep from crying out at the feel of him, all smooth delving piercing hardness.

It definitely felt wetter than before, and stickier, but there was something in that, in the truth that it was Agmund who'd done that, and who was now inside her again, about to do it again. And it was enough to set her hips rocking against him, oh gods, and he instantly met her in it, his own hips rolling up, and—Selby couldn't help a strangled groan—his other hand coming to her other hip, guiding her down as he came up, keeping her in his rhythm.

The images were still there, of course, swimming through his head into hers, but maybe Selby had gotten a bit inured to them by now, or maybe Agmund just thought less in the mornings. In any case, there was thankfully no actual murdering in them, mostly just snippets of his dreams, of his father, the forest, a cliff, a river. While his body kept slamming up and up, so hard that Selby cried out, far too loud. Until Agmund abruptly stopped, and clapped his overlarge hand over her mouth.

"Shut up for a minute," he breathed, as his other hand—his casting hand—came up. And suddenly Selby could *feel* the magic flowing out of him, purposeful, powerful, intentional this time. It was a spell to change the air's density—to suppress sound, his thoughts supplied—and gods, it felt good, unfurling out of him like that, and Selby couldn't stop another harsh groan, even as Agmund's fingers slackened against her mouth, his lips curling into a smug little smile.

"Now screech all you want," he said coolly, and Selby glared at him, snatched his hand off her mouth—and then, unthinkingly, put it down to her breast instead. Because she wanted to feel that again, because he owed her that, because he was such an utter bastard and he felt so damned *good*—

His hand cupped tighter around her breast, his other hand gripping her hip, holding her there as he fucked her. And curse it, Selby's mouth was still betraying her, crying out far too loud, but then Agmund was the one gasping, his eyes rolling back—and Selby could feel that beautiful smooth cock firing off inside her, pumping her full of his pleasure.

Gods, it was good, even still. And even the feel of the mess he'd made of her was good too, so full and heavy and slick, and Selby let herself sag down on him, revelling in the sensation of it. That cock slowly softening inside, those hands still held too tight on her skin.

But then the hands drew away, leaving only cool air in their wake, and then a light little slap to her hip. "Up," Agmund said, and though Selby should have been offended, she still felt too damn good to care.

"Might be messy," she told him instead, but Agmund only shrugged, and waved her up anyway. So she moved her body upwards, wincing at the loss of him, and then again at the wet sound it made, the strings of sticky white oozing between them, the shiny wet sheen of his ruddy half-hard cock.

If Selby wasn't mistaken, Agmund was looking too, and there was an unmistakable replying twitch from that cock. But then he shoved up and out of bed, holding up his loose trousers as he stalked toward the water closet, and slammed the door behind him.

Well. Selby looked at the closed door for a long minute, feeling his mess now slipping down her thighs, and then she dropped herself back to the bed and pressed her hands to her eyes, hard. Gods, how could he feel so good, and still be so awful, and was she really thinking of sitting up again, with her breasts bare to the air, just to see if he would look—

But she didn't move, and when Agmund stalked out again, looking freshly scrubbed, with his trousers properly tied around his waist, he didn't even glance at her. Just went and pulled on a clean tunic from the wardrobe, and strode toward the door.

"You're leaving?" Selby asked, stupidly, to his back, before she could stop herself. "For the whole day?"

Agmund hesitated, his hand on the latch, his face straight ahead toward the door. "Ketill's sending me scouting," he said. "But I'll be back by supper. Meet me here after that?"

Selby nodded, which Agmund couldn't see, but he was still standing there, still with his hand on the door. "And look," he added, flatter now. "Just—stay out of certain people's way, all right?"

Selby swallowed, but gave another nod he couldn't see. And then he left, taking care not to open the door too far as he went. No doubt to make sure that if any of his friends were outside, they wouldn't notice Selby's unwelcome pedlar presence in his bedroom.

It wasn't a great start to the day, a feeling that only intensified as Selby dressed and washed, and then stepped out into the corridor. Which—she gagged, and clapped a hand over her mouth—stank like nothing she'd ever smelled before. Like a sickening wall of putrid, rotting death.

She bolted back inside the bedroom, and then straight into the water closet. Where she spent far too long kneeling over the latrine, gasping for air, her body shuddering all over with an awful cold sweat.

By the time it was finally done, and Selby's beleaguered stomach had somewhat settled again, an ugly, nagging question had arisen in her thoughts. Perhaps the smell had something to do with her? Perhaps it was *targeting* her?

It didn't seem possible, but once she had cleaned herself up, she carefully crept back out of the water closet, and over to Agmund's shelf. To her most meaningful possessions, with their undeniable little aura of clarity still surrounding them, and she reached and picked up Scarper's skull, stroked it carefully in her fingers.

And it was—better. Better, here in Agmund's room, and better, the closer she was to her possessions. So maybe—Selby reached out a tentative finger to touch the nearest wall, and then hissed at the foul taste of it—maybe this *was* magic.

Unkind magic. Magic that was perhaps targeted specifically toward her.

It was a deeply appalling prospect, but the more she considered it, the more it seemed the only possible answer. She was the only person affected by the smell, the only one to even notice it. And though she wasn't familiar with spells like this, she'd heard whispers about them, like everyone had. Spells to weaken people, to haunt people. Spells that could use a person's own magic against them.

There was no provision in her contract for illness, Selby knew, and none for malignant spells, either. Gods, she hadn't even thought of those as possible outcomes, and she rubbed her eyes, tried to think. If she became too sick to carry out her Agmund-fucking duties, would she need to leave after all? Would she need to give the coin back? Pay those penalties?

She looked down at Scarper's skull in her hands, and then reached to touch at her mother's lock of hair, and Simon's whistle. What would they say if she failed? If all the coin had to be returned? What would happen to them then?

No, no, curse it, *no*, and Selby grasped for the hair and the whistle, and gripped them tight. She wasn't going to back down. She would find out who was targeting her, and why.

And with another deep breath, she lurched to her feet, braced herself, and opened the door.

13

Selby spent the rest of the morning wandering around Coven Manor, poking her head into all the places she didn't belong. Going over every single floor, touching every single wall, and earning for her trouble multiple suspicious looks, and a colourful variety of snickers, whispers, and not-unintelligible insults.

"Does this place have any crawl spaces?" she asked a skittish-looking housemaid, who had tried dodging off in the opposite direction when she'd seen Selby approach. But Selby had been quicker, and she bodily blocked the maid from moving, and fixed her with a grim smile. "Or maybe a basement?"

"No, miss," the maid said, keeping her eyes on the floor, while her slippered feet angled sideways. "There used to be a basement, years ago, but it's been completely filled in."

That wasn't helpful, and Selby whipped out a piece of paper and charcoal that she'd snitched from Agmund's desk drawer. "Can you tell me who this room belongs to, then?" she asked, jabbing the charcoal at the rough map she'd started drawing. "Or this one?"

The maid babbled out some names, which Selby jotted

down with the others she'd collected so far. It didn't mean much, at the moment, but it was a start. And so far, her explorations had discovered that the smell seemed slightly stronger here, on the manor's bottom floor. And in addition to the dining hall and main entrance, the bottom floor also housed all five directors' offices, the servants' quarters, a large meeting room, and apparently, a makeshift morgue, seemingly for the personal use of one Runar Alariaq.

It seemed unlikely that the servants could be responsible for the smell, but given their deeply hostile reactions to Selby so far, they couldn't easily be eliminated, either. And neither could Runar, or the directors—which included Ketill, of course. But would Ketill truly try to sabotage her like that? After all the time and coin he'd expended to bring her here?

"Ms. Seng," interrupted a too-familiar voice, and when Selby whirled around, there was the white-robed, highly unwelcome sight of Ketill himself. "Come with me, please," he said. "There's someone I'd like you to meet."

Selby nodded, grudgingly tucking away her map and charcoal, and followed Ketill around the corner. Into a spacious, well-appointed room, with a small sitting area, a heavy, well-constructed desk, and shelves and shelves of books lining the walls.

It was Ketill's office, Selby knew, and—she couldn't help a convulsive twitch—Agmund had been inside it. Recently. She'd been trying to ignore her constant awareness of Agmund's movements, but looking back over the morning, she could follow where he'd gone to breakfast, then back up to his room, and then here, where he'd paced back and forth, lingering in this very spot. And then he'd gone out, due north. Scouting, he'd said.

"Ms. Seng, yes?" interrupted another voice, and Selby belatedly noticed that there was a second person here, a woman she didn't recognize. She had short dark hair and a tall, slim build, and she was perhaps Ketill's age, maybe not quite to her sixtieth year. "I'm Augusta Morley," the woman said, with a smile. "Director of the earth-magic department. I've heard a lot about you, Ms. Seng."

Her smile was warm, and surprisingly genuine, and Selby managed a smile back. "I'm sure you have," she dryly replied. "Nice to meet you. And please, call me Selby."

Morley's smile widened into an actual grin, and she gave a pointed glance toward Ketill behind them. "I assure you, Selby, I've only heard good things," she said. "Klaus tells me you're already working wonders with Mr. Agmund. Like I've always said, Klaus"—she elbowed at Ketill's side—"you air-mages need us earth-users around to keep you properly grounded."

Ketill's eyes looked forbidding, but he slightly inclined his head. "I will admit, Ms. Seng's affinity with Regin is among the strongest I've ever encountered," he replied. "The results have been highly impressive. Enough that Regin is finally able to be useful again."

Useful. The word rankled, and Selby's head tilted, her eyes narrowing on Ketill's face. "Why can't he be useful without his magic?" she asked, without at all intending to. "Can't he teach? Or advise? Or support other air-mages?"

Something twitched on Ketill's mouth, almost like a smile. "Regin is not an academic or a teacher, Ms. Seng," he said. "He will be the first to tell you he lacks both book learning and patience. He is far better utilized on the field, in action."

It sounded so smug, so unbelievably condescending, and Selby had to clamp her mouth shut as Ketill kept talking. "Now the reason I've asked you here, Ms. Seng, is that Ms. Morley is currently understaffed. She may be able to make some use of your skills."

Selby was still frowning, but she glanced back at Morley, who was giving her a rueful, almost knowing look. "Klaus says you have some skill in object analysis," she said. "I unfortunately don't have any budget to pay you"—her eyes flicked briefly to Ketill—"but if you'd like to work with us as a volunteer, I'm sure we could find some projects for you. Which may help you with future job prospects, as well."

Ketill gave a stiff nod of approval, and Selby fought to objectively consider Morley's words. They were being kind, perhaps. Giving her something meaningful to do. A way to say, *I was volunteering with the Coven for Magical Advancement, doing real earth-mage work, and not just fucking Regin Agmund.*

"That's very kind of you," Selby said finally, with an attempted smile toward Morley. "I'd be honoured. Of course."

"Excellent," Morley replied. "Why don't you accompany me over to my office—my team workroom, really—and we'll get started?"

Selby nodded, all too eager to take her leave of Ketill, and followed Morley to another one of the rooms she'd previously identified as directors' offices, a few doors down. And Morley's workroom—Selby's mouth dropped open as she stepped inside—was quite possibly the most fascinating room she had ever seen.

It was very like a garden, with its ivy-covered walls, large window, and packed earthen floor—but also like a laboratory, with its rows of wooden shelves crammed full of stones and jars and plants. More plants hung from the ceiling, their vines trailing down onto the room's large central table, and Selby was almost certain the tree in the corner was growing out of the floor.

There was already someone sitting at the table—it was Kal, looking stiff—and Morley went to take a seat beside him, waving Selby toward the chair opposite. "So, object analysis," Morley said thoughtfully. "You know, we don't see a lot of that around these days. Though of course you'll have heard of Mr. Kyte, or Ms. Leighton?"

Neither of those names meant anything to Selby, and Morley clearly caught that, flashing her an apologetic smile as she spread a few rocks and leaves across the table. "Mr. Kyte is one of the Coven's principal investigative agents," she explained. "He can discern who's been in any room within the previous twelvemonth. And Ms. Leighton is an appraiser, in demand by every gallery and museum in the country."

Selby couldn't deny a flare of interest at that, and Morley gave her another understanding smile. "Both worthwhile careers for an object specialist," she continued, "though it does depend whether you specialize in true inanimate objects, or with living things, or things that were once alive. Which do you prefer?"

Selby's thoughts darted to Ketill's many dire warnings, and she nodded toward the rocks and leaves on the table. "Objects, mostly," she replied. "Usually the kinds of items my family would sell in our shop. Jewelry and semiprecious stones, clothing, tools."

"Makes perfect sense," Morley said, giving a wave at the items on the table. "Why don't you tell us about each of these?"

Selby obediently picked up the first rock, turning it over in her fingers. "This one's from a volcano," she said. "It used to be hot and liquid, once. And then it was buried under the earth for thousands of years."

Morley nodded, looking pleased, and Selby touched at the next objects in the row, a set of similar-looking leaves. "You grew these," she said, with a quick glance toward one of the room's hanging plants. "Um, from that plant, there? You've had it for a long time."

"Right again," Morley replied, with satisfaction. "And this?"

This was another rock—or, rather, what seemed to be a rock. But Selby knew better, she'd felt these before, and she turned it over once, twice, before speaking. "It's a bone," she said slowly, carefully. "One that's been buried so long it's turned to stone."

Morley nodded eagerly, leaning forward across the table. "Can you tell what it's from?"

Dangerous, Selby's thoughts shouted, even though she liked Morley, and knew that telling her the truth could possibly be to her benefit. But Ketill's slimy face was looming in her brain, and finally she settled for part of it, a piece of it.

"It's human," she said. "A piece of a leg bone. And it's very, very old."

"Can you tell me anything about the person?" Morley asked, leaning even closer, and Selby swallowed, turned the stone over again. The images were faint and foggy, but still *there*, hunting, snow, a tribe, a family, and he had been killed by a running herd of huge, strange animals, his last moment had been one of deafening noise—

"Not much," Selby said finally. "It's from a man, I think."

Morley sat back in her chair, her eyes looking oddly intent for an instant, but then she waved at Kal beside her. "Your turn, Kal," she said. "Give her something I don't know about."

Kal's brow furrowed, but finally he pulled a gold ring off his middle finger, and slid it across the table. And when Selby took it in hand, she almost winced, because it had been Kal's father's, and his father's before him, a long unbroken line of earth-mages who had married earth-mage wives to keep the line pure, to keep it in the family, *you're destined for greatness, boy, you've been planned, see that you keep it that way—*

Selby hurriedly handed the ring back, and tried to smile. "It's made of gold, with a bit of copper for strength," she said. "Both mined from the north of Sifjar, more than a hundred years ago. It would earn a high price at market—a really lovely piece."

That last part was a lie, and maybe Kal knew it, because he didn't betray any acknowledgement as he slipped the ring back on his finger. But when Morley glanced at him, with an obvious question in her eyes, he twitched a curt nod.

"Well, I'm impressed," said Morley, and it sounded like she meant it. "I'm thinking, to begin, you could work on plant classification and analysis. Between our greenhouses and the garden, there's a lot to keep track of, and it would be a great help."

Selby was willing, of course, and soon found herself confronted with a pile of stems and leaves to sort and label, according to a list of criteria Morley had identified. Age, source, type, any notable properties.

It was real work, and Selby should have been glad to do it. But as the minutes crept by, filled with leaf after leaf, her circling thoughts seemed to return, again and again, toward Agmund. She couldn't taste his magic at all anymore—he was far off to the north—and that shouldn't feel so disconcerting, should it? Just like all his unpleasantness this morning shouldn't bother her, either. *Get on with it, I don't have all day...*

"So are you enjoying working with Mr. Agmund so far?" Morley asked, halfway through the afternoon, once Kal had gone off somewhere else. "Has he been fair to you?"

Selby twitched, and shot Morley a swift, uncertain look. "Um," she said, and looked back down at the leaf in her hand. "It's been—all right."

Morley gave a snort, a too-knowing roll of her eyes. "Let me guess. Klaus had you sign away your firstborn in some iron-clad Coven contract, and if you so much as dare to express a true opinion on the subject, you'll suffer the consequences."

Selby blinked, twice, and Morley smiled back, a little grim. "We all know how he works," she added. "And how Agmund works, too."

Selby's heartbeat picked up, and she turned over the leaf in her fingers. "How Agmund works?" she asked, carefully. "In what way?"

Morley leaned back in her chair, crossing her arms over her chest. "Mr. Agmund is—he was—the best air-mage in the country," she said slowly. "And that isn't a position that just falls into one's lap. To reach that level, Agmund has had to be ruthless."

Ruthless. Selby's heart pounded faster, her fingers still turning over that leaf. "How so?"

Morley sighed. "Word is that he has never once refused a

job. He never asks questions. He obeys Klaus in all matters, even if the matter is intensely personal, and hurts those closest to him."

She nodded pointedly toward Selby, and Selby's thoughts flitted to this morning—*get on with it*, he'd said, *finish it*—and then to last night, to all those things he'd said. *I'm just following orders. Doing my job.*

"I say this not to alarm you," Morley added, softer now. "But to warn you. Agmund can be very convincing and charming when he wants to be. But you would be wise not to trust him."

Selby nodded, biting her lip, blinking hard. "Yes, I can see that. Thank you."

Morley waved it away, and stood to her feet. "You're welcome to come here as often as you like," she said. "And if you ever need help, or even just someone to talk to, my door is always open."

It was very kind, and Selby was very grateful, and she spent the rest of the afternoon sorting leaves with as much enthusiasm as she could muster. She even went and brought her supper back to the workroom, sorting as she ate, and tried not to notice the too-powerful feeling of Agmund's magic finally coming back from the forest, growing stronger and stronger with every second that passed.

It was after dark when Agmund finally walked through Coven Manor's front door. Going first to Ketill's office, and then to the dining hall, and then—Selby followed every single step, her breath coming short and shallow—up to his bedroom.

That was without question Selby's cue—she'd agreed to after supper, and it was now long past that—so she took her leave of Morley, and climbed slowly up the stairs. Noticing, as she trailed her fingers along the wall, that the smell seemed weaker than it had earlier in the day. Unpleasant, yes, but no longer nauseating.

She was still considering that when she stepped inside the room, and found Agmund. He'd been pacing back and forth—Selby could even feel where—and his head snapped to look at her, his eyes narrow and flinty. "You're late."

Selby blinked, and shut the door tightly behind her. "I thought you wanted me to avoid your friends," she said. "And stay out of your room when you weren't here."

Agmund's eyes went even narrower, and an irritated-sounding growl rumbled from his throat. "Look, I told you that was fine, didn't I? I'd rather you were in here than—"

He didn't finish, snapping his mouth shut, but his sentiments were very clear, and Selby crossed her arms, and frowned back at him. "Walking around reminding people of my unwanted pedlar presence?" she asked flatly. "Which, incidentally, is only here because it's helping *you*?"

Agmund didn't reply, his eyebrows furrowing lower on his forehead, and Selby stepped closer, and glowered up into his stupid angular face. "And for your information," she continued, "I was in Morley's workroom all day. Working."

Agmund didn't move, still frowning down his nose at her, but something changed in his eyes, hinting toward surprise, or disbelief. "You were working?"

"Yes, *working*," Selby shot back, and gods, he was an asshole, and how did she keep forgetting this? "I know it may come as a shock to you, seeing how you're the centre of the universe and all, but other people can use magic too, and occasionally even do useful things with it!"

Agmund's eyes shifted again, and he arched an eyebrow, like there was no way Selby could do anything useful. "Oh yeah?" he said coolly. "Like what? Fortune-telling? Ferreting out people's secrets? And sure, that's useful, if you're running a fucking *scam*—"

The rage surged so strong it swallowed Selby's breath, and she lurched another step closer to him, her hands in fists. "You *bastard*," she breathed, "you fucking odious *swine*, how *dare* you, pedlars are *not* fortune-tellers, and I have *never* scammed anyone in my life. I ran a *shop*, I *sold* things, I tried to make people's lives better and put food in my family's mouths, and even if you're Regin fucking Agmund, I don't deserve your damned *disrespect!*"

She was hollering at the end, loud enough that she could feel Agmund's sound-suppressing spell, unfurling through the room—but he didn't reply. Just kept staring down at her, like he still didn't believe her, and had he really thought she was a *fortune-teller* all this time—

"You have no idea," Selby continued, and suddenly the anger seemed to crack, leaking into something else. "What it's like, to know the truth behind every damned thing you touch. Or how dangerous it is, because some people are *awful*, and not only do you get their bilge in your head, but they might turn on you for having it, too! They might even run off and report you, because you're sharing their mess, and sharing magic is *illegal*, and those are *exactly* the same thing, and"—she had to pause, gulp back a breath—"even if they don't do any of that, they still might decide you're useful, and if you don't give them what they want, they'll try to take it instead!"

There was a moment's stillness, and then—how *dare* he—Agmund's eyes darted downwards, toward Selby's breasts under her dress. Clearly admitting what he wanted from her, and the rage bloomed again, almost dizzying in Selby's head.

"And *you*," she choked out, "are just the same as all the rest. Or even worse, maybe, because you *do* always get whatever the hell you want, don't you?"

And to make her point—or maybe something else—her feet kicked off her boots, and her hands went to the front of her dress, fumbling from one button to the next. Shoving the dress off entirely, onto the floor, and then yanking her white shift off, too. Leaving her standing there, naked and exposed, in the middle of Agmund's bedroom.

"There," she snapped. "Better, asshole? This what you want?"

Agmund's eyes darted downwards again, a red flush

creeping up his cheeks. But he didn't deny it, didn't move, and somehow that only seemed to make Selby even angrier. "Well?" she demanded.

He still didn't speak, and with the next surge of anger Selby jabbed her fingers into his bony chest, and shoved him backwards, toward the bed. He went, staggering a little, his gaze flicking between her hand and her face, and Selby kept shoving until he was sitting, looking up at her with strange blue eyes.

"Down," she snapped at him, the way he'd said *up* to her earlier that day, and though again he hesitated, blinking at her, he finally did it. Lying back on the bed, fully clothed, his eyes unreadable, his face now a deep shade of red.

He'd let Selby touch him earlier—just that morning, and gods, it felt like so long ago—so she touched him again. Reaching down to loosen the tie of his trousers, and then tugging them downward, just enough to let out his swollen, hungry cock.

She had to close her eyes at the sight of it, try to breathe through the anger the hunger the heat—and then she mounted him, a little unsteady. And she couldn't look at his face anymore, so she looked down instead, to where her hands were lifting his cock, guiding it up toward her.

And while she wanted to take it slow, take her time feeling him, getting used to him, she understood now that he liked it harder, faster, slamming it in, getting it over with. So that's what she did, biting her lip and squeezing her eyes shut, trying to block the suddenly swarming mess of his thoughts, guilt and exhaustion and *need, need more magic, not enough, never enough*—

Selby thrust her body down, hard, and abruptly the thoughts stopped, and shattered, and reformed into something else. Mountains, now, from years ago, when Agmund had run away. Living for weeks in caves, and setting off rockslides, and feeling the fierce furious joy of a lightning bolt smashing into the highest strongest peak—

But he wasn't touching her, wasn't moving under her, and it was only Selby in this, gritting her teeth as she rode him hard, the way he liked. Hissing at the repeating slick fullness of it, the raw bare thrusting of it, just going and going and going, not looking, until he just—

There it was, thank the gods, and Selby gasped her relief at the truth of it, the pleasure of it, even now. Regin Agmund spurting out inside her, doing his duty, fucking his harlot, and she waited until she felt his cock slackening to pull herself off. To slide away onto the other side of his bed, turn her back to him, curl herself up, don't move, don't think.

Agmund wasn't moving either, but for the heavy rise and fall of his breath beside her, and for some stupid reason, that flared even more mess through Selby's head. He'd gotten what he wanted, now he would roll over and go to sleep and fire off some lightning, tomorrow she would have to do it all over again, and again, and again—

Her eyes were wet, suddenly, leaking onto his bed, and even though she tried to silence it there was still the distinct, irrepressible sound of her nose giving a short little sniff. And the sobs kept threatening to rise, the heaving gasps lurking in her throat, oh gods, she couldn't start bawling, not here, not in front of him—

There was a harsh exhale from Agmund beside her, and she could feel him shifting on the bed, almost like he was turning to face her. "Look, Seng," he said, and his voice was low, hoarse. "I—I shouldn't have assumed. Or should have asked. All right? I really thought pedlars, well, and especially with your skills—"

He didn't finish, which was just as well, because it was just so fucking typical, that a sheltered lauded hero from the backwoods wouldn't have even bothered to question his ridiculous assumptions, had probably never bothered talking to a pedlar in his entire damned life.

"And look, I know I shouldn't have said it anyway, all right?"

he continued, to Selby's vague surprise. "I know it was shitty. It's just—when I get low on magic I just hate everybody, hate the fucking *world*."

"Fine, well, that still doesn't give you the right to treat me like absolute rubbish," Selby's thin voice hissed back. "Even if you are Regin fucking Agmund."

He sighed again, and this time there was a hint of a groan in it. "Will you stop calling me that?" he said, sounding strangely weary. "It's not like I ever asked to be famous, or to have people fall all over me like they do. You don't think I can't see through that bullshit? Or that they don't want a lot from me too?"

Selby didn't reply, and without warning, there was the feel of Agmund's warm hand, brushing against her bare shoulder. And—her breath caught hard in her throat—once again, here were his thoughts. His memories. His truth.

Will you sign my portrait, one woman shouted. *Will you come back to my place*, asked another. *Will you explode my neighbour's house, will you catch the thief who stole from me, will you give me a baby. I know Regin Agmund, my niece's friend's uncle knew Regin Agmund, my mother raised Regin Agmund before he was famous, let me tell you everything I know about Regin Agmund. Would Regin Agmund support this, will Regin Agmund eat this, what happened to Regin Agmund's family, where did he grow up, he didn't write me back, where does he live, where can I find him—*

It broke off just as quickly, the warmth of his hand gone, though Selby could feel his slow, shaky exhale. "And yeah," he continued, lower now, "I guess I do want this from you, all right? And I'm sorry for that, but it is what it is, because my magic is everything to me, and yeah, I'll do almost anything to get it back. But that doesn't mean I want to—to force you, or be owed it, or whatever. I'd really rather—"

He broke off there, and Selby opened her eyes, waited. "What."

He sighed again, shifted his body on the bed. "I'd rather

you wanted it," he said finally, quiet. "Like before. Not like—just now."

Oh. The heat suddenly flooded through Selby's cheeks, and other places, too—and she swallowed, blinked her eyes in the dark. "Well, if that's really what you want," she replied, her voice cracking, "you need to scale back your assumptions, and your pedlar-hating, and especially your comments about hurrying it up and getting it over with!"

Her voice had cracked again, because yes, Agmund saying that earlier today had hurt, maybe more than she'd wanted to admit. Because after the lovely quiet tautness, the willing silence as her hands had explored him, it had felt almost like a betrayal. A denial that it had ever happened at all.

"Sorry," came Agmund's quiet voice, again surprising enough that Selby blinked. "About this morning, I mean. Just—let's be honest, you're being *paid* to do this with me, all right? And yeah, I do want to be civil about it, and fair to you, but you have to accept that I'm never going to be all sweet and cuddly with you, either. You're doing your *job*, I'm doing mine. That's all."

Right. Back to this again. He was just doing his duty, Selby was just his harlot, he was never going to really like her or trust her, and that still hurt, too. Even though it was true, of course it was true, and it was Selby who couldn't keep it separate, couldn't keep herself from wanting more.

There was another long sigh from Agmund behind her, a brief nudge against her back. "And look," he said, "if we're in the middle of this, and I say something you don't like—tell you to hurry up, or whatever—why can't you just give my shit back to me? You already seem pretty damn comfortable mouthing off at me about everything else, why's this any different?"

What? Selby blinked in the dark again, and then finally turned herself around to where Agmund was facing her, barely visible in the dim light, his head propped up on his hand.

"So what, you can just say whatever you want to me?" she

demanded. "So you can appease your guilty conscience about this, or whatever? And I'm supposed to just ignore you, and do whatever I want anyway? When you tell me to hurry up, I just say *fuck you*, and grab your balls and hold you there?"

There was a sound from Agmund that might have been a laugh, breathless and short. "What, you'd have a problem with that?"

She'd have a problem. And the heat surged through Selby's body all at once, because Agmund was giving her—permission. Because maybe some part of him, however distant, did actually want this, the bastard.

And gods, Selby was fucked, because her traitorous hand was already sliding under the blankets toward him. And—oh, *gods*—finding that hard smooth cock, and then those soft round bollocks just below.

"Fine then, asshole," she said, as she curled her fingers close. "Not a problem at all."

14

This time, Agmund didn't protest Selby taking her good time with him. Letting her hands run all over him, wandering everywhere she wanted to touch.

And there was so much to touch, to explore. Not just the delectable contrast of hard and soft, obvious and secret, between his legs—but also his smooth belly, those pebbly pink nipples, the ridges of his ribs, the sharp angles of his shoulders. It was only when Selby reached his face that he got cagey, his jaw clenching tight under her fingers, so she kept her hands lower, went everywhere but there.

She took him slow, too, riding quiet above him in the dark, feeling the heat of his strong fingers digging into her hips. Tilting her forward a little, even, and then there was the thrilling revelation that she could do this and lie all the way down on top of him, feel all that bare skin, so smooth and warm against her as they fucked.

Gods, it was good. And when the pleasure finally coiled and exploded, Selby buried her face in his neck, cried out against him—and he didn't resist that, either. Just digging those fingers deeper, driving his hips up and up until he was gasping, too, firing off yet more of himself deep between her legs.

Afterwards it felt easy, warm, content. Even when Selby pre-emptively put his arm beneath her, to keep the lightning at bay, his complaining was halfhearted, and he left off entirely when Selby instead pulled the arm over her, and wrapped both arms tight around it.

"You can really sleep like that?" was his last comment, to which Selby snorted, and curled closer against his heat.

"If I have to choose between this, and lightning storms while I sleep, I'll take this," she replied. "Every time."

Agmund could have protested there, said this wasn't going to happen every time, but he didn't. And then he slept, and Selby slept too, all the night through, better than she had yet in this odious place.

Morning came slow and easy, too, without any words from Agmund—but that was fine, because he was hard again, and at the moment, that was all Selby wanted. Just to experience that again, lying low over him, breathing in the succulent scent of his neck, while his hips rocked up, and his cock did impossible and wonderful things inside.

He thought about magic again, too—but like the morning before, his thoughts seemed slower, quieter. Hinting at the dreams he'd had the night before, and the forest, the river. That damned river again, and once the pleasure had uncoiled, exploded, and then faded again, Selby was still lingering on it, even as Agmund elbowed her off and stood to his feet, tying up his trousers.

"What's the river?" she asked, without actually expecting an answer—but Agmund hesitated, glanced over his shoulder as he yanked on a clean tunic.

"It's the closest I ever came to being dead," he replied, voice flat. "Me and water don't mix like that. At all."

That made sense, what with the lightning, and Selby propped her head up to look at him. "Ever?"

He frowned, shrugged. "I said, at all, didn't I? As in, never."

And Selby was ignoring his moods, she was, so she kept

watching, considering that. "But when you cast, isn't the lightning far away from you? So shouldn't you be safe?"

Agmund shrugged again. "I'm still the source, so it still somehow connects to me, which means it'll still kill me. Ketill can explain it, if you really need to know."

He'd finished dressing, now running both hands through his mussed-up hair, and Selby's eyes caught on the ease of his movements, how his tunic tightened over his chest. "So you don't even take baths, then?"

Agmund shot her a dark look, his lip curling. "You don't have to bury yourself in water to get clean, do you?" he snapped. "Especially when one wrong move could get you electrocuted?"

But Selby still wasn't rising to his rubbish, not now, and she shook her head. "No, of course not," she said. "It makes perfect sense. I just never thought about it before. And you seem very clean to me."

She said the last with a hopeful smile, like a peace offering, and in reply Agmund snorted, and walked out. Without so much as a goodbye, or a *we'll do this tonight*, but as Selby let herself fall back onto his bed again, she was still smiling, and giving a stupid little shake of her head.

However, her good mood lasted only as long as it took to step out into the corridor, and inhale its awful, overpowering stench. And by the time she went down for breakfast, and sat at a table with Thora and Runar, she was feeling truly ill, and could only pick at her still-full plate of food.

"Please stop trying to eat, sweetheart," Runar said, his eyes flicking lazily toward the vicinity of Selby's stomach. "We'd much prefer you didn't vomit on the table."

Thora elbowed Runar in the side, and her head tilted with interest, or perhaps concern. "Is it that smell again?"

Selby had almost forgotten she'd told Thora about the smell, and she nodded, took a few slow, shallow breaths. "I know it sounds ridiculous, but it's really been bothering me, and I haven't been able to make much sense of it. It seems especially bad in the mornings."

Thora looked nonplussed, and Runar's eyes glanced toward Selby's belly again. "Not pregnant," he said, with a smirk. "Not for a lack of trying, though, I see."

Selby's face flooded with heat, her eyes darting across the room toward where Agmund was currently sitting in his usual spot, surrounded by the usual air-mages. And gods, she could still feel him inside, sparking low and deep, and could Runar really *see* that—

Thora elbowed Runar again, harder this time, and he grimaced at his breakfast. "Sorry," he said. "Rude habit, I know. What's the smell like?"

Selby swallowed, frowned down at her plate. "Like something rotten. Like... death."

Neither Runar nor Thora replied, and Selby remembered, again, what Kal had said out in the garden. And also, what she'd seen in Runar's workroom, and about that morgue, for his own personal use, just a few corridors away.

"Um, Runar," Selby began, with an uneasy glance toward him, "is there any chance your work could leave a smell like that?"

Runar's handsome face stilled, something peculiar in his eyes—but then he smiled again, stunning, if not quite genuine. "No, there isn't," he said coolly. "I follow all the proper protocols for cadaver storage and disposal. And let's be frank here, sweetheart"—his smile sharpened—"is there any chance that hoarding remains in your bedroom might have anything to do with your smell?"

Oh. *Oh.* Selby's face burned again, the nausea roiling higher in her gut. How the hell would Runar have known that? She could usually tell when other people had been in her space, and as far as she'd noticed, there'd only been her and Agmund in that room these past few days. Which should have been a relief, but that meant—it had been *Agmund* saying that. Agmund telling people she hoarded dead things on his shelf.

The truth of that seemed to swallow everything that had happened that morning, and last night, and when Selby glanced over at Agmund again—he was laughing at something Njall had said—there was a sharp, twisting knot in her stomach. Were they talking about her? About how barbaric she was, how hideous, how bleach-worthy?

"What else has Agmund said?" Selby asked, with surprising bitterness in her voice. "That I steal his things when he's not looking? Or maybe that I've set up a fortune-telling scam out of his bedroom?"

Thora winced, but Runar's eyes on Selby were intent, and he pointed at her with his loaded fork. "Sorry to say," he replied, "but there *was* something about the fortune-telling, too. Something about touching people to ferret out their secrets?"

He was half-smiling again, as though that had to be a joke, but Selby's entire body had gone cold, her eyes frozen on Runar's handsome face. Agmund had been *telling* people that? Of all things? Especially after he'd *said* he wouldn't talk about her? And, after all Ketill's dire warnings on the subject?

"*Runar*," Thora said, a low warning in her voice this time, but Runar just shrugged, and kept eating.

"What, she deserves to know," he replied. "It won't do her any good to think Agmund's not using her, because he is."

Runar was right, of course he was, and Selby suddenly felt too sick to even look at any more food, and shoved her plate away. "Right. I should actually go. See you both later."

She'd already stood, about to leave, when there was an odd twitching feeling on her arm, like someone had flicked it with a finger. "Wait," came Runar's voice, and Selby frowned down at her arm, and then back at Runar, who was busy swallowing the mouthful of food he'd been chewing.

"Look," he said, "if you're really smelling something, and it doesn't have anything to do with your hoard of death"—he made a face, which was a bit rich, considering—"then you'd probably be wise to turn your attention to our resident air-mage dream team. Especially the ones who specialize in localized gaseous manipulation."

He might as well have been speaking another language, but his eyes angled a pointed look toward Agmund's table, and—if Selby wasn't mistaken—toward Greta, who was currently sitting beside Njall, and leaning in to whisper something into his ear. And wait, Greta specialized in—in *localized gaseous manipulation*? Whatever the hell that was? And that could be responsible for the smell?

"It's kind of the difference between huge outdoor weather spells, like Agmund does," Thora supplied, "and smaller, localized spells that change the air in a particular place. Specialists will sometimes work in mines, or in factories and forges, to make sure people can breathe."

Or not breathe, maybe, in Selby's case, and she shot another glance over her shoulder toward Greta. And maybe Greta felt it, because her eyes met Selby's for an instant, and the bare, visceral hatred in them was strong enough to make Selby flinch.

"And could you make a smell follow someone?" she asked, shaky, now. "Even if you couldn't see them?"

"Maybe," Runar replied, around another bite of food. "I mean, that would take some real skill, and let's be honest, Greta's not exactly rolling in that. But the spells *are* out there, if you know how to use them. If you've got the right incentive, maybe."

Gods, that was an unsettling thought, and Selby darted one last, uneasy look over her shoulder as she walked out. Greta was probably sabotaging her, and Agmund was telling people about her, being the self-absorbed petty arse that he was. He was ruthless, he couldn't be trusted, even he kept saying this was all about the magic, and why couldn't she seem to remember that?

When she got to Morley's workroom, she was still flustered and distracted, but Morley only greeted her with a warm smile, and another pile of leaves. And at the moment, Morley was rapidly becoming Selby's favourite person in this entire cursed place, and she managed a smile back, and gratefully set to work.

The leaf identification still wasn't the most exciting of tasks, and if she was honest, it was already starting to become tedious—but it was something to do, something to focus on that didn't involve Regin Agmund. And she liked the easy camaraderie between Morley and her earth-mages, the mutual working equality that seemed entirely at odds with what Selby had seen of Ketill and Agmund so far.

"Selby, I want to introduce you to Fasta Valgeirr and Henrik Hallen," Morley said around midday, when two fair-haired mages strode into the workroom. "My resident structural and architectural geniuses. Give these two a heap of rubble, and they'll have you a palace within a week."

The girl—Fasta—looked unaffected by such praise, but this Henrik grinned, crinkling the corners of his grey eyes, and held out a big, work-roughened hand toward Selby. "Morley exaggerates," he said. "We might be able to get you a cabin. And the roof would probably leak."

Selby smiled back and shook his hand, as the requisite surge of images briefly filtered through his fingers. Enough to show that this Henrik seemed an easy, cheerful fellow—at least, with everything except his work, which was an incomprehensible tangle of materials and quarries and construction techniques, tinted all through with Fasta. Days and weeks and years spent working with Fasta, watching Fasta, impressing Fasta, on hundreds of construction sites.

Fasta's smile wasn't nearly as easy as Henrik's, but she shook

Selby's hand too, swarming her with even more equations, and the weight of hours and hours spent bent over a desk, her long blonde braid trailing on the paper beneath her. So she was the planner, maybe, while Henrik did the implementing, and Selby could see that while it suited Fasta, there was still something unsatisfactory about it. Relating, perhaps, to the fact that Fasta had actually brought Henrik in to work for the Coven, and was somehow responsible for keeping him there, and therefore tried very hard not to notice his eyes, his grin, the strength of his broad shoulders, how damned *good* he was at his job, and—

"Nice to meet you, Selby," Fasta said, withdrawing her hand, and though her faint smile had vanished, the words felt genuine. "Morley says your specialty is object analysis?"

Selby nodded, and soon found herself embroiled in a lengthy discussion about building materials, and how accurately she could determine the age and structural integrity of various types of stone and wood and earth. It ended with Henrik promising to bring Selby a selection of samples in the morning, and giving her a disconcerting list of all the various qualities they'd like to have identified.

"So is this your entire team?" Selby asked Morley, once Fasta and Henrik had left. "Kal, and those two?"

"More or less," Morley replied. "I have a few mages out on assignment with the Coven, and a few more on contract for specific jobs. But in terms of full-time, that's it. And even Fasta and Henrik are off-site taking contracts half the time."

Morley's voice had gone flat, and Selby considered her, and then the pile of leaves still on the table. "But—aren't there something like twenty air-mages working here?"

"Twenty-one, actually," came Morley's clipped reply. "But growing and building things doesn't have quite the same appeal as electrocuting them and setting them on fire, does it?"

Right, Selby could see that, and she could easily empathize with the telltale glint of anger in Morley's eyes. Especially when Agmund finally came back from the forest, late in the afternoon, and made straight for Ketill's office. Where he stayed for several interminable hours, while the sun slowly edged lower and lower through the window.

Selby ate her supper in the workroom again, trying to ignore the feel of Agmund going to the dining hall, and then finally back up to his room. Where she was no doubt supposed to be too, and Selby finally set aside her leaves and followed him up toward it, her heart hammering louder and louder in her ribs.

The vile smell had seemed to fade again throughout the day, at least—maybe because Greta had been too busy to keep casting it?—until Selby reached the third-floor landing. And there, suddenly, the smell was strong again, pungent and odious, but also—different. Like it was coming from a single source this time, over toward what she now knew to be the servants' back stairs.

Selby glanced up to where she could feel Agmund pacing, waiting—but then she turned and crept, slowly and quietly, toward that back staircase. It was dimly lit, and at first she didn't see anything, just narrow steps and tiled floors and the ubiquitous wood-panelled walls.

But then—Selby squinted in the dim light, stepped closer—there was a fair-haired person, huddled on a stair. And for an instant, Selby thought it had to be Greta, maybe following her around and casting her stink-spells, because the smell was getting stronger, like maybe this person was *creating* it—

The floor creaked under Selby's foot, and the figure jumped up, and whirled around. And it wasn't Greta, though this girl had the same kind of hair, and her eyes on Selby in the dim light were very wide, with something that might have been shock, or fear.

"Hey," Selby said carefully. "I'm Selby. I don't think I've seen you around here before?"

She hadn't been sure of that, at first—but the more she

looked at the girl, the more certain she became. Not only was the girl's face unfamiliar, but her clothes were also different—not the neatly pressed uniforms the servants wore, or the well-tailored items worn by the well-paid mages. Instead, her dress was shabby and stained, and the jacket over it was ill-fitting, with fraying patches on the sleeves.

The girl hadn't yet spoken, just kept staring at Selby with those too-wide eyes, and Selby stepped closer, and winced at the strength of that smell. Maybe Greta had put the spell on this girl too, maybe she was another one of Agmund's exes or something—

"Do you live here?" Selby asked, trying for a smile. "Or work here?"

The girl's entire body twitched, and her eyes went even wider, enough that Selby could see the whites of them all around. "Yes," she said, and twitched again. "No."

Selby's eyebrows furrowed together, and she reached, without thinking, to touch at the girl's arm—but then the girl leapt away, her body visibly trembling. "No," she said again. "No. Don't tell them you saw me. *Please.*"

And with that, she turned and sprinted back down the stairs, the sound of her pattering feet fading as she went.

15

"Where have you been?" Agmund demanded, once Selby had finally made her way to his room, and shut the door behind her. "I thought we agreed, after supper?"

Not this again, already, and Selby was already too unsettled to ignore his rubbish. She'd just spent a good half-hour tracing that girl's awful smell, following it down the back stairs to the first floor, and finding that it had disappeared, suddenly and disconcertingly, into nothing. There had been no door there, no nearby exits that Selby had seen, and it made no sense, there was nowhere she could have gone.

"There was something important I had to deal with," Selby snapped, because Agmund didn't actually care about her answer, did he? "And while we're on the subject, I thought we *also* agreed that you're not going to talk shit about me to your friends. Who seem to be spreading it around that I touch people to dig out their secrets, and hoard dead bodies in your bedroom!"

Agmund's eyes blinked, once, and then angled toward Selby's shelf. He'd loosened the neck of his tunic again, Selby's whispering thoughts pointed out, and his feet were bare, and gods damn it he was an asshole, ruthless, she *had* to remember that this time—

"Yeah, well, that's not talking shit, because it's true, isn't it?" Agmund shot back, with a wave at the shelf. "And I *didn't* tell anyone about the fortune-telling, except for—"

He abruptly snapped his mouth shut, something moving in his eyes, and Selby felt a muscle in her jaw twitch. Of course. Of fucking *course*.

"Except for Greta," she supplied flatly. "And has it never occurred to you, asshole, that telling your ex-girlfriend information like that about the new girl you're fucking might make her want to take some kind of action? Might give her even more reason to want to get rid of me?"

Agmund blinked again, and Selby could see the sudden tension in his shoulders, that familiar dislike flicking across his eyes. "Are you really accusing Greta of trying to get rid of you?" he demanded. "That is such bullshit, Seng, of course she's not going to like you, but there's no way in hell she'd sabotage my career like that!"

Selby barked a low, disbelieving laugh—Agmund couldn't truly be this dense, could he?—but maybe he was, because he came a swift step closer, his frown going even deeper.

"Look, Seng," he said, the warning too clear in his voice. "If you want to be like this to me, fine, go ahead, have at it. But if you try that shit on *any* of my friends"—he came another step closer, looming tall over her—"I'll haul you up in front of Ketill so fast, your head will still be fucking spinning while you're crawling home to your wagon!"

Selby couldn't deny the sudden jolt of fear—Agmund wouldn't really send her away, would he? What about the penalties, the payment, his magic?—and she had to search her thoughts, find her breath again.

"I'm not accusing Greta," she said, though maybe that was a lie. "I just—this place keeps making me feel sick, the awful smell keeps following me everywhere, it *has* to be magic, but nobody else even notices it! Doesn't that seem suspicious to you? Doesn't it seem like making me too sick to—to do my job—would be a damned good way to get rid of me?"

Agmund's eyes narrowed, his arms folding tight over his chest. "Are you?" he asked, voice stiff. "Too sick to—work?"

"No," Selby replied, just as stiffly, and grimaced at the responding look on his face. "I mean, not yet, but it's really strong, and it feels like it's getting stronger. The only reason it's not fully affecting me is because of my"—she waved toward that shelf, took a breath—"my things. Because they have protective effects."

Agmund was gazing at her with clear skepticism, his eyebrows arched high on his forehead. "They have protective effects."

"Yes," Selby said, and she pulled at her hair, trying to think of a way to explain this. "I don't know how it works, exactly. But when something is—connected to you, and you take a lot of comfort from its presence, when you're around it, you're—better. Stronger. And maybe it's just you being happier because it's there, or maybe there are some properties inherent to the object, I don't know. But it makes a difference."

Agmund's eyebrows rose even higher, but he wasn't protesting, and maybe this was Selby's chance to actually fix some of this, if he was truly listening. "And if—if you really don't want me to get too sick to work," she ventured, "maybe you could let me bring out a few more of my things? To make the protection stronger?"

Agmund kept staring at her, his arms still too tight over his chest, and Selby saw something white and crackling, sparking bright in his fist. "Can you honestly even *hear* yourself right now?" he finally asked, his voice cold, incredulous. "You smell something you don't like, so you come to me and say Greta's trying to *curse* you? And that I need to let you put out even more *dead shit* in my bedroom, so it'll protect you from her?"

Selby swallowed hard, lifted her chin. "Not exactly," she began. "I mean—"

But Agmund broke her off with a laugh, cool and mocking. "Nice try, Seng," he said. "Play sweet for a night or two, make me think you're not all that bad, and then you come out with this absolute *lunacy*. And you wonder"—he came a step closer—"why people think pedlars are all trying to fucking *scam* them!"

The words felt like physical blows, one after the other, and Selby backed away from him, until she was up against the door. "I'm not lying," she protested, though it sounded faint, weak. "And I'm not trying to scam you. I *have* smelled it, ever since I've gotten here. And just now there was a new girl out in the hallway, and she smelled like it too, and then she ran away, and I followed her, and that's why I—"

She was losing it, damn it, getting into that on top of everything else, and Agmund stared at her like she'd completely lost her mind. "Really?" he demanded, voice grim. "Now we're blaming the random girl in the hallway? Surely you can do better than that?"

"I'm not lying," Selby insisted, but it sounded even weaker than before, and Agmund laughed again. "Bullshit," he snapped. "This is total bullshit, from start to end, and whether you like it or not, I'm still the strongest air-mage on this fucking *continent*! You don't think I'd notice if there were any changes to the air around you? You don't think I'd be able to tell if it had anything to do with my girlfriend of almost two entire fucking *years*?"

Oh gods, curse Selby, because Agmund probably *would* be able to tell, and maybe she should have just asked. But then again, maybe he was a part of it, he was ruthless, maybe he *knew*—

But Agmund didn't look like he knew now, he just looked furious, and he stalked toward the door, and waved Selby aside to yank it open behind her. "I've had enough of this bullshit for one day," he said, voice clipped. "Get out. Come back in the morning, once you've sobered the fuck up."

Selby stared at him, her whole body snapped still, because he couldn't really want her to *leave*? But Agmund's face looked ugly now, twisted with anger, his eyes narrow slits in his too-pale face. "I said, out!" he shouted, more blinding white sparking in his fist, so this time, Selby went. Fleeing out into the hallway, and down the stairs, not thinking, not thinking...

It wasn't until she was in front of Morley's workroom that she realized where she'd gone, and though she'd already begun to back away, the door opened, and there was Morley behind it. Taking one look at Selby's face, and ushering her inside.

"What is it, Selby?" she said, shutting the door quietly behind them. "Is everything all right?"

"I just—" Selby gasped, and then pulled in a heaving breath. "Could I—would you mind if I stayed in here? For a while?"

Her eyes darted around the already-familiar room, now lit with a few flickering lanterns, its plants and jars making it look cozy and welcoming. A place that still stank, but Agmund wasn't here, and that, maybe, was enough.

"Of course," Morley said, and her eyes on Selby were full of sympathy, and warmth, and safety. "Stay as long as you like."

16

Selby ended up sleeping alone in Morley's workroom, slumped over the table, with her head on her arms. She'd worked on Morley's pile of leaves long after dark, well after Morley had gone off to bed, until the exhaustion had become so strong that there'd been no more thoughts to think.

But when morning came, it was with a reeking stink so powerful that Selby could barely breathe. She had to desperately dodge for Morley's little adjacent water closet, and barely grabbed the latrine before hurling the remaining contents of her stomach into it.

Her stomach kept heaving, long after there was nothing left to bring up, and when it finally stopped, Selby was shaky and shivering and cold. Too weak to even stand, for the moment, so she just sat there on the floor, with her head on her knees, and her arms wrapped around them.

And then she jolted up again, because that was the feeling of—*Agmund*. Leaving his bedroom, and he'd told her to come back in the morning, and what the hell time was it, gods he would be *so* furious—

But when Selby shoved herself to her feet, she staggered sideways, straight into the wall. Hard enough that her fingers scraped painfully against it, her head bouncing off the solid wood, and the nausea flared again, like a furious punch to her already-screaming stomach.

She ended up curled over the latrine for another good hour, while Agmund went first to the dining hall, and then to Ketill's office. And then—Selby's stomach lurched again—outside, walking further, and further, and further away.

"Selby?" came Morley's voice, eventually, once Selby had crawled out to the main workroom again, and curled herself up on the bare earth under the tree. "Is everything all right?"

Selby tried to reply, but it only came out as a groan, and Morley cursed under her breath, and then knelt down beside her. "Dear gods, Selby," she said, "what's wrong? Are you ill?"

Selby shook her head, enough to make the room spin, because what did it mean if she *was* ill, too ill to work? But Morley made a hushing noise, and soon returned with a warm blanket, draping it over Selby's shoulders.

It helped, a little, but the panic had started rising now too, shouting in Selby's head. Saying things like *get out* and *your head will still be fucking spinning while you're crawling home to your wagon*. And maybe Agmund would make her leave, and the payment and her mother and *Simon*—

Morley was still hovering, asking if she should alert Ketill, or call for a healer, but Selby waved it away. "Just a bit of flu," she managed. "Just need some rest."

Morley huffed a bit more, but finally brought over some water, and a plate of bread and fruit. Telling Selby she had a few meetings, but to let her or any of her earth-mages know if there was anything she needed.

The rest of the day passed in a haze, broken only by the occasional staggering trip back to the water closet. And Agmund was still gone, Morley was gone, and by late afternoon, when a hand shook her shoulder, Selby couldn't seem to move at all.

"Selby," said a voice—Fasta's voice, Selby noted, and why

hadn't she known that from her touch? "Hey. Are you all right?"

"She doesn't look so good," said another voice, Henrik's. "Her face isn't supposed to be that colour, is it?"

"Of course not," replied Fasta's voice, and her hand shook Selby's shoulder again, harder this time. "Hey. Selby."

But the movement only seemed to wrench up the nausea in Selby's stomach, her whole body convulsing with it, and her hazy vision registered the incongruous sight of an earthen bowl flying from the nearest shelf toward her. Just in time, thank the gods, for her to empty her stomach into it.

"She needs a healer," Fasta said firmly, and Selby could feel Henrik standing to his feet—but then there was something else, faint, beyond him. The taste of Agmund, walking through the front door, and how had she not even noticed...

"Agmund," Selby croaked, and at this point she didn't care if he would be furious, if he would send her away. "Need Agmund."

There was an instant's hesitation, a faint flicker of Fasta's surprise through her hand on Selby's shoulder. "Really? Is Agmund even here?"

Selby tried to nod, but even that hurt, everything hurt, oh gods. "He is," she rasped. "Just back."

There was the sound of footsteps, of Henrik walking away, and then an interminable silence. Broken only by the feel of Fasta rubbing her shoulder, Fasta's thoughts now just slightly stronger behind it, *why would she want Agmund, what's made her so sick, what's taking Harry so long, is he talking to Ilsa again...*

But Selby's own thoughts were trapped on that feeling of Agmund, finally coming closer, and closer. Until the door banged back against the wall, because Regin Agmund was here, the taste of him almost mouthwatering in the air, oh gods.

"What the *fuck*," his voice hissed, and now his hands were here, strong, touching her. Tilting up her face toward him, like he had a right to do that, and maybe he did, because gods, his touch was everything, everything.

"She's coming with me," he said. "*Now*."

17

Selby stayed in bed for three days.

The world had become strange, stilted, dim. Like time had lost its meaning entirely, and had been replaced by the difference between Regin Agmund being there, and not.

"Stay," Selby had begged him, thickly, once someone—Henrik, maybe—had carried her up to Agmund's room, and deposited her in his bed. Because Agmund couldn't be seen touching her in the hallways, even now, but Selby didn't care, just needed him touching her now, didn't care what that meant.

"You sure?" he'd said, his voice hitching, but Selby had grasped for his hand, and pulled him closer, onto the bed.

He'd done it, curling his body warm all down the back of her, a dizzying swaying relief—until the images, new and raw, swarmed into Selby's thoughts. Memories of the day Regin Agmund had spent, furious at her, furious at Ketill, furious at the world. Fighting with Ketill, shouting at Ketill, already low on magic and sinking ever lower, walking toward his target, his jaw set, his hands in fists.

Are they in position, he'd said, to the scouts who'd

accompanied him, to the uniformed man—the army lieutenant—behind him.

Yes, the man had said. *Ready to fire, sir.*

And then Regin Agmund—this one, lying here holding her, so warm, so alive—had moved closer, stepping quiet through the trees, using that same sound-suppressing spell. Seeing those targets—two men, one woman—standing in a circle, talking, no idea he was there...

His magic—the magic he'd gotten by touching Selby—had been weaker than he'd wanted, than it should have been. So weak he'd barely been able to get enough heat, enough force and wind and pull, *come on, come on*...

The clouds had swirled above, too slow and too obvious, enough that the woman had looked up, and screamed. And Agmund had to finish it, had to, couldn't leave it like this, *come on*...

It should have been over in an instant. There should have been three white forks of lightning striking at once, the boom of thunder reverberating through the nearby trees. And then, three bodies, lying still and empty on the ground.

But somewhere, there was the distinct sound of a child, wailing. And Agmund had closed his eyes against it, had felt the storm, the lightning, waiting, ready, so close, *there*—

And then he'd dropped his hand. And the storm above had fizzled and faded, warm air blending with cool, clouds flattening and dissipating. The screaming people were already fleeing, toward a nearby cabin, and the uniformed lieutenant had come running, *what happened, why didn't you finish the job*—

Agmund had said something about his magic, *not strong enough yet, fucked up on me again*—but it had been a lie. He'd had enough magic. It had been that damn kid crying, five months since a kill, *do you promise you won't use my magic to kill people*...

"I didn't do it," Agmund's hoarse voice whispered, close against Selby's neck. "I failed."

He'd failed. Something clenched hard in Selby's chest, and despite all the reasons to still be furious with Agmund, she felt her hands on his arm tighten, pulling him closer. "You didn't fail," her shaky voice whispered back. "Thank you."

The world faded again, after that, twisting in and out of dreams, and at one point there were voices, one that sounded a lot like Ketill, and another that didn't belong to anyone Selby knew. And then, hours later, there was the touch of that blessed familiar hand again, wide against her arm—and again Selby dragged it close, needed it close. So much that she almost sobbed when it came, Regin Agmund settling his warm body down all behind her, his arm close and familiar over her waist, his thoughts carefully whispering of mountains and forests and sky.

Another night and day passed, with Agmund there almost all through it, and there was the distant awareness of him helping her drink, tilting the waterskin gentle against her mouth, and again talking to those voices. Yelling, at one point, while his hand kept gripping Selby's shoulder, but his touch was all that mattered, so she turned toward it, and slept.

After that Agmund left again, for how long Selby couldn't quite identify. But when she awoke again it was dark, and quiet, and she was alone.

She sat up carefully in the bed, feeling its solidness beneath her, and then put a tentative foot to the floor. The room remained still, her stomach quiet, though the taste in her mouth was thoroughly revolting, and she could still smell a twinge of the manor's usual awful stench, emanating from the nearby wall.

She climbed carefully to her feet, holding onto the bed for balance, and then stripped off her dress and shift, and staggered to the water closet. Where she scrubbed herself all over, and rinsed out her mouth until it finally tasted clean again.

She'd just finished putting on a clean shift when Agmund walked back into the bedroom. He looked tired, and strained, and more gaunt than before, almost like those hollows in his cheeks had deepened overnight.

And Selby should have yelled at him. Should have called him out on taking that awful mission in the first place, and not telling her, and shouting at her before he'd left, and a dozen other things. But instead, there was an appalling, uncontrollable part of her that just walked straight toward him, until she was close enough to touch, circling her arms around the slim taut warmth of his waist.

He didn't touch back—not even a finger—but he didn't resist, either, or speak. And when Selby tugged him toward the bed, arms still around his waist, he went easily, kicking off his boots, and then dropping down onto his back, and pulling her on top.

There was no talking, but there was touching, as Selby's hands slid first to his tunic, pulling it up and off over his head. And then down to his trousers, carefully lifting them over the bulge of his beautiful hard cock, and then her hands stayed there, stroking him, seemingly on their own. While she kept her eyes shut, not wanting to see him, perhaps not able to bear seeing him, right now.

But his breath was gasping under her fingers, his body warm and willing, his hands briefly ghosting along her waist. And that was enough, Selby distantly thought, and as she stroked that thick hardness she knelt over him, and then—to her own vague astonishment—lowered her head, and touched her mouth to that smooth chest. Letting her tongue linger on the salty silken skin of him, the scrape of hair on her tongue, the jolting shocking feel of his hard nipple, jutting up between her lips.

The hunger was too strong to be denied, now, the closeness too real, too intense. And Agmund was gasping, with every upward stroke of her hand, and Selby was gasping with him, feeling it, tasting it. Rising, finally, to the thrilling musky skin of his neck, and breathing that, tasting that, lying half on top of him now, while her hand brought him up and up, higher and higher, her teeth biting down on smooth skin, her body rutting up against the perfect hard thickness of his thigh—

And then it collapsed back down again, the heat the high the gods-damned screaming relief, and Selby arched up into Agmund as he pulsed out, spilling sticky wetness out onto her fist, into the now-shaking clutch of her fingers.

"Fuck," Agmund gasped, quiet enough that he probably hadn't meant Selby to hear it—but she had, and it did something to her insides, to where she was supposed to be hurt, and betrayed, and angry.

But Selby's exhausted brain didn't seem to care, and when she didn't move her sticky hand, Agmund didn't seem to care, either. Just shifted and stretched under her, and then pulled in a long, heavy breath, making her rise and fall against his chest.

And when his dreams came, they were of a shouting Ketill, of an unfinished storm, the sound of that child wailing—but Selby replaced them with his forest, with the gently exploding trees, and fell, once more, to sleep.

18

It was a strange, surreal night. One that had Selby waking, halfway through, feeling hot and hungry and uncomfortable, with snippets of dreams swirling through her head—and then putting her hands to Agmund's naked body, and feeling those dreams snap apart into a million forgotten pieces.

They fucked slow and quiet in the dark, with Selby lying on top, and if not for Agmund's hands on her arse, she'd have almost thought he was still asleep. But when he finished he moaned aloud, his hips canting hard up against hers, and afterwards he didn't even push her off, just let her fall back asleep against the easy rise and fall of his chest.

The lightning woke her up again, maybe an hour or two later, but she just grasped for his hand, twined his fingers with hers. And then settled soft into his chest again, his heartbeat slowing under her ear, his breath even and steady beneath her.

When morning came he was half-hard again, jutting into Selby's leg, and it was too easy to slide over, to take him back inside. To feel him there, twitching and filling, deep between her legs, while she gasped, revelled in the astonishing pleasure of it. And then she put her hands back to his hard thighs behind her, showing him her bouncing, jiggling breasts as she rode him until he came.

Afterwards she was sore, and sweaty, and full of his thick stickiness—but she felt better, so much better, almost like herself again. And the still-lingering smell from the walls was just annoying, not disgusting or sickening, especially when she collapsed down on Agmund again, and inhaled that musky, delicious scent of his neck.

"So I told Ketill," Agmund said, out of nowhere, his voice hoarse, "there's no way I'm going out again. Not for a few months, at least. Magic's not reliable enough yet."

Selby raised her head to look at him, blinking, because she knew, and he knew, that it had been enough, more than enough. But his eyes were purposely looking away, his mouth set, and curse her but Selby touched at his thoughts, at the mass of his memories from the past few days.

And now that she was awake, and properly thinking again, the visions seemed startlingly vivid, unnervingly close. Agmund walking back from that failed job, his hands clenched, his head pounding, silently shouting the shame of it, the weakness of it. Agmund walking into the manor, running into Morley's workroom, staring aghast at Selby's limp, crumpled body under that tree. Agmund panicking, fighting for air, hollering at Ketill, *I am not going again, I leave for one fucking day, we are bringing in another healer now, what if she never wakes up, what if she leaves...*

"You did the right thing, with the mission," Selby heard herself say, her voice still unsteadier than it should have been. "You did. You'd have dreamed about that kid crying for months. *Years.*"

Agmund shot her a strange, uneasy glance, and then looked intently away again. "It wasn't that," he replied, his voice flat. "It wasn't me doing the right thing in the least. And you know it."

And maybe—maybe Selby did know. Because Agmund still wasn't hiding his thoughts, wasn't hiding anything, and the real reason he hadn't let those lightning bolts strike had been—this. Here. Selby. Because she would have seen exactly what he'd done, in all its brutal detail. And if she'd decided to turn around, and walk away for good, she would have taken all Agmund's magic with her. Maybe forever.

Selby swallowed, her shoulder giving a funny little shrug. "It was still the right thing," she said. "You keeping your magic is worth more than you following some horrible orders. A lot more."

Agmund blinked at her, and there was an odd twitch of his hands against her skin. "It isn't, though," he replied. "My job *is* my magic. It's the reason I even *have* magic, like this. It's what I'm needed for. What I'm meant to *do* with my life."

He truly believed that, Selby could see it, but all the same, there was a hint of something like helplessness, curdling deep below. And when she touched toward it, beyond it, there were again just—faces. Bodies. *People*, lying still and blank and ruined on the earth. Sometimes one, sometimes many, that one day hundreds, a sea of death under his feet—

But then his thoughts shoved them further downward, changing instead into the reasons, the orders, the just cause behind every one. Insisting that it was fine, he was doing his job, he was needed, important, keeping peace, keep his head down, there was no escape anyway. No running from the cold chasing darkness that would keep clawing, keep dragging until he drowned...

It was bleak enough, unsettling enough, that Selby flinched all over, her thoughts recoiling away from him entirely. Back into the blessed, comparatively simple silence of her own head, and she frowned as she studied him, took in the truth of his shuttered, uneasy eyes.

Regin Agmund *wasn't* ruthless. Regin Agmund was conflicted, unhappy, and desperately lonely. Regin Agmund had thought, more than once this past year, that the world would be a better place without him in it at all.

"Hey," Selby said, letting her thoughts twine back toward his, which were now carefully fixated on here, this minute. On her, looking down at him with her head cocked, her hair askew, her face tinged with concern, the weight of her body warm and strangely reassuring on his.

"Fine, so you put yourself ahead of your job *one* damned time," she told him, as lightly as she could. "Out of hundreds. Give yourself a break, asshole. And maybe try accepting the fact that you're a huge self-absorbed prick, and that's bound to come out once in a while."

There was an instant's stillness as Agmund stared at her—but there was no mistaking the faint flare of brightness in his thoughts, and then the small, relieved twitch at the corner of his mouth. "Huge, eh?" he said, with a meaningful glance downwards. "You really think so?"

Selby's face flooded with sudden heat, and she gave a sharp elbow into his ribs. "No," she snapped. "Absolutely not."

But Agmund was smiling now, brief and genuine, his eyes warm and almost grateful on hers—but then his thoughts shifted again, hesitating on the truth of her words. He *had* been an arrogant prick. And he needed to deal with it.

"And look, I want to apologize for not believing you were sick," he said. "I just—my magic was already low, I was already in a foul mood, and when you blamed Greta, I completely lost it, and didn't listen to anything else you said. I should have."

Selby couldn't seem to reply to that, and Agmund cleared his throat. "And you know I'm done with Greta," he continued, "and that's not going to change—but we were still together for two whole *years*. And I'm not trying to justify being an asshole, but the truth is, I haven't even known you for a month. And you're being *paid* to be here. You're fucking me for the *coin*."

His voice had gone flat, maybe even angry, and Selby swallowed hard, because the nausea had roiled again, deep in her gut. He was saying that she still couldn't be trusted. That if it ever came down to Greta's word against hers, Greta's would always win.

And gods, it hurt, and gods, why was Selby still so caught in this, in him. Why couldn't she keep it apart, why was there only this moment, the heat of his skin against hers, the strength of his hands against her back. The truth of his most shameful, painful thoughts laid bare, for her.

"I'm sorry I accused Greta like that," Selby said finally, closing her eyes, dropping her head back to the warm comfort of his chest. "I just—I heard that it was her kind of magic, and something she might be able to do. I haven't been able to figure out anything else to explain the smell so far, and it—it just seemed like it fit."

Her breath was coming too fast, her heartbeat pounding too loud, and she heard Agmund sigh, felt his fingers spread on her back. "Well, we brought in three different healers to look at you," he replied. "And none of them could find anything. Ketill thinks it's got something to do with this"—those fingers tapped against her back, meaning this, them fucking, maybe—"since it seems better when I'm around, right?"

Selby hesitated, but then nodded, and his chest beneath her rose, and fell. "Well, if you'd just *tell* me if you're feeling shitty," he added, lightly now, "maybe we wouldn't have had this problem. Total honesty, remember?"

Selby raised her head to glare at him, because he was the one who'd taken off to go *murdering* people, without telling her, like he'd promised he would. And in return Agmund grimaced, and let out a heavy breath. "I was going to tell you about the job," he said. "That morning."

Selby blinked at him, tilting her head, because she could feel the truth behind that. He'd actually looked for her, in the dining hall and the garden, and he'd even asked Thora and Runar if they'd seen her, when he'd run into them in the hallway.

"Oh," Selby said, blankly, and in reply Agmund gave her a

smug smile, and shoved her off sideways, onto the bed. His hands familiar and proprietary on her bare hips, lingering for an instant too long—and then he was up, out of bed, and going for his wardrobe.

Selby didn't protest, just silently watched as he pulled out a clean pair of trousers, and yanked them up over his naked arse. Giving her quite the view, but he purposely wasn't looking at her, and she swallowed, fixed her eyes on the mess of his hair. "You know," she said, "I never really considered that how I feel could be directly related to you."

Agmund gave her a swift, sideways look, tying up the trousers' cord with quick fingers. "Why wouldn't it be?" he replied, as he turned to rummage in his wardrobe for a tunic. "Gods know I didn't believe Ketill at first, but there really is something to this affinity shit."

Selby rolled over onto her side to better look at him, and now that her thoughts were somewhat functioning again, she could pull together how maybe—possibly—Agmund's presence had affected how she felt, and the smell, too. How not-fucking him these past few days had felt utterly awful, and now, how bringing him off three times in a night had her feeling quite possibly the best she'd felt since she'd arrived here.

"But what would that have to do with the smell?" she asked, earning another brief, sidelong look from him before he pulled on his tunic. "I mean, I understand feeling good when you touch me, but then smelling something vile and getting horribly ill when you're gone? That seems excessive, right?"

"Maybe," Agmund replied with a shrug, now bending over, and pulling on his boots. "But then again, you're pretty excessive, Seng. If fucking you didn't give me my magic back, it would barely be worth the bullshit."

His eyes were a little saucy as he arose, making Selby blink—but then there was the warm, swarming realization of what he'd just said. *Barely worth.* Meaning it still would be worth it, even if she didn't give him his magic back. Even if—

she stared at him again, frowning—he didn't even look better from it too, healthier and pinker and less bony than the night before.

"Any chance you'd be up for one more round, then?" Selby's voice asked, shocking enough that she immediately clamped her mouth shut, her face furiously flushing—but Agmund actually, honest-to-gods grinned at her, flashing her a row of even white teeth, and it was so stunning, so unexpected, that Selby could barely breathe.

"Nah, thanks, but I'm late for Ketill," he said. "Tonight, though? And on time for once, for fuck's sakes?"

Selby was still too busy blushing to speak, but nodded, and let her eyes openly linger on his straight back, the tantalizing curve of his arse. And with one last long, knowing look over his shoulder, he stepped out the door, and yanked it shut it behind him.

19

Runar was not impressed.

"So you and Agmund are at it again already, I see?" he demanded at Selby. "Don't you think that's a *little* premature?"

He'd dragged Selby and Thora up into his chilly second-floor workroom, which was currently free of anything dead-looking. And at his insistence, Selby had lain back on his cold steel table, while he hovered his gloved hands over her, moving from her head to her feet.

"Uh, is it premature?" Selby asked, looking to Thora for help, but Thora's hand was firmly clamped to Runar's shoulder, her deep blue eyes distant and glazed. "Why?"

"Because you've been gravely ill?" Runar shot back, his hand lingering in the vicinity of Selby's stomach. "And magic exhaustion or not, Agmund should be able to keep his dick to himself for at least a day or two?"

"Wait, Agmund had magic exhaustion?" Selby asked, frowning up toward Runar's face. "Really?"

Runar frowned back at her, his lip curling. "Not the important point, sweetheart," he replied. "But yes, he was practically falling over himself when he came down here, hollering at me to come fix you. *He* should have been in bed, too."

His frown deepened with the memory, but the words twisted something tight and warm in Selby's belly. "He was actually that upset?" she heard her traitorous voice ask. "And he tried to get you to help me?"

"Oh, for fuck's sakes, Selby," Runar snapped. "You need to re-examine your priorities. Don't worry about Agmund, worry about yourself, and your health. And the fact that a lot of people around here are spreading a *lot* of nasty and quite frankly dangerous rumours about you—and now you come down with *this*?"

He gave a sharp, irritated wave toward her, seeming to encompass her entire body—but beside him Thora leaned closer, and murmured something unintelligible. To which Runar gave a heavy sigh, and an elaborate roll of his eyes.

"And yes, Agmund brought me in to help you," he said flatly. "Along with two other healers, when I couldn't find anything. One of them was Holben, who's a useless hack, but the other was Kace, from the city, and she's actually competent, though she charged them an exorbitant price to tell them exactly the same thing I did. But no expense spared for Regin Agmund's meal ticket."

Selby made a face, but Runar didn't seem to notice, hovering his gloved hand over her neck. "And no, there's no apparent physical cause," he continued darkly, "though our resident air-mage experts refused to even *consider* the obvious alternate conclusion."

He meant a magical attack—maybe he meant Greta—and Selby took a breath, let it out. "I did mention to Agmund the possibility of Greta causing this," she said carefully. "He really, *really* doesn't think that's possible. He says he'd recognize the taste of her magic."

Runar snorted again, his hand coming up over Selby's face, filling her nostrils with the strong smell of antiseptic. "Says the air-mage whose magic's been shot for a year," he snapped. "Did he consider the possibility that it might have been one of his twenty other air-mage minions? Either alone, or helping her?"

It was a fair point, but Selby couldn't help feeling doubtful. Agmund's magic *was* coming back, there was no question about that, and surely he'd be able to recognize his friends' magic too? And also—Selby studied Runar's angry, narrowed eyes—Runar had had a lot to say about Greta and the smell, hadn't he? And in jumping to that conclusion, Selby had overlooked another still-real possibility, because Runar *did* work with bodies, he *did* have that morgue downstairs. And even if he and Thora had both denied it, he *had* been awfully touchy about it, hadn't he?

But then, there'd also been the girl in the stairwell, and Selby considered that, cleared her throat. "Listen, another thing," she began, "a few nights ago in the corridor, I came across a girl I didn't recognize. And it seemed like that smell was stronger around her—but when I followed her, she disappeared."

Thora's head turned at that, her forehead furrowing, and her hand moved from Runar's shoulder to Selby's. "What did the girl look like?" she asked, so Selby described the blonde hair, the patched clothes. Making Thora's forehead furrow deeper, and beside her Runar shook his head.

"The only girl here who wears patched clothes is *you*, sweetheart," he said, toward Selby. "None of the others would be caught dead in a getup like that. Including you, Thora, thank the gods, since I have to look at you all day."

He flashed Thora a brief, crooked smile, bringing an unmistakable flush to her already-pink cheeks. "Well, maybe I'll scrounge up some rags for tomorrow," she replied, dropping her hand from Selby's shoulder. "And also, I think we're good. She'll be fine, at least for now."

She gave a distracted smile toward Selby, and Runar nodded, and yanked off his gloves, and tossed them into a nearby bucket. "For *now*," he said. "But take it easy, Selby, you hear me? And tell Agmund where to shove his dick if you don't feel up to it. And also, Thora"—he strode to the washbasin, shot her a smirk over his shoulder—"if you dare show up here tomorrow wearing rags, you're working naked."

Thora's face flushed even deeper, her mouth opening, but her reply was cut off by a loud knock on the door behind them. And when she went over to open it, there was—Ketill. Frowning over his spectacles toward them, and striding inside the room like he owned it.

"I trust Ms. Seng is on the mend, Alariaq?" he asked coolly. "And that she is able to resume her usual duties?"

The look on Runar's face was something straddling politeness and loathing, but he gave a curt nod. "Within reason," he replied, just as coolly. "However, Mr. Agmund needs to be considerate about said *duties*, and willing to accept no for an answer."

Ketill didn't reply, and his eyes moved purposely to Selby. "If you are indeed well again, Ms. Seng," he said, "I'd like to speak with you in my office."

There wasn't any plausible reason to refuse, and after a quick, earnest thank-you to Runar and Thora, Selby followed Ketill out. Down the stairs, around the corner, into his roomy, shelf-lined office.

"How is your smell?" Ketill asked, once he'd sat down behind his desk, with Selby in the chair across from it. "Are you still experiencing it?"

He was gazing across the desk toward her, his grey eyes carefully blank. And he couldn't be trusted, Selby knew that, but the smell had been ever-present all morning, just like always, so she shrugged, and frowned down at the polished expanse of wood between them.

"It's still there," she replied. "It's always here, as long as I'm in this building. When Agmund is around, it's better, but"—Selby took a breath, said the truth that had been growing in her thoughts all morning—"I really don't think it's otherwise connected to him. It's not like his absence is *causing* it, if that makes sense. I smelled it here before I ever even *met* him."

Ketill's eyes didn't change, though he slowly folded his hands in front of him. "Does it feel like magic? Or like a physical property?"

"It's magic," Selby said, and she was sure of that, too. "And it's stronger in the manor's walls. And down here, on the bottom floor."

And the wall point alone, Selby thought now, should have made her question Greta's involvement, because would air-magic be able to affect the walls? What would be able to affect walls?

"I conducted several comprehensive sweeps of the entire manor yesterday," Ketill said. "I searched for any kind of magical source that could explain such an effect on you. I found nothing."

Selby's eyes dropped back to the desk, and she nodded. "I'm not surprised. I haven't been able to find anything either."

There was an instant's silence, broken only by Ketill's fingers drumming on the desk. "Have you considered, Ms. Seng," he said, "that perhaps you are creating the smell yourself?"

What? Selby twitched, but Ketill kept talking, his voice smooth and implacable. "I'm not accusing you of untruths, of course. However, self-induced illness is a proven phenomenon, particularly when under duress. And the fact that this smell only affects you, and seems to be tied to the manor, suggests to me that it could be magic created by you, on a subconscious level, and experienced only by you."

Selby twitched again, because even worse than the suggestion itself was the fact that maybe—possibly—he could be right. Could the smell be her own body, hating being here, and trying to sabotage it? Could that explain why it was better around Agmund, after bedding Agmund, because that was—she could admit—the part of all this she liked best?

"But my magic has never done anything without my knowledge before," Selby countered. "And it connects to objects. Not buildings."

"I think perhaps you're short-selling your abilities, Ms. Seng," replied Ketill's maddeningly steady voice. "You have had a profound effect on Regin, and correct me if I'm wrong, but that is not an intentional magical effort on your part, is it? And what is a building if not simply a larger object? And does it not stand to reason that if an object can appeal to you, that it could also repel you?"

Selby blinked up toward him, to where his face was too calm, too understanding. "I would suggest you spend some time reflecting on your place here," he continued. "And on the fact that your presence, and your work with Regin, is a matter of immense importance to our Coven and our country. There is nothing shameful in it. Nothing to require any amount of doubt or guilt or self-flagellation on your part."

The words were steady, reasonable, perhaps even true, but Selby's thoughts had flicked back to that girl in the hallway. And if she was making all this up, why would she have attached any meaning to that girl, who she'd never met before, and if anything, had looked more like her than any other person in the place?

She opened her mouth to ask about that, but Ketill kept on speaking, his voice flatter now. "I have also generously conceded to Regin's request to avoid off-site assignments for the immediate future," he said. "He has been adamant that they will only worsen your distress. I hope you will be grateful for his efforts on your behalf, and respond in kind."

Selby nodded. "I will," she said, and to her vague surprise, she meant it. "I'm very grateful to him—and to you—for that."

Ketill inclined his head. "I'm happy to hear it," he replied. "Now, I would like to return to the incontrovertible fact that despite some recent setbacks, your work with Regin has still yielded even better results than expected. Consequently"—he pulled out a sheaf of paper from a drawer, and slid it across the desk—"I would like to extend your contract with us for another six months."

It was like he'd suddenly dumped ice down Selby's back, and she gaped at him, at that appalling stack of paper—that new contract—on the table. "Another six months?!" she demanded, her voice shrill. "With all due respect, sir, I can't. Absolutely not. I'm needed by my family. I have to go home."

Ketill's eyes narrowed, and his mouth did something that might have been intended as a smile. "I am sure your family could continue on quite well with the payment we are willing to provide," he said. "We are prepared to quadruple our previous payment for the six-month term, paid immediately upon signing. And delivered directly to your family, just as last time, if you prefer."

Selby was still staring—*quadruple* their previous payment?—and Ketill gave her another of those disconcerting smiles. "I will remind you, Ms. Seng, that many young mages spend their entire lives attempting to gain placements in this facility, and only a precious few are accepted each year. I am offering you excellent wages for important work with the most famous mage in the country, and it will open many, many doors to you in the future. You would be wise to accept it."

The words, on their face, perhaps couldn't be argued—but to Selby, there seemed to be a low hint of warning in them, too. A threat, even. Just the same as when he'd made the offer the first time, out east at their wagon.

"Regin has not been unpleasant to you, has he?" Ketill inquired blandly, cutting through Selby's thoughts. "Because if he has been, that can be addressed."

There was a sudden, full-blown shudder up Selby's back, because that sounded like a threat, too. And even if Agmund *was* still an asshole, and *had* been unpleasant, Selby found herself recalling, too strongly, that bleak, sinking desperation in his thoughts. The untold misery he'd already endured under Ketill and this cursed Coven.

"No," she snapped, the word almost surprising in its vehemence. "He and I have—an understanding."

Ketill didn't contest that, and gave a slow, satisfied nod. "I am pleased to hear it," he said. "And please consider my offer, Ms. Seng. You would do well to accept it, especially given the health of your family."

Wait. That was new, that was even more ice down Selby's back, and her hands tightened to fists. "The health of my family?" she repeated. "What do you mean?"

Ketill looked down his nose at her, and shifted in his chair. "A salary like the one I am offering you will guarantee their standing for many years," he replied, his voice far too smooth. "You disagree, Ms. Seng?"

Selby stared at him, at those cold soulless eyes, and slowly shook her head. "No, sir."

"Good," he said, as he pulled the contract back toward him. "You're dismissed. Let me know when you've changed your mind."

There was no response to that, only the overpowering need to get out of his sight, and with one last, uncertain look over her shoulder, Selby went.

20

Agmund didn't mention Ketill's offer that night, or the next morning. Didn't mention Ketill at all, in fact, though he did ask, a little stiffly, how Selby was feeling.

And he kept asking, in the nights and mornings after, each time before he touched her. Even when he was obviously irritable and exhausted from a long day of Ketill's endless drills and exercises—still no killing, thank the gods—Agmund would close his eyes, take a breath, and ask.

It meant something, and strangely enough, it seemed to make Selby crave him even more. Seemed to make the ever-present smell and its accompanying nausea fade behind the all-consuming hunger, the need to touch him, to slide her hands against his chest, his back, his arse. To feel him looking at her like that, and to know, with utter certainty, now, that Regin Agmund wanted her.

Of course it was still Selby doing all the actual taking, with Agmund on his back, and her on top. But his hands were always there, often of his own volition, now, on her breasts or her waist or her arse. And when Selby slept on him at nights, or took the liberty of yanking off his trousers or his tunic, or putting her hands wherever she pleased, he never protested, never resisted, never complained.

And even if he still spent plenty of time with his friends, and avoided being seen with Selby in public, she couldn't seem to muster up more than a mild annoyance about it. Because when they were alone, the world's greatest air-mage was almost entirely hers for the taking, all the way from his lean, expressive body down to the most mundane thoughts in his head.

Regin Agmund hated green vegetables and tight clothes. He liked getting up early, with the sun. He loathed reading, studying, sitting still, making polite conversation, and he much preferred being outdoors, being busy, learning and sharpening the magic he loved. He thought of magic almost constantly, new spells and better spells and backwards spells, and even though his magic hadn't yet returned to its previous heights, he'd never been so desperately grateful for it as he was now, after so many months spent starving for it.

But, oddly enough, for all the space magic occupied in Agmund's brain, he rarely spoke of it. Only to Ketill, or very occasionally to his friends, when asked. He told more to Njall than the rest, perhaps—but that, Selby now understood, wasn't because Agmund was closer to Njall than the others. Rather, it was because Agmund's friend Mik—a truly decent air-mage, who Agmund had often worked with—had left Coven Manor last year, leaving Njall as the single best air-mage remaining. And therefore, Njall was the one other person, beyond Ketill, who sometimes actually understood what Agmund was talking about.

But no one else understood what Agmund was talking about—even Greta hadn't, those entire two years—and Agmund had always just found it easier to say what they wanted, to supply what was expected of him. Wry comments and cocky swagger and an easy smile, never even a hint of loneliness or despair or those constant horrifying nightmares, because of course the world's greatest air-mage should be content with his privileged lot in life, shouldn't he?

And simmering beneath it all was Agmund's ever-present awareness that if he drove off his friends, he had no one left. No childhood friends who'd known him before he was famous. No family members who hadn't tried to profit from his fame. No one except, perhaps, for Ketill.

It was strangely unsettling to see, to experience, and it had given Selby a new, deep-seated appreciation for her own family, and the certainty their support had given her. She'd always been accepted, and listened to, and cared for, just as she was. And after Agmund left each morning, Selby had begun spending some time kneeling by her shelf, thinking of her family, touching their things. Praying for her mother's safety, for Simon's health, for good weather and good luck.

And while she was there, she'd also begun reflecting, like Ketill had suggested, on her own place here, her own purpose. And though she was loath to admit it, the more she thought about it, the more she was willing to consider the possibility that maybe—maybe—Coven Manor's ever-present stench was her own doing, after all. That maybe Ketill was right, and once she accepted her role here, came to terms with it, the smell would go away.

There were parts of it that were easy to come to terms with. Like working with Morley and Kal identifying plants, and now also with Fasta and Henrik, identifying woods and grains and types of stone. And then eating meals with Runar and Thora, and spending time each day out in the garden. Even the outright mockery from the other mages had faded somewhat, and had been replaced by sullen, suspicious looks that were far easier to ignore.

And, of course, the easiest part of all was Agmund. Since Selby's sickness, she'd made a point of being there early in his room every evening, lounging about in only her shift, ready and waiting for when he showed up. A development which had seemed to mitigate the worst of his end-of-day moods, and therefore headed off a multitude of problems between them.

But then, fewer problems with Agmund meant more time in bed with Agmund, getting along with Agmund, sharing snarky but companionable conversations with Agmund, spending more and more time in Agmund's thoughts and dreams. And even becoming accustomed to the ever-increasing moments when instead of speaking out loud, Agmund would just say what he wanted without words, touching his thoughts directly into hers.

Are you sure you're not just pregnant? he silently asked one morning in bed, when the smell-induced nausea felt particularly strong, and Selby's head snapped up to stare at him. The question had felt furtive, not something he would have ever asked aloud, but she could feel that he'd meant it, his blue eyes oddly intent in the dim morning light.

"Oh, I'm sure," Selby replied, as evenly as she could, over the curious new lurch in her stomach. "Ketill had that sorted, remember? And believe me, I would know."

Agmund's mouth twitched up, his long body stretching out beneath her. *Right*, his silent thoughts said back. *Having something alive inside you. Probably drive you round the bend, hearing it thinking in there all day.*

It was true, and a deeply alarming prospect—but Agmund didn't seem overly alarmed, and Selby frowned down at him. "Shouldn't you be more upset about the idea of that? You *hated* those women who tried to have your kids."

Too late she clamped her mouth shut, because Agmund had never actually told her that, but he only shrugged against the blanket. "It's different, you're not trying," he said dismissively. "And you can still fuck when you're pregnant, can't you?"

Selby pulled herself up further, making zero effort to avoid digging her elbows into his bare chest, which had rather filled out these past few weeks, his ribs now barely visible under his skin. "Really?" she demanded. "*That's* what you're worried about? Ketill would have your *head*, you fool. And"—her voice dropped lower—"he'd make me get rid of it. Right?"

That prospect was alarming too, for reasons Selby couldn't quite explain, but Agmund's thoughts and eyes had gone distant, and he absently nudged her elbows off his chest, and onto the bed instead. "Maybe," he said. "But if you really wanted it, I'd deal with him."

Oh. Selby kept staring at him, feeling thoroughly dumbfounded, and Agmund twitched a faint smile at her. "Don't go getting any ideas, though," he added. "I mean that. I'd be a terrible father."

Behind those words was a memory, of course featuring an exasperated Ketill, saying *I hope to gods you don't ever have children of your own, Regin*. And there had in fact been a few very close calls that a bitterly furious Agmund had demanded Ketill deal with, before Agmund had settled down with Greta—and Selby was disconcertingly caught off guard by the truth of that, and also, by the accompanying surge of entirely irrational jealousy.

"Oh bullshit," Selby snapped, perhaps at herself, or Ketill, or both. "You'd be a passable father, there's loads worse. Also, you're rolling in coin, and that's a huge help."

Agmund didn't like talking—or even thinking—about his wealth, Selby knew, but by now she was well aware that he had more than enough to live out the rest of his life in absolute luxury. Though at least he never tried to diminish the power his coin had, the many ways it made life easier, and she could feel his thoughts silently conceding her point. Saying, *yeah, fair, that would help.*

"Still just passable, though?" he said out loud, raising his eyebrows at her. "You sure know how to flatter a guy, Seng."

Selby gave him her most winning smile, and drummed her fingers on his chest. "Yep. Total honesty, remember?"

Of course Agmund remembered, since it had become a recurring theme between them these past weeks. Not quite reaching to certain major points—Agmund's job, Selby's family, that ten-page contract between them, with its looming three-month deadline—but to the daily, constant things. *Where are you going, when will you be back, what did you do today, why are you being such an asshole right now. Is this all right, do you care if it makes a mess, do you want to do it again, are you sure you feel up to it, fuck yes.*

And a few times, it did go a little deeper, too. One night, Agmund asked her to tell him more about pedlars, about the shops and trade routes and stereotypes. And another night, he asked, with an odd glint in his eyes, if anyone had bothered her lately—and behind the question, Selby had caught an involuntary flicker of memories. Memories of Agmund snapping at Coven staff, at servants, even at his friends, the irritation sharp and genuine in his thoughts. *I told you, pedlars aren't scammers. She hasn't stolen anything. She's just doing her job, and helping me. I don't want to hear it. Fuck off with that shit.*

It somehow twisted the longing even deeper into Selby's chest, disorienting and all-consuming, unlike anything else she'd ever experienced in her life. And though she desperately fought to stay distant, stay professional, it felt more impossible with every day that passed. Every day that Agmund's hands, Agmund's body, Agmund's thoughts, touched hers, entwined with hers, did things to hers that no one else had ever done before.

It didn't help that Agmund wasn't always professional, either, and it had been maybe six weeks since Selby's illness when he stayed out late one night, later than he ever had before. Selby had been waiting, her irritation increasing with every dragging hour, because she could feel him lingering out in the forest, doing nothing, for no discernible reason. And when he finally came in, well after midnight, said reason suddenly became clear, because the reek of ale on him was almost strong enough to drown out the walls' ever-present stink in Selby's nostrils.

"Don' whinge at me," Agmund warned, his words slurring a little as he staggered inside, and slammed the door behind him. "I didn' know. Surprise party, for me. Can' very well leave, can I?"

He looked annoyed in the dim candlelight, his bottom lip jutting out in an almost-comical pout. Almost as if he would have preferred to leave his friends, and spend the evening with Selby instead. And despite her lingering irritation, she stepped closer, and began untying the laces of his tunic with hands that easily betrayed her in their eagerness.

"Surprise party?" she asked, as he raised his arms up, and she pulled the tunic off. "What, is it your birthday or something?"

"Nah," he replied, and kicked absently at the floor in the way that Selby now knew meant he was uncomfortable. "Yesterday I hit a target at three leagues."

He didn't elaborate, but Selby considered him for an instant, her hands flat up against the warm, silken rise and fall of his bare chest. Because first off, he'd hit a target at three leagues—even given his ridiculously godlike abilities, that seemed absurdly impossible—but also, because maybe there was an implication in the way he'd said it, or thought it. That he'd been able to do that, before, and hadn't again, until now.

"What, so an Agmund-finally-has-all-his-magic-back party?" Selby asked, a little thin. "How lovely for you."

Agmund clearly caught the sarcasm in her voice, and his eyes narrowed at her, even as she untied his trousers, and pulled them down to reveal the hard cock behind them, now pointing straight and thick out toward her. "Don' start with me, Seng," he snapped. "If I'd've known, I would've invited you."

Selby bitterly laughed at that, her eyes briefly angling up to meet his. "And don't you lie to me, asshole," she replied, even as she stepped closer, and lightly circled her fingers around that hard pulsing shaft, tasting of his raw, undeniable hunger. "No way in hell would you have invited me to a party like that."

Agmund didn't argue, thankfully, and didn't resist as Selby nudged him backwards, toward the bed. He still had his boots on, and his trousers were still trapped around his ankles, so it was awkward going, but he didn't complain about that either, and let her push him down to seated.

"I would've invited you," he repeated thickly, as he watched Selby get to her knees, and start pulling off his boots. "If it was somewhere else."

That was the key point, of course, because he still held to that don't-be-seen-together-outside-the-bedroom rule, and once Selby had finished with his boots, and his socks and trousers, she sat back on her heels, and looked at him. "Bullshit," she said, voice flat. "You'd only have invited me if it was somewhere else, and also, if *nobody* you knew was going to be there."

Agmund groaned aloud, and his bare foot kicked lightly at Selby's arse through her shift. "So much talking," he said. "So much whinging. Tell me, Seng, why d'you never do anything halfway worthwhile with that smart mouth o' yours?"

Selby's eyes darted up to Agmund's face, and then back to his still-engorged cock, because was he really saying what she thought she was saying? But then his hand went downwards, adjusting himself a little, and Selby swallowed at the sight, felt her tongue dart out to lick her lips.

"Yeah, you know what I mean," Agmund's low voice drawled, making something fire deep in Selby's groin. "Why haven't you?"

Selby's face felt very hot, and she glanced up at his eyes, oddly dark and dazed in the candlelight. "Um, because," she began, "you've never asked?"

Agmund made a sound that might have been a snort, or a laugh. "I don' ask for shit with you," he said. "Matter o' principle, ain' it? But it don' ever stop you doin' anything else."

Now those were interesting words, sending even more flares of heat to Selby's groin. And she couldn't seem to find a reply, could only look at that swollen, hungry cock, still pointing straight toward her. Waiting.

"So it's not that it might make you feel sicker, then?" he asked, voice even lower. "Or that you don' like it?"

Selby had no idea whether she liked it or not, thanks to her highly lacking past experience, but looking at him now, oh gods, was too compelling, almost overpowering. And she could just lean forward, could fit herself right between his spread thighs, could find out exactly what Regin Agmund tasted like...

"No," she whispered, and with the word, that waiting cock visibly flared, bobbing up a little toward her. Wanting her, proving that he wanted this, and suddenly Selby's heart was pounding out of her chest, echoing in her ears.

"Why, then?" Agmund murmured, so soft that she almost couldn't hear it. "Tell me."

Selby dragged her eyes back up to his, searched for something, anything. "Because," she said, breathless, "you haven't let me put out more of my things."

Those eyes blinked, incredulous, for an instant—and then he groaned, rubbing at his face with his palms. "You're kidding me, wench," he said, almost a growl. "You won' suck me until I let you put more *dead shit* on my shelf?"

Selby should have been offended, but suddenly she found that she was almost enjoying this, that the heat in her face and her groin were matched by the husky heat in her voice. "That's it, asshole. You give me another shelf, I suck you off."

Agmund groaned again, digging his palms in deeper, and then dropped his hands, and glared down at her. "You do it once?" he asked. "Or more, after that?"

Oh *gods*, he wanted it more, and Selby fought to grasp at her racing thoughts for an answer. "Possibly more," she breathed. "Maybe."

And then there was the warm, thrilling feel of Agmund's hand, gripping under her chin, tilting her head up, making her meet his eyes. "You promise me more," he replied, voice gone harder, "and you can have your damn shelf. *If*"—his forehead furrowed, his grip tightening—"there's no new bones, or dead shit. Deal?"

Selby swallowed, and pulled in a slow, shaky breath. "Deal," she whispered, and there was an unmistakable flash of something like triumph in Agmund's eyes. And eagerness, too, and when he dropped his hand from her chin, he also dropped his knees open wider. Saying, *I'm waiting.*

Selby's heartbeat hammered even louder, and she crawled a little closer between his knees, almost enough to touch. Drinking in the sight of that swollen jutting cock, the smooth ruddy head, the small sheen of wetness pooling at the tip.

"So why's this better?" she murmured, as she finally, carefully, stroked a finger down the beautiful thick length of him, felt the flaring heat of his craving behind it. "Than the usual, I mean?"

She let her touch become more familiar with the words, circling around him, and suddenly there was a brief, clearly involuntary memory of Greta asking a similar question, months ago. *Why the hell is this so important for you, what does it matter, why do you always—*

The memory broke off, abruptly, and Agmund leaned back a little on the bed, let his legs fall open wider. "It's not better," he replied. "But different, in a good way. An' I love any kind of fucking I can get. Always have."

As if in confirmation of those words, his hips bucked up slightly, thrusting him deeper into Selby's fingers, so she let her grip tighten more, brought up her other hand to slide against the soft hair of his thigh. "Why am I not surprised," she murmured. "Does it always have to be multiple times a day, too?"

Agmund huffed a low chuckle, and bucked his hips up again, smooth hot friction between Selby's fingers. "Yeah, sure, if I'm feelin' it," he said. "An' I usually am. My record, if you care, is twelve in a single day. Coulda done thirteen."

The words were smug, satisfied, and behind them was the barest flicker of the memory of that. A year or two before Greta, in a posh room in the middle of the capital, a school of some kind. And the women had just kept coming in, one after the other, sometimes several at once, and Agmund hadn't even gotten dressed in between, or bothered asking their names.

"Congratulations, asshole," Selby hissed, though her hands kept stroking, slick against that smooth skin. "How very convenient that you're the most famous mage in the world. How many women have you had, hundreds?"

She couldn't quite believe she'd said that, or just how bitter it had sounded coming out—but when she glanced up, Agmund hadn't seemed to take offense, and instead was watching her through half-lidded eyes.

"Maybe," he said finally. "Haven't counted. But it doesn't actually mean it's any good. If you want the truth, a lot of it's been shit."

Selby's hands on him stilled for an instant, because the words seemed entirely at odds with that memory, all those eager beautiful women. But Agmund's thoughts were nudging at her now—*why'd you stop*—and Selby made her hands move again, one still stroking smooth up that cock, the other brushing over the soft skin of his firm bollocks below.

"But how could it possibly be shit?" Selby asked, sounding genuinely curious, because it did seem unfathomable. "They'd probably do anything you want, as often as you want, any way you want. You're—"

She shut her mouth just in time, but there was a hard curl on his lip. "Regin fucking Agmund, I know," he said, voice clipped. "It doesn't mean I'm stupid, or I can't tell why people want to fuck me. Or why they'd never say no to me, even if they didn't really want it."

Ah. That did make sense, and behind it there were more memories, even one of Agmund that next morning, scrubbing himself off, in that same posh room. Almost hating himself, and hating those nameless women he'd taken all that pleasure with. Women who wanted him only for his status and fame, for the bragging rights of saying they'd bedded Regin Agmund. Women who had no idea who he actually was. Women he would never be able to trust.

So that had to explain why Agmund had settled down with Greta, right? And that should have made him happy? But then Selby's thoughts darted back to that brief, betraying memory she'd just seen of Greta—along with multiple others she'd caught, these past weeks—and there was the slick hurtling certainty, or maybe even satisfaction, that Agmund definitely hadn't always been happy with Greta, either.

"Don't judge me, Seng," Agmund snapped, perhaps reading into the look in her eyes, the way her hands had once again hesitated on his glorious smooth skin. "You love it, too."

It took Selby an instant to adjust to that, to give him a swift, furtive look. "Do not," she managed, but Agmund laughed, a little harder, perhaps more mocking, than before.

"Oh, don't try and deny it to me," he said coolly. "I know better. Out of anyone I've been with, you have more reason than all of them to just grin and bear it—but you don't. You're never happier than when there's a big fat cock deep between your legs, pumping you full of its spunk."

My big fat cock, he was saying, and *my spunk*, and Selby betrayed an involuntary gasp, a clench of her fingers around him. And fuck, he was an asshole, but he just laughed again, and gods she was so *completely* fucked with this—

"Or, between your lips, maybe," Agmund continued, breathless now, and his hand was on Selby's chin again, tilting her gaze up to meet his. "Can't say for sure until we find out, can we? But to my mind, odds are, you'll like a nice hard cock spraying down your throat, too."

Selby's mouth gasped again, but she managed a glare up at him, a too-tight squeeze of his cock in her fingers—though in reply he just made a show of spreading his legs even wider, of reaching down to tug the skin up over the smooth, ruddy head of him.

"I'm waiting," he said, low and husky. "Gonna lose your shelf, if you don't get to it."

Selby swallowed, felt it convulse hard in her throat. "You are *such* an arrogant asshole," she breathed, but her eyes had dropped again, watching her fingers give a slow slide up that perfect cock, silently betraying her words. While Agmund let out a rich, rolling laugh, and there was the sudden, thrilling feel of his hand, brushing brief against her hair, tasting all through of his heavy jolting hunger.

"An asshole," he murmured, "whose cock you're gonna suck, witch."

At this rate Selby was going to bite him, the bastard, but at the look on her face he only laughed again, his head tilting backward, showing off the long line of his neck. And fuck, he was gorgeous, and Selby finally drew close to that hard waiting cock, and kissed it.

Agmund hissed through his teeth at the contact, the smile immediately vanishing, and though Selby should have gloated, or something, she was far too distracted in this, too caught. In feeling that soft, warm, pliable skin under her lips, and how it slid easily away, exposing the smooth bulging head underneath. And how his slit felt and tasted under her tongue, hard and salty and slick, vibrating between her lips.

Fuck. Selby had to taste that again, feel that again, so she gave it another slow, careful kiss, watching Agmund's face this time. Watching his lips come apart, his eyelashes fluttering closed, his chest heaving deep with the shudders of his breath.

That meant it was good for him too, and the swirling thoughts behind his skin confirmed it, so Selby kissed him again, this time letting her tongue linger. Wishing, irrationally, that she could kiss his mouth like this, but that was something she'd still never dared to do, because he always tensed, or turned away, when she got too close—but he wasn't tensing now, wasn't refusing now, was actually letting out a low groan as Selby's kiss went deeper, as she took more of him inside her mouth.

That felt good too, tasted so good, so she took a little more, using just a touch of suction this time. His gasp at that was audible, his fingers fluttering against her hair, so Selby sucked him inside deeper, harder. And then groaned around him at the feel of those fingers tightening on her head, guiding her closer, wanting her to take all of him, oh gods—so Selby tried to do it, deeper and deeper, until he was wedged up tight against the back of her throat.

The taste of it, the feel of it, had somehow drowned out most of the images of it—but now that Agmund was so far inside her, bearing down on her throat, stretching out her mouth, it was like his thoughts were swarming directly from his cock into her brain. Memories of this, of so many of those girls doing this, as an overture, or an advantage, or a notch on their belts—but no girl doing it for a shelf. No girl calling him an asshole while she knelt between his legs, and softly stroked his cock and balls. No girl who didn't give a shit that he was Regin fucking Agmund—

Selby groaned around him again, and then louder when he pulled out a little, and then slid back inside. He liked the movement, she realized, liked sinking home into her throat, and the images in his cock liked it, too. Feeding back a strange hazy loop of herself, still wearing her shift, her face flushed, her eyelashes thick and dark against her cheeks, her hot, slick mouth stretched wide around Agmund's pale-looking cock—

Oh, *gods*. Selby sucked harder, moved faster, shivering all over, while Agmund's gasps rose to steady, strangled groans. The images streamed faster and messier too, shouting how much he craved this, how many months he'd gone without this. How the blood just kept pooling and pulsing in his cock, filling him to the point where it was almost painful, and how good her hot little mouth on him felt, how he desperately needed more. Needed more of her mouth, her hands, needed her stroking at his balls and other places, too...

So Selby moaned and did that, too, taking advantage of Agmund's spread legs to caress and explore anywhere she wanted. While the stream of his thoughts and his pleasure surged harder, not giving a damn what she did, as long as there was more of it, more of her, why the hell did she have all those clothes still on, what would she do if he grabbed her head with both hands and had at it—

Selby blinked up at him, hazy and frantic—he *wanted* that?—and then she yanked backwards, all the way off, and fumbled for her shift. Hurling it off and away, fully baring herself for Agmund's dazed, staring eyes. And giving him a damned good view of her bulging, pressed-together breasts as she slid both hands back between his legs, and sucked his hungry cock down her throat.

"*Fuuuck*," Agmund breathed, his hips snapping up hard, and Selby spared an exploring hand long enough to grab at his hands, and press them flat against her head, on either side. Giving him permission, or maybe an order, and Agmund groaned again as he obliged, sinking his fingers deep and possessive into her hair.

Gods, it was good. So good that Selby couldn't make out the images anymore, couldn't even begin to protest as Agmund guided her head back and forth, sliding her mouth up and down. Slow at first, maybe letting them both get a feel for it, but then faster, harder, deeper. Until she was close to gagging with it, but she couldn't have cared less, because Regin Agmund was fucking her mouth, gasping with every thrust, the images the heat the hair of his crotch in her face, the smell of him, the taste of him, the feel of that silken skin slamming again and again between her lips—

"Gon' come," he gasped, his voice hoarse, broken—and the words made Selby groan aloud, made her suck harder, could feel the rise the rise the rise, the screeching teetering ecstasy, whirling high and taut and furious—

And then it collapsed, in bright, surging bursts of pleasure. So strong that Agmund cried out, his body bending double over her, while his cock shuddered and flared out deep in her mouth, sending stream after stream of thick, salty-bitter liquid deep down her throat.

It was all Selby could do to swallow it, to keep it from spilling out her mouth, but he didn't let her go, didn't release the pressure. It wasn't until she'd finally finished swallowing, taking the last of it with effort down her throat, that he finally sagged backwards on the bed, enough to let his cock slip out between her lips.

"Fuck," he breathed again, and Selby realized that his hands were still in her hair, and that they were trembling. And she was still breathing hard too, feeling the new thick numbness of her lips, the ache in her jaw. And most of all the pounding pulse between her legs, still hungry and eager and soaking-wet.

She'd been staring at his cock, she realized, at how it had gone a little soft against that coarse dark hair, and belatedly she blinked, looked up to his face. To where he was looking back down at her, his pupils blown wide, his eyes hazy and hungry and approving.

"Thought so," he murmured, as one of his hands slid down her cheek, his thumb brushing up against her lip. "Been denyin' both of us, Seng."

Selby rolled her eyes at him, though she couldn't stop her head from leaning into the touch of that hand. "Been denying myself a shelf, you mean," she said, and in reply Agmund laughed, rich and throaty and warm.

"Witch," he said, but the word was low, affectionate. "Think you can do it again?"

What? He wanted it *again*? Selby's breath caught, the heat swarming to her groin so fast she almost felt dizzy with it.

"Asshole," she managed. "Aren't you supposed to need time in between?"

Agmund laughed again, and *gods* he looked good when he laughed, his eyes crinkling, his mouth wide and a little wry. "That's why it's a challenge," he said, voice teasing. "You bring me off again, you get a prize. And"—he leaned forward, his voice lowering to a conspiratorial whisper—"it's one that'll have you screeching my name, wench."

Selby's mouth dropped open—he couldn't possibly mean that, could he?—but he raised his eyebrows, gave another brush of his thumb against her lip. "Give you a tip," he murmured. "I like it even better when it's messy. Sloppy. Lots of tongue."

It was like Selby's body had taken over, stealing her away from her brain, because her throat let out a low groan, her too-sensitive, too-swollen groin throbbing with every word out of his mouth. *Wet. Sloppy. Lots of tongue. Screeching my name.*

And before she'd realized it, she rose up, and shoved Agmund back on the bed. Climbing over him onto it, straddling him in their usual familiar position, but this time she had her weight on her hands, pressing down on his shoulders, holding him there.

"Bastard," she whispered, but Agmund only laughed again, his eyes still warm, and maybe a little expectant. Wanting to see what she would do next.

She began with his neck, licking and kissing, breathing in the succulent musky smell of him as her tongue explored his ear, his throat, his collarbone. And then she tilted his head back to do the other side, and shuddered all over at the impossible sight of that. Regin Agmund ready, pliable, blond head arched back, neck bared for her touch.

Then it was back to kissing and licking and tasting, while her hands stroked his smooth bare chest, played with those pink nipples, and then slipped further down. Revelling in the feel of his chest heaving under her, the occasional twitch of a muscle, the telltale trail of gooseflesh she left behind as she went lower, and lower.

Agmund's hands had found Selby's head again, long fingers sinking back into her hair, and when he guided her even lower, she went willingly, maybe even eagerly. Running her tongue against the hard muscle of his abdomen, tasting his navel, feeling that coarse hair under her lips. And then—she shuddered again—finding his cock already hard and hungry, still a little wet, smelling of musk and spunk.

Selby held Agmund's eyes as she kissed it this time, and then sucked it inside. Making sure to keep it wetter, sloppier, her mouth open and soft and languorous as she slid down, and up, and down again. This angle was easier, her distant thoughts noted, and she let her hands wander further as she sucked, let them move in time with her tongue. And fuck this was good, fuck he looked good, Regin Agmund naked and spread-eagled on his bed, his hazy eyes watching her, his hard cock deep in her mouth—

There was no warning when he came this time, just the sudden spurting liquid filling her mouth, and Selby couldn't hold it all in, had to pull off, gasping for air, fighting to swallow that thickness down her throat. Agmund was gasping too, his eyes still on her, staring as she licked at the last of it, wiped at her swollen wet lips.

"Sorry," he breathed, and his hand still on her hair tightened. "Thought I had another minute. You coulda spit."

Selby wiped at her mouth again, tried to find her voice. "Didn't want to lose my prize," she managed. "Do I still get one?"

There was a flicker in Agmund's eyes, an instant's stillness in his body beneath her, and Selby realized, too late, that the prize had probably just been him talking drunken gibberish. And gods knew what he'd even meant by it anyway, and her stupid whispering hope that he'd get hard again, finally let her fuck him, was probably just that, stupid, and driven only by the fact that the swollen throbbing ache between her legs was almost painful, now, shouting at her for something, anything, *please*.

"Never mind," she said, though she couldn't quite look at him, and dropped her eyes to his still-heaving chest instead. "You're probably tired, I'll just—"

She gave a vague wave toward the water closet, because at least there, she could shut the door, hide from him, get some kind of relief—but then Agmund cleared his throat, loudly. And when Selby glanced back at his face, he looked determined, maybe a little grim.

"Look, if you want to have me do the same," he said, "I won't stop you."

He wouldn't stop her. Selby blinked down at him, at his suddenly wary eyes, and tried to put that together. If she wanted to have him do the same—

He sighed, sounding exasperated now, like Selby was being intentionally stupid, but she truly wasn't following what he meant. "I can fuck you?" she asked, tentative, hopeful, because yes, that was exactly what she wanted—but he grimaced, something moving again in those eyes.

"My mouth," he said, curt. "If you want."

What? Selby's heart jolted, and she put her trembling hands to either side of him on the bed. "Um," she said, and suddenly there was the vision of that, the possibility of that, she could fuck his mouth, what the *hell*, there was no way he meant what she thought he meant—

But Agmund's eyes were steady, waiting, and Selby's breath was coming too fast, her head giving a frantic shake. "No way," she breathed. "You don't mean that, you're drunk, you can't actually *want* that—"

There was a flicker of annoyance on Agmund's face now, and as if to refute that point, his hand gripped at Selby's arm, tugging her upwards. "I wouldn't have offered if I didn't," he said, voice flat. "Now get on with it, before I change my mind."

The protests were already rising in Selby's throat, things like *I can't do that, can't show you that, can't let you taste that*—but her body was shouting otherwise, and the image of it, the prospect of it, was suddenly wildly, impossibly thrilling. Regin Agmund was offering to let her fuck his mouth, he wouldn't have offered it if he didn't want it, this might be her only chance to do this, ever, and at this point her dripping-wet body was almost screaming for it—

So she moved herself up him, until she was straddling his waist, her knees up under his arms—but then she hesitated again, risking a swift, uncertain glance at his still-forbidding eyes. Asking, maybe, what she was supposed to do next, and in reply he gave a longsuffering sigh, and yanked a little on her waist this time. Saying, *come on.*

Selby's heart was pounding so loud she was sure Agmund could hear it, and her legs shook as they moved up over his shoulders, as her crotch now hovered appallingly close to his face. And an ashamed, whispering part of her was trying to keep it away from him, leaning back toward his chest, but he sighed again, and gave an irritated roll of his eyes.

"I said my mouth, Seng," he murmured, and though there was impatience in his voice, there was something else, too. And that was enough, maybe, to make Selby maneuver herself over his face, her legs spread wide apart, showing him everything that was supposed to be hidden, covered, safe.

Her cheeks were burning hot, her arms and legs shaking as she held herself there, and took in the shocking realization that he was actually *looking* down there, his eyes dark and intent. And in reply her swollen body was pulsing and clenching for him, the wetness actually audible, the shame flooding her with heat—

But then there was the sudden, searing feel of both Agmund's hands, coming up to tighten on her arse. And now pulling her down, closer, and Selby gaped at the impossible, mind-bending sight of her open body lowering over his mouth, his lips parting, as if to take her in—

And oh gods, oh fuck, holy fucking *hell*, that was Regin Agmund's mouth, his *tongue*. And Selby yanked herself away, staring and heaving and shuddering all over, feeling the shock of it still trembling through her limbs. *Fuck*.

But Agmund's thoughts behind it had been hot, hazy, hungry. *Want to see you take this*, they whispered, and when his hands pulled downward again, with perhaps a twitch more impatience in them, Selby dragged in a long, fortifying breath, and relented. Back to the impossible, gut-swarming feel of his mouth between her legs, his tongue, licking up flat against the most intimate of places—

She had to yank herself away again, dragging in breath, but it already felt like she was on fire, like every nerve was screaming for more. And when Agmund's hands pulled back down she went easier this time, and squeezed her eyes shut and made herself stay, made herself feel that, the kiss of his lips, the pressure of his sliding tongue, warm, wet, *wonderful*—

He tilted her more, pulled her down tighter, and then actually slid his slick, sinuous tongue a little inside. Making Selby cry out, her hands fluttering, shaky, her body silently shouting its disbelief, and now his tongue was flicking, in and out—*knew you'd love this*, it whispered—and oh gods that felt good, felt impossible, felt like she was breaking and blasting apart—

"Agmund," she gasped, "you—you—"

There was an odd sound from his mouth between her legs, almost like a laugh, and then he began sucking, soft and wet, just at the top of her crease. Against the single most sensitive place, against the place that was drawing in everything, shutting off every other part of Selby's body, and she was gasping out loud now, pleading. "P-please, oh gods, please, Agmund, oh *fuck*—"

Her gasps were broken by a cry, sharp and shocked, because one of Agmund's hands had come further down behind her, and there was the impossible, unspeakable feeling of a long single finger, sliding deep into her grasping quivering wetness, just where she needed it, craved it. Making her entire body arch forward onto him, up against where his mouth was still sucking on her, he was impossible outrageous the world howling and screaming between her legs—

And then Selby was the one screaming, while her body shuddered and keened. Gripping her again and again in spasms of furious screeching ecstasy, in deliverance finally given, in a swirling sinking shaking relief.

When the world finally returned again, Selby was on her hands and knees over him, still gasping for breath, still trembling with the aftershocks. And Agmund—Agmund was looking up at her, his mouth and chin still shiny with her wetness, and his eyes were lazy, maybe even satisfied.

"All right there, Seng?" he asked, a little mocking, and though Selby tried for a growl down at him, it came out sounding like a moan instead. Making his still-wet mouth quirk up, and for a dizzying, hanging instant she was caught on the sight of that mouth, on the truth of what it had just done, oh *gods*.

Agmund was actually smirking now, the bastard, and Selby carefully maneuvered her shaky body back downwards, and let herself collapse against his side. She felt weak and rubbery all over, but there was also a slowly spiralling contentment, a sudden surging warmth toward him that couldn't quite be denied.

"Decent prize, then?" he asked, his voice rumbling into her face against his neck, and she breathed in that smell of him, let out a shaky laugh.

"*Gods*, yes," she whispered. "*Fuck*. I had no idea anything could ever feel so good."

There was another rumble of laughter through his neck, but then his body shifted against hers. "You have done that before, though," he said. "Right?"

His voice sounded careful, or even wary, and it was the tone that made Selby tense first, before the words themselves knit together in her head. *You have done that before.*

And maybe she should lie, maybe Agmund didn't want to be the first, maybe that was awkward—but he'd already nudged his shoulder up under her head, wanting her to look at him. "Have you?"

Selby couldn't read his thoughts, or the look in his eyes, but suddenly she couldn't bear lying to him, not now. "Um," she began, "no. Should I have told you first?"

Agmund's shoulder gave a jerky shrug, saying *I guess not, whatever*—but his mouth had gone thin, and his eyes on her were speculative, suspicious. "But you have done the rest of it," he said slowly, carefully. "Before me. Right?"

Selby's body stilled, because he was supposed to know all that, wasn't he? But the way he was looking at her said maybe he didn't, and he didn't like it, and Selby was already feeling entirely lost—

"Um," she said again. "Well, I've done—some of it?"

There was a shift in Agmund's eyes, a flash of something like disbelief, and he shoved up to look at her, propping his head on his hand. "What did you do, Seng," he said, his voice suddenly hard, commanding, not sounding drunk anymore in the least. "Tell me."

The room flickered around them, and Selby swallowed, searched for words. "Well," she replied, "kissing, and touching. And"—she took a breath—"using hands. To, well, you know."

Agmund stared at her, still with that disbelief in his eyes, and then he closed them, briefly, as if his head hurt. "Gods damn it," his thin voice said. "Are you fucking *kidding* me? You were a *virgin* when you came here?"

Selby's mouth opened, but the words wouldn't come, and Agmund stared at her again, his eyes narrow and intent. "But the first time we did it," he said quickly, like he was grasping for the words. "You weren't in pain, there was no blood, nothing.

And I sure as hell didn't try to make it good for you. So how—?"

How could it truly have been her first time, he meant, when there'd been no proof of it, and there was something tight in Selby's throat, now, threatening to escape. "Well, I knew why I was coming here, right?" she said, her voice cracking. "Ketill and the contract both made that very damned clear. So I did whatever I could to—to deal with it."

Agmund's eyes closed again, like he really was in pain now, and he pinched the bridge of his nose. "You should have told me," he said. "Before."

The lump in Selby's throat was rising, turning into something oddly like panic, and she shook her head. "I thought you knew! And you hated me, you could barely stand to touch me, why would I have brought up something like that?"

Agmund's body against hers flinched, and he let out a slow, silent breath. "Did Ketill know?" he asked. "When he—recruited you?"

He was studying her closely, his thoughts carefully unreadable, and Selby nodded, tried to speak through that tightness in her throat. "He said it was ideal," she replied. "That it made me an even better candidate. And it was in my contract that I couldn't touch anyone else, I had to give you my virginity, and I thought you saw my contract, I thought you knew!"

Agmund blinked, once, and then he let his body drop back to the bed, and put his palms to his eyes. "I didn't," he said, quiet. "I didn't want to read it. Shit, Seng, I'm sorry."

He was sorry. Selby was still staring at him, digesting that, when abruptly he turned over on his side, facing away from her. And for some reason that made the panic swing up higher, louder, and Selby's hand went, on its own, to the sharp line of his shoulder.

"Agmund," she said, a little helpless, because the other words were too tricky, and perhaps entirely unwarranted.

Things like *It's all right* and *I forgive you* and *I'm over it* and *I still like it, I still like you*—

"Regin," his voice said, suddenly, and Selby's hand on his shoulder twitched. "Call me Regin, for fuck's sakes."

Regin. He still wasn't turning to look at her, wasn't thinking anything she could follow—but Selby's breaths came slower, the tightness easing off in her throat. "Selby, then," she whispered, letting her hand slide down his arm. "If you don't mind."

There was a jerky shrug from his shoulder, saying no, he didn't. And that was enough, maybe, for now, and Selby lay carefully back against his reassuring heat, and drifted, finally, to sleep.

21

Morning came abruptly, with the cold, unfamiliar feel of Agmund sitting up, and getting out of bed.

Selby blinked her bleary eyes open and rolled over, reaching to where his warm body was supposed to be. But he wasn't there, and instead he had his back to her, yanking on his trousers.

"You have somewhere to be?" Selby asked, her voice a bit scratchy, and maybe hurt, because she couldn't remember the last time he'd left bed without their usual morning activities—but he barely glanced over his shoulder as he pulled on a tunic.

"Yeah," he said, already striding for the door. "Might be back in a while, though. Maybe."

He didn't wait for a reply before he walked out, shutting the door quietly behind him. Leaving Selby staring after him, and feeling cold, and tired, and uneasy.

She tried to go back to sleep, but she was used to having Agmund's warm body to curl up against, and him not being there was setting her thoughts racing, jolting from one strand to the next. From what Agmund had done last night, to what she'd done last night, to what he'd said after, to this—

It didn't help that Selby could feel him down in Ketill's

office, pacing back and forth, or that the smell seemed particularly pungent today. So much that she lay back down on the bed again, taking slow, deep breaths. Willing the nausea to settle, waiting for the pounding in her head to fade...

But without warning here was Agmund, stalking back into the room, and slamming the door shut behind him. Meaning he was upset about something, or low on magic, or both, and Selby sat up to look at him, felt the room slowly spin around the bed.

"What is it?" she asked, but already he'd come over, standing too close, looming over her. Looking undeniably angry, with his hands and shoulders clenched, and though Selby was still supposed to be ignoring his moods—and getting quite good at it, actually—something in this made her heartbeat pick up, her stomach twisting painfully in her gut. "What?"

"You said you were doing this for the coin," he said, voice flat. "Didn't you?"

"Um," Selby said, blinking up at him, trying to think. "Yes?"

Agmund's jaw twitched, and he crossed his arms over his chest. "Yeah, well, I just had a long talk with Ketill about all this," he snapped. "And according to him, *you* followed *him*, and begged him to bring you here. And you told him you'd always liked me, because you had one of my portraits, and thought I was *hot!*"

He spat out the last word, like it was a curse, and Selby had to close her eyes against that, against the sudden screeching fury in her head. Fuck Ketill, that smug soulless manipulative bastard, how *dare* he—

"So is that it?" Agmund said, voice hard. "Did you read my thoughts, and knew I wouldn't like hearing that tripe, so you made up some doing-it-for-the-coin bullshit? Are you fucking *scamming* me with this?"

Was she *scamming* him, oh gods, and Selby put her hands to her aching, churning stomach. "Of course I'm not scamming you, you asshole," she shot back, though the words came out wavering, thin. "I told Ketill what he wanted to hear. He said an attraction was crucial for the project's success, so I made one up! And yes, I did beg him to bring me, because like I told you, I *needed the fucking coin!*"

Agmund's eyes were still flinty, his lip curling. "Yeah, well, if it's coin you're after, Ketill also said he's offered to extend your contract. For *four times* the pay. And so far, you've refused to sign!"

The tone in his voice changed at that, as if he was insulted somehow, or hurt, and Selby shook her throbbing head. "Ketill offered once, weeks ago," she corrected him. "And at that point you were still being awful to me, and also, this place has made me feel horrible ever since I got here! Why the hell would I have agreed to sign up for six more months of that?"

Agmund's eyes shifted, his arms tightening over his chest. "Because you need the coin," he snapped back. "Supposedly."

Selby let out an exasperated groan, rubbed her hands against her aching head. "I said, I *needed* the coin. As in, past tense. And I got it, for this, all right?"

Agmund still didn't look like he believed her, his mouth too thin, his eyes grim and angry. "Why."

Why. And Selby still hated thinking about it, couldn't bear thinking about it, and she stared across the room, toward her shelf. Toward her father's box, Scarper's skull, Simon's whistle, the lock of her mother's hair.

"Because a week after Ketill first made that offer, our shop wagons caught fire," she said, in a voice that didn't sound like hers. "We lost everything. The horses, both wagons, all our stock. And Simon—my little brother—his lungs have always been bad, but after that he could barely breathe without coughing, he needed a healer, and ongoing treatments, and you know how much that costs, so—"

She couldn't finish, but she gave a helpless wave toward Agmund, the room, this entire cursed manor. While the nausea roiled harder and faster in her gut, and with it were those awful memories, burned stark into her brain. The screaming horses, the blinding orange light, the sound of Simon coughing and coughing, her mother with her face in her hands...

Selby's stomach spasmed, and she leapt unsteadily to her feet, staggered sideways around Agmund's too-still body. And thank the gods, she made it to the latrine, just in time to empty her stomach down into it.

When she finally wiped her mouth and leaned back again, Agmund was standing beside her, with a cup of water in his hand. Selby took it, swishing it again and again in her mouth, and finally she managed to stagger up to the washbasin, to clean off her too-hot, too-sticky face.

Agmund kept standing there, watching her, but Selby didn't look at him. Just let herself sink back down to the floor opposite the latrine, flinching at the foul taste of the wall as she leaned her shaky body against it. But her stomach had slightly settled, at least, and she took one long, fortifying breath, and then another.

Agmund still hadn't moved, his boots not far from Selby's feet, and when she finally looked up he was studying her, mouth grim. "So you're honestly telling me," he said, "you came here, and did this with me, because your brother was seriously ill, and your family was fucking *destitute*?"

He had the truth of it, and Selby gave a weary nod. Which was perhaps a mistake, because Agmund's staring eyes had gone angry and appalled, and there was a too-bright spark of electricity, flaring from his fingers.

"What the fuck, Seng!" he shouted, making Selby wince, and then he sighed, kicked at the floor. "Sorry," he said, quieter this time. "What the *fuck*, Selby."

Selby. It sounded fluid, pleading, *beautiful* on his mouth, and Selby had to close her eyes, try to put the words together. "I—I didn't hold it against you, or even Ketill. I don't. You gave me an opportunity when I needed one. I just—did what I had to do."

There was an instant's silence from Agmund, and then a low, harsh noise from his throat. "But you wouldn't have done it, if you'd had another option," he said. "And you didn't want me. Didn't think I was hot."

Selby shot him a furtive look, but his eyes were intently on his feet, and she sighed. "No."

There was more silence, feeling almost oppressive, now, and his boot kicked at the floor again. "Did you get new wagons?" he asked finally. "And horses? And your brother's treatments?"

Selby drew in a breath, and jerked a nod. "Ketill paid me for the entire three months in advance. Got it all arranged before I came here."

"Wait," Agmund said, sharply now. "So you haven't gotten paid since you came here, either? And you don't have anything left?"

Selby sighed, shook her head. "No."

Agmund gave a loud, exasperated groan, and when Selby looked up again, his mouth was a thin line, his eyes closed. "So what do you want."

What did she want. Selby stared at him, at that look on his face, and felt something swoop in her stomach. "What do you mean?"

"I mean, what do you want," Agmund repeated, voice flat. "From me. Do you want more coin? I could pay you myself."

He could pay. Selby's stomach flipped again, and she shook her head, so vehement that the room seemed to flicker around her. "No. *Gods*, no. I don't want payment from you. I *can't*."

There was another instant's silence, and thankfully, Agmund didn't ask Selby to explain why. Why she could take the Coven's payment, but not his, how taking coin from him now would feel like a slap in the face, a transaction between a god and his harlot.

"Well," Agmund said, "does that mean you'd rather just"—he paused, his chest rising and falling—"not do this anymore?"

What? Selby gaped at him, and she felt the nausea rise again, sudden and sharp. "You don't actually *mean* that?" she demanded, her voice shrill. "What about the contract? And your magic?"

"What about it?" Agmund snapped back. "You're apparently here under duress, against your will, and you won't take my coin, and you say you're not attracted to me, so how the *fuck* do you expect me to touch you after all this?!"

The room seemed to be tilting sideways under Selby's body, and she pressed her hands flat to the floor, tried to think. "But—I thought you said you'd do anything for your magic."

Agmund gave a hard laugh, another kick at the floor. "Yeah, well, I guess there's a line somewhere. Forcing myself on someone who doesn't want it is beyond me, even if I am Regin fucking Agmund."

The bitterness in his voice was palpable, almost painful, and Selby swallowed hard, shook her head. "Look, the thing is, I—" she began, and swallowed again. "I *do* want it, all right? You know I do."

Agmund's eyes snapped to hers, unmoving and watchful, but he didn't move, didn't speak. So Selby dragged in air, searched for courage to say it, for truth.

"And I know I don't have a lot of experience, but"—she breathed deep again—"but it's still good, right? I mean, it is for me. And it's gotten a lot better between us in general, and you have let up on your asshole tendencies somewhat, and I like that we're honest with each other, and you, uh, talk to me like you do, and don't think it's weird. And"—she couldn't meet his eyes—"you might be a tiny bit hot. In person."

There was more silence, but when Selby glanced up, she could see Agmund's shoulders and hands relaxing, his eyes briefly fluttering closed with something that could only be relief.

"It was really those stupid portraits," Selby added, for reasons she couldn't quite explain. "Made you look like such a smarmy, spoiled-rotten pretty-boy. The kind who'd cast one spell, and then sit back and expect to be fawned over for weeks afterwards. And who'd be a selfish prick in bed, besides."

She didn't know why she'd said that last part, but there was something strange in Agmund's eyes, on his mouth. "Yeah, well, I hate those fucking portraits," he said. "I actually blew up at the last artist over it, but Ketill made me leave it, because it's good publicity, or some such shit. Also"—he hesitated, gave a heavy sigh—"I *have* been a selfish prick in bed, haven't I?"

Selby opened her mouth to argue that, but then shut it again, because maybe that would be giving him credit he didn't deserve. Because other than last night, it had always been her doing all the touching, the taking, even making all the advances toward him in the first place.

Agmund had clearly followed that, because he sighed again, and that strangeness was still shifting in his eyes. "Look, are you still feeling sick?"

Selby blinked up at him, but shook her head—and suddenly Agmund stepped forward, too close, and reached out his hand.

"C'mon, then," he said. "Let me make it up to you."

22

Selby followed Agmund to the bed in silence, her eyes on his straight back, her heartbeat thudding in her chest. What had he meant, *make it up to you*? With what?

But then he turned around, standing so close that she had to raise her chin to look up at him. "This is just once," he said, his eyes oddly hard. "Just—what I should have done, the first time. All right?"

Selby's head nodded, her eyes still uncertain on his, and then—her entire body twitched—Agmund's hand came up, and stroked gently at her face, her cheek. Making her eyes flutter closed, until there was the thrilling, unexpected feel of his other hand, on her other cheek, both of his hands now carefully cupping her face between them.

It felt suddenly, painfully intimate, firing a sharp thrill down Selby's back, and then again when Agmund leaned down, and—oh *gods*—pressed his lips to her forehead. His mouth soft, warm, and then moving down to one cheek, and then the other. And then, light, to the tip of her nose.

That made Selby smile, unwillingly, but Agmund was already tilting her head, and doing it to her neck. Pressing a series of soft, slow kisses down the side of her throat, each one a single perfect jolt of pleasure, and when he reached the crook of her neck she couldn't help a gasp, couldn't stop her trembling hands from settling against his chest.

Agmund's own hand had come to rest lightly over her shift on the small of her back, even as his other hand tilted her head further, giving him better access. His mouth now sucking a little on her skin, with an unmistakable brush of his tongue, oh gods, and Selby was already shivering all over, swaying on her feet.

He moved to the other side, and that felt even better, and when Selby moaned aloud he huffed a short, silent laugh. And then kept going, kissing lower, while his hands eased further downwards, skimming over her breasts, her waist, her hips.

His thoughts were very carefully distant, and he still hadn't kissed her mouth, but at this point Selby couldn't have cared less. Just kept trying to breathe, to stay upright, while Agmund's hands began sliding upwards again, crumpling her shift with them. Undressing her, oh hell, and Selby tilted her head back, silently pleading for more of his lips, his tongue.

Agmund kept sliding the shift further up, over her groin, her waist, her breasts, and this time she was the one lifting her arms, letting him pull the shift off over her head. Which he did, dropping it to the floor, and then putting his hands back to her waist, guiding her toward the bed.

There was no thought of resisting, just another surge of deep, disbelieving pleasure as Agmund set her down, lowered her onto her back. Until he was the one straddling her, oh gods, his face his eyes his hands, those hands gliding up the curves of her bare body with something almost like reverence.

Then Agmund leaned low over her, like she so often did to him, and kissed again at her ear, her neck, her collarbone. Moving lower, slow but inexorable, kissing gently as he went, until his mouth was brushing against her too-sensitive nipple, and—Selby dragged in a gasping breath—he sucked it into that warm slick heat, flicking it with his tongue.

Fuck, that was good, and Agmund kept at it, even as his hands kept stroking, caressing. Down over her waist, her thighs, back up to take the other breast in hand, to flutter his fingers over her nipple, while Selby heaved under him, fighting for air, oh *gods*.

He slowly moved down further, his kisses warm and whispering against her surprisingly sensitive belly, and then into the creases of her thighs. Mouthing at her coarse hair now, oh gods, and he couldn't want to do this *again*, no fucking way—

But he nudged her legs apart, settling his still-clothed body in between them, and at the first impossible touch of that impossible tongue between her legs Selby cried out, shuddering hard beneath him. But he didn't stop, just wrapped his arms around both her thighs, pulling them apart, and did it again, and again, and again.

Oh gods, oh *fuck*, Selby writhed and moaned under the barrage of it, all her nerves firing at once, but Agmund kept holding her still, in place. And all she could do was cling to him, grab at his hair, too much too strong, his tongue so hot so wet so deep, and she was so close she could *taste* it—

He eased off, suddenly, going back to kisses, light and warm and teasing. And then he met her eyes, maybe for the first time in all this, and his expression was almost playful, his thoughts finally speaking to her, saying what, *what do you want now—*

Selby growled and yanked on him, yanked him up, and once he was there she pulled at his tunic, needing, craving the feel of his bare skin. And thank the gods, he easily obliged, sitting up over her to take the tunic off, holding her gaze with saucy, beautiful blue eyes.

It was too much, so much, and Selby's shaky hands were already at the top of his trousers, untying them with too much force. "Please," she breathed, "please, Ag—Regin. *Please*, fuck me."

Something flared in those eyes, and he kicked the trousers off with almost alarming speed—and now it was his warm skin all over her, all on top of her, and when she pulled down it was his wonderful heavy weight, pressing her to the bed. And her arms curled up around him, her head up against his neck, and his head was in her neck too, his mouth kissing hard and hungry and with maybe even a touch of teeth.

"Oh," Selby gasped, because the visions in her head were all of lightning and strength and forests, while his knees guided her legs apart, settling between them. And oh fuck, that was the feel of his hard cock, just brushing up between her legs, and she was fighting to reach it, to drag him downwards, her hands tight on his arse while he gave a low, husky chuckle into her neck—

And then he was there, the smooth rounded head of him nudging right where she wanted it, craved it. Her hips tilting to take him, silently begging him, please, while his eyes held hers, compelled hers, and he started to sink slow and smooth inside.

Fuck, that was good, Regin Agmund in charge driving into her commanding the sky, firing her alive from the inside out. Making her take him, sinking into her spreading her legs wider, until his coarse hair and hard bone was flush up against her, his balls pressing below, his cock buried deep inside.

It was unlike anything Selby had ever felt, between the sheer sensation of it, the pressure, the visions of his magic, the safe warm enclosing heat of his body, all over hers. His mouth kissing at her neck again, his breath harsh and gasping against her ear.

All right? his thoughts whispered, and in reply Selby gave a fervent nod, a deep, involuntary clench against his cock inside her. Feeling him flare up against her in reply, oh gods, and she let out a desperate moan, grasped her hands hard to his arse, pulled him deeper—

He obliged, his hips giving a firm little circle, his cock doing the same inside, and Selby cried out into his neck, and then louder as he did it again, and again. Going harder, faster each time, until he was thrusting deep the way he liked, and it was all Selby could do to hold on, to keep breathing, to keep her mouth from screaming, or maybe sobbing.

"Want to feel you come," he breathed, his voice rough, his eyes brief and hard on hers—and oh, Selby's body was heating gripping clinging at him, Regin Agmund everywhere, his words his voice his thoughts his massive fucking cock—

She arched back with a shout, her entire body heaving as it wrung itself out around him, against him, under him—and now it was him doing the same, bearing down against her as he pulsed out over and over again, filling her deep and hot and glorious.

It left Selby limp and shaky and gasping, her trembly hands skittering up to his messy bowed head. His eyes were closed, his breath exhaling hard against her neck, and in that stolen, hanging instant, it was like something had tilted in Selby's being, piercing low in her belly. Regin Agmund had made love to her, Regin Agmund was the most beautiful human on this earth, Regin Agmund was *everything*.

The certainty of those thoughts was appalling, and rather terrifying, and so was the way Selby's mouth had gone to Agmund's neck again, kissing him soft and still a little hungry. "Gods, Ag—Regin," her voice breathed between kisses, low and husky. "Fuck. Fucking *incredible*. *Thank* you. *Gods*."

She was half-expecting him to be offended, or distant, but he was still there, still here, still inside her. And Selby was revelling in this, had perhaps never felt so content as this, and when Agmund finally lifted his head to look at her, she smiled up at him, slow and warm. "Still not that hot, though," she murmured. "Don't let it go to your head."

He half-laughed, half-growled, and let his head fall back against her neck. "You lie, witch," he said, his voice hoarse. "I know better. I could do this five times a day, and you'd still be wanting more."

"Would not," Selby protested, but her body had betrayed her, clenching up tight around him. And in reply he laughed again, and his cock vibrated as it filled a little fuller, stretching out inside her, and she couldn't help a breathless groan, her hands and hips pressing up taut against him.

"Would you?" she whispered now, too brazen. "Do it again?"

Agmund's cock flared again, his own hips rocking back toward her—but then he let out a slow, shaky breath, and pulled out of her, away. Moving himself over, and off to the side, and Selby had to make herself let go, keep from trying to pull him back.

"I can't, all right?" he said, quiet, his eyes looking straight up at the ceiling. "Just a one-time thing. Like I said."

Oh. He didn't say why, but the whispers of it were still there, twining through his thoughts. Selby had still been paid to do this with him. She hadn't told him the truth about why she'd come here, even after she'd promised to be honest. She couldn't be trusted. No one could.

Selby felt a sudden wetness behind her eyes, and she blinked it away, fought to keep her voice steady. "I should have told you," she said. "I'm sorry, Regin."

Agmund's eyes closed, and he gave a jerky shrug of his shoulder against her. "Not your fault," he whispered, and again there was that deep piercing twist, low in Selby's belly. And maybe she was pushing it, but she suddenly needed to touch him, craved it, and she slowly slid her arm back over him, curled herself against his smooth warm heat.

He didn't touch her back, but didn't resist, didn't make any move to get up. And suddenly Selby knew what that meant, what he wanted, what he couldn't say.

So she slid herself on top of him, running her hands up over his chest, spreading her still-dripping body over the thick length of his hard cock. Feeling the sticky-slick wetness of it—he'd just made love to her, just filled her—and she gasped as it twitched up hard against her, wanting her, proving it.

She was still wet enough, still open enough, that she didn't even need to use her hands, could just lean forward over him, angle herself, wedge that hard slick head up into her own hungry heat. And then sink down as he flared up, feel their bodies finding each other, knowing each other, belonging together.

Agmund didn't touch her at all this time, but Selby didn't care, because she had his cock, had his seed. And could have it, nearly any damn time she pleased, and she groaned as she ground down, shot herself full of that impossible beautiful strength.

But Agmund wasn't thinking of lightning this time, or magic. And instead, for the first time in a long time, he was thinking of Greta. Of how Greta had always liked it best that way too, with him fucking her on top, her hands clinging at his back—but how with her, he'd always been the one to offer, to caress, to make the first move. Because that's how it had always been with them, Agmund pursuing and Greta evading, and it had been so heady and thrilling at first, so different from being propositioned and fawned over and used—

Selby should have told Agmund to fuck off, to stop thinking this, but a twisted, awful part of her couldn't bear to break it. Instead, she just kept riding him, rocking her body hard up against him, while he thought about how slim and lithe Greta was in comparison, how he'd always thought Greta's body was perfect, a pristine temple at which he'd eagerly bowed and worshipped. But you couldn't get a temple dirty, either, couldn't fuck in your own spunk or before you'd washed or down her throat or when she was on the rag, could never call her a wench and expect her to still want it—

But Greta hadn't cared about Regin Agmund either, had proven that when she'd kept refusing him, made him work for it for months, until they'd really, truly known each other. Or at least, that had been what Agmund had thought, and he'd finally let his guard down, and handed Greta his body and his heart and his soul. And he'd made love to her just that same way, whispering his devotion and his fidelity, until—

Selby's mouth let out a choking sound, her body on Agmund's halting as she tried to breathe, to block the truth of that—and then she felt Agmund's hands on her hips, fingers gripping tight.

"Sorry," he said, his eyes too knowing, too regretful on hers. "Sorry. I'll stop."

And he did, the shift immediate, and almost breathtaking. Lightning streaking down from the sky, smashing sharp and furious against a pyre of rock, making the earth itself shake beneath his feet—

It was better, so much better, but those memories of Greta were still there, painfully rattling inside Selby's skull. And her body kept moving, but maybe more on its own than anything, just because she needed to fuck him, needed to at least prove to him that she would do anything, probably everything he ever asked—

But then, without warning, the vision changed again. Went from the lightning to a memory of Agmund staggering up the stairs, in the dark, with only one purpose in his head—and finding it, there. Waiting for him in his bedroom, yanking off his clothes, looking up at him from between his spread legs with hungry, eager brown eyes.

An asshole whose cock you're gonna suck, witch, he'd said, words he'd never imagined himself saying to a girl in his life, but then she'd actually fucking done it, kissed and licked and suckled at his cock like it was a gift from the gods. Like there was nothing she wanted more than to feel it jamming in her throat, to feel it pumping her mouth full of so much spunk she could barely keep it all in—

Selby gasped, gaping down at him, but his eyes were looking at her breasts, noticing how they bounced and jiggled when they moved. How last night she'd openly taunted him with them, and how they'd looked while he'd used his mouth on her, how they'd heaved and quivered over him. And how one of these nights he was going to spray off all over them, see what that fucking *looked* like—

Gods, Agmund couldn't actually *think* these things, he *couldn't*—but now here was the memory of him, in that very water closet, with the door closed, and Selby still in his bed. And they'd just fucked, she'd just gotten naked for the first time, and Agmund's cock was still dripping wet with her, with them, and already hard, again. And he'd taken himself firmly in hand, and emptied out to the image of smooth skin, gorgeous full tits, that fat round ass that just screamed *fuck me*—

Oh gods, the image of that, the *thought* of that, and Selby's body was already convulsing around Agmund again, pulsing out its pleasure, its shuddery shaking relief. And one, two, three more thrusts, his hands driving her hips down hard—and he was doing the same, pumping her even fuller of him, again, again, again.

When he finished this time he waved her off, his eyes suddenly distant, remote. So Selby lifted herself up, though a twisted part of her didn't bother trying to keep the mess inside, let it leak out onto him, slipping all over his hip as she moved off over to the side.

Agmund looked at it—at her—for an instant too long, but then he jolted out of bed, to his feet. Grabbing for a rag from the wardrobe to wipe himself off with, and then yanking his clothes on, and turning toward the door.

"You're leaving?" Selby asked, her voice wavering, and Agmund hesitated and looked back, his eyes lingering on where she was still sprawled out naked on his bed.

"Yeah, I've got to go," he said, rubbing at the back of his neck. "But we still need to talk, all right? Tonight?"

Right. Something lurched in Selby's gut, but she nodded,

and so did he. And then he left, striding out the door, and Selby dug her palms into her eyes, tried to breathe, because what the hell had all that been, what did it mean, what the hell did he want to talk about, *why*—

She could feel Agmund going down toward Ketill's office again, but then stopping in the corridor, perhaps to talk to someone. Perhaps Greta, and the thought of that immediately dredged up those memories of Agmund's, swirling and shouting through Selby's head. Agmund had wanted Greta. Agmund had loved Greta. Agmund had trusted Greta. And between what Greta had done, and this entire situation—including the fact that Selby hadn't told him the truth about her reasons for being here—Agmund couldn't trust Selby. And probably never would.

Gods, it was hard to think about, and lying in Agmund's bed only made it worse, and finally Selby dragged herself up to the water closet, and then, after a good long scrubbing, out into the corridor. It was still only late morning, and blessedly quiet, though the stench in the air seemed to have become even more powerful, almost enough to make her retch.

Down the corridor the smell was worse, and worse still when Selby had gone down one flight of stairs, and then two. It almost seemed to emanate from one spot again, and rather than stopping at Morley's workroom, Selby kept going, kept following it, around toward the baths, behind the dining hall, down a narrow little hallway—

Until she stopped up short, because there—was the girl. The same girl Selby had met in the back stairwell, with the patched clothes and blonde hair, and smelling like death.

The girl was sitting up against the wall, with her head tilted oddly to one side, her eyes staring straight ahead, her legs sprawled out. And even before Selby had taken another breath, she knew.

She was dead.

23

Selby should have run away. Should have called for help. Should have done something, anything other than kneeling down beside this poor girl's body, and looking at her.

She'd touched dead bodies a few times before, and knew what to expect—but when she reached, brushed a finger against the girl's cold cheek, it still set her heart hammering, her teeth clenching tight together. Not just from the stillness, the coldness, but also, the memories.

They were of darkness. Working in darkness, casting spells. Or one spell, rather, over and over and over again. Complex, exhausting, head hanging, draw the magic, use the magic, beg pour *need* the magic—

Selby yanked her hand away, shaking it a little, because stronger than the memories, than that spell, had been the despair. The certainty of failure, the desperate need to do better, the constant endless working that never worked, never enough—

There was suddenly the sound of someone behind Selby, and yelling, and now more people, and more. Their rising voices finally cutting through the rushing in her ears, *what's*

Agmund's pedlar doing here and who's that girl and is she dead, did the pedlar actually kill her?

Selby stumbled backward, far too late, and shook her hands, her head. "I didn't," she said, helpless, toward the watching faces. "Do anything. I just—found her."

They didn't believe it, not with their shifting feet shifting eyes, and Selby would never have thought herself so happy to see Ketill, striding down the hallway, with no Agmund in sight. Agmund had gone out toward the forest, her distant thoughts shouted, and Ketill was here, brushing her aside, putting a hand to the dead girl's neck.

"Call for Holben," he ordered the onlookers. "And Alariaq. Now!"

Alariaq was Runar, Selby could register that much, and Holben was the staff healer. And at least when Holben finally came round the corner, with his drawn mouth and pale hair, he didn't look at Selby, didn't accuse her, and when Runar showed up, minutes later, he gave her arm a brief, reassuring squeeze on the way by.

"It's a combination of magic loss and physical exhaustion," Runar announced toward the onlookers, once he'd knelt in front of the girl, and put both hands to her head. "Not murder, you fools. Has anyone seen her around before?"

The onlookers seemed to collectively shrug, murmuring amongst themselves, and Selby made herself step forward, made herself speak. "I saw her in the servants' stairwell, once," she said. "I didn't know who she was. I tried to talk to her, and she ran away."

There were a few missing details in that, of course, but it was enough to bring Runar's eyes angling sharply toward her. Remembering, maybe, that Selby had told him and Thora about that girl, and about the smell, which was currently so powerful that Selby was very near to vomiting again.

"Regardless, the body should be taken to Holben's office for further examination," came Ketill's voice, calm and implacable. "Holben, I will accompany you."

With a twitch of Ketill's fingers, the air around them seemed to thicken and change. Making the dead girl's body float upwards from the floor, hovering in midair, staring blank-eyed up toward the ceiling.

"The rest of you, please resume your usual responsibilities," Ketill's cool voice said. "I am certain this is but a sad accident, and nothing more. We will keep you informed of any further developments."

With that, he turned and walked away, while the girl's dead body floated along behind him, her head now lolling sideways, her hair hanging down toward the floor. And suddenly Selby wanted to follow, desperately needed to see those memories again—but here was Runar, holding her still, his hand grasping too tight to her arm.

"This way," he said, steering her down the corridor, and Selby couldn't seem to resist. Not even when he guided her up the stairs, into an unfamiliar, unused-feeling room, with a long single table in the middle of it, and no other furnishings to be seen.

"Don't look now, sweetheart," Runar said, "but you're in shock. Close your eyes, take deep breaths, and kindly tell me how you found that girl, and why the *fuck* you thought it was a good idea to touch her!"

He seemed oddly, irrationally angry, and Selby couldn't think, or find words. "How—how did you know?" she stammered. "That I touched her?"

"Because any healer worth their shit will see your magic's residue," he snapped. "And Holben, while mediocre, will certainly see it, too—and believe me, he will have no qualms telling the entire Coven about it. And the next thing you know, you'll be out on your arse for *murder*!"

Selby's thoughts were racing, swerving, smashing into one another, and she frantically shook her head. "No, that's impossible, I only touched her," she said, too quickly. "She was already dead when I got there, I only even found her because she smelled like the rest of this place, but worse. I told you about her before, remember?"

The look in Runar's eyes said he did remember, and he stalked across the room, and back again. "Do you have an alibi?" he demanded. "Somebody who could account for you being elsewhere right before this happened?"

Selby twitched, gave another distracted shake of her head. "I was with Agmund, but then he left, and I was alone for probably half an hour, and I—"

"So no," Runar supplied, with a low groan. "Damn it, Selby. This is bad."

"Why?" Selby demanded at him. "Why is it bad? I haven't *done* anything!"

"No, you found a dead body, and you touched it, and you admitted to seeing the person before," Runar replied flatly. "And I know you're just living in your happy little Agmund-fucking bubble, and I'm not blaming you for that, do what you have to do—but if you paid even the *slightest* attention, you would know that almost everyone here is *still* saying awful things about you, and they're still *deeply* suspicious of you, and they're going to take this in the absolute *worst* way possible!"

Selby shook her head again, fought to think. "Why? What way?"

Runar rolled his eyes, gave a longsuffering sigh. "Think about it, Selby. Agmund's magic is dead, all the experts say so, there's talk of shelving him for good. And then *you* show up, a poor pedlar, with those *clothes*, and you use a highly questionable branch of magic, and you keep remains in your bedroom. And suddenly Agmund's nearly good as new again, and it makes no sense, nobody knows how you're doing it, there's nothing in the literature to support this. And *then*, there's a dead girl in the corridor, wearing the same kind of clothes as you, with you touching her, and her magic drained? It doesn't take much to make a few connections there, and I guarantee you, people are already doing it!"

Gods damn it, and Selby rubbed at her face, her eyes. "Well, it's not like they can actually prove anything, can they? And what could they do to me with no proof? Besides kick me out?"

"Haul you up before the Coven's thick-witted Magical Regulatory Committee," said Runar's clipped voice. "They don't need proof. And I've been there before, sweetheart, it's not fun, and if you make it out of there with your magic still even remotely usable, you'll be one of the lucky ones."

What? "They can't do that," Selby's strained voice protested. "Can they?"

"People can do a whole lot of fucked-up things with magic," Runar replied grimly. "I mean, just look at yours. You don't think if somebody can give someone else magic, somebody else could take it away?"

Selby gaped at him, because she'd never even once considered that as a possibility, and the thought of life without magic was suddenly so horrifying that her entire body had started quaking, her stomach cramping alarmingly in her gut, and she desperately needed something to vomit in, now—

But Runar's hand abruptly reached out to touch her back, fingers spread wide, and immediately her stomach seemed to simmer down, back to its usual uneasiness. "Sorry to alarm you, sweetheart," his voice said, lower now. "But it's better that you know. If I were you, I'd be getting ready to run. Sooner rather than later."

Those words should have been alarming too, but Runar's hand on her back seemed to be having some kind of calming influence, making Selby's thoughts come slower, with less panic and more creeping resignation. She could run. She should. But what about Agmund?

And maybe Runar was fucking with her head more than she thought, because suddenly Agmund was here. Throwing the door of the room open, and stalking inside like he owned it, while his eyes caught and held on Runar's hand on Selby's back, and fired with unmistakable anger.

"What's this?" he demanded, with a sharp wave of his hand between them. "And what's this I hear about you and some *dead* girl?"

Runar's hand snatched away from Selby's back, and he stared coolly toward Agmund across the table. "Selby was feeling ill, so I've calmed her nausea," he supplied, voice distant, professional. "And, she found a dead body in the downstairs corridor, and *touched* it."

Agmund's eyes darted to Selby's, but the anger in them had faded, shifting into something else. "Of course she did, she always touches everything," he snapped, though his head tilted, his eyes gone speculative, now. "Did you find anything out? Could you tell how she died?"

Runar audibly gasped, but Selby's eyes were held to Agmund's, on the strangely reassuring certainty of his being here. Of his not blaming her, not even seeming to consider that it could have been her fault.

"I'm not sure," Selby said, slowly. "Runar says she died of magic exhaustion, and that makes sense, because in the memories she was just casting a spell, over and over again. And the spell was so difficult, and she was so tired..."

Selby's voice caught, and beside her Runar loudly cleared his throat. "I was just pointing out to Selby the obvious ramifications of this *disaster*," he said, "and the fact that it will not end well for her. And that at this point, her wisest course of action is to leave. Immediately."

"Leave?" Agmund echoed. "Why the hell would she *leave*?"

"Because the rumours about her are already vicious," Runar shot back, "no thanks to *you*. And she obviously deals in magic loss, and is quite comfortable with death, and has miraculously and mysteriously brought your magic back. Put all that together and what do you get?"

Agmund's hands were gripping at the table, his eyes

flicking between Selby and Runar. "Ketill will protect her," he said tightly. "I'll protect her."

The words sent a funny swooping through Selby's gut, but Runar's lip curled, his eyes contemptuous. "Even Regin Agmund isn't above the laws about using magic," he coldly replied. "Especially when you're not out unleashing death and destruction on demand, like you're supposed to be. And also, the rules apply differently to people who don't belong, and especially to poor people. I'd give it a week until Selby's under questioning. If that."

Agmund's face had gone paler than usual, and he gave a jerky twitch of his head toward the door. "Are you done?" he demanded toward Runar. "Is there any reason you're still in my workroom?"

His workroom? But Runar didn't argue, and instead shot Agmund a look of purest loathing before turning on his heel and stalking out, leaving Selby and Agmund alone.

"Is this really *your* room?" Selby asked, into the sudden silence, and though it was the stupidest question, it was all she could seem to say. "It doesn't feel like you at all."

"Yeah, well, I never use it," Agmund replied, a little distractedly. "I hate being cooped up in this hole all fucking day. Ketill makes me keep it, for the optics, or some such shit."

Right. The mention of Ketill sent a chill up Selby's back, and she dragged in a breath. "Do you think Runar's right? Am I going to be blamed for that girl's death?"

Agmund let out a low growl, and then pinched the bridge of his nose. "Look, I wish you wouldn't hang around with him," he said. "He doesn't exactly have the best reputation himself, you know."

"What, because he's not pale enough, either?" Selby said back, her voice strained. "Or rich enough?"

But Agmund rolled his eyes, shook his head. "No," he replied, "because he gets off on cutting up dead bodies, and whatever he's been working on here for the past five years is some deep secret shit. *And*, he fucks around more than almost anybody else here, and given the chance would be up your skirt in seconds, I fucking *guarantee* you!"

He actually sounded angry about that, and Selby frowned right back. "Yes, well, I wouldn't, because Thora likes him," she countered, "and also, I have a ten-page contract that says I'm only allowed to fuck *you*!"

Agmund's jaw twitched, that telltale electricity sparking in his hand, and he gazed at her across the table, his eyes distant, unreadable. "Is that what you want from me, then? Permission to fuck other people?"

He was back to their unfinished conversation that morning, to what Selby wanted from him, and she rubbed hard at her eyes, felt her shoulders sagging. "No," she said wearily, "what I want is for you to answer my damned question. Am I going to be accused of this? Of murdering that poor girl for her magic?"

Agmund was briefly silent, and then he kicked the table between them, hard enough to set it skittering. "I don't know," he said. "I need to talk to Ketill."

He didn't *know*? "But Runar says—he says the Coven can take away my magic," Selby said, her voice suddenly high-pitched, panicky. "Can they really do that? Without any proof? I didn't do anything, I swear I didn't!"

Her eyes were pleading on Agmund, begging him to say of course she didn't, of course they couldn't take her magic away for no reason—but he was carefully looking away, his hands in fists, shoulders hunched.

"They *can*?!" Selby asked, her breath coming too fast, too frantic. "Oh gods, oh gods, Runar's right, I should go, I have to leave, before—"

She was already moving, lurching for the door, but suddenly Agmund was here, in front of her, his hands gripping her arms. "I said, I'll talk to Ketill, all right?" he said, voice oddly thick. "We'll do whatever we can to keep you out of it. And look, I know this is going to come off in the most selfish way possible, but I had Ketill walk me through your whole contract this morning, and you leaving right now could have extremely shitty consequences too, all right? Maybe even worse than being accused of murder. And how's it going to look if you *are* under suspicion for murder, and then you up and run? You don't think they'd just let you go?"

Selby's body wilted under his grip, her eyes blinking at his chest. "So that's it, then?" she asked, hollow. "I just—sit here, and wait for them to come for me?"

She could feel Agmund's breath, in and out, and his hands on her arms pulled her closer, until she was almost touching him. "No," he said. "No. We'll figure it out. We find out why this girl died, what killed her, and we'll clear you of all of it. All right?"

Selby didn't see how that could be possible, but there was something in his voice, in the grim angry determination in his eyes, the solid familiar warmth of his presence. And though she couldn't seem to speak, she closed the small distance between them, and slid her arms tight around his waist.

He didn't refuse, didn't even twitch, and Selby exhaled at the warm, unmistakable feel of his hand, widening flat against her back. "It'll be fine," he said, soft, and in that moment, Selby could almost believe it. "You'll see."

24

Selby spent the next hour alone in Agmund's bedroom, trying not to panic.

Agmund had needed to talk to Ketill, or so he'd said, and he'd indeed gone down to Ketill's office, where he'd been ever since. And the longer he stayed there, the louder the whispers in Selby's head became.

Maybe Agmund wasn't going to help her. Maybe he'd just been spouting whatever it took to make her stay. Maybe they'd look for someone else to bring back his magic, someone new who he could trust, who didn't have any questionable accusations against them. Someone who wasn't at risk of losing her own magic.

It still felt impossible, surreal, and Selby repeatedly tried to calm herself down, to convince herself that Runar had been overreacting. Or maybe lying, covering his own tracks, because he worked in death too, didn't he? *Deep secret shit*, Agmund had said, and Runar's morgue had been just a short walk away from where Selby had found that girl...

Or—maybe it was all just a sad mistake, like Ketill had said. And Ketill would fix it, Agmund would fix it, there was no way anyone would question anything that gave Regin Agmund his magic back...

But when Agmund finally showed up again, he looked unusually subdued, his mouth a thin line, his hands in his pockets. And rather than meeting Selby's eyes, he glanced at the shelf, and gave a purposeful nod toward it.

"Thought you were going to put out more of your stuff," he said. "Good luck, or whatever."

Good luck. The panic was rising again, Selby's breath coming fast and harsh, and after an instant's looking at her, Agmund jerked his head toward the door. "You got a coat?" he asked. "I got permission from Ketill to take you out for a bit."

Selby blinked, but the prospect of getting outside, away from this odious place, was suddenly almost mouthwateringly appealing. So she nodded, and yanked on her cloak, and followed Agmund down the stairs, and out the front door.

They got a few odd looks along the way, but no one commented, and once they were outside, Selby sucked in a long, dragging breath of the crisp clean air. Gods, it smelled good, and when Agmund nudged her in the direction of the forest, she went willingly, drinking in the sight of sky and trees and bright afternoon sun.

Agmund clearly had a destination in mind, and as they approached it, Selby realized that she'd often felt him here, around these coordinates. And it turned out to be an astonishing, beautiful little grove, enclosed by a close-set ring of soaring oaks and pines. There was a soft green carpet of moss underfoot, a smattering of colourful wildflowers throughout, and a few small grey boulders under the trees, just the right height for sitting.

"Like it?" Agmund asked. "Good, right?"

Selby nodded, slowly spinning to drink in the sight of it. "It's beautiful. The best thing I've seen in *months*."

Agmund's mouth twitched up, and he waved toward a

nearby pair of boulders. "Figured it'd be nice for you to go somewhere that doesn't make you want to hurl for once."

Selby couldn't help a swift, genuine grin at him, her hand reaching to brush against his arm. "Thank you."

But Agmund only looked away, rubbing at the back of his neck, and Selby's thoughts sank again, twisting into something dark and afraid. He'd talked to Ketill, and now he was being overly kind, and none of this could be good...

"So what did Ketill say?" she asked, as she sank onto the closest rock, felt the reassuring twinge of its ancient strength. "Does he think I'm in trouble over this?"

Agmund still wasn't looking at her, and he sat on the rock opposite, kicking at the moss beneath it with his boot. "He doesn't know," he said slowly. "Holben has to file his report with the Coven today, and it sounds like that's going to need to have your name on it. And since the cause of death was magic exhaustion, and they don't have any other suspects, there's bound to be some kind of investigation—and you're bound to be brought into it."

Fuck. Selby's breath collapsed from her lungs, and she gripped her fingers together. "In what way?"

Agmund sighed. "Ketill said they'll want to do an inquiry. They'll do some research into your magic, ask you some questions, analyze you to see if you're telling the truth."

The fear jolted even higher, and Selby fought to breathe, to feel that solid rock beneath her. "And what if they find that I can do magic that isn't sanctioned?" she asked, quiet. "Magic that's against their rules?"

Agmund sighed again, frowning down at his boots. "I don't know," he said. "Ketill's already trying to lay some groundwork, talk to his contacts. He's got a lot of reach, you know, and he says he should have been able to hush all this up, but—"

He abruptly stopped, his eyes darting up and then away again, and Selby wasn't breathing now, couldn't. "But *what*?"

There was a brief spark in Agmund's hand, and he closed his fist, clenching tight. "But apparently there've been a lot of nasty rumours flying around about you, and how you're bringing my magic back. Even beyond this place, in Ketill's circles, in the Coven, in the government. For *months*. People have been saying you're"—he took a breath, let it out—"a necromancer. Killing people, to bring my magic back."

What?! So Runar had been right after all, oh gods, oh *gods*. "But *why*?" Selby asked helplessly, her hands coming shaky to her face. "How? I mean, I know nobody here really *likes* me, but who would *say* that?"

"Damned if I know," Agmund replied, with a jerky shrug of his shoulder, a furtive glance at Selby's eyes. "And look, I know I told Greta about you seeing my memories that time, and she didn't keep it quiet. But before you blame her for this, I already tore into her about it, and she swears up and down she hasn't said a word."

Selby hadn't been about to blame Greta—she was not making that mistake again—and she shook her head, tried to think. "But Ketill *knew* about my magic," she said. "When he recruited me. He said nothing I can do is actually illegal, and as long as I didn't talk about it, it shouldn't be an issue!"

"I know," Agmund said, frowning back down at his boots. "And believe me, Ketill's furious. I haven't seen him rage like that in a long time. He said he never thought it would come out, and why would it, right? All you're supposed to be doing is fucking me."

He gave a short laugh, hard and strangely bitter, winding the fear up tighter in Selby's gut. "I shouldn't have touched her," she whispered. "She just—smelled so much like the smell, like what's making me sick, I thought maybe I could find out—"

The words choked in her throat, and she blinked hard, down at Agmund's boots. At where one of those boots was now reaching over, and nudging against her own.

"So this dead girl had that smell too?" Agmund asked, sharper. "And that's why you touched her?"

Selby nodded miserably, but across from her Agmund sat up straighter. "Then tell me about it," he said. "About this girl, your magic, the smell. *Everything.*"

25

For the rest of the afternoon, Selby talked, and Regin Agmund listened.

She spoke unsteadily at first, the words coming out disjointed and uncertain—but the longer Agmund listened, the easier it seemed to become. He asked questions in the right places, frowned in the right places, and for once, Selby almost appreciated that he was such a suspicious and cranky bastard, with all his enraged force seemingly on her side for once.

"Ketill honestly told you that *you* were making the smell?" he demanded, once Selby had shared that particular point. "Why the hell didn't you tell me? And *why*, for fuck's sakes, would you make a smell that made you sick?"

"Because I need to punish myself?" Selby replied, giving a wan half-smile toward him. "Because I feel guilty about what I'm doing?"

Agmund snorted, and rolled his eyes. "Typical Ketill bullshit," he said flatly. "You *love* what you're doing."

He seemed very certain of that fact, suddenly, his eyes hard and steady on hers, as if daring her to deny it—but Selby wasn't about to try, was already being betrayed by the heat pooling in her cheeks. "Well," she said, and searched carefully for the next words. "Do you think, then—is there any chance Ketill might have anything to do with all this?"

Agmund's head tilted, his forehead furrowed. "What do you mean?"

"Well," Selby replied, slow, "on top of that, isn't it a bit suspicious that he told me there'd be no problems, and brought me here anyway? When he *knew* full well that I could still be accused of something like this?"

Agmund sighed, and his mouth had gone tight, his eyes grim. "Look, I hate to say this," he began, "'cause I've worked with Ketill for half my life—but even if he knew *for sure* you'd get called on this, he'd probably still have brought you here. That awful contract of yours doesn't even hint at what your magic really does, right? Just tells you to keep quiet? And I guarantee you, that was on purpose. So if it ever came out, Ketill could say he knew nothing."

What? The nausea roiled in Selby's gut again, after being so blessedly absent these past few hours, and she stared at Agmund, at the certainty glinting in his blue eyes. "You mean that?" she demanded. "Ketill would sacrifice me—my magic, my body, my *life*—just so *you* could get your magic back for a while?"

Agmund looked distinctly uncomfortable, but he gave a jerky shrug. "I'm the Coven's best mage, right? They need me too much. The country needs me."

Of course, the great Regin fucking Agmund was so utterly *essential*, worth so much more than a lowly replaceable pedlar, and the fury screeched through Selby's head, drowning out everything else. "That is so unbelievably vile," she snapped, as she leapt to her feet, and paced across the clearing. "The government and the Coven are supposed to look after their people, not treat them like pawns in some horrible game! If I'm disposable once I've served my purpose, then what about you? What happens when your magic goes away for good? Does Ketill just throw *you* away, too?!"

Agmund was still sitting on the rock, frowning up at her, and suddenly it was crucial that he see this, that he understand. "It *will* happen," Selby continued, harder now. "Maybe not now, but someday, I guarantee you. Because they already see you as a commodity, like their pet attack dog that they can just set onto whatever target they please! It doesn't matter what *you* want, only what you can do for *them*!"

Agmund's arms crossed over his chest, his lip curling. "I'm not forced to do anything," he replied, voice flat. "I haven't done any actual jobs in months now, remember? And if you think I'm tied here with a contract like yours, well you're wrong, because I'm not. I'm here because I damn well *want* to be."

What? Selby's brows snapped up, and she gave an incredulous shake of her head. "No, actually, you don't," she shot back. "In case you haven't noticed, you hate being in that manor just as much as I do. It's *never* been home to you, and the only things you do in there are eating and fucking and sleeping, and dealing with Ketill. And if you could do all that out in this forest, too, you probably would!"

The anger had risen in Agmund's eyes as she spoke—but at the last it slipped, betraying him. And Selby gave a grim smile, stepping a little closer, making him look up at her. "And you don't even *like* the work the Coven's had you doing all these years. You never have. It's made you feel guilty, and miserable, and *trapped*."

Agmund frowned away from her, not meeting her eyes, but Selby was still committed to this, to the truth. "And you shouldn't have to do it," she added, quieter. "They have plenty of coin and resources, don't they? There's no reason they can't use other means to work out this country's problems. But instead they've been using you—Ketill's been using you—to make their jobs easier. They don't give a damn about what *you* want."

Agmund kept glowering away from her, his shoulders square and tense. "Oh, fuck off with this," he said. "Yeah, maybe I don't like living in the manor, but who gives a damn, I don't like being inside anywhere all the time. And what I *do* like is using my magic, being useful with it, doing shit that's important, that needs getting done! And Ketill's the best, the people here are the best, so of *course* I want to be here, being the best!"

Good gods, Selby was so done with this, and she groaned aloud, rolled her eyes at the blue sky overhead. "The people here aren't the best, they're well-funded rich kids who've had their parents pay their way! And if *you* really want to be the best, and do important work, there are a hundred other ways to do that without being cooped up here, and being let out just long enough to go kill some people!"

"Bullshit," Agmund said, his eyes snapping contemptuous to hers. "Give me *one* fucking example of something else I could do. And don't you *dare* say teaching or writing books and shit, I'd go jump in that river first!"

Selby threw her arms up, and gave another exasperated groan. "Oh my gods, Regin," she said, "you're tall and gorgeous and rich and white and male, you're the most famous mage in the entire *country*, your options are *endless*! If you really wanted to keep taking jobs, you could at least get out from under Ketill's thumb, and pick assignments that don't make you miserable. Or"—she stepped closer to the rock, glared down at his eyes—"you could get away from that altogether, you could manage forests or clear land or fertilize fields. You could work with scientists on ways to use lightning, to maybe channel it, do something useful with it, you could study the ways it affects earth and water and people, you could even create art with it, because it's *beautiful*. Or, you could take the easy route and travel around and put on shows, sign autographs, bask in the adoration, and rake in obscene amounts of coin!"

Agmund was staring up at her, not speaking, and something in his eyes made Selby's voice drop. "Or with all the coin you have, you could just—take a break. Spend some time travelling, off in the woods, and think about it."

Agmund's throat convulsed, and his eyes finally flicked away from Selby's, looking at something beyond her. "Look, if I walk away from this, do any of that," he said slowly, "I'm a failure."

A failure. Selby couldn't speak, suddenly, could only shake her head at him. "You can't honestly think—" she began, tried again. "No. You'll never be a failure, Regin. Ever. Even if you never cast a spell again."

Agmund's eyes darted back to hers, and it occurred to her, too late, that maybe this was saying too much, admitting far more than he wanted to know. And he was rubbing at the back of his neck, now, confirming that, and Selby took a swift step backwards, away.

"Well, what about you, then?" Agmund said, and the sudden sharpness in his words made her take another step back. "I don't see you walking away from your responsibilities to live out some bullshit fantasy."

Selby should have snapped back at him, but instead she let out a bitter, disbelieving laugh. "Um," she said, "isn't that exactly what I did, coming here? And exactly what I'd really rather do at this point, too? Leave this horrible place behind, leave *your* sorry arse behind, and run for it?"

Agmund grimaced, and his hand rubbed again at his neck. "Wench," he said, but his voice was quiet, his breath coming out slow. "I wouldn't even miss you."

Selby laughed again, and this time it was almost genuine. "Who's lying now?" she said coolly. "You'd miss me real quick, once your magic stopped working."

"No, I'd miss my magic," Agmund countered. "Not you."

But he *was* lying, even if it was just a little, because something in his eyes betrayed it. And when Selby took a step back toward him, those eyes betrayed it even more, flicking down to her chest under her dress, and back up again.

"You keep telling yourself that," Selby said, softer now, and she was close enough to touch, to brush a single finger under his chin. "Asshole."

"Witch," he replied, but his voice and eyes were mild, and he leaned back on the rock, on his hands. Almost as if in silent invitation, and when Selby glanced down at his trousers, and that telltale bulge in front, she was sure of it, enough to close that last space between them.

"Hypocrite," she murmured, as her audacious hands went down to untie his trousers, to pull out the hard swollen length of him. Looking so oddly incongruous against his otherwise fully clothed body, against the rock and the clearing and the trees, but looking right, too, beautiful. Like he belonged, like of course Regin Agmund should fuck in the forest, all straw-haired and blue-eyed and one with the open air.

"Not like you're one to talk," he said, looking up at her under those blond eyelashes, and for an instant Selby was so distracted that she couldn't follow what he meant. And her body seemed to be acting on its own, putting one knee to the rock on one side of him, and then the other.

"I'm only doing my duty," she said, as haughtily as she could, even as she scooted forward, closer, and pulled up her skirts, bunched them up to give some padding under her knees. "Fulfilling the terms of my contract, and all that."

The corner of Agmund's mouth quirked, and he leaned back a little more, watched with lazy eyes as she positioned herself over him. "Sure you are," he said, soft. "'Cause as ridiculous as your contract is, it sure as hell doesn't say anything about fucking me out in the open like this, where anybody could see you. Like the greedy, shameless little cocktease you are."

What? Selby was taking that as an insult, and glowered down at him even as she reached under her skirts, took his warm willing cock in hand, guided it toward her own hungry wet heat.

"You are such a smug self-absorbed *disaster*," she breathed, and then gasped aloud at the feel of him there, at that hard smooth head slowly delving its way inside. "Such a spoiled arrogant entitled *troll*, without that fucking contract I wouldn't look at you *twice*."

His cock, now halfway up inside her, had actually shuddered with the words, like he actually *liked* them—and the look on his face was betraying it too, all half-lidded indolent godsdamned *amusement*. "Such an ungrateful wench," he said, his voice not quite steady as he raised his hips a little, sank himself deeper. "You should be thanking me."

Selby scoffed a laugh, though perhaps it came out more as a groan as she settled herself all the way down on him, skin to skin. "For what?" she said, breathless, blinking against those sudden surging images of blazing lightning, striking down in this very forest. "Being a total dick?"

Agmund laughed too, even as his hips circled up against hers, grinding hard, just where she craved it. "No, for *giving* you such good dick," he said, husky. "For making this tight little cunt of yours happier than it's ever been in your entire fucking *life*."

Oh *gods*, and when Selby gasped aloud, grinding back down against him, he laughed again, softer this time. "You can't lie to me," he murmured. "I *know*."

He knew. The hunger and the heat were swirling, now, pooling hard between her legs, all around his hardness deep inside. So good, damn him, and Selby gave a vehement shake of her head, even as she ground down again, took him deeper, oh *gods*.

"Any dick would be better than yours, asshole," she choked out, fighting to glare at him through her fluttering eyelashes. "I'd still rather have the drunken town mummer's."

"You fucking would *not*," Agmund shot back, through gritted teeth, and he put his hands to her hips, moved her faster. "No fucking way will you be satisfied with his limp wrinkly prick twice a week, after you've been having mine twice every day."

Selby was riding him hard now, desperate and brutal, and maybe he was right, oh gods, because it was so good, shockingly good, with the clear air in her lungs and Regin Agmund all in her eyes and pounding so deep inside her. And the images in his head had flipped, briefly, from forest-lightning-crash to *why-the-fuck-aren't-those-tits-out*, and Selby's trembly hands were already there, unbuttoning her dress to the waist. Pulling out both breasts over the low neck of her shift, bunching them up high and round, nipples puckered and hard in the cool air—

Agmund's eyes glinted on the sight, his hips bucking up harder, more erratic. And he even pulled himself up closer, his lips parting as he stared, his breath coming out harsh enough that Selby could feel it on her bouncing breasts, now almost dangerously close to his face...

"Such a damned hypocrite," Selby breathed, and without thinking, without warning, she gripped a hand at the back of his head, and drew him even closer. And he didn't blink, didn't make the slightest effort to pull away—not even when Selby cupped one of her breasts, and thrust its hard hungry nipple between his warm parted lips.

"Suck on it, asshole," she gasped, and when he actually obliged, she gasped again, grinding down harder, faster. Shivering beneath that tongue, that suction, that wet warm heat on her skin, oh gods, oh *fuck*—

And then she pulled it away, fed him her other breast, revelled at the impossible sight of Regin Agmund willingly taking her nipple into his mouth, and suckling it. His eyes closed, his hands gripping so tight on her hips it was almost painful, his huge hard cock slamming up again and again and again—

"Come for me, witch," he ordered, between sucks, those blue eyes angling up brief toward hers. "You know you want to, want to prove to me just how good my dick is, how it fucking *owns* you—"

Oh gods, oh, he was not saying this, was not sucking her breast even deeper into his mouth—but he *was*, and the tension the tightness the cursed furious glory was shuddering out all through her, all around him. Proving it to him, showing him, and the triumph flared in his eyes, his teeth lightly scraping her nipple as he pulled off.

"That's right, my filthy little wench," he said, as he gripped her hips even tighter, drove up again and again and again. "Ride me harder, show me, touch yourself, *show me*—"

Selby was doing all of it, riding him harder, crying out her pleasure, caressing her too-sensitive breasts while he watched. While he slammed in harder and harder, while his eyes rolled back and he let out a strangled yelping groan, a bright, succulent surge of magic—

There was a sudden sharp streak of light, the deafening boom of thunder, as a massive white bolt came down behind him, meeting the highest tip of the nearest tallest tree. And Selby gaped at it, felt that pulsing-out cock plunge up even deeper inside her, and oh gods it was so good, so impossible, and her own body convulsed again in reply, drinking him in, drinking him up, please, please, *please*.

When it finally finished Selby couldn't meet Agmund's eyes, couldn't seem to speak. He didn't speak either, but that familiar little slap to her hips was clear enough, and she pulled her shaky body off him, stood on limp rubbery legs as she put her dress back together, tucked everything safely away again.

Agmund was doing the same, the silence between them stretching taut, now, and Selby recalled, belatedly, that they'd come out here to talk, not to fuck. And she was still in danger, her magic was in danger, and she'd ignored all that so she could ride Agmund out in the open, just like a filthy little wench, where anyone could see her—

But no one would have, she thought now, because like

always, Agmund had been using his sound-suppressing spell, and she'd have felt someone approaching, and probably so would he. And despite everything he'd said, he'd wanted it too, he'd essentially been the one to suggest it, him and his gods-damned *my dick fucking owns you*, and *gods* she was so fucked with this—

"You actually upset, then?" came Agmund's voice, rough enough that Selby twitched, blinked up to where he was watching her, his hand rubbing the back of his neck. "Look, I'm sorry, but if you don't want me to mouth off like that at you, you could just fucking *say* so."

What? Selby blinked at him again, tried to reorient her brain. "No, you asshole," she said back, a little distractedly, pulling her hair out of her face. "Of all the infuriating things you've come out with this past hour, anything you just said is at the very bottom of the list."

Agmund half-smiled, looking almost relieved, and then glanced away. "You really don't care?" he asked, his voice carefully casual. "You're sure?"

Selby pulled in a breath, made herself speak truth. "No. It's kind of hot, don't you think?"

Agmund didn't reply to that, still intently looking away through the forest. And when he waved Selby back in the direction of the manor, she went, walking beside him through the trees in the dimming evening light.

"Then what's bothering you?" he said finally. "All the other bullshit?"

Selby nodded, and beside her he sighed, kicked an errant stone out of his path. "Look," he began, "I asked Ketill for the day off tomorrow, and I was thinking—"

But then he halted, mid-step, his eyes fixing on something—nothing—in front of them, and an instant later, Selby felt it too. Someone was there, in the forest, and walking out toward them.

"Damn it," he said, quiet. "Can you maybe—"

He jerked a wave off to the west, into the thicker trees, and Selby gaped at him, blank and disbelieving. Was he actually suggesting she go *hide* in there? From what?

But that question was decisively answered by the sights and sounds of a group of perhaps six or seven air-mages, walking toward them. Agmund's friends, including Njall and Tomik, and a perfectly coiffed blonde head. Greta.

"*No*," Selby replied, sharp, but just as quiet. "If any of them are even adequate air-mages, they'll know I'm here anyway."

The mulish look on Agmund's face suggested that perhaps they weren't adequate air-mages, but it was already too late, because Njall had caught sight of them, raising a hand. "Hey, Regin!" he called. "Thought we heard you casting out here."

Heard him cast—oh. Right. And Agmund was such a terrible liar, rubbing at where that telltale red was creeping up his neck, and he quickly stepped forward, close in front of Selby, as if he could block her from their view.

"Yeah, just getting in a bit of practice," Agmund replied, his voice light. "What's going on?"

The group had fully reached them now, and Selby could tell the instant when they caught sight of her. Their steps faltering, their eyes giving uneasy glances toward each other, and Selby was already wishing she had run after all, had just vanished into those trees.

"We were all going to meet up for supper, remember?" Njall said, with a barely perceptible flick of his eyes toward Selby. "Catch up on things."

Oh. And suddenly the reason they were here was abundantly clear, because the whole manor had to be abuzz with gossip about the dead girl, and Regin Agmund's pedlar being caught red-handed at the scene. And clearly they were here to either get the latest news, or else to rescue Agmund from Selby's evil clutches, or both.

And Agmund clearly knew that too, and Selby didn't miss the sudden clench of his jaw, the harsh exhale of his breath.

But then he jerked a nod, even as his eyes betrayed a telltale swift glance over his shoulder. And his hand surreptitiously came behind him, brushing brief against Selby's wrist, saying, *Sorry. Meet me back in my room, after supper?*

Selby couldn't seem to acknowledge it, couldn't even look at him, because it meant he was choosing them, over her, *now*, when she suddenly, desperately needed him. So she looked intently away, wishing herself invisible, fighting and failing to ignore the unmistakable feel of Agmund's thick wetness, seeping down her thigh under her dress.

"Yeah, I'm getting pretty hungry," Agmund said aloud, as he took an abrupt step forward, away from Selby. "What's on for supper, do you know?"

Njall gave some kind of reply, but Selby didn't hear it, because they were leaving, of course they were leaving. Some of them angling dark, uneasy glances over their shoulders toward her as they went, but Agmund didn't give a single look back, not one.

The tightness in Selby's throat had become almost painful, and she rushed unseeing for the nearest tree, putting both hands to its reassuring solid bulk. Breathing, and breathing again, fighting to slow her thundering heartbeat. Agmund didn't trust her, he never would, and clearly his offer to help her—even his making love to her, earlier—was just him doing his duty by her, and that was all. And Selby *knew* that, so why did it hurt so much, why did it matter—

But it did matter. And Selby was sure of that, somehow, and the strange, jolting certainty had her spinning around, striding back for that little grove. Walking past the boulders this time, and straight toward that tree, the one Agmund had struck with lightning as he'd emptied himself out inside her.

And this tree—Selby closed her eyes, took a gasping shuddery breath—this tree had Agmund all over it. Agmund's magic, his smell, even the sheer strength of his hunger, and Selby clung to that, to the bare undeniable fact of that. Regin

Agmund had wanted her, in that moment. He'd wanted her so much that he'd struck a tree full of the truth of it.

Selby tried not to think as she snapped a twig off the tree, put it in her pocket. Tried to keep her head entirely blank as she stepped further into the forest, reaching out her hands, brushing the tree trunks as she passed.

And then, suddenly, there was another one, tasting of Agmund's lightning, his magic. With this one, he'd been in a calculating mood, perhaps trying to hit this smaller tree amidst a number of larger others, and Selby let her fingers linger, spread wide, before moving again.

Soon there was another, and another. And Selby circled the clearing again and again, making wider circles each time, taking care to touch each and every trunk she passed.

Some of the trees tasted speculative. Some jovial, some angry. But nearly all of them had that same focused calculation, that serious intense concentration. Working hard, hitting targets, doing his job.

But no other tree tasted of Regin Agmund's hunger. Not a single one. And finally Selby went back to that lone tree, and sat up against it, still not thinking, until the sky faded, and faded, and finally went black.

26

Selby must have dozed, out there alone in the forest, because the next thing she heard was the angry sound of stomping, crunching boots.

She blinked awake, and found herself staring into the dazzling light of a lantern, hovering near her face. A lantern that was being held by—Selby sighed, tried to ignore the skip in her heartbeat—Regin Agmund.

He was alone, thankfully, and squinting up at his flickery face in the lamplight, it occurred to Selby that he was angry. Downright furious, in fact. About what now, gods only knew, and Selby climbed unsteadily to her feet, put her hands to her hips.

"What?" she said. "What'd I do now?"

Agmund's mouth opened and closed uselessly, a sight that might have been comical if he didn't look about to electrocute someone, probably her. "Where," he ground out, "the *fuck* have you been?"

The unfairness of this was already rankling, and Selby rubbed at her still-scratchy eyes. "Um, right here? Why?"

"You've just been sitting out here for three fucking *hours*?"

he shouted, waving the lantern erratically. "Why the fuck didn't you come inside?!"

Selby stepped back from him, put a hand to the solid trunk of that tree behind her. "Because I've been trapped in that hellhole for more than two months now?" she said slowly, clearly. "And it makes me feel sick? And you were obviously doing more important things with your friends? Why would I go back in there if I didn't have to?"

"Because you *did* have to!" Agmund bellowed. "I told you to meet me in my room, remember? You're not allowed to be out here without permission! Do you know how much *shit* Ketill and the Coven would have given me if they found out?"

"Well, if it was that important, you could have *told* me!" Selby shot back. "Total honesty, remember? Or does that only matter until your friends show up?"

The words landed in silence, and Agmund's lantern jerked in midair. "I would have stayed," he snarled, "but I wanted to go shut down the rumours myself, before they got out of hand! Do you think we need even more stupid gossip flying around about this right now?"

It skittered something in Selby's stomach—he'd gone with his friends to try to help? But no, no, he'd still wanted to hide her from them, he still didn't want to be seen with her in public, and that wild fury was still flashing in his eyes. "And also," he growled, "coming back in should have just been common fucking *sense*. You were just doing this to punish me!"

Dear gods, he was infuriating, and Selby pressed her hands to her eyes. "I had no intention of punishing you," she snapped. "For anything."

"Bullshit," Agmund snarled. "You were mad at me for going in, so you thought you'd play this shitty little game as revenge!"

"What shitty game?!" Selby demanded. "Getting fresh air?"

"No, making me think you *left*!" Agmund shouted, and there was suddenly a blinding, crackling white, appearing and disappearing in his free hand. "That you just up and fucking *ran!*"

That you ran. And suddenly this was making a whole lot more sense, and Selby rubbed at her eyes again, harder this time. "Fine, fine," she said, through her teeth. "I wasn't trying to punish you, or make you think I took off, I really wasn't. It's just really lovely out here, and I've had an awful day, and I just—I wanted some space from you, all right?"

She squeezed her eyes shut, reached again for the tree behind her. Waiting, because Agmund had gone silent, the only sound the slow sharpness of his breath.

"Why," he said finally, stubbornly, and Selby sighed, blinked her eyes back open, searched for an answer. And then decided to finally just tell him, because she was already so fucked with this already, and why the hell did it matter now?

"Well, it's still not exactly pleasant for me to face the truth that you still can't even *speak* to me in front of your friends," she said. "I mean, I know they don't like me, I know I was paid to be here, I know you think you can't trust me. But it still doesn't give you permission to keep treating me like yesterday's rubbish!"

Agmund visibly twitched, his eyes narrow and shadowed on hers, and he abruptly set down the lantern, came a step closer. "Gods," he muttered, "if this is still about that shit I said to you earlier, I already apologized, all right? Look, I'm sorry. I won't do it again."

The words came out bitter, petulant, and Selby couldn't help an exasperated groan. "This has nothing to do with that, you asshole," she snapped. "I already told you, I *liked* that. This has everything to do with you being a raging fucking *hypocrite*. Saying how much you care about my *total honesty*, and then turning around and pretending like you don't even *know* me, like I mean *nothing* to you!"

Agmund's eyes in the flickering light were cold, distant,

enraged. "You *don't* mean anything to me beyond my magic," he said, voice thin. "I thought I've made that very fucking clear!"

Gods, he was the absolute *worst*, and how did Selby keep forgetting this, how did it keep hurting so much? "Right, really fucking clear, asshole," she managed. "Making love to me, going down on me, practically begging me to suck you off. Wanting me all over you every time we're in the same damned room!"

"Yeah, because I like fucking, and fucking you gives me my magic back!" Agmund bellowed, straight into her face. "And that's *all*!"

Selby was struggling to breathe now, to find truth in this, and she swallowed hard, pulled herself up straighter. "You're lying," she said, a little desperate. "You've never done it with anybody else like you do with me. You've lived here for *years*, but you've *never* brought anybody else out here like you did with me today, and shot off lightning when you came!"

Agmund's hand yanked angrily through his hair, and above him the air was crackling again, a flare of blinding white in Selby's eyes. "No, I haven't!" he shouted back. "These aren't the kinds of girls you can just take out and fuck on a rock in public!"

It was like Selby's thoughts had turned to ice, her entire body frozen and brittle, and she lifted her chin higher, blinked through the lingering white still behind her eyes. "Oh?" she said. "And who is that kind of girl? A greedy, filthy wench?"

Agmund let out a low snarl, like she'd gone and insulted *him*, somehow, and gods, Selby was finished with him. Why did she keep putting up with him, why did she keep forgetting, why had he been so *kind* these past weeks...

So she turned, abruptly, and walked away. Away from his eyes, his voice, his face, and instead, strode deeper into the trees. Thinking, with a stilted distant clarity, that yes, she really should have been using her time out here to run, to get a head start on her escape. Agmund clearly wouldn't have wanted to admit to anyone that he'd lost her, and she could have had a good three hours behind her. But with no coin or supplies or food, and if she was really going to do this...

She halted in place, and then whirled around to the sight of Agmund coming up behind her, with the lantern in hand. He'd stopped too, a short distance away, watching her with wary, angry eyes, and Selby squared her shoulders, touched for the nearest tree, felt its quiet solid strength.

"You asked earlier if I wanted payment," she said, her voice a thin rasp. "I've changed my mind. I presume you have funds in the capital's principal bank? I would be very grateful if you could instruct them to give me a small sum, to be picked up within two weeks."

She didn't wait for his answer, just turned again, and kept walking. Travelling alone at night would be risky, dangerous, but at least she had her magic, and her cloak. It would be enough to keep her warm, and avoid any bandits, but then, suddenly, there was the awful, horrible thought of all her things, sitting back there in Agmund's room, possibly being thrown out, forgotten, once she was gone.

"And," she said, turning around again, to where Agmund was *still* behind her, "Instead of disposing of my things, if you could send them back to my family, I would be deeply grateful to you. My mother won't be easy to find, but you could send them to my uncle, Artimus Balen, in Kaynr, he'll see that she gets them."

She turned again, kept walking, and walking, not thinking—but now Agmund was close, too close. Right behind her, his hand gripping at her arm, and—Selby twitched—he tasted suddenly of desperation, of a cold curdling miserable fear.

"Selby," Agmund said, and his voice was different, now, rougher. "Don't do this."

Selby just kept walking, her arm shaking a little to rid itself of that awful lingering misery—but there it was again, even worse this time, and in a swift, jolting motion Agmund swung around in front of her, blocking her path.

"Please," he breathed. "Don't."

Selby stopped walking, closed her eyes against the prickling wetness behind them. "Why shouldn't I," she said, her voice wavering, betraying her. "Your Coven is going to accuse me of murder, and try to take away my magic, and you freely admit that I don't mean anything to you, and your so-called honesty doesn't mean anything either. So why the *hell* should I trust you, why should I risk myself for you, why should I believe a single word that comes out of your lying fucking *mouth*!"

Agmund's body was very still, and his eyes blinked, once. And Selby realized, too late, that the cursed wetness was escaping from her own eyes, and she angrily wiped it away, went to step around him. But he was here *again*, why was Regin Agmund always fucking *everywhere*, and now both his hands were on Selby's shoulders, jolting her all through with sheer sweeping terrified desperation.

"I'm sorry," he said, his voice thick. "I'm sorry. I shouldn't have said that, all right?"

Selby's shoulder gave a jerky shrug under his hand, her eyes looking past him, into the murky darkness. "Yes, you should have," she replied, hollow, "because at least now I know the actual truth, and can make an informed decision about my future with you. Or lack thereof."

There was an instant's heavy silence, and Selby shook Agmund's hands off her, and kept walking. Not thinking, not stopping, just had to get away as fast as possible, before the pain caught up, before it broke her under its weight.

"Wait," said Agmund's voice, breathless, too close, and he was here again, once more blocking Selby's path, the lantern left behind. "Look, I—" he began, and his face looked strangely etched in the shadows, his eyes shutting tight. "I know the truth about you is more than I've been letting on. I *know*. All right?"

Selby set her jaw, frowned at his shadowy face. "Then why. Why don't I *exist*."

His shoulders rose and fell, and his eyes opened again, glittering oddly in the flickering light. "Because you're going to *leave!*" he choked out. "Whether it's now, or in a month, you're going to walk out of here forever, and take my magic and my *life* with you. *You* get to go on, and be happy, and forget all about me, and I—"

He didn't finish, and gods curse her, but Selby's hand reached out to touch him, pressing flat against his heaving chest. And behind it, in the surging miserable tangle of his thoughts, his voice was there, alive, shouting with a clarity that was almost painful.

I can't afford to care about you, it said. *I can't afford to lose the only people I have left for you. I can't afford to trust you, or let you into my life even more than I already have. I can't. You'll ruin me.*

You'll ruin me.

Oh. Selby blinked at him and swallowed hard, her thoughts wildly spinning. She would ruin him. Not just because she held the inexplicable key to his magic, but also because—

Because he *did* care. He *wanted* to trust her. He *had* let her into his life. And Regin Agmund couldn't afford to do that again, not after Greta, not after his father, not after almost every person he'd ever met. Not when he knew exactly how it would end.

"But Regin," Selby heard herself say, her voice hoarse. "I wouldn't do that. To you."

Agmund gave a brittle laugh, a vehement shake of his head. "Sure you wouldn't," he said. "Says the girl who *just* tried to *leave* me! And Ketill offered you that fucking extension, and you said *no!* And if you would just *sign* the fucking thing, if you would just agree to *stay*—"

If she would just agree to stay. He broke off there, but the words were still strong enough, stunning enough, to make

Selby recoil, gaping at his glittering eyes. Feeling it in his hands, in the sudden twisting damned *hopefulness*.

"Stay," she repeated, slowly, deliberately. "Here? With pay? On another contract?"

Agmund nodded, his jaw tight, and the earth under Selby seemed to shift, her eyes trapped on his. "For how long?" she heard herself say. "Another six months?"

Agmund's throat convulsed, and the hopefulness twisted higher, sharper, deeper under Selby's skin. And one of his hands slipped up, brushing against her cheek, and the world tipped again, swooped deep in Selby's chest.

"Longer, if you want," he said, quiet, like he meant it. "For as long as you possibly can."

27

Selby felt rooted in place, like she couldn't speak or move or think. Like she'd become part of the earth itself, with Regin Agmund for its sun.

Stay, he'd said. *As long as you possibly can.* And he was somehow infecting her, because suddenly the temptation was almost breathtakingly powerful. Stay. Sleep with him every night, wake up with him every morning, ride him in the dark in the light in the open air, suck him off straddle his mouth oh *gods*—

"Regin," Selby said, around a shaky, unreliable breath, "you just told me you didn't care about me, remember? And now—now you're asking me to—to be your permanent paid *mistress*, or something? For as long as I want? Don't you hear what you're saying? What if I wanted *forever*?"

Agmund's eyes on her didn't change, didn't even blink. "I could probably handle that," he said, as if making an attempt at lightness, but Selby's mouth fell open, her head shaking hard enough to whip her hair in her face.

"You're confused," she breathed. "You're just thinking about your magic, all right? And I know how important your magic is to you, and I want you to keep it too—but you sure as *hell* don't want to pay me to do this *forever*. You don't trust me, you don't want me in your life, you barely even *like* me, you *just* fucking said so!"

Her hand was still against Agmund's chest, now clenched into his tunic, and his thoughts behind it were suddenly steady, sure of themselves. "Look, that was just me losing my temper, and you know it," he said back, sounding almost as breathless as she did. "And I thought you knew to ignore my shit by now?"

"Oh, fuck off," Selby snapped back, but it came out sounding strange, uncertain, and she took one bracing breath, and then another. "I can ignore most of your shit, but you telling me you don't give a fuck about me is pretty damned vile, even for you! And"—she dragged in another breath—"I'm flattered that you think you can tolerate me for the rest of your entire *life*, but you must see there's no way in *hell* I'm ever going to sign up for that!"

Agmund blinked at her, looking taken aback. "Why not?"

"Honestly?" Selby demanded, her voice cracking, "You think I'd be happy having to always hide, to pretend, to be gossiped about forever as Regin Agmund's harlot? Having to watch while you live your *real* life with your *real* friends, your *real* job? What if you decide you want a real wife, too? Or a real family?"

Agmund blinked again, but then shrugged, both with his shoulder, and his thoughts. "Well, I wouldn't stop you from having kids," he said. "If that's what you wanted."

What? And was that why he'd asked, that time, about Selby being pregnant? He *wanted* her to have his kids? Wanted her *trapped*?

"What—the—*fuck*," Selby sputtered, and the rage was so strong, so overpowering, she could barely speak. "So you'd have an entire secret fucking *family*? You'd bring innocent *children* into this, who'd be raised up *knowing* they were second-rate, born to your *harlot*, who's being *paid* to fuck you for your magic? I thought you wanted to be a *good* father!"

She could feel Agmund's flinch, and that familiar stubbornness flared in his eyes, in his thoughts. "I'm not saying you'd *have* to do that, I'm saying you *could*," he shot back. "I'm saying you'd have coin, and options. You could still have your own family, if that's what you want. Or, you could live in luxury, travel the world, do research, pick out your own projects, everything you nagged at me earlier about!"

Oh, so they were back at this again, and Selby jabbed a finger into his chest, glared up at his shadowy face. "Yes, everything you could still do, if you had a damned backbone!" she said, her voice shrill. "And you know what? If you ever found the guts to finally give up this hellhole, and come away with me, do all that with me, I would happily fuck you as much as you want, and maybe even have your kids, for *free*. But when this contract is done, I promise you, I am *done* being Regin Agmund's harlot!"

Agmund's eyes were distant, stony, and Selby could feel the fury blazing up again behind his touch, sudden and wild and forceful. And it occurred to her, all at once, that he was low on magic, this was how it always felt, maybe *that* was why he was saying all these ridiculous things...

Her hand snapped down to his trousers, yanking them open, thrusting them downwards. While Agmund twitched and stared, his anger shifting, hesitating. "What the fuck," he growled, "are you doing."

Selby drew in breath, shot him a cold, brittle smile. "I'm doing you a much-needed favour, asshole," she replied, and then sank to her knees on the damp ground. To where his groin was barely visible in the flickering lantern light, but she could see that his cock was soft for once, curving gently over the bulge of the heavy bollocks below.

The sight of it was suddenly, strangely arousing, and Selby leaned in, inhaled the musky scent of him. Felt that soft cock give a hopeful twitch in reply, and she let out a hard husky laugh, and sucked him into her mouth.

Agmund gasped aloud, his hips bucking, and he was already filling up, becoming thicker and harder and longer between her lips, growing deep into her throat. And gods, that was good, and *he* was good, and suddenly there was the vision of lightning, striking down strong and true, and Selby gasped, too. Not just at how it looked, how it felt, but also at the truth that he always did that, was considerate with that, knew she liked it. *Stay*, he'd said—

So she sucked him back harder, deeper, sloppier, using one hand on the base of him, the other to delve at his thigh, his hip, those heavy hanging balls, and further back. Groaning around him as he swelled even fuller, as his hips gave a sharp little thrust toward her face.

Gods, that was good too, and so was the feel of his hand, coming to rest against her hair. Making her suck harder, deeper, moving in earnest now, sliding him in and out, and she needed to drag out his spunk, needed to feel it pour down her throat...

She gripped a hand at his bare arse, driving his hips closer, faster—and he instantly met her in it, gripping both hands to her head. Using his thick cock to fuck her mouth now, slamming rough into her throat, bringing her head forward again and again.

"Suck harder, witch," he breathed, his voice unsteady, and Selby moaned around him, let him feel the barest touch of teeth. But he only cursed and thrust even faster, and saliva was dripping down her chin, but she didn't care, he wanted her to *stay*—

"Gon' come," he gasped, his hips bucking harder, uneven, desperate. "Look at me, look up, let me see you take it—"

Selby was already moaning, blinking up at him in the dark, holding his watching eyes as his huge demanding cock fucked her face. And with one last gouging thrust he was shouting, spurting out, making her gag as he filled her throat with his thick, bitter-salt seed. But he didn't let off, didn't pull back, and

Selby moaned again as she fought to swallow, to keep it inside, there was so *much*, oh gods…

She finally had to push him away, her throat still working to swallow, to drink down the last of it. But he kept his hand on her face as she did it, and once she'd finished and looked up again, he brushed his thumb soft against her swollen lips, and then guided his still-dripping, mostly-hard cock back between them.

"Clean up your mess," he whispered. "Filthy wench."

A shudder trembled up Selby's back, and she obeyed, holding Agmund's eyes as she licked at him, suckled on him, rolled him around in her mouth. Doing everything with him that she wanted, that he wanted, *Fuck this is good*, his thoughts unwillingly whispered, and it *was* good, he was good, he wanted her to stay…

Finally he was the one who pulled away again, giving a soft, regretful groan. "Better stop," he murmured, "else I'll just be wanting it all over again, and I've already been asshole enough for one day, haven't I?"

Selby staggered up to her feet, stumbling a little, but Agmund grabbed her arm, steadying her. And then he kept his hand there, as if to keep her from moving, and behind it Selby could taste the churning, determined mass of his thoughts, now intentionally speaking into hers. *Don't go, please, I'm sorry, thank you, I didn't deserve that, I needed that, needed you.*

"I really am sorry," he said aloud, darting a swift, uncertain look toward her eyes. "And I"—he swallowed, hard enough that she could hear it—"I do want you to stay. At least for the rest of this contract. Please."

But maybe what they'd just done had cleared Selby's own head, too, because she turned to look over her shoulder, toward the blackness behind them. Her magic was at risk. Her future was at risk. The smart thing, the right thing, would be to run.

"Please, fuck, *don't*," came Agmund's cracking voice, as his other hand clenched on her shoulder. "Not like this, not now.

They'll track you within hours, and you'll look guilty by default, and it'll all be that much worse for you, and your family. Why in the *fuck* you agreed to fucking *servitude* if you walk out on this, for the love of the *gods*, I could have gotten you out of it before, but now—"

His thoughts swirled higher and louder as he spoke, shouting the nearness of his panic, and his hands gave Selby a little shake as he moved around to block her line of sight, to lock her eyes to his. "Please," he said again. "Not now. Not like this. I understand if you don't want to be my—my lover anymore, after all this. But if they catch you, and enslave you, or *hurt* you, I won't—"

His eyes closed, the words breaking off in his throat, but they finished in his thoughts, too strong and too clear. *I won't be able to live with myself. Please.*

Selby's heart plummeted—his *lover*, he'd said, he wouldn't be able to live with himself—but then she tore her gaze away from his face, back to the trees. Yes, if she was tracked and caught, it would be bad. But what if she wasn't caught? What if she could escape? Make a new life, a new beginning, somewhere else?

"And you have nothing," Agmund continued, his panic hardening into a tense, tight resolve. "No clothes, no coin, no food. And yeah, I'll give you coin if I can, but if you think they'd let you just waltz into the bank in the capital and take it, you're full of shit."

Selby resented that, and she frowned up at him, her bottom lip jutting out. "All right, yes, maybe that was a bad plan," she said, "but I'm not *helpless*. If I can avoid being caught, I'll be fine."

"Oh really?" Agmund shot back. "In the woods, by yourself, with no food or shelter or defense, out in the open like that? You'd be lost and dead in a *week*."

"I would *not*," Selby countered. "You're not the only one here who's spent half their life in the woods, asshole. And you're right, it wouldn't be fun—but as long as I still have my magic, I can track and hide and find good food, I can sneak into places a lot of people can't. And I can feel where people and animals have been, and know if they want to hurt me or not, or what they plan to do next."

Agmund's thoughts under his hands had gone oddly still, his eyes searching hers. "Oh," he said, a funny tilt to his voice. "Right. Yeah. I guess I didn't think of that."

Selby tried for a shrug, but she couldn't seem to move, not with his hands still clenching on her like that, his thoughts caught in that strange, stilted loop. "You've never told me any of that, though," he added. "Why?"

Selby shrugged again, let out a slow exhale. "You never asked. Just like you've never actually asked about my life before I came here, or my family, either."

She could feel the regret blooming through Agmund's thoughts, sharp and swift—and with it, the reason he'd never asked. Because Selby had never pried into his past, or his father, or the hell that his childhood had been after his father's death. And Agmund had been unspeakably grateful to her for that, and had wanted to return the courtesy.

"Yes, well, I saw it all in your head, and on your stuff," Selby told him, more bitterly than she meant. "I didn't have to ask."

But there wasn't any censure in Agmund's thoughts, just that funny loop again, and he swallowed hard, shook his head. "Then tell me," he said. "What's your family like? And—do you really *like* being on your own in the woods? Most girls hate that kind of thing."

Selby eyed him with suspicion, glancing again into the blackness of the forest behind them. "You mean, *these* girls hate that kind of thing," she corrected him. "And also, you're stalling. Trying to keep me from running."

She both heard Agmund's sigh, and felt it under his hands. "Yeah, I am," he replied, "because unless there's something else you're not telling me, you still can't erase your trail, or keep yourself from being followed, or actually fight back if you're attacked. The Coven has a *lot* of good mages, and they'll catch you, and please, just"—his thoughts floundered, turned sideways—"look, all right, please, if you're that set on running, at least let me fucking *help* you."

Wait. He would—help? Regin Agmund would help Selby break her contract? Help commit what was probably treason? Help cut off his own magic for good, *forever*?

But the confirmation of it was there, here behind his hands, soaring straight from his thoughts to her own. "Come back with me to the manor for now," he said firmly, "and we'll come up with an actual plan. I'll give you whatever coin I can, pack you food and clothes, give you the names of a few places you could lie low for a while. And you can tell me exactly how to find your family, and hopefully I can get to them in time to tell them to run too, so the Coven doesn't go looking for them next. All right?"

Oh, gods *curse* Selby, because she hadn't even considered the dangers to her family in all this. How maybe—maybe the Coven would go after them for the coin she owed, if she broke her contract. Maybe the Coven would lie to them, try to use them to contact her. Maybe the Coven would decide to take *them* as indentured labourers, instead…

Selby's body betrayed a hard, sustained shudder, strong enough that Agmund felt it, his hands tightening almost painfully on her arms. "Or," he said, "you come back with me tonight, and like I promised you before, we face this bullshit inquiry head-on, and deal with it. We figure it out, together."

Together. And it would be ridiculous of Selby to trust him—he'd *just* said he didn't even *like* her, not even an hour ago, right?—but his thoughts behind his hands were still wide-open, nothing to hide. "Please," he said, "just—walk with me, and think about it, and tell me about your brother. Simon, right? How old is he? Ten? Twelve?"

Selby shot one more look over her shoulder, but Agmund

had picked up the lantern again, and was half-guiding, half-dragging her in the direction of the manor. And curse her, but Selby let herself be dragged, caught in his thoughts that pleaded *They'll catch you, you can't outrun them without a plan, please, I know I'm an asshole but I mean this, how the fuck old is he.*

"Thirteen," she said, unwillingly, earning a look of sheer, grateful relief from Agmund's watching eyes.

And? his silent voice prompted. *What's he like? Does he have magic too?*

"No magic," Selby replied, with a reluctant smile. "But he's a sharp little fighter, I've seen him take out men twice his size. And he works hard, speaks his mind, doesn't take anything from anyone. And when he's angry, watch out."

Agmund's hand tightened on her arm, still guiding her through the trees, and he huffed a low chuckle. "Like his sister, then," he said, quiet. "You miss him."

There was a pang in Selby's chest at the thought, and she nodded, glanced sideways at Agmund's shadowy face. "But he's growing up now too, you know? Even before I left, he was always wanting to go off with his friends—or take off leading a caravan of his own. I think Ma will only get a year or two more out of him, if that."

"Yeah?" Agmund asked. "And what happens then?"

He was still trying to distract her, Selby knew very well, but the question was something she had intentionally avoided thinking about for months, maybe even years. And now, for some ridiculous reason, with multiple horrible fates looming over her head, and Regin Agmund actually listening beside her in the dark, it seemed easier to face it. To be honest.

"I don't know if I—would continue," she said, slowly. "With Simon gone. I'm glad I've been able to help Ma all these years, and I'll probably always still see myself as a pedlar, but"—she took a breath—"the shop is still her life, her choices, not mine. And it's felt more—constricting, somehow, for a while now. Like a door that keeps closing, and if I don't escape now, maybe I never will. You know what I mean?"

Agmund didn't speak, but his hand gave a brief squeeze to her arm. Tasting undeniably of sympathy, of understanding—and then the silent whisper of agreement, saying, *Yeah. I know.*

"So how would your ma get by without you?" he asked, out loud. "I bet you keep a lot of the operation going, with all your brilliant stuff-touching skills?"

Selby shrugged, but couldn't help a wry little half-grin toward him. "Well, before I left, I used the last of Ketill's coin to bring on my other uncle, and his son," she said. "They've both been wanting to get off the longer shipping routes, and they're hard workers, who can do other jobs on the side to help out. I really hope it's working. For them, and Ma too."

There was another brief, companionable flare of agreement from Agmund, the lantern bobbing as they walked. "Why don't you write them and find out?" he asked. "You said you had another uncle you could send things through."

"No coin," Selby replied, with another shrug. "Remember?"

Agmund's steps faltered, and the touch behind his hand surged with disbelief, perhaps even anger. "Oh for fuck's sakes," he snapped. "You could have just asked. You didn't think I'd give you enough to send some letters home?"

"But," Selby began, shaking her head. "I don't want—"

But Agmund cut her off with a harsh, exasperated groan. "Yeah, yeah, you don't want my coin," he said. "Look, for something like that I'd give it to a complete fucking *stranger*, of course I'd want to give it to you. And not as payment for anything, either, so don't even start!"

A sudden ripple of warmth ran up Selby's back, and she felt her lips quirking up. "Not even a little?" she asked. "Surely we can get into at least one more raging quarrel before we get back?"

Agmund snorted, or maybe laughed, as his hand released Selby's arm, and slipped close and almost proprietary around her waist. "Fuck off, wench," he said, but his voice was light. "The writing shit's in my desk drawer, though you probably already know that. I want to see a letter by tomorrow, leave it for me and I'll get it posted for you."

Selby shivered beneath another flare of warmth, tasting dangerously close to affection—but then it flattened again as she caught a glimpse of Coven Manor's looming bulk through the trees. Agmund was taking her back. Agmund wanted her to stay, and risk a Coven inquiry, and losing her magic for good. Or, he would help her run. He would try to help her family.

He seemed to sense her hesitation—how had Regin Agmund gotten so good at reading her thoughts?—and his arm tightened around her waist, pulling her to a stop. "One other thing, I should have said," he began, his eyes uneasy in the lantern's flickering light. "I didn't want to upset you even more, but"—he took a breath—"those investigators I mentioned earlier? It sounds like they're going to be here tomorrow."

Tomorrow. Selby flinched and staggered, her breath choking in her throat, and suddenly the dread and the fear flared up again, pounding in fierce, dizzying waves. Tomorrow, why hadn't he said, *why*—

But in a single smooth step, Agmund was here. Folding her whole body close against his, without even a twitch of hesitation, his arms tight and strong and warm against her back.

"But like I said," he whispered, close, husky in her ear. "If you stay, we'll figure it out. All right? Tonight. We're going to stay up all night, and dig through this whole damned manor. You're going to walk me through everything, we're going to break into a shit ton of places, and enrage a bunch of people. It'll be our own little adventure."

Selby's breath escaped in a shaky half-laugh, but she couldn't seem to speak. While the dread kept pounding louder, what if they found her guilty, what if they took away her magic, what if everything Runar had said would come true...

"Or," Agmund said, and he leaned back again, enough to

meet her eyes. "If you still want to run, say so. And we'll have you out the door, or"—his head tilted, his mouth grimacing—"probably my window, by morning."

Selby stared at his face in the flickering lantern's light, saw and felt and tasted all the thoughts he betrayed. He meant it, he really did, and gods curse her, because she couldn't pull away, couldn't look away. Regin Agmund was offering an escape, he was offering freedom, he truly meant it, and damn it, Selby wanted—an adventure.

"No," she said. "I'll stay."

28

For the rest of the night, Regin Agmund kept his word, and took Selby on an adventure.

It began with sneaking up on the manor's back gate, well away from the watching eyes of the front gatekeeper. And then—Selby almost shouted her astonishment—an impossible, invisible mass of air came up under her feet, and levitated her and Agmund up over the gate, and gently dropped them down on the opposite side.

"What the hell," she gasped at Agmund, staring. "I thought you specialized in *lightning* magic. I've never even seen you *think* about—about *flying*."

He grinned back, though his hands looked a little shaky, his face paler than before. "Yeah, well, I've never liked it," he said. "Feels almost as bad as water, being all floaty and ungrounded like that. But I'm still the best air-mage on the continent, wench, I can do any damn spell I want."

Selby choked a reluctant laugh, even as she reached for his still-shaky hand, and felt his stuttering, unsettled thoughts swirling behind it. "Well, just because you *can*, asshole, doesn't mean you *should*."

Agmund shrugged, flashed her another brief, sideways

grin. "Most times, maybe," he said, "but I just got a halfway decent cocksucking back there, so I'm feeling pretty damn good."

Selby blinked, and then scoffed at him, thrusting his hand away from hers. "*Halfway* decent?" she demanded. "Don't count on more of it anytime soon, then. Arrogant *troll*."

Agmund only grinned again, the sight of it making something flip low in Selby's belly, and she willingly crept after him around to the manor's front door. Which he somehow easily opened, with even more admittedly impressive air-magic that she'd never seen him use before.

Inside the manor it was quiet and dark, with no wandering people to be seen, but the smell was an awful wall of putrid foulness, almost staggeringly powerful after having been free of it for so long. Selby had to take short, shallow breaths, while Agmund stayed close, rubbed at her back, and when she stepped even closer to him, breathed in the far superior musky scent of him instead, he didn't resist, his hands coming easy to her hips.

"So, plan of attack," he whispered, once Selby could somewhat breathe again, and he'd begun leading her through the dim main-floor corridor, lit only by the light of the occasional flickering sconce. "We need to figure out where the girl came in, and what the hell she was doing here. So I think we start with you touching every single wall in the hallways, and tracking everywhere she's been."

It made sense, so with Agmund trailing behind her, Selby proceeded to investigate every corridor in the entire damned building. And though it was faint, she was able to trace the girl's signature around the front door, and the main-floor corridor with the directors' offices, and the chilly steel door to Runar's morgue. Also, there was still a trace of her on the back stairwell, on both the first and second floors, though just like that night Selby had followed her, it seemed to connect to nothing else.

"Well, I say we start with the morgue," Agmund said, pulling Selby back by the hand toward its imposing steel door. "Alariaq's the death-dealer around here. And he's good enough to cover his tracks, if needed."

Selby found she didn't at all like the thought of Runar being involved—he and Thora had become her closest friends here, beyond Agmund—and she eyed the door warily. "Wouldn't they have brought the girl's body down here, though? That would explain the smell being here, right?"

"Maybe, but it sounded like they took her body away for testing," Agmund replied, not meeting her eyes. "Ketill wouldn't tell me where."

That didn't bode well, and Selby frowned at Agmund as he ran his hands along the door's seamless edge, maybe feeling for the latch inside. "Did *Ketill* find out the girl's name?" she asked him. "Or where she was from, or why she was here?"

"I don't think so," Agmund replied, as the taste of his magic flared out, and the door made a distinct-sounding *click*. "It sounded like they were running spells, trying to trace her. But when I talked to Ketill after supper, they hadn't found anything yet. Not even what kind of magic she used."

Selby grimaced, watching where the steel door was slowly swinging open, letting out a gust of cold, antiseptic-smelling air. The room beyond it was pitch-black, but with a spark from Agmund's fingers, a nearby wall lamp sputtered to life, revealing a cold, sterile-looking room, not unlike Runar's regular workroom upstairs. A disconcerting array of metal tools lined one wall, a variety of bottles and jars lined another, and in the room's middle were three large steel tables, one of which—Selby twitched—held the unmistakable, unsettling shape of a human body, thankfully covered by a sheet.

Selby felt rooted in place, just inside the steel door, and Agmund nudged her inside, and shut the door behind them. Making Selby twitch again, though a glance up at his face showed him looking even more uneasy than she felt. "Go on, then," he said, eyeing that sheet-draped table. "Can you feel her in here?"

Selby wrinkled her nose against the smell—combined with the manor's usual stench, it was particularly noxious—and stepped further into the room. Trailing her fingers along the walls, first, as far away from that body as possible, and then touching at the cold, empty tables, and the two stools beside them. Tasting alternately of Runar and Thora, and Selby sat down on one of the stools, closed her eyes, let the images wash over her. The two of them working, concentrating, talking, magic, had to keep working, keep trying or else, not a single trace of the dead girl, but—

Selby opened one eye, and studied the draped, still body on the table, now close enough to touch. And it wasn't possible, or was it, and Selby ignored Agmund's distant sputtered curse as she reached a hand, carefully, and touched it.

The images swarmed her in a flood, a man a soldier a life, now dead, except. And Selby staggered back off the stool, already expecting it, but still flinching at the sight of the body—*moving*, under the sheet. And then, as she stared, a grey, mottled arm slid from beneath the sheet's white edge. Reaching. Out. Toward her.

Agmund's shout behind her was bloodcurdlingly shrill, and Selby felt his hand—warm, alive, oh gods—gripping her arm, and yanking her toward the door. Out of the cold stench, into the corridor's warmer stench, and Selby felt the surge of his sound-spell just as the door slammed shut behind them with an echoing, near-deafening thud.

"What. The. *Fuck*," Agmund gasped, over his shoulder, as he dragged Selby down the corridor, his fear streaking genuine and powerful through his fingers. "It was *alive*."

But Selby shook her head, and pulled Agmund to a stop in the middle of the corridor, breathing hard. "It wasn't alive," she said. "It was just"—she cast through those visions, those memories—"functioning. A bit."

"Functioning?!" Agmund demanded at her. "What in the *fuck*? It could have *killed* you!"

His hands were visibly trembling, his face gone very pale, and Selby instinctively lurched toward him, her arms circling around his waist. "It couldn't have done anything of the sort," she told him. "They've only reactivated"—she had to take a breath, marvel at the skill behind that—"part of its brain. It was only responding to my touch."

"What in the *fuck*," Agmund said again, his hands gripping too tight against Selby's back. "Did you *know* they were doing that? Fucking *necromancy*?"

Selby shook her head against his chest, but the thought was a strangely lowering one. Why were Runar and Thora working on a project like that? Had they gotten permission, somehow? And Runar had been the one to tell Selby how dangerous a Coven trial could be, right? *I've been there before, it's not fun...*

"It's not—as bad as it sounds," Selby said, pulling back to look at Agmund's too-wide eyes. "Really. It's just—science. Exploring the human body. There's no malicious intent whatsoever. And also, our dead girl was never in there, if that helps."

The shock surged through Agmund's thoughts again, but Selby was distantly gratified to note that there was less actual fear in it, and more disbelief. "You are *fucked*, wench," he said, putting his hand to her face, and giving it a little shake. "Touching two dead bodies in one fucking day. And saying the one that *moves* isn't malicious? And you don't even *try* to run?"

Selby couldn't find an argument for that, not with Agmund's clammy hand gripping her face like this, his eyes locked on hers. "Don't you *ever* scare me like that again," he said, through clenched teeth. "I mean that. *Fuck*."

He did mean it, Selby could feel the strength of it all through him, and she nodded. To which he nodded in return, the movement curt, though perhaps relieved, too.

"Just about gave me a heart attack," he said now, looking

past her, distractedly running a hand against his hair. "I need—"

He broke off there, his thoughts all twisted and jumbling, not unlike when he had those horrible dreams of his. And just like she did with the dreams, Selby carefully touched at them, replaced them with calm, with focus, with visions of exploding green trees.

"You need what?" she said, as coolly as she could, attempting to ignore the odd, watchful look Agmund gave her. But then he closed his eyes, took another breath, let it out.

"You'll see," he said. "Come on."

29

The next leg of their adventure, Selby soon discovered, was breaking into the kitchen.

"Are we allowed to be here after hours?" she asked, once Agmund had blown a bit of air at the dining hall's locked door, and waved her in with a flourish.

"Nope," he replied, as he guided Selby over toward the adjoining kitchen. "C'mon."

The kitchen was far too dark to see in, let alone peruse food options, but another blinding little flare of electricity from Agmund's fingers lit the nearest lamp. Revealing what looked like an entire wall of food, a pantry stocked from top to bottom with cakes and fruit and bread and dried meats, more food than Selby had ever seen in one place in her life.

"Eat up," Agmund said, plunking a pastry into Selby's hand. "After the unholy nightmare that was, we need it. Gods *damn* it."

He was giving her that look again, part incredulous, part relieved, and Selby meekly took a bite of the pastry he'd given her. It was delicious, and she could feel Agmund relaxing as they sat side by side on the kitchen's counter, passing cakes and fruit and desserts back and forth. Eating until Selby's stomach felt close to bursting, while Agmund beside her just kept going, packing away an astonishing amount of food, and eventually Selby just sat there and watched, half-amused, half-amazed.

"How in the gods' green earth were you so skinny before?" she demanded. "When I first got here?"

Agmund's sideways glance was furtive, his throat working to swallow the huge bite of cake in his mouth. "Just—wasn't hungry," he said. "Couldn't make myself care. About anything."

Oh. He was very intently looking away from her, like he was ashamed of that. And when Selby gently touched a hand to his thigh, behind it were his memories of that whispering darkness, the bleak clawing desperation. The steadily rising suspicion that the world might be better off without him in it at all.

Selby fought back a grimace, and felt her hand moving, running slow and suggestive down his thigh. "Well, keep eating, asshole," she murmured, her voice thick, husky, appalling. "And, um, say, if I were to"—she took a fortifying breath, met his eyes—"suck you off again right now, would you get crumbs in my hair?"

Agmund blinked, looking genuinely taken aback—but then the warmth in his eyes, in his too-betraying thoughts, made Selby's furiously flushing face almost worth it. "Nah," he replied, his voice just as husky as hers. "I'll use a plate."

And he did, the arrogant bastard, just kept on eating, while Selby knelt in front of the counter, and kissed and sucked and licked his gorgeous hard cock. Making him gasp, and shudder, until finally he almost choked on his cake, and set it aside in favour of sinking both hands deep into Selby's undoubtedly crumb-filled hair, and thrusting her head up and down his slick heat, slamming it into her throat again and again and again.

He came with a choked cry, his elbow knocking against his plate, and sending it off the counter to smash in a hundred pieces on the floor. While Selby eagerly swallowed him back, oh *gods* why did she like this so much, and then she shot him a smug little grin as she stood up again, licked her lips, and tucked him back into his trousers.

"Better?" she asked, and in return, Agmund's fingers stroked warm and close and familiar against her mouth, her face. While his eyes looked almost reverently into hers, making something twist sharp and deep in her gut, and he opened his mouth, as if to speak—but then he moved his eyes, and his thoughts, purposely away.

"Yeah," he said finally. "Thanks. But we should keep going, all right? Lots to do still."

Right. Selby swallowed, her lightness dropping, because she kept managing to forget that. She'd chosen not to run, she was under investigation for murder, there would be an interrogation tomorrow, the possible consequences were horrible, and here she was awakening dead bodies, devouring a shocking quantity of snacks, and sucking Regin Agmund off in a kitchen.

"I think next we should go through the visitor logs," Agmund said, a little stilted, once he'd done some other elaborate air-spell, meant to supposedly erase their signatures from the kitchen. "They'll have checked the logs already, but they probably only went back a few weeks, right? You said you saw the girl a month or two ago?"

Selby nodded, and followed Agmund back toward the manor's main entrance, into the locked, empty gatekeeper's office. It was a tiny, cluttered room, lined with shelves and boxes, all stuffed haphazardly with books and papers, in no discernible order.

"Visitor logs," Agmund muttered, prowling around the room, pulling out random piles of paper, and stuffing them back again. "Visitor logs, where would you be..."

He was already making a mess, wafting several wayward sheets of paper to the floor, and after watching for another minute Selby elbowed him out of the way, and off into a corner. And then she put her hands to the desk, feeling the wood the maker the gatekeeper, the work, the writing, the logs, putting them away...

"Over here," she said, going for a crooked stack of books, and flipping the first one open. It was indeed a list of dates and names and signatures, and Selby couldn't help a satisfied smile at Agmund's look of obvious disbelief.

"Earth magic to the rescue," she said, as she handed him the next book in the pile. "Again."

He quirked a reluctant-looking grin at her, his hand brushing hers tasting of something she couldn't quite decipher. And then he opened the book, running his finger down the line of names and dates. "Would you recognize the girl's name, if you saw it?" he asked. "Or felt it?"

That was an idea, because each visitor's name was accompanied by their mark, in their own hand. So Selby closed her eyes, and began running her finger down the list of names, briefly feeling the taste of every single one.

There was nothing on the first page, or the second, or indeed the entire first book. Or the second book, or the third, so many twitches of different people different lives, and Selby's thoughts were already starting to swim as Agmund handed over the fourth.

"Are you sure you haven't just missed it?" he asked, but Selby shot him a sharp look, and kept going. She wouldn't have missed it, there was no way, that girl was burned into her brain—

"There," she said, suddenly, as her finger came to an abrupt halt, halfway down the page. "There, oh gods. That's her."

Her hand was shaking on the paper, and Agmund swatted it away, leaned over her shoulder to get a closer look. *Anabel Smit*, it said, in an angled, purposeful script, beside a date and time.

"Almost a year ago," Agmund murmured, quiet. "And it doesn't say when she left."

He was right, it didn't, and that was peculiar, because most of the names did have a time of exit, as well as entry. A few others didn't, though, suggesting that it could have been just an error, the gatekeeper forgetting to make the proper note.

"Can you tell anything else from touching it?" Agmund asked, and Selby put her trembly hand back to the signature. Back to where Anabel had walked in here, naive and determined and hopeful, hoping for—what?

"I think," Selby began, "It almost feels like she—had a purpose here. Like she was coming here to do something. It was supposed to be something good. Something... happy."

Agmund's eyes were a little strange on Selby's, but he nodded. "Like some kind of work, or project?"

"Yes, just like that," Selby said slowly. "Like she had a—a purpose here. Not just a job, not like in the kitchens, or cleaning, or whatever—but something important. Something that held real meaning to her."

Agmund was silent for a minute, his fingers absently tapping on Selby's shoulder. "And did you get any of that when you saw her in person? When you touched her?"

Selby shook her head, dropping her eyes down to the book. "No," she said, quiet. "It was almost like—she'd failed. At whatever it was she was brought here to do."

"Brought here?" Agmund repeated, sharply. "By somebody else? Someone who was already here?"

Selby considered that, turning the memories over in her thoughts. "I think so. But I didn't catch any hints as to who it might have been. Not Runar or Thora, I know that much."

"Well, it could have been any of the mages working here, right?" Agmund said, slower now. "Lots of them bring extra people around for short-term projects or research. So the real question is still *where*?"

Selby had no answers for that, and didn't resist as Agmund plucked the book out of her hands, and piled it back on the shelf with the rest. And then he clasped her hand and drew her out again, back toward the stairs.

Until he halted, so abruptly Selby almost ran into his back—but then she felt it, too. They hadn't yet encountered a single other person in their explorations so far, but now someone was coming, too quickly, and there was nowhere to hide—

Here, Agmund's thoughts whispered, and in a flurry of movement Selby was pinned flat to the stone wall, with Agmund leaning close over her. His breath hot against her ear, his hips grinding up against her, and oh gods was he hard *already*, and Selby's hands fluttered to his arse, her whole body arching up into him—

"Selby?" a familiar voice said, and Selby jolted away, and found—Morley. She was carrying a large box in her arms, and though she looked rather tired and drawn in the flickering lamplight, she gave a wry wink, and stepped sideways around them. "My apologies, you two," she said. "Didn't intend to interrupt."

Selby's face felt very hot, and beside her Agmund was the epitome of faked innocence, running a hand through his hair. "Sorry," he replied. "We were just, uh, on our way to bed. Do you need help with that box?"

Gods, Agmund was such a hopeless liar, especially with that still-visible bulge in his trousers, but Morley nodded and willingly handed the box over. "Thank you. I was just heading to my workroom."

Agmund led the way, leaving Selby and Morley to walk together, and it occurred to Selby, suddenly, that she hadn't yet talked to Morley about any of this, and that she probably should have. "Listen, Morley," she said, tentative, "do you know anything about this investigation tomorrow? I've been hearing a lot of rumours about my involvement, and I'm starting to be—worried."

Morley's eyes were grim in the dim light, and she unlocked her workroom door with a wave of her hand, and led them inside. "I'm afraid I've also been hearing some unfortunate rumours," she said, as she turned to light her lamp. "But I'm sure the incoming investigation will clear up any misunderstandings. The Coven's investigators are some of the best mages in the country."

She gave Selby a smile that was clearly meant to be reassuring, but Selby couldn't seem to smile back. "But I don't really belong here," she countered. "I'm not one of you, I didn't come here in the usual way, and I have a different sort of magic. They're not likely to be charitable toward me, are they?"

Agmund had set Morley's box on the workroom table, and Morley murmured her thanks before studying Selby again. "I don't think you need to worry about that in the context of the investigation," Morley said. "I know some people still carry around those old prejudices, but most of us—at least those of us in the Coven's leadership—are well beyond that. I can personally vouch for your reliability and work ethic, and I know Ketill is pleased with your work as well. And, of course"—she gave a brief smile toward Agmund—"your positive association with Mr. Agmund can only bolster your case."

Selby winced—so far that hadn't bolstered anything with anyone around here—but Morley didn't seem to notice. "If you'd like someone to be with you during your questioning tomorrow, I'm currently planning to be there," she added, "I'd be happy to help however I can."

Selby's heartbeat picked up its pace—tomorrow was only a few short hours away now, right?—and beside her Agmund cleared his throat. "Nope, not necessary," he said, his voice clipped, sure of itself. "I'll be with her."

Selby couldn't read the look Morley gave Agmund, but then Morley nodded. "Well, if there's anything else I can do, please let me know."

That seemed to be the end of that, and Selby followed Agmund out into the corridor. "Weren't you kind of rude?" she said in a whisper, as she followed him toward another door. It was Ketill's office, and Selby frowned as Agmund waved a hand at the latch, and walked straight in.

"Just want a place to think for a minute," he said, shutting the door behind them with a gust of air, and then casting his usual sound-spell. "And Morley was rude, too. She was dismissive of your concerns. And she's never liked me."

"Well, she's one of the only people here who's actually been kind to me," Selby replied stubbornly. "Just because there's bad blood between her and Ketill, or whatever, doesn't mean you have to take his side."

"I'm not taking his side," Agmund replied, as he sprawled his tall body out in Ketill's large chair, his hands behind his head. "I'm taking *your* side. She should have taken you more seriously. And I don't think she's been taking your skills seriously all this time, either."

Selby blinked at him, because they'd talked about her work with Morley rarely, if at all, but Agmund leaned back more in the chair, propping his foot up on the desk. "She has you sorting plants and rocks and shit all day, right?" he said. "Making lists?"

Selby nodded, slowly, and Agmund raised his eyebrows, and waved irritably toward the room, or maybe the building at large. "You can do *this*," he continued, "you can read minds, and see people's memories and dreams, and even figure out *dead* people—and she has you sorting fucking *plants*? Why the hell did I even bother?"

Why did he even bother. Selby's head tilted, considering that—and rather than asking, saying those tenuous words aloud, she reached over, and touched her hand to his booted foot on the desk. And even through the thick leather, there was the memory, weeks ago, Agmund in this very office, telling Ketill, *You need to find Seng some real work, you can't possibly expect her to sit around here and wait for me all the time.*

Agmund's eyes were oddly steady on hers—he'd really done that, he'd meant for her to see it—and Selby looked back down at the boot, gave a funny little shake of it, still under her hand. Regin Agmund, such an asshole, and still—she swallowed—still.

"So," Agmund said, clearing his throat. "We know Anabel's name, we know when she came here, we know she was working on a specific project. What we don't know is who brought her here, or where the hell she actually *was* in here. And until we know that"—he frowned up at the ceiling—"we still don't have a case, or a sweet fucking *clue* who's really responsible for her death."

That was the truth of it, and suddenly Agmund's other foot kicked hard at Ketill's desk, making it skid against the floor. "Gods *damn* it," he said, pressing his hands to his eyes. "There's got to be something else we can do tonight. Maybe we can try to find out where Anabel was from, go talk to her family, figure out what she was doing here. Or we could go around and start waking up people, ask them questions about her while you touch them—"

Selby shook her head, a little frantic, because she'd never dared to use her magic like that before, and she could just imagine the horrible rumours that would spring from it, just in time for her questioning. And there was no way they'd be able to find and contact Anabel's family tonight either, but tomorrow would be too late, maybe forever...

But there was one other thing. And Agmund wasn't likely to like it, but there more Selby thought about it, the more it was the only option left.

"Then let's go back upstairs," she said. "I know who can help."

30

Soon Selby was standing in the middle of the upstairs corridor, and knocking on Henrik's bedroom door.

"I still don't think this is a good idea," Agmund muttered, as Selby knocked again, louder this time. "What if *he's* the one who brought Anabel in?"

Selby frowned at Agmund, and knocked again, because she could feel Henrik in there, probably sleeping. "Henrik doesn't plan things," she murmured back. "Fasta does. And also, they do most of their actual construction work off-site, so why would they bring Anabel here?"

Agmund didn't look convinced, but he put his hand to the door beside Selby's, and sighed. "Fine," he said. "You might want to close your eyes."

Selby didn't follow, but after another wave of his hand, Agmund swung the door open, and strode into Henrik's room. And Selby realized, too late, that Henrik wasn't alone, and the girl with her arms around him in bed wasn't Fasta, but one of the ubiquitous blonde air-mages.

"Hey, Tana," Agmund said, his voice smooth. "Hallen, we need to borrow you."

Henrik's blond curls were standing all up on end, and he

sat up in the bed, showing off a pale, barrel-shaped chest. "Uh, what?" he said, his voice thick. "Now?"

"Yep," Agmund replied. "For the rest of the night. Sorry, Tana, you'll have to find some other bed to crash. Pretty sure Njall wouldn't say no."

With that, Agmund ducked outside and shut the door, with Selby close behind. "Really?" she whispered. "Do you know how much hell you'd have given Henrik if he walked in on *you* and said that?"

"Yeah, well, I'm doing him a favour," Agmund whispered back. "She's a boring fuck, and it'll be nonstop drama for weeks afterwards."

"You *slept* with her?" Selby hissed, more stung by that than she wanted to admit. "And *you*, of all people, have the gall to call someone *else* a boring fuck, with nonstop drama?"

Agmund shot her a look, and elbowed her further up the hall. "I'm not boring, I have *principles*, because you were *paid*," he hissed back. "And you know I fucked around a lot before, and it fucked with my head, right? Do you see me still doing it now?"

Selby opened her mouth to dispute that—but then closed it again, because yes, she'd spent far too much time in Agmund's head by now, and knew very well that he'd been remarkably faithful to Greta during their two years together. And, to be fair, he'd actually been legitimately faithful to Selby these past months, too.

"Fine, fine," Selby said, looking purposely away from him, as she knocked on another door. "Still nonstop drama, though."

Agmund snorted, but an instant later the door was opened by none other than Thora, blinking between them as she pulled a white dressing-gown haphazardly over her slim frame.

"Selby?" she sleepily asked. "What's going on?"

Selby explained the situation as quickly as she could, and Thora was a genuinely generous person, because she instantly agreed. "But you're getting Runar, too," she said. "Right?"

Selby ignored Agmund's groan beside her, and jerked a nod. "Sure," she replied. "If you think it would help."

Thora did, obviously, so next Selby went to rap at Runar's door. Runar opened it almost immediately, although he was stripped to the waist, wearing low-hanging trousers, and looking lithe and smooth and admittedly gorgeous in the dim corridor lamplight.

"What?" he demanded, his eyes flicking back and forth between Selby and Agmund. "This had better be good."

Agmund was eyeing Runar with something not unlike revulsion, no doubt thinking about that moving dead body downstairs. "Selby wants your help," he snapped. "For an hour or two, tops."

Runar's eyes narrowed, lingering on Agmund with equally obvious dislike. "Having to do with the forthcoming investigation, I presume?" he asked coolly. "Finally worried about losing your meal ticket, are you?"

Something flashed in Agmund's hand, and suddenly he seemed very tall, leaning down over Runar with fury all over his face. "You have some nerve judging *me*, you lawbreaking prick," he growled. "And she's not my fucking *meal ticket*, and she's supposed to be your *friend*, so why don't you shut your big mouth, and put a fucking shirt on!"

Runar blinked, clearly catching that *lawbreaking* bit, and looked about to reply in kind—but then Thora came up behind them, wearing a white blouse and trousers, with her hair pulled into a long, messy braid. Her eyes looked shadowed in the dim light, her skin very pale, and Runar's eyes snapped to her, and stayed there.

"They woke you up, too?" he said, quieter. "You really need your sleep, Thora."

Thora gave a dismissive shrug, but a telltale redness had crept up into her cheeks, and Selby noted that Runar had made no effort to get a shirt, and in fact had stepped out into the hallway between them, and reached a hand to trace down Thora's cheekbone. A gesture which obviously wasn't unfamiliar to her, or indeed unwelcome, judging by the way her eyelashes fluttered, the tension seeping away from around her mouth.

"That'll give you an hour," Runar told her, with another dark look toward Agmund. "And *only* an hour, is that clear?"

Agmund replied with a frown, and an impatient wave of his hand back toward Runar's bedroom. And after an exasperated sigh, Runar stalked inside, and soon reappeared wearing a slim-fitting, low-cut silken tunic.

"Fine," he snapped. "So what's the reason for this?"

Henrik had walked up to join them, and Agmund groaned again at the sight of Fasta beside Henrik, looking perfectly poised, as though getting woken in the depths of the night for mysterious reasons was an entirely expected occurrence. "Yes," she said, "what's our objective?"

Selby shot a brief, grateful smile toward Fasta, and took a breath. "Well, I'm going to be interrogated tomorrow," she replied. "About the murder of a girl named Anabel Smit. We know Anabel worked here in the manor for more than a year, but we can't sort out where. I was hoping"—she took another breath, felt Agmund's warm hand on her back—"you could help me."

The words were followed by an instant's silence, during which Fasta and Henrik exchanged dubious glances. "You expect us to trace this girl somehow?" Fasta asked. "You'd likely be better at that than we are, Selby."

"Thanks, but I've already tried, with no luck," Selby replied. "All I've been able to tell is that Anabel was downstairs, and then the trail seems to disappear. So I'd like to know if there are any places in the manor she could have been hidden? Any other ways in or out?"

Henrik's eyebrows furrowed, and he shook his shaggy head.

"Sorry, Selby," he said, "but Fass and I have both lived here for years now. We'd have noticed anything like that ages ago."

Selby could feel Agmund stiffening beside her, his irritation prickling through his fingers into her back. "Look, just humour us, all right?" he snapped. "Selby's magic *is* good at this shit, and hers says that Anabel was here—and also, that there's something off about this building, these walls, in general. Something to do with magic, and it's strong enough to make her feel sick. So I want you to prove her wrong."

Agmund gave Selby a sideways glance as he spoke, with a silent *don't take this personally*, and Selby found herself twitching a smile back. Because again, Agmund was actually giving serious credence to her magic, to her words, and acting accordingly.

"And I can help too," Thora said, around a huge yawn, as she waved toward Fasta and Henrik. "If you two don't mind me touching you occasionally as you look. I'll try to project the most promising possibilities."

Runar frowned at Thora, his foot tapping on the floor. "And why am I here again? Just to keep Thora from passing out, which, by the way, she absolutely *should* be doing?"

"Well," Agmund replied, voice just as sharp, "you can supposedly tell if people are lying, right? From their heartbeat, or anxiety levels, or some shit? Don't try and deny it, I know Ketill's used you for it before."

Runar didn't deny it, though his chin lifted. "And who am I monitoring?"

"Them," Agmund said, with a jerk of his head toward Henrik and Fasta, which immediately set Henrik sputtering. "Sorry, you two, but it's useful, because your alliances might be questionable. Now, can we get the hell on with it? And stay together, inside my sound-spell, so we can talk freely, all right?"

There was something about his certainty on this, his determination, and Selby leaned into him as they followed Henrik and Fasta down the hallway. Watching Henrik stop every few steps to press his hand flat to the wall, while he and Fasta murmured back and forth about support beams and joists and various builders' signatures.

"It's all structurally sound," Henrik said, once they'd gone around the entire upper floor. "Every room along here is the way it should be. No traces of magic, no recent renovations, no crawl spaces or inconsistent dimensions."

"And you agree?" Agmund cut in, eyes angling toward Runar. "He's telling the truth?"

"He is," Runar coolly replied. "At least, what he believes to be the truth."

Henrik darted Runar a furious look, which Runar immediately returned, and Selby cleared her throat. "And Thora," she said, "can you tell at all whether this is what we should be doing?"

"I think so," Thora replied, her head tilted, her eyes with that glazed distance in them. "But perhaps—further down."

She didn't elaborate, and together they slowly, painstakingly, made their way down the back staircase, and all around the third and second floors, with equally unhelpful results. Until Selby was beginning to feel like maybe this had all been a mistake, and she'd have been better off just going back to Agmund's room, and getting some damned sleep.

"The smell's getting stronger again," she told Agmund, quietly, as they climbed down to the first floor. "It's always stronger at night, and down here."

He nodded, looking grim, and tired, too. "Pay special attention down here," he ordered Henrik and Fasta. "And especially round the front."

They did, taking obvious care with the front hallway, and the main staircase. And then kept going, and going, touching every wall, while Selby's tiredness grew and grew, her head bobbing with every step.

They did the back staircase last, near the area where they'd found Anabel's body, and at this point, Selby had very little expectation of finding anything unusual—but then Henrik hesitated, right at the base of the back stairwell.

"What?" Selby asked, just as Thora's breath caught, and she waved for Henrik to continue. But he hesitated again, pulling back, frowning up at the wall.

"It's nothing, really," he said finally. "It's just a place that's been walled in. Looks like it used to go to the basement."

"The basement?" Selby repeated, voice sharp. "I was told the basement had been filled in."

"It was, years ago," Henrik replied. "Long before our time. There was apparently an earth shift that made it unsafe."

"You're sure of that?" Agmund demanded. "And that it's actually filled in?"

Henrik nodded. "Absolutely. You can feel it, right, Fass? Solid compacted rock underneath this whole building. Good earth-mage work."

Fasta nodded too, her eyes intent on the wall Henrik was touching. "It was a good decision, too," she said. "It's made the whole structure much more stable. It's held up very well, in excellent condition."

"Well, can we get behind this wall?" Agmund asked. "Without being detected?"

"Probably," Henrik replied, sliding both hands over it. "But it doesn't go anywhere, the mass of rock's not far beyond it. And we're not getting through that without making a mess."

Agmund shrugged, and waved Henrik forward. "Well, let's take a look, at least. Unless, Thora, you disagree? Or Runar?"

Runar shook his head, and beside him Thora did the same, her eyes still distant. "No," she said. "We should try."

Henrik and Fasta were already conferring, deliberating over what the load-bearing beams were, which one to move first, how to keep the integrity of the plaster, and so forth. And once they'd seemed to settle it, they raised their hands to the wall in unison, and counted to three.

And then, incredibly, the entire wall—*moved*. Not just a

piece of it, but the entire damned wall, sliding out toward them on an angle. Opening it up at the corner, almost as if opening the cover of a closed book. And once Selby had caught her breath, she darted over to the opening, and looked inside.

And there, in the middle of where the wall should have been, was a staircase. A narrow set of dark steps, going downward, and ending with a sheer wall of solid rock.

Selby jogged down the stairs, trailing her fingers along the rough-hewn stone on both sides. Until she stopped up short, fighting back the bile suddenly surging in her throat.

"She was here," she gasped. "Anabel was *here*."

31

Two hours later, Henrik and Fasta still hadn't found a way through the mass of rock.

"There has to be a way," Selby kept saying, and couldn't seem to stop saying, even after they'd tried one thing, and another, and another. Cutting into the rock, digging through it, coming at it from different directions, even from outside.

"There isn't," Fasta said, for the third or fourth time, looking as bleary-eyed as Selby felt. "It's part of the manor's structural support system. You can't just knock it out without affecting the entire building."

Agmund was looking at Runar—he'd been looking at Runar a lot these past two hours—and Runar nodded. Which in turn had Agmund looking at Thora, brows raised, and Thora sighed, and twisted her hands together.

"I don't know," she said. "I think Selby's right, and there's something—but it doesn't seem like this is the way. Fasta's right too, if we smash our way through here somehow, at best, we have thirty people in this corridor in two minutes."

It was a miracle that they hadn't run into more people, actually, and Runar glanced at Agmund again. "How long can you keep up the repulsion spell *and* the sound-suppressing spell?" he asked, and Selby gaped at Agmund, because he'd been doing that all this time? And what the hell was a *repulsion spell*, anyway, and was that why he'd become increasingly curt this past hour, barely speaking to her or anyone else?

"Not long," he said, voice flat, in answer to Runar's question. "Thora, what are the chances of us sorting this out tonight?"

"Not good," Thora tentatively replied. "Sorry."

Agmund sighed, yanked a hand through his hair. "What about tomorrow, then. We all get some sleep, and reconvene?"

Thora's eyes flicked uncertainly toward Runar, and across from them Henrik looked downright forbidding, his eyebrows heavy, shoulders hunched. "Looking at it any more isn't going to do jack squat," he said. "This is just an abandoned corridor that leads to a filled-in basement. There's nothing else to see."

But suddenly Runar whirled around to face Henrik, his mouth curling into a not-so-nice smile. "And you were doing so *well*," he drawled. "Just so we're all clear, you don't actually believe that last bit there, do you?"

Henrik exchanged a brief glance with Fasta, and then he shrugged, looking defiant. "I'm not lying. It *is* just an abandoned corridor and a filled-in basement."

"Yes, yes," Runar said, impatient. "I'm not calling you on that. I'm calling you on there being nothing else to see. What else is there to see that you're not telling us?"

Henrik didn't answer, and Agmund jerked forward, and grabbed the front of Henrik's tunic. "My patience is getting very fucking thin," he growled. "Tell us, what the *fuck* else is it!"

Henrik shoved at Agmund, enough to make him put a foot back, but he didn't let go of Henrik's tunic. "*Now*, Hallen," Agmund snarled, "or we start talking about that pretty little cottage of yours out in the woods, and when it's going to see its next lightning storm!"

Selby had no idea what Agmund was talking about, but alarm flashed through Henrik's eyes, and Fasta's, too. And now

Fasta was the one stepping forward, and elbowing Agmund away from Henrik. "Listen, fine!" she said. "It's just—"

Agmund took a step backwards, though his hands clutched to fists, his eyes murderous. "*What.*"

"It's just—" Fasta took a breath. "There are still traces of magic in the stone, that's all. It's probably nothing."

Agmund shot an angry glare at Runar, who twitched back a nod. "*She* believes that," he said, under his breath. "But..."

Agmund whirled back toward Henrik, his glower even fiercer than before. "What do *you* believe, then, Hallen?" he hissed. "And do *you* recognize the magic?"

There was another instant's silence, in which Henrik glared back at Agmund—until again, it was Fasta who spoke. "Morley. It's Morley's magic."

Selby's breath caught, her eyes darting to meet Agmund's. *Morley* had been here? Was she part of this, somehow?

"The thing is," Fasta continued, louder now, "Morley would have been consulted when they filled this in, right? She's been here that long, she's an expert in her field, so of course they'd have worked with her on it."

"But," interrupted Runar. "There's something, isn't there?"

Fasta sighed. "It's just—a bit stronger than you'd expect," she said, "for work being done more than ten years ago. But she's probably been reinforcing it, checking on it over the years. It *is* in excellent shape. So it's really likely nothing."

"Then let's go ask her," Agmund snapped, spinning around toward Morley's workroom—until Thora's hand snapped out, and grasped tightly at Agmund's arm.

"No," she said, her eyes gone distant, dazed. "Selby's being questioned tomorrow, and Morley will be there. You can't."

"Oh yes I can!" Agmund retorted, yanking his arm away, but now it was Runar who grabbed him by the shoulder, pulling him backwards.

"Oh no, you can't," he growled. "You dragged Thora around here all night long, she knows what she's doing, and you're sure as hell not going to decide to ignore what she says now. And you're sure, Thora, right? This fool and his raging temper need to stay the hell away from Morley right now, or Selby pays the consequences at this trial tomorrow?"

Thora nodded emphatically beside him, but Agmund was looming over Runar, glaring between him and Thora. "What kind of *consequences*," he snapped. "What the hell does she mean!"

Thora was wringing her hands again, shaking her head, looking visibly distressed. "I can't," she said, her voice rising. "I can't, I'm sorry, you know I would, I want to help, it's against the, the, the—"

She broke off there, because Runar had whirled around to grasp at both her shoulders. "Stop," he ordered, his eyes close and intent on hers. "Look at me. Breathe with me."

Thora's eyes were wide and almost fearful on his face, but she gave a quivery nod, and audibly gulped for air as Runar's shoulders purposely rose, and fell. "You're fine," he said, his voice gone low and soothing. "Everything will be fine. All right?"

But Thora's fearful eyes kept darting over Runar's shoulder, and Runar gave a longsuffering sigh, and spun around to face Agmund again. "There are limits on what Thora's allowed to tell people about the future," he said. "But I can follow the activity in her brain, so *I'm* going to tell you. Morley's not involved in this. At *all*. And if you go down there and start yelling at her, you're going to permanently destroy any chance you have of getting Selby out of this unscathed. So if you even *try*, I'm putting you to sleep *this fucking instant*, for all our sakes."

Agmund let out a sound not unlike a strangled roar, and Selby reached to grip at his hand, and glanced helplessly toward the rest of them. "Look, there has to be something else we can do," she said. "Some other way to get down through this wall, and find out what's going on."

Nobody looked convinced—Thora still looked nearly on the verge of tears—and Runar stepped close beside her, and slid his arm around her shoulder. "Well, it's been great fun," he said, eyes narrowing at Agmund, "but Thora needs to sleep before she collapses on us. We can talk again tomorrow if we must. All right?"

Agmund didn't reply, but Runar tugged Thora away, and she went, with one last apologetic look over her shoulder. While Henrik and Fasta raised their hands, counted to three, and slid the wall back into place with a rumbling *crunch*.

Agmund still looked furious, almost helpless, and while Selby felt the same—like that wall closing was an end, somehow—she was also exhausted, and so nauseous it was becoming hard to breathe.

"Can we go back to your room for a few minutes and talk this over?" she asked Agmund, threading her fingers through his. "Please?"

He didn't reply, but didn't resist, and Selby pulled him toward the stairs. Calling back a quiet thank-you behind her, to where Fasta was wordlessly disappearing the dust on the floor, while Henrik sealed the corner where the wall had opened. Fasta nodded back, but Henrik didn't look up, and Selby tried not to grimace as she yanked Agmund up the stairs, and up, and up.

"This is such bullshit," Agmund growled, once they were alone in his candlelit bedroom. "We were onto something, they were fucking *lying* to us, and you just want to *give up*? And not even *try* to check out Morley again? When those assholes are coming for you tomorrow?!"

Coming for you. It was his mood, his magic, it had to be, and Selby tried to ignore it, went for the ties of his tunic, pulling them apart with fumbling fingers. "Knocking down the whole manor wasn't a good plan, either," she said, as she slid her hands up under his tunic, up against that smooth warm skin. "And Runar said Morley doesn't have anything to do with it, remember? If anything, I think it's more likely to be Ketill."

"Yeah, well, that's because you're in denial!" Agmund shot back, even as Selby yanked the tunic off, and went for his trousers. "I told you, Ketill wouldn't risk it, and we both know Runar's word isn't worth *shit*. The fact is, there's a secret hidden basement with Morley's magic on it, with Anabel's magic on it, and that's awfully fucking suspicious. And just because Morley's nice to you doesn't mean a single fucking *thing*!"

Selby had pulled down his trousers, exhaling at the sight of his hard cock bobbing out toward her, and then knelt down, untied his boots. "Fine," she said, pulling off one boot, and then glancing up, past that too-close, too-hard cock. "You're right, it is suspicious. But even if you don't believe Runar, Thora thought it was a bad plan too, right? Which it *is*, because if you barge in there yelling at Morley, of course she's going to have a perfectly reasonable explanation, and who's going to question her on it? Would Ketill? Who does Morley even report to?"

Agmund grimaced, and he kicked off his other boot, watching as Selby pulled off his socks. "Ketill can't do anything to Morley," he said thinly. "He's tried. She's too close to a few certain people on the Coven's main governing Council."

"Does that include the people in charge of this investigation?" Selby asked, looking up again as she unbuttoned her dress, shoved it behind her to the floor, and then yanked off her shift, too. "Maybe that would actually help me, then, don't you think?"

Agmund didn't reply, his eyes gone still on hers, and Selby realized, with a jolting thrill, that he was naked, and hard, with her naked on her knees before him, his swollen cock just a handsbreadth from her mouth. And it was so easy, way too easy, to lean forward, to drop a soft, open-mouthed kiss to the end of it.

"There's got to be another explanation," she said, once

she'd pulled off, but Agmund twitched, so she did it again. Sucking him in a little this time, tasting him, feeling her eyelashes flutter closed at the salty smooth hardness of it, delving deeper into her mouth.

"Maybe Anabel was an earth-mage too," she added, pulling off briefly, licking her lips. "She could have found a way into the basement herself. Maybe someone else hired her, maybe Ketill or the servants or your horrible *friends*—"

The words were broken by Agmund's cock, sinking between her open lips. "Then why's Morley's magic on it," he said, a little breathless. "And why didn't Morley notice someone fucking around down there. And where the *fuck* is your smell coming from!"

It didn't make sense, and between the taste and feel of Agmund in her mouth, the scattered images of lightning storms all mixed up with his anger, and the strange hungry tiredness in her head, Selby couldn't think, couldn't answer. Could only keep sucking, keep kissing, take him deeper, because this was the only thing right now, the only thing, *my lover*, he'd said, *stay*...

"You're too generous," he said now. "Too forgiving. Somebody's a tiny bit nice to you, probably just using you to benefit them, and you keep getting on your knees for them, taking their cock down your throat."

As if to make his point, he sank himself deeper, almost enough to make Selby gag, but oddly enough she didn't feel sick, felt better than she had in hours. So she just gave a long, deep swallow around him, swirling her tongue against him, sliding her hands up against his hard thighs.

"But what if I like it," she whispered, pulling off again, swallowing through her now-tender throat. "What if it feels—"

She broke off there, not quite meeting his eyes, and suddenly Agmund pulled her up to her feet, and back toward the bed. Dropping his naked body down onto it, and then dragging her down on top of him, all skin to heated skin, warm and breathless and stunning.

"What," he whispered, as he roughly manhandled her, spreading her legs over him. "How's it feel."

Selby couldn't seem to speak, especially when his hand slipped down between them, and brushed up gentle against her hungry swollen wetness. Making her shudder and gasp, and he did it again, this time letting his fingers linger, nudging up just a little between. "What," he said. "Tell me."

Selby's mouth wouldn't work, her thoughts wouldn't work, and oh fuck there were two of his long fingers, sliding slow, purposeful inside. Curling forward, rubbing exactly where she craved it, making her gasp aloud, her whole body clenching so hard against him that the room spun.

"What," he said again, bringing down his other hand, rubbing his thumb up against that hard little nub, and Selby cried out this time, her head swarming with the impossible realization that Regin Agmund was touching her, Regin Agmund was playing with her, Regin Agmund's fingers were on her and in her and soaking wet with her, oh *fuck*—

Too abruptly those fingers slid out, and Selby whimpered, her body convulsing against the loss of them—but then they pulled her apart, open, wider. And Agmund's fluttering eyes were watching, held between her legs, while he guided her down, raised his hips up, and impaled her, slow and deep, onto his massive swollen cock.

"How's it feel," he whispered, even as that cock twitched hard, right up against where his fingers had been, filling even fuller inside her, showing her a single stark lightning bolt, soaring from the sky. And oh gods, oh please, that was it, that was everything, and Selby cried out, grinding down on him as her body shuddered its release, repeatedly gripping at him, craving him, pleading him begging him praying him for more.

It left the world still spinning, the air and sense all vanished, and Selby put her hands to him, looked at those beautiful eyes, flickering in the candlelight. "Wonderful," she said, because that was the only word, the only truth. "The best I've ever felt in my *life*."

Agmund's eyes shifted, changed, and his hands were on her hips now, spread wide and maybe even possessive. "You'd get used to it," he replied, and it took Selby an instant to realize he meant this, him. "You'd want to explore a bit. Try other guys."

This barely made sense, and Selby blinked at him, tried to think. "Why," she gasped, even as he twitched again inside her, as her whole body quivered in response. "You do just fine. Better than fine."

Agmund betrayed a husky chuckle, another twitch of that cock. "Nah, I'm a boring fuck. Remember?"

The words didn't work, Selby's brain didn't work, and she shook her head, searched for truth. "Was just giving you grief," she breathed. "You're an asshole, a bastard, an entitled arrogant *troll*. But not boring. At anything."

Agmund's fingers on her hips spread wider, digging a little tighter. "Better watch yourself, wench. Almost sounds like you *like* me."

Selby should have denied it, but at the moment she was too tired, too thrilled and stunned and caught in this to care. "'Course I like you. Why do you think I keep putting up with your mess?"

There was another shift in Agmund's eyes, something changed. "'Cause you have a contract," he said, and his hips rolled up under hers. "You were paid."

Oh gods, he was still talking, but this seemed important, though Selby couldn't stop her own body from meeting the next roll of his hips, her mouth letting out a strangled gasp. "Already told you, I'd do it for free," she replied, breathless. "With conditions."

Agmund's eyes narrowed, saying something Selby couldn't follow, but his thoughts were carefully distant now, his hips coming up harder, his cock circling inside, impossibly deep. "Why," he said. "'Cause you like my dick, right? Feels good?"

And he did feel good, oh gods, even him saying that felt good, but the words weren't right, weren't quite true. "You know it does," she whispered back. "But there's the rest of it, too."

"Rest of what," Agmund said, harder now, matching the distracting demanding grind of his hips. "My magic, the lightning? Or"—he ground up again, almost painful this time—"you think I'm hot?"

Selby had to shake her head, her breath hissing out through her teeth as she met him again, again. "Your magic *is* good," she managed. "The lightning's hot. But like I said before, *you're* not, not really. Not like that."

Agmund laughed again, and it seemed almost cold, or sarcastic. "Bullshit," he shot back. "You said it, earlier. Called me gorgeous."

She had? Selby blinked at him, gasped at him, tried to remember through the constant driving distraction of that beautiful hard cock. "Did not. Did I?"

"You did," he replied, and Selby had no idea how he was remembering this, how he could keep talking when it felt like this, like that, like this. "When you were raging at me for being white, and rich, and not having a fucking backbone."

Ah. That. The memory was cloudy and vague, and fuck he felt so good, and Selby shook her head again, grasped for words. "Well, you know what I meant," she said helplessly. "You're on portraits, people obsess over you, you're Regin fucking Agmund. You're not actually really—handsome, or pretty, like—"

It was too much, entirely too much, but that cock was still driving up, and up, setting aflame every thought, every nerve under Selby's skin. "Like *what*."

Gods, they were still on this, and Selby's mouth was just talking now, saying things it absolutely should not have said.

"Like Runar, maybe. Like something in a painting. A real one. Not your trash portraits."

Agmund's eyes changed again, into something Selby wasn't sure she liked, and he was driving up so hard now that her body jolted with every thrust. "You *like* him?" he breathed, the words heavy, laced with dislike. "Thought I saw you looking at him, fucking little dead-raising sorcerer *shite*—"

And how could he say things like this, and still feel so damn good, and Selby growled, and shook her head. "Don't like him, you asshole, already told you, I like *you*!"

The pounding was harder, faster, unrelenting, everywhere, everything. "Why," Agmund hissed. "For fuck's sakes, *why*."

His hips drove up again and again and again, his body invading her owning her, and this was important, and she couldn't *think*, and with gritted teeth and scrunched-shut eyes she clamped down on him, on the frenzy on his cock on his body, on everything.

"Stop," she gasped. "Just stop, Regin. *Please*."

He did stop, thank the gods, so sudden that Selby's head was still spinning, that she had to put her hands to either side of his head. Looking down at him, at his unreadable eyes, while she tried to breathe, to follow, to think.

"I like you," she said, between breaths, holding his eyes, "because I want you, sure, and you're *very* good at this, and your magic is brilliant, and you're very tall and you have this cock and this body and these eyes. But"—she took another breath, drew out truth—"you're also—consistent. Honourable. Considerate. I can—rely on you. Trust you."

"Bullshit," Agmund snapped back, his chest heaving under her. "I've treated you like shit. Told you I didn't care about you. Talked about you to other people. Pretended you don't exist around my friends."

His mouth twisted, his thoughts gone dark and bitter, with something almost like self-loathing—and Selby didn't argue it, still holding his eyes. "Yes, that's all true," she said, hoarse. "But you've also been—honest with me. You ask how I feel. You let me take the lead. And you were right, you *have* had principles about this"—she gave a vague, shaky wave downwards—"because even from the start you never pushed me, never demanded anything, never made me feel guilty or ashamed about it. You were—a gentleman."

Agmund didn't speak, just looking at her, and Selby swallowed, kept saying it. "You come to me when you say you will. You're here every night, every morning. You've been understanding when I've been sick. You believe what I tell you. You offered to help me run. You stayed up for hours tonight trying to help me. Giving me an adventure."

His eyes flickered on hers, and Selby couldn't help a soft little rock against that still-hard, glorious cock. "You work so hard," she breathed. "You look like a fae in the forest. You sign trees with lightning, your favourite place is a grove, you dream about your regrets. And you"—she paused, dragged in another breath—"you kept trying when you lost your magic, you want to make a difference, you want to do something that matters. You want to *live*."

Agmund's body inside hers shuddered, perhaps giving its silent agreement, and Selby shuddered back, grinding down harder, pressing deeper. Feeling him do the same, meeting her in this, and this was something too, something too strong to leave unsaid.

"You fuck like you mean it," she whispered now, letting herself arch against him, revelling in the feel of him. "You're *with* me, in it. You call me names and pout and gripe at me, and make me feel like I'm the only girl in the entire *world*."

The last word came out like a gasp, or maybe a sob, and she couldn't look at him anymore, couldn't bear to meet his eyes. And thank the gods, he was driving up again, driving all those thoughts out of her head, the fear the misery the loneliness. Just filling it with this, with him, saying *I am with you, right now, this minute, you're the only one, you're mine, mine, mine*—

"More," Selby gasped, pleaded, as she sank down to lie against him, clinging to him, to his shoulders, his driving pounding hips. "More, harder, please, Regin, *please*—"

There was a glance from his eyes, a swift jolting stillness—and then a flurry of movement, a twisting of limbs, of weight. And then Agmund was above her, looking down at her, his body close and heavy and warm, his breath hot, hungry, *here* on her neck.

"Oh gods," Selby moaned, her entire body clutching up against him, shuddering at the impossible feel of him meeting her, slamming against her, plunging into her with all his weight. "Oh gods, Regin, oh fuck, oh please please *please*—"

He nodded, once, and kept driving higher, brighter, his muscles taut tense glorious. Saying, with every slam of his hips, that he was here, with her, he meant it, in all of this he meant it, and Selby buried her face in his neck, gasped against the strength of it, the blinding wheeling truth of it.

"Please," she said again, in a whisper, a gulping strangled sob. "*Please*, Regin."

He nodded again, blond hair moving silken against her face, his body pulling up tighter, firing in deeper, as far as he could go—and then he was gasping too, groaning into her ear as his cock pulsed and trembled, obeying her, filling her, pumping her full of everything she wanted, needed, adored.

Finally he went still over her, with her gone still beneath him, but for their gasping-together breaths. Until he propped himself up on his elbows, looking down at her, and it was almost unbearable, impossible to meet his intent, searching eyes.

"Look at me," he whispered, so she did, though she couldn't stop blinking, couldn't stop the wetness streaking out the corner of her eye. And she kept blinking, praying to the gods that he'd missed it, but he hadn't, and his thumb came to brush it away, his hand resting soft against her face.

"You deserve better," he whispered now, or perhaps he just

mouthed the words, or said them with his eyes. "So much better."

And then, without warning, for the first time ever, Regin Agmund put his mouth to hers, and—kissed her.

It was soft, warm, sweet, his tongue and lips easy and natural and wonderful on hers. Like they'd been doing this all this time, a hundred times, like their mouths were made to fit together, like a dream where Regin Agmund tasted like a god, like Selby could keep drinking and drinking and never ever be full.

Her hands had gone up to his head, sliding against that cropped hair, pulling him down harder, deeper. And he did, his tongue sinking further into her mouth, tangling against hers, like he owned her, like he was entitled to this. And maybe he was, because the only thing in Selby's head was more of this, more of him, clinging to him so hard she would never have to let go.

It was him who pulled away first, eyes glazed and distant, and he dropped his head down against her shoulder, where she couldn't see him, couldn't follow. His breath still coming too heavy, his chest heaving against hers, and Selby's hands stroked at his back, committing the feel of it to memory, revering it.

"Should sleep," he mumbled finally, into her ear, and Selby swallowed, tried to nod. Not wanting this to be over, not wanting that to be true—but when he lifted himself off he was still facing her, and he yanked her close, tucked her all up against his solid silken heat.

"Night," he whispered, and Selby tried to whisper back, but there were no words, nothing left to say at all.

32

Selby woke to the sound of a sharp rap on the door, and the brightness of the afternoon sun streaming through the window.

"Shit," Agmund's voice said, too close, and he jostled Selby as he leapt out of bed, and yanked on his trousers from the mess of clothes on the floor. And then opened the door, while still tying the trousers, and speaking with someone in low tones that Selby couldn't follow.

When he shut the door again he was looking grim, his eyes not quite meeting hers. "Ketill," he said. "Those investigators are here. Wanting to meet with us in a half-hour."

Fuck. The fear suddenly hammered in Selby's head, too strong behind her eyes, and she stared at Agmund, tried to breathe. And in three long steps he was there, his hand coming to her head in something that, any other time, would have been lovely, reassuring, kind.

But at this point it felt almost painful, almost making it worse, and Selby reached and pulled at it, at him. Pulling him back onto the bed, fumbling with his trousers, and he didn't resist as she yanked the trousers down, shoved him back onto the bed, and slid herself on top.

It was too rushed, too quiet, and Selby couldn't bear looking at his eyes as she did it, so she sank down over him, buried her face in his neck. Felt the slow rhythmic rock of his hips, his fingers gripping wide on her back, his body and his thoughts sinking deep inside her, where they should be, where they belonged.

He groaned aloud as he came, his hands pulling her down hard against him, and Selby closed her eyes, tried to keep herself there, on the feeling of this, of how good it was—but the rest of it was already trickling back, faster and faster until it was almost a roar, a constant pounding shout of fear in her head.

"It'll be fine," Agmund's voice said, a little gruff, and though Selby appreciated the kindness, she couldn't seem to reply, or even look at him. He was the one who hadn't wanted to stop searching last night, and now she was desperately wishing she'd listened, maybe they could have found something, maybe...

"You all right?" he asked now, quieter, and Selby suddenly couldn't bear it, and pulled herself away, off. Going first for the wardrobe, grabbing her cleanest clothes, and then into the water closet, where she shut the door and scrubbed at her face until it hurt.

When she came out again Agmund was fully dressed, and looking finer than she'd ever seen him, in a tunic of white silk, and grey woollen trousers, with his hair brushed and gleaming. Looking not unlike the Regin Agmund of portrait fame, and Selby couldn't help a touch at the tunic, all busy insects and careful tailoring and Ketill saying, *It matters how you look, Regin.*

Selby winced at that, because her own clothes still loudly proclaimed her a pedlar, and she couldn't help trying to smooth out the old fabric of her dress—but Agmund grasped her hand, pulled it away. "You look fine," he said. "You'll be fine."

He was being so kind, far too kind, and that only made it

worse. And worse still was when he pulled Selby out the door, and kept holding her hand as they went down the corridor, like he wasn't ashamed, like he truly didn't care who knew.

Greta was nowhere to be seen, thank the gods, but many of the other mages were, and all of them looked, stared. While Agmund ignored them all, didn't make any sign of acknowledging anyone until they'd reached the bottom floor, and found Ketill, standing in front of the main-floor meeting room.

"You're late," he muttered to Agmund, barely loud enough for Selby to hear, and she couldn't catch what Agmund muttered back. But he kept going, leading her inside the room, and Selby gripped his hand as she stared at the sight of a table full of people, staring back at her.

There had to be ten or twelve of them, all strangers, though Selby's darting eyes caught sight of Morley, at one end of the room. Morley gave a reassuring smile, but Selby couldn't smile back, not with so many pairs of unfriendly eyes assessing her, running from her head downwards, and back up again.

"Mr. Agmund," one of them said, a fair-haired, middle-aged man with drooping ears. "And Ms. Seng, I presume. Please be seated."

There were two empty chairs on the nearest side of the table, and Selby sat, her body twitching at the feel of the chair beneath her, whispering echoes of many meetings long past. Agmund dropped into in the empty chair beside her, while Ketill strode over to the other side, and sank into a seat beside Morley.

"I am Captain Ludwen," the fair-haired man continued, "the head of the Coven's Magical Regulatory Committee. We have asked you here today to testify concerning the recent unexplained death here at Coven Manor. Are you willing to answer our questions truthfully, to the best of your knowledge, and without the interference of any magic on your part?"

His eyes held to Selby's, waiting, and after a swift look at Morley, who was giving a tiny nod, Selby nodded too. "Yes, sir."

Ludwen gave a cold little smile, and glanced down at where a heavy notebook was opened on the table in front of him. "Excellent," he said. "My colleague Mr. Bekkan"—he waved a hand at a short, skinny man across the table—"will observe you for any signs of falsehoods. Ms. Seng, can you begin by telling us when and how you discovered the corpse?"

Selby swallowed, and darted a sideways glance at Agmund—he was staring straight ahead, his eyes blank—but his hand was still on hers, and it gave a little squeeze. *You can do this*, it said. *Just be honest. You've got nothing to hide.*

So Selby began speaking, her voice halting at first. Telling the story of how she'd come down that morning, how she'd followed the smell. How she'd touched Anabel.

At her mention of Anabel's name, Ludwen's eyes sharpened, and he and several others made notes. "And how, exactly, do you know the victim's name, Ms. Seng?"

Selby hesitated, as the fear lurched up—but Agmund gave her hand another squeeze, and cleared his throat. "We looked through the visitor logs, and found Anabel's name," he interjected, voice curt. "Last night."

Ludwen gave Agmund a disapproving glance, though there was a twinge of deference in it, too. "Did you obtain the proper permissions for such a search, Mr. Agmund?"

"No," Agmund replied, his voice even, cool. "I didn't."

Ludwen's eyes dropped, back down to his notebook. "Then, Ms. Seng, can you enlighten us how you determined which entry in what was presumably an extensive visitor log belonged to the victim?"

He'd already been informed about Selby's magic, that was clear, but with Agmund still gripping her hand, Selby told them what they already knew. How she could infer information about people and objects by touching them, and how people could leave a trace after they'd gone.

"And when you do this, Ms. Seng, do you ever draw magic

from your subject?" Ludwen asked, his voice carefully remote. "Or give magic? Transfer it?"

"No," Selby replied, and thank the gods her voice was steady, firm in the truth of it. "Never."

The room was very quiet, with all the eyes in it but Agmund's on hers, and Ludwen's head tilted, his gaze searching, suspicious. "However, your magic is decidedly unusual, Ms. Seng. And we have been informed by several reliable sources that you seem to draw sustenance—or perhaps even health—from objects that were once alive."

There it was, damn him, and the faces around the room looked expectant, now. Like this was exactly where all this was supposed to lead, and Agmund gave another squeeze of Selby's hand, another silent kindness that helped her take in a breath, let it out again.

"Since I can detect traces of an object's history," she said, "I sometimes find certain objects comforting, especially if that history involves a shared memory or person. But there's never any transfer of magic involved."

"But what is to say that your comfort, or your memories, are not fuelled by magic?" Ludwen asked, in a tone that was perhaps meant to be reasonable, but still flashed ice down Selby's spine. "And how can you explain your health being affected by the possession of such items?"

Selby opened her mouth to deny that, to say that her health hadn't been affected in the least by anything—but suddenly the ice was drowning her, because with this building, with the smell, her possessions *had* helped. How often had she relied on them, on their small pocket of reliably clear air, over these past weeks?

"I believe it's a mental effect," she said, a little desperate. "It's comforting to be reminded of home."

Ludwen's eyes angled down the table to Mr. Bekkan, who gave a wave of his hand that said *maybe, maybe not*. Pounding more fear through Selby's skull—she did believe that, she *did*—

but there was a look she didn't like on Ludwen's eyes, something not unlike satisfaction.

"Mr. Agmund," he said now, folding his fingers together. "We would also like to ask you a few questions."

Agmund's hand in Selby's twitched—he hadn't expected to be interrogated, too—and she caught him glancing at Ketill, who gave an almost infinitesimal nod. Which made sense, of course—refusing to answer questions at this point would only raise more suspicion—so Agmund shrugged, though Selby recognized that wary, narrow-eyed look on his face. "Fine."

"Excellent," said Ludwen. "First, kindly inform us precisely what happens to your magic when you touch Ms. Seng."

Agmund's face didn't change, his jaw set. "My access to magic increases. I can draw more from my environment."

The assembled faces glanced at one another, and Ludwen gave a conciliatory nod. "Fascinating. And how much does it increase? And for how long?"

"It depends," Agmund replied, his voice short. "On the frequency and length of contact."

Ludwen's eyebrows went up, in a clearly put-upon gesture. "And what kind of contact would this be, Mr. Agmund? Simply touching one another?"

Selby's stomach flipped in her gut, but Agmund didn't move, didn't flinch. "Sometimes," he said. "But as I'm sure you're aware, Mr. Ludwen, effective use of a magical affinity requires more intimate contact."

"More intimate contact," Ludwen repeated, deadpan. "In what way, Mr. Agmund?"

Agmund's hand in Selby's twitched again, that familiar dislike now curling his lip. "Do we really need to get into specifics?"

"Yes, I'm afraid so," said Ludwen, with an entirely unconvincing gravity. "Your failure to truthfully answer our questions could have grave repercussions for Ms. Seng. I'm sure you don't wish to impede our investigation?"

Agmund's eyes flicked once more to Ketill, but Ketill's face was impassive, and Selby could feel Agmund pulling in a breath, could taste the anger under his fingers. "Sex," he said flatly. "Fucking."

Several people shifted in their chairs around the room, but Ludwen didn't seem to notice. "And did Ms. Seng seem opposed to, ah, performing such *activities* with you in exchange for payment? Did she seem reluctant, perhaps, or embarrassed?"

The anger snapped through Agmund's fingers again, and he hesitated, for long enough that Ludwen leaned a little forward, eyebrows raised high on his pale forehead. "Your honest answer, please."

Ketill gave that infinitesimal nod again, and finally Agmund swallowed. "At first, a little. But not after that."

Selby's face was burning, her hand gone clammy in Agmund's, but Ludwen was still smiling. "How often did Ms. Seng initiate said—activities? Never? Occasionally? Always?"

Oh gods, Agmund couldn't answer that, and the look on his face, the feel in his fingers, said that maybe he wouldn't—but then he glanced at Ketill again, and took another breath. "Almost always," he said. "But I made it clear that she needed to. She was doing her job."

"Of course, of course," Ludwen said, voice cool. "And how often, precisely, would Ms. Seng initiate?"

Selby's heart thudded in her chest, her entire body gone hot and humiliated in her chair, and she couldn't even keep her eyes on Ludwen as Agmund sighed, spoke truth. "A few times a day."

There were a few titters around the room, and when Ludwen spoke again there was amusement in his voice, too. "And you didn't find anything unusual about such—er—enthusiasm, Mr. Agmund? Perhaps due to your—ah—celebrity, that is typical behaviour, where you're concerned?"

Agmund was briefly silent, and perhaps Ludwen waved for

him to continue, because he sighed again. "Not usually," he replied. "Not from the same girl, long-term."

Gods curse Agmund, curse *her*, and even a squeeze of his hand didn't help, couldn't make Selby look up. "Look, I wanted it too," he added, a little rushed. "I was attracted to her. I made my interest very clear."

"Of course," Ludwen said again, his tone too understanding. "But that would likely have been driven by your desire for your magic, yes? Did you ever have relations with Ms. Seng *without* thinking of regaining your magic?"

There was another instant's silence, another exhale of Agmund's breath beside her. "No," he said.

No. And though Selby should have known that, should have expected that, it still hurt, so much that she couldn't breathe. "And also," Ludwen's implacable voice continued, "you didn't allow yourself to be seen with Ms. Seng in public, and you reportedly confided to several of your colleagues that you were only associating with her for the magic. Correct?"

"Correct," said Agmund's quiet voice, and despite the surge of regret behind his fingers, the single word felt like a wrenching, hammering punch to Selby's already-churning stomach.

"With all that in mind," Ludwen continued, kindly now, "did it never occur to you, Mr. Agmund, that perhaps there was something suspicious about Ms. Seng? That perhaps she might have had ulterior motives in pursuing these—ah—*activities* with you? Or that her means of delivering your magic may have been suspect?"

Agmund beside her had gone very stiff, his hand now gripping almost painfully on hers, the anger swelling even stronger than before. "I was suspicious, at first," he said flatly. "But not now. I absolutely believe she's here for the reasons already stated. And that's *all*."

"And why do you believe this, Mr. Agmund?" asked Ludwen's grating voice. "What could possibly inspire such confidence in a woman who—forgive me—only demanded a relatively small sum to make herself extensively available to you, and did so with unprecedented eagerness? A woman with whom you were not willing to publicly be associated with, and who has shown an unusual affinity for corpses, and who is now under investigation for murder?"

There was something in Agmund's hand against Selby's that felt a lot like a spark, and he leaned forward, the fury flushing his face, pounding through his fingers. "You're making a lot of assumptions here, Ludwen," he snapped. "A lack of boredom in the bedroom and a few relics on a shelf have jack *squat* to do with your trumped-up murder charges! She's an innocent girl making the best of a bad situation, and that's all. Would you talk like this about your own daughter? Show some fucking *respect*!"

Ludwen's mouth smiled, at total odds with his cool, glinting eyes. "Your chivalry is admirable, Mr. Agmund. Now please, answer the question. Why do you place such confidence in a woman whose motives are, at best, admittedly questionable?"

Agmund's eyes had briefly closed, his mouth tight. "Because," he said slowly, "she refused Ketill's offer to come here, multiple times. And kept refusing, until she had no choice but to accept."

"Indeed?" Ludwen asked. "In what way, Mr. Agmund?"

There was another twitch of Agmund's hand in Selby's, though his thoughts were carefully distant behind his fingers. "Her family's business was lost to fire," Agmund replied, his voice strangely careful. "And her brother taken very ill."

"Questionable," interrupted another voice—the truth-seeker Mr. Bekkan, his eyes alarmingly alight on Agmund's. "Or perhaps incomplete."

Ludwen's eyes darted between Mr. Bekkan and Agmund, his mouth curling back into that cool smile. "Please reiterate your last statement, Mr. Agmund," he said. "And include the full truth this time."

There was more silence from Agmund, and Selby

realized, belatedly, that perhaps for the first time since he'd started speaking, his eyes were on her. Saying something she couldn't quite read, and then looking away again, toward Ketill.

"Selby refused Ketill's offer to help me," Agmund replied, his voice low, resigned. "And then her circumstances deteriorated until she was obliged to accept it."

They were the same words, or were they, and Selby stared at Agmund, her breath locked in her throat. "*Obliged*?" she repeated, and for an instant the entire room vanished, and there was only Agmund's stiff body, his too-betraying eyes. "By who? *You*?!"

Agmund winced, and jerked a sharp shake of his head. "I had no magic," he said, too quickly. "No idea who you were."

But he'd glanced at Ketill again, sitting there so safe and smug and fucking *untouchable* across the table, and Selby gaped at Ketill, at that truth of it in his eyes. "*You* did that?" she gasped, between her suddenly lurching breaths. "You burned my wagon? Killed my horses? Made my little brother so sick he almost *died*?"

She was shaking, oh gods, and though Agmund tried to keep hold of her hand she shoved it off, put her hands to her face. Ketill had done that, Ketill had singlehandedly gifted her that soul-crushing night of horrified terror, and the endless, despairing weeks afterwards, he had almost *killed* Simon, what the *fuck*—

"And you *knew*?" Selby croaked at Agmund, because that was impossible, she *trusted* him, he would have *said*—but his eyes were guilty, oh gods, he was guilty, he'd known that and he'd still fucked her, had lied to her, had taken *everything*—

"Not at first," he said, desperate, or maybe pleading. "Not until you told me."

Until she'd told him. Yesterday morning. And after that he'd left, he'd said they had to talk again, but that had been when she'd found Anabel's body, and things had gone all awry—but then afterwards, they'd talked in the forest, and last night, he hadn't said, had never even *hinted*—

"Why don't we break for a few minutes?" said a familiar voice, and when Selby glanced over it was Morley, her eyes watching, sympathetic. "Reexamine the available evidence, and meet again in an hour?"

No one protested, thank the gods, because Selby had already stumbled to her feet, staggering for the door. Desperately needing to escape, to go somewhere where she could cry, or scream, or both—

"Selby," said Agmund's voice behind her, low and frantic. "Wait."

But Selby wasn't waiting, couldn't. And she rushed out the door, and shut it behind her, and ran.

33

Selby ended up in Agmund's room, pacing back and forth across it, clenching her fists so tight it hurt.

She should have run. Should have escaped while she had the chance. Because now, under so much suspicion, with all these higher-ups here, in the middle of the day, the chances of actually getting away would be almost hopeless. And Agmund had surely been right, her running would be seen as immediate admission of her guilt, as proof that she'd murdered Anabel—and Selby still couldn't even comprehend why, or how, she was supposed to have done such a thing. How they could possibly imply that *anyone* would ever want to drain magic from an innocent girl, and fuck it into Agmund, who *knew* what Ketill had done to her?

She couldn't keep it straight, couldn't focus couldn't breathe, and when Agmund finally came running up the stairs, and barging into the room, it was almost a relief to see his lying scheming face, to have something, anything else, to fuel the sheer shouting incoherent rage.

"What the *fuck*," Selby breathed, already rounding on him, "was that about? Why didn't you *tell* me?!"

Agmund looked just as furious as she felt, and his face was

white as he slammed the door shut behind him. "I *was* going to tell you," he shot back. "It's just been a bit busy, if you haven't noticed, what with you getting hauled up for *murder*!"

"I didn't murder anyone!" Selby shouted back. "I only touched her! I did *nothing*!"

"I *know*!" Agmund replied, his too-tall body looming too close, too angry. "This entire thing is total bullshit, somebody is aiming for me, for *you*, and for the life of me I can't figure out fucking *why*!"

He'd bellowed the last part, straight into her face, and Selby pulled herself tall, glared straight back. "Maybe look at the upstanding man," she gasped, "who destroyed my livelihood and almost *murdered* my brother and manipulated me into selling myself to you, so he could keep on pulling the strings with these smug leering old assholes!"

Agmund dragged a heavy hand through his hair, and gave a vehement shake of his head. "No," he said. "It's not Ketill. I would know. And yeah, it was vile of him to do what he did to you, but you have to see, he would never do that to *me*!"

"Oh like *hell* he won't," Selby snarled. "He'll do it in a second once you finally stop being useful. You just wait and see!"

Agmund's shoulders hunched, his eyes gone flinty and cold. "Sure, whatever, fine," he snapped. "But he's still sure as hell not going to set me up like this, with a full-on investigation, stirring up a public scandal with the Coven! This is embarrassing for him, and downright dangerous, there's no fucking *way* he'd risk it! He's way too smart, and even he can't find a way out of this mess, so where the hell does that leave us?"

Selby pulled hard at her hair, shaking her head, trying to think. "They have no proof," she said. "Can they charge me without any actual proof? All they actually have is me touching her, right? And me being a filthy pedlar harlot, which I still don't understand how that has *anything* to do with this?!"

Agmund's hand had gone to hers, snatching it out of her

hair. "Don't call yourself that shit. And the case they're trying to make is that you're using illegal means to power me, and your unwarranted enthusiasm is a reflection of that. Because good girls can't actually want to fuck that much, right?"

His voice had gone bitter at the end, and Selby felt the anger jolt again, twisting deep in her gut. "Not with men like them, they don't! And it still doesn't even make *sense*, *why* would I do that, *why* would I risk breaking their laws to help you!"

Agmund gave a jerky shrug, kicked hard at the floor with his boot. "Because I'm Regin fucking Agmund. Or because people do wild shit to try to get in this place all the time. Or because you're trying to set up Ketill, or maybe they even think Ketill's in on it, and paying you more than you're letting on. Or promising future benefits. Or something. There could be a million fucking reasons, and it seems like every asshole in that damned room is ready and willing to be convinced of any of them, or all of them!"

Selby blinked at the floor now, staring down at his familiar black boots. "Because I'm a pedlar," she said, quiet. "And I've sold myself to you for payment, even when you made it very clear that you weren't committing to me in any way. That you were only in it for the magic."

Agmund let out a sharp breath, and those boots stepped closer, his hand coming to slide against her arm. "Fuck *off* with that, will you?" he said, and suddenly he just sounded tired, strained. "You know I wasn't just in it for the magic. Gods, I told them as much, and they didn't call me out on lying, did they?"

That was true, and the too-strong images behind his hand confirmed it—but then Selby shook her head, hard. "Yes, but you still thought about getting your magic back," she said bitterly. "Every single time, you said. And they didn't call you on that, either."

Agmund gave a muffled groan, a little shake of Selby's arm. "Of course I thought about it," he snapped. "I think about it pretty much every second of every fucking day, all right? It's always, *always* there. But that doesn't mean I didn't want you."

Oh. And maybe that was some kind of admission, some kind of truth, and when Selby glanced up, his blue eyes were steady, certain, sure of themselves. "Thought you knew that," he said, quieter now. "Didn't you see?"

Selby had to look away, bite her lip. "Sure, yes, fine," she managed. "But you just like fucking, remember? And so do I. But it doesn't actually mean anything. It doesn't *change* anything."

There was silence from Agmund above her, silence that maybe meant agreement, and Selby's entire body slumped. It didn't change anything, none of it did, and it was finally starting to sink in that maybe she was truly doomed with this, maybe lack of proof meant nothing...

Agmund's hands gripped at both her arms, but then he twitched, and his body angled toward the door. His thoughts recognizing that someone was there, and Selby sighed as he let out a low groan. It was Ketill. Of course.

"Damn it," he muttered, grimacing. "Give me a minute, all right?"

There was no refusing, because Agmund was already going, sidling out the door. Leaving Selby alone again, feeling his presence just beyond the door, but of course he had his sound-spell on again, making sure she couldn't hear a single word they spoke.

He'd said a minute, but it was definitely already longer than a minute, and Selby finally sat down on the bed, twisting her hands together. Looking at her things across the room, and wanting to touch them, but Ludwen's words were still shouting in her head, *you seem to draw sustenance from objects that were once alive...*

By the time Agmund came in again, Selby was half-frantic again, and she leapt to her feet at the sight of him, because focusing on him, on anything, was easier than the chaos currently pounding through her thoughts. "So?" she demanded. "What did he want?"

Agmund shot her a harassed look, and opened his mouth—and then closed it again, and kicked at the floor. "He thinks I should go try and talk to Hendersson," he said. "See if he can try to sway things."

"Who's Hendersson?" Selby asked, nonplussed. "And why would he help?"

Agmund made a face, shoved his hands in his pockets. "He's Greta's father," he replied. "He's on the Committee. One of the old guys downstairs."

Greta's father was downstairs. And Selby stared at Agmund again, her mouth falling open, because first of all, Greta's father was really one of those awful men, and also, Agmund had *known* that? All this time? And he hadn't bothered to even *mention* that crucially relevant fact?!

"I'm not going to talk to him," Agmund said, too quickly. "I can't stand the sight of him anymore, and it wouldn't be any help anyway, not after everything I said down there."

What? And in all of this, in so much ongoing horror today, this seemed to lodge deepest in Selby's head, in her gut. "What the *fuck*, asshole?" she said, her voice sounding strange, shrill. "You're telling me that your testimony down there ruined your chances to cozy up with your ex-girlfriend's *father*? Who just *happens* to be on the committee that's trying to charge me with *murder*?"

Agmund at least looked away, rubbing awkwardly at the back of his neck in his *yeah-fine-I-fucked-up* tell, but the anger, the injustice, the gods-damned betrayal was pounding louder now, so strong that Selby's head ached.

"You are one cold bastard, you know that?" she hissed. "Greta's father is charging me with *murder*, Ketill has willingly destroyed my *life*, all those assholes downstairs are judging and humiliating me, and one of them clearly has a *massive* agenda in getting rid of me for good, and gods only know what the hell they're going to do with me next! And meanwhile you've been letting on that everything will be fine, that I should *stay,* and you'll *help* me? When you *knew* all that, and didn't *tell* me?"

Agmund shot her that look again, all helpless thwarted innocence, and Selby had no patience for this, for him. "You are *fucked*," she breathed. "You say you can't trust anybody, you want people to care about *you*, and then you turn around and throw this kind of betrayal on somebody who actually *does* care? While you bow and grovel to these selfish as fuck *assholes* who will use you up and spit you out without a second *thought*?!"

The anger was finally flaring up in Agmund's eyes, his jaw twitching. "Look, I didn't know for sure Hendersson would be here," he said, voice hard. "I thought he would excuse himself, because yeah, it's way too personal—but he hasn't, so we're stuck with it, and I was *going* to tell you, if you'd lay off me for five minutes! And Ketill's not trying to use me up, he's trying to fucking *help* me!"

"Oh, *sure*," Selby drawled. "Why, he's trying to help you so much that he lied to you about me, didn't tell you what he'd done to bring me here, or that it might be a short-term fix and not to get your hopes up, because I might be charged with using illegal magic! Even if he *isn't* behind this mess of a trial, he's still fucking you over, and you know it!"

Agmund was shaking his head, his eyes narrow and glittering, but Selby wasn't done, not even close. "Why the fuck are you still defending him?" she demanded. "Or any of these horrible people? They don't know you, they don't care about you, they don't care that you hate it here, that you've barely been away from this hellhole in an entire fucking *year*!"

That blazed more anger through Agmund's eyes, and he lurched a step closer, glowering down at her. "You don't know what you're talking about," he snapped. "It's complicated."

But Selby had this, she wasn't letting go, and though it was probably intrusive or inappropriate, she snapped up a hand against his cheek, fingers spreading wide. Looking this time, searching, and it was enough to see exactly what *complicated* meant, and she gave a hard, bitter laugh.

"Of *course*," she said, making no effort to keep the derision out of her eyes, her voice. "Too busy, too important, the Coven needs you, Vakra needs you, same old same old *drivel*. What does it matter if you've been miserable, if your nightmares are horrifying, if you even stopped *eating*! If you're all but a *prisoner* in this awful horrible place, doing an awful horrible job that eats away at your fucking *soul*!"

She was going too far, and she knew it, but some wild part of her was glad of it, not willing to stop, until everything was out between them. "You're deluding yourself, asshole," she continued, her voice almost triumphant, carrying through the room. "You're too wrapped up in your own self-importance to see what's right in front of your face! I guarantee you, you're going to wake up in twenty years and realize that you're alone, and you're miserable, and you've spent your entire *life* doing things that you didn't actually want to do, living in a place you hate, and pleasing people who couldn't care less about you!"

The fury was firing through Agmund's eyes now, crackling in the air all around them, and Selby somehow smiled at him, past the desperate sweeping rage shouting in her own head. "You'll think fondly of me," she said coolly, "and remember I said this, and wonder why the hell you didn't listen."

There was a low, harsh growl, deep in Agmund's throat. "Bullshit," he shot back. "I'm not going to think fondly of you about anything, I probably won't think about you at *all*!"

"Oh, shut your lying mouth," Selby replied, her voice clipped. "You asked me to stay, to be your *lover*, forever! To have your fucking *children*! You don't just get to take that back and pretend anymore like you don't give a damn about me!"

Agmund's mouth opened and closed, working uselessly, probably about to spout some tripe about her bringing back his magic, but Selby wasn't having it. "You know what I think?" she asked, and she reached for him again, pressing a hand to his heaving chest. "You actually *need* someone like me. You *need* someone to finally be honest with you, and tell you the truth. You need to be called an asshole, a self-absorbed short-sighted *troll*, because that's what you really fucking *are!*"

There was a satisfying spark of light in Agmund's right hand, and he was sputtering, breathing hard. "You little *witch*," he growled. "You have no right to call me anything, you're being paid to fuck me, and that's *all!*"

And that was something, and that twisted part of Selby suddenly grabbed at the front of his trousers—and found, surprise surprise, that he was hard, that this was *arousing* him, holy mother of fuck.

"You lying *snake*," she breathed at him, even as she yanked down his trousers, pulled out that swollen cock, gripping it with familiar fingers. "You let them call me a harlot, what the *fuck* are you?"

There was another sharp growl in his throat, guttural and furious, and suddenly Selby was being half-shoved, half-dragged to the bed. And she didn't resist in the slightest, not even when Agmund pushed her down onto it, on her knees, facing away from him.

"I'm your biggest fucking fantasy, witch," he hissed. "I'm everything you've ever wanted, don't even try and deny it, because I fucking *know!*"

His hand yanked at Selby's skirts, bunching them up, and suddenly there was the shocking feel of cool air on exposed skin, all the way from her waist to her legs, still half-encased in her boots. "Tell me, wench," he growled, and oh gods he was spreading her legs apart, pulling her arse up, exposing her to him, exposing everything. "Tell me you don't want it."

With the words there was a hand, brushing up against Selby's bare exposed heat, and she could actually hear her wetness, could feel it on his fingers. "Yeah, thought so,"

Agmund drawled, and now he was the one laughing, cold and hard and triumphant. "Already soaking wet for it, like always."

Selby's traitorous body betrayed a desperate, too-obvious clench against his fingers, and he laughed again, even colder this time. "Tell me you want it," he ordered, and he pulled her up higher, spread her wider. "Say it."

Selby wasn't saying it, she wasn't, but she still wanted it so damned much, needed it, yes, please—and suddenly, oh gods, there was the shocking feel of that familiar slick rounded hardness. Just nudging up against her, and Selby choked and gasped, shuddered deep inside at the impossible thrill of it.

"Tell me, witch," Agmund insisted, and that hardness pulled away, then nudged back against her again. "Tell me you want it. You want *me*."

Oh hell, Selby's hips canted back, trying to take him deeper, more, *yes*—but his hands were there, strong and familiar, holding her still. "Not a fucking chance. Not until you say."

Selby still wasn't saying, but he'd delved in a little deeper, using both hands on her arse to pull her wet body wider, further apart. Like he was looking at this, like he wanted to see this, and Selby couldn't help a strangled moan as he pulled out, slid the hard slick length of his cock all up and down the wet crease of her. "Tell me."

Selby couldn't, she wouldn't, more, yes, *please*, and Agmund huffed another one of those laughs. "Such a stubborn little wench," he breathed. "You should see yourself, your skirts all up with your legs spread and your dripping wet cunt out, practically begging me for my dick."

Oh gods, Selby *loathed* the bastard, but when Agmund sank a little inside again, her body reflexively clamped on him, fought to keep him there. "Yeah, you like that," he gasped, "you love it, this hungry little cunt of yours would take my dick any way I'd give it to you, wouldn't it? You want to be fucked, witch?"

Selby writhed all over, but still didn't reply—so Agmund

yanked out, and gave a light slap of that cock against her, oh fuck. Making her tremble all over, so good, so fucking good, yes, damn him.

"Tell me," Agmund's raspy voice ordered, "or you won't get it. Say it."

Selby groaned aloud, her cursed body fighting to impale itself on him, fighting to hold him there. And there was the shocking, thrilling feel of another slap of that cock, and she groaned again, her arms shaking under her, her thoughts full of nothing but this, *please*...

"Say it," Agmund breathed, with a circling, delving dip of that cock inside. "Say, 'fuck me, Regin.'"

Oh, gods, yes, and he kept doing it, dragging up more gasps, more groans, from Selby's throat. "Say it," he hissed again, and he was making shallow thrusts now, sinking just barely inside. "Say it, or I'm going to blow just like this, and this is all you'll get, I swear to fuck."

He wouldn't dare, the asshole, but the panic the craving was here, everywhere, and Selby fought to swallow, to breathe. "Fine," she gasped, even as he delved inside again, as her body gripped at him, hard. "Fuck me, Regin. Please. *Please.*"

He gave a low groan, a twitch of his fingers on her hips—and then he plunged deep inside. So fierce and full and wonderful that Selby shouted, maybe even screamed, because oh he was everywhere, everything, how could anything be so huge, so completely overwhelming—

He held himself there, making her feel it, and she ground hard and desperate back against him. Feeling his bollocks pressing low between her legs, his cock circling deep in her belly, and fuck it was so *good* like this and why the *fuck* hadn't they done it before—

"Thank me, witch," came his strangled voice behind her. "Say 'thank you, Regin', and I'll fuck you properly."

Oh gods, he was going to fuck her properly, and Selby's

gasping breath just said it, couldn't stop. "Thank you, Regin. Thank you, fuck me, *please*."

And that was it, because he gave a harsh, helpless growl, and dragged himself out—and then slammed back in. Making Selby's eyes roll back, her arms trembling dangerously, but he held her still, and did it again, and again. Driving deep and strong and furious, fucking her owning her *everything*.

"Tell me you like it," he breathed, between thrusts. "Tell me you like me."

Oh gods, oh please, and Selby was too far gone to notice, to care. "I like it," she gasped back, even as he sank deeper, harder, angry bright beautiful. "Oh gods, I like it, I love it. I love *you*."

I love you.

There was an aching hanging stillness, an instant where he hesitated, sunk deep inside—and then he was spraying into her, pouring out that warm wetness while he groaned, long and loud enough that it went all the way to Selby's bones.

And without warning Selby's body flared up too, needing him taking him craving him, pulsing out frenzied and reckless and wonderful all around him. With a relief that was almost stunning, head-spinning, shattering the bed, the room, the world.

Agmund hadn't moved, maybe waiting for her to finish, and there was another silent hanging instant, his fingers spreading on her skin—and then he cleared his throat, swallowed loud enough that Selby could hear it. And then he drew backwards, away from her, *no*—but when she whirled around to look, he was already yanking up his trousers with fumbling hands, his face a furious shade of red.

"Sorry," he mumbled, not looking at her. "Fuck, I'm sorry. Lost my temper, shouldn't have—"

He couldn't actually be apologizing, like that hadn't been quite possibly the most glorious fuck of Selby's life, in an ever-increasing line of also-glorious fucks. And in an instant she was off the bed, yanking down her skirts, standing on shaky legs, and touching him.

"Don't," she said, desperate, clinging to him. "Don't you *dare* apologize to me for that. I *wanted* that."

It was appalling, maybe, and Selby should have been embarrassed, ashamed. Especially since Agmund obviously was, giving a twitchy shake of his head, and pulling his trouser ties too tight, and refusing to meet her eyes.

"I wanted that," Selby repeated, gripping at his tunic, and suddenly she needed to make him see it, to hurl out the last of the truth between them. "And maybe—maybe I even wanted you angry, I was winding you up on purpose, all right? Because this"—she waved wildly at him, the room—"this isn't going to continue, Regin, all right? You have to see that. They're going to get rid of me in some way or another, and it's going to be very soon, and"—suddenly her breath felt dangerous, frantic, lurking in her throat—"and after that I'll probably never see you again. So why not end it with what we both wanted?"

Agmund stared down toward her, his eyes blinking, once, and again. "They're not going to get rid of you," he said, but nothing about that was convincing, not his voice, his face, his eyes. "We'll figure it out. They have no right. No proof."

Selby attempted a shrug, because hadn't he been the one to say, earlier, that it didn't matter? That they had a million made-up reasons, and surely one of them would stick? And Greta's father was there, sitting in judgement over her, and what the hell else was there to say?

"Look, if you wanted," Agmund said, thick, "you'd see me again."

Selby tried to smile, to let on that she believed that, but it didn't quite work, and now her voice was just saying it, anyway. "You might as well be honest, Regin, you're not really ever going to leave your life as the world's greatest air-mage to go hang around with a pedlar, are you? And even if I get out of this with my magic intact, I'm not going to be set up as your secret harlot, and watch while you live your real life with someone else. I can't"—she dragged in air—"I wouldn't be able to bear it. All right? So once this is done, it's done."

Agmund was staring at her again, his eyes strange, and he opened his mouth to speak—but then there was a knock on the door, and he groaned aloud, his eyes squeezing shut. "It's Ketill again," he said, voice thin. "We'll be wanted back downstairs."

The sudden surging fear was cold, then hot, then cold again, and Selby twitched a shaky nod. While Agmund strode to the door and yanked it open, said something curt to Ketill, and shut it again.

"We're late," he said, his voice distracted, his hand yanking through his hair. "But look—this isn't done, not yet, all right? We'll fight it, get out of it, no matter what happens, it's going to be *fine*."

It sounded slightly more convincing this time, like maybe he really did believe that, and Selby didn't have the will to argue. Just nodded, and then dropped her eyes, and went for the door.

Agmund didn't hold her hand this time, but he stroked her back once they reached the meeting room, and found Ketill's stiff form waiting outside it. Looking at them like *they'd* done something wrong, the conniving lying *bastard*, but Selby raised her chin, and walked past him as though he wasn't there.

But too soon they were back inside that room, sitting in those chairs, being stared at by those same faces. Like it was a recurring dream, a nightmare that didn't end, and Selby was wishing again that she'd run for it, after all, that she'd taken that time just now to do something productive, anything, rather than fucking Agmund, saying goodbye—

Her breath was coming too fast, too shallow, and even Agmund's hand gripping hers didn't help. Especially when Ludwen leaned over the table, and gave Selby a smile that made her skin crawl.

"I'm afraid, Ms. Seng," he said, "that further evidence has

come to light. And on behalf of this Committee and our esteemed Coven, it is my regretful responsibility to charge you with murder."

34

Murder.

Selby should have expected it, should have braced herself, but maybe she'd thought they would come at it from a roundabout way, with hints and implications. But this—*charge* you, he'd said—was so shocking, so suddenly terrifying, that Selby could only stare at Ludwen, while her heartbeat screamed in her ears. Murder. *Murder.*

"Murder," Agmund repeated, sounding blank, distant. "But you have no proof!"

Ludwen turned his smile on Agmund, and it was indulgent, almost sympathetic. "My dear boy," he said, "I'm very sorry to tell you this—but we do."

They did. Agmund's hand on Selby's clamped very tight, and she was deeply, distantly grateful when he spoke again. "What," he demanded. "Tell me."

Ludwen smiled again, and gestured across the table to one of the interchangeable men. "Mr. Dainn is our earth-magic specialist," he said. "Please, tell us what your team has found."

Mr. Dainn was pale and mousy-haired, and his light eyes glinted unkindly on Selby's face. "One of our biggest questions, of course," he said, "was how the victim accessed Coven

Manor—and Ms. Seng—without being detected. The manor is structurally sound, with excellent security precautions—however, we were told that Ms. Seng has spent considerable time in the garden."

Selby stared at him, not following, and Mr. Dainn inclined his head across the table, toward where Morley was sitting, her eyes strangely grim. "With Augusta's help," he continued, "we found a very cleverly concealed underground tunnel. A passageway, leading from the garden, out into the forest."

A *tunnel*? Selby blinked, swallowed, fought to find her voice. "What does that have to do with me?" she asked. "That isn't my kind of magic, I can't even dig a hole, let alone a tunnel!"

The disdain flared in Mr. Dainn's eyes, and he gave a dismissive sniff. "The evidence contradicts you, Ms. Seng. Traces of your magic were all over the passageway, on multiple items. Suggesting that even if you didn't create it yourself, you used it, multiple times."

What? Selby flinched all over, and wildly shook her head. "I never even heard of a passageway," she told him, helpless, choked. "I have never used one. Ever."

Mr. Dainn's eyes didn't change, still gleaming with that dislike, and beside Selby, Agmund cleared his throat. "And look, even if she had used it," he said, "what would that prove? That she found a tunnel? Big fucking deal."

Ludwen gestured at Mr. Dainn, who spoke again. "The passageway also held multiple traces of our victim. Suggesting that it was used for clandestine meetings between the victim and Ms. Seng, no doubt to exchange magic. Magic that Ms. Seng would then transfer to Mr. Agmund."

It was preposterous, impossible, and Selby shook her head, so hard the room spun. "I only saw Anabel twice," she said. "That's all. I never exchanged anything with her. I *swear*."

"Wrong again, Ms. Seng," countered Ludwen, and Selby stared as he smiled again, and pulled something out from under the table. It was a little bundle, wrapped in cloth, and Ludwen unfolded it to reveal a small, grey stone.

"Do you recognize this, Ms. Seng?" he asked, and though Selby should have lied, should have tried, she could only seem to nod. It was one of her rocks, one of the many that had been put away into storage that first day, with all her other things.

"It—it was mine," she stammered, quiet. "But it was in storage. I haven't seen it or touched it since I came here."

"Perhaps the first truth you've told us today, Ms. Seng," said Ludwen's smug voice. "At least, partially. This stone was found on the victim's corpse, and our analysis suggests it had been with her for several months—precisely since when you arrived."

What? Selby couldn't *think*, because how would Anabel have gotten that? Could she have broken into the storage room somehow...

"Maybe someone broke in, and took it," Selby said, high-pitched. "I didn't give it to anyone. I'm not lying, I swear it, aren't you supposed to be able to *tell*?"

She shot a frantic look over at Mr. Bekkan, the one who was supposedly evaluating them for signs of untruthfulness, and he made a face that was distasteful, or disapproving. "Under ideal conditions, yes," he replied. "But when a subject's body is flooded with an anxious response, as yours is now, the variations between truth and untruth are often too subtle to be admitted into an official investigation."

What the *fuck*, and Selby glared at him, her hand gripping desperately onto Agmund's. "So you're saying it only counts when it benefits you?" she demanded. "Or that you're not good enough to tell the difference? Why don't you get Runar Alariaq down here and see if *he's* good enough!"

That was absolutely the wrong thing to say, judging by Agmund's quelling look, and the exchanged glances around the table. Because of course, Runar wasn't one of them either, and there was so much fear and fury shrieking in Selby's head that she wanted to scream.

"So Anabel came across a rock that Selby had once," Agmund's voice said, quickly. "So what. How is that proof of anything."

"Because, Mr. Agmund," said Ludwen, placidly, his finger stroking at the rock, "this is not just any rock. This rock"—he looked at Selby, eyes suddenly sharp—"came from the sky. Didn't it, Ms. Seng?"

This sounded like an accusation of some kind, but Selby couldn't see why, couldn't stop her head from nodding. "Yes. That's why I kept it."

"Indeed," said Ludwen. "And as I'm sure you're aware, rocks like this one are in very high demand, particularly with smiths working in machining, and weaponry. A rock like this"—he lifted it higher, squinted at it—"would have fetched a tidy sum at auction. More than a year's wages, for a person of your position."

A person of her position. The rage surged again, almost too shrill to be ignored, and Selby fought to think, to find recourse. "How would I have known that?" she countered. "I don't work with smiths, they buy from foundries and mines, not pedlars! I just found a rock I liked, and kept it!"

"And gave it to your victim," Ludwen said smugly. "As payment for her services. Until you drained too much magic from her, and killed her!"

No, no, no, this wasn't happening, and Selby shook her head, frantic, bewildered. "I didn't. I swear I didn't."

"As we have already noted, Ms. Seng," said Ludwen, smooth, implacable, "the evidence disagrees with you. And perhaps the most damning evidence of all is Mr. Agmund's magic itself!"

Mr. Agmund's magic. Agmund shot a swift, uncertain glance at Selby, perhaps just as confused as she felt, while Ludwen kept talking, digging her ever deeper. "We have studied Mr.

Agmund's magic, Ms. Seng," he added, "as found in numerous traces around this facility, from his various exercises and projects these past weeks. And Mr. Agmund's magic shows considerable evidence of being tainted. Contaminated. With large amounts of your victim's magic."

What? That was impossible, absolutely absurd, but Agmund shot Selby another brief, searching look. And for the first time since they'd stepped foot in this room, there was doubt in his eyes, behind his fingers on hers, something wary, unsure.

"And those amounts have been considerable enough," continued Ludwen, "to suggest that they have been infiltrated into Mr. Agmund's magic regularly. Over the course of months."

Months. Selby's head was truly aching now, shouting pounding whirling the room around her. Months? Someone had been infiltrating Agmund's magic with Anabel's for months? How? *Why*?

"Do you deny it, Ms. Seng?" said Ludwen, his voice now almost conciliatory, sympathetic. "Will you confess? If you do, you may qualify for a reduced sentence."

A reduced sentence. And despite everything, something leapt in Selby's gut, maybe they would let her go, maybe—

"What kind of reduced sentence?" she heard herself say, and Agmund's eyes, Agmund's eyes were killing her, destroying her. While the satisfaction in Ludwen's was almost palpable, something alive.

"You may be permitted to keep your magic," Ludwen said. "Or at least, some facets of it."

Her magic. Of course that was what was at stake, then, and the strangled sinking in Selby's gut twisted even deeper. "And would I be imprisoned as well?" she asked, in a voice that didn't sound like hers. "Confined?"

"You are being convicted of murder, Ms. Seng," replied Ludwen's implacable voice. "It is beyond any of our power to allow you to roam free. However, you may qualify for early release, if you cooperate with certain conditions. Your magic is quite fascinating, and may, perhaps, lead to work that is useful."

Oh. Oh, gods. She would be using her magic to work for the Coven, she would be just like Agmund, but without the wealth, the status, the freedom. And Agmund was still looking at her, and his eyes, oh gods, oh gods.

Just confess it, then, he said, too clear through his fingers. *I understand. Keep your magic.*

What? He wanted her to *confess*?! Selby spun and stared at him, blinking—and then, all in a rush, finally, *finally*, she understood. *That* was the choice Agmund had made. Stay here, stay trapped, stay imprisoned. Keep obeying, keep doing work he hated, keep his head down—for the magic. For Ketill's brilliance, for access to researchers, for anything that might help. For *hope*.

And the magic was so much. So many things. And such a crucial part of Selby's existence that the prospect of losing it, forever, was staggering, horrifying, so painful that she almost couldn't bear the thought.

But then, the alternative? To be trapped in a place like this? To work for people like this? To become what Agmund had become, what she'd condemned him for? What they'd fought about gods knew how many times?

Selby swallowed hard, and then pulled herself straight in her chair, lifted her chin, and met Ludwen's eyes. She would face her fear, her future, her truth. Total honesty.

"No," she said. "Never. I won't."

35

Selby's refusal set off a chorus of muttering, grey heads conferring, saying words she couldn't hear. While Agmund just stared at her, his eyes glimmering with shock, or maybe fear.

"You have to," he breathed, out loud, his hand on hers gone clammy and hot. "Don't you see, it's not just your magic they'll take away—"

But Selby was not confessing to a murder she hadn't committed, she was *not*. Not even when Ludwen rose to his feet, puffed out his chest, and looked down his nose at her with barely veiled disgust.

"Very well," he said, clipped. "In that case, Ms. Seng, you will be escorted to the capital for sentencing and magic-draining and imprisonment. You have a half-hour to put your affairs in order before we depart."

Imprisonment. *Draining*. And though Selby had known, already, that this was her future, she couldn't seem to move. Couldn't even watch as Ludwen swept from the room, as Agmund roughly shoved his chair back, leapt to his feet, and followed.

Ketill immediately stood up too, rushing out after Agmund,

and slowly the rest of the room filtered out, some of them giving Selby little shakes of their head as they passed. All sadly disapproving of the lying pedlar harlot, all not caring about her fate beyond this, and Selby blankly wondered which one was Greta's father, which one could now rest content in the fact that he'd inflicted a proper punishment on the Agmund-stealing pedlar.

It left Selby sitting there alone, staring at her hands, while her breaths came shorter, quicker. Imprisonment. Draining. Sentencing. So no more magic, then, no more outdoors, no more hope of seeing Simon and her mother again. No more feeling the truth behind anything anymore, no more memories, and a hard shudder clamped down her back, the grief choking strong in her throat.

"Hey," said a quiet, familiar voice, and when Selby glanced up there was Morley, looking down at her with sympathy in her eyes. "I'll come with you to collect your things, if you like."

Right. A half-hour, to put her affairs in order. So Selby nodded, wiped at her damp eyes, and stood. Staggering slightly as she followed Morley out the door, as she walked away from the too-strong feeling of Agmund, just a few doors down, furiously pacing back and forth across Ketill's office.

But there was nothing he could do, or Ketill could do, that had been very clear, and Selby wiped at her eyes again as she silently followed Morley up the stairs, toward Agmund's room. Passing gods knew how many people along the way, all giving her looks that were mocking or curious or even triumphant, and Selby didn't even look, didn't care. Not even when Greta's tall form passed by, arm in arm with another blonde girl, and together they merrily laughed, the sounds ringing down the corridor after them.

"Arrogant brats," Morley said, with feeling, once they'd passed, but Selby couldn't even muster up the energy to agree. Agmund would never go back to Greta, that had been very clear, but gods knew what else he would do instead, and something bubbled up in Selby's throat, too close to a sob.

"Can I," she began, once they'd reached Agmund's room, and she'd touched the closed door. "Could you just—give me a minute, alone? Please?"

Morley hesitated but nodded, again with that sympathy in her eyes, and Selby slipped inside the room, shut the door, and leaned back against it. Tried to breathe, to find focus balance *something*, but there was nothing there, nothing inside. Only the strangled lurking sobs, the breaths coming so fast there were stars sparking behind her eyes.

She lurched for the shelf, her steps sideways and staggering, and then dropped to her knees beside it, touching, holding, cradling her things. Her father's box, Scarper's skull, Simon's whistle, her mother's hair, and there was no way she could risk taking any of these with her, where they might be used against her, or carelessly thrown away, or lost.

"Oh, Papa," she whispered, putting the box to her cheek, and finally there were the gasping, broken sobs, escaping out her quivering mouth. "What am I going to do, they're taking away my magic, taking away Regin, taking everything—"

There was no answer, of course, but Selby kissed the box, let the feel of it filter into her skin. The love, the warmth, the affection, all things she had had, once. Things that were still with her, even if she couldn't feel them, even if everything else had gone.

It was enough, maybe, to let her stand and stumble over, still with the box in hand, to open Agmund's desk drawer. Finding the paper and a quill there, and ink, and Selby's fumbling hands pulled them out, smoothed out a sheet, opened the inkwell, dipped the quill into it.

Dear Ma and Simon, she wrote, the letters looking wobbly, wrong. *I have been accused of a crime, and it seems I will be locked away, and my magic lost.*

The sobs again swallowed her, wracking out her throat, and

Selby gripped at her father's box with her other hand, took gasping breaths until she could write again.

I hope you won't worry, she wrote. *I hope none of this returns to affect you in any way. I hope you will carry on and do well and make me proud. Simon, I hope you will keep practicing until you are the greatest fighter in the world.*

Selby's hand was shaking again, and she made to shove away the quill—but then she swallowed, and put it back to the paper.

I hope Regin will return my things to you, she added. *And I hope you will place no blame on him for any of this, as he has been good to me. I love you both. Goodbye.*

The last words came out shaky, almost unintelligible, and Selby wiped off the quill, put the stopper back in the ink. And then tucked it all away in the drawer again, with her letter on top, and a silent prayer that Agmund would find it, and send it.

"Selby?" came Morley's voice, and with it, a soft knock on the door. "Almost done?"

Right, damn it, and Selby propelled her trembly body to the wardrobe, and pulled her few things out of it. Her shifts, her dresses, her cloak. And her bags were still in storage, so there was nothing to put any of it into, but there was a ratty-looking old satchel in the bottom of the wardrobe, and with a silent apology to Agmund Selby took it, and started stuffing her clothes inside.

But the stupid satchel, of all things, tasted so strongly of Agmund, reeked of Agmund—he must have travelled with it often, kept it close with him—and Selby's breaths were strangling again, catching hard in her throat. She'd probably never see him again, he'd go on to live his life without her, but maybe he'd lose his brilliant magic for good, just like she was about to lose hers, and the sobs were escaping again, wracking out ragged and desperate, and refusing to stop.

There was another knock on the door—Morley again—but Selby couldn't seem to open it, couldn't move. Just stood there, bawling, in the middle of the room, until Morley finally opened the door, and stepped inside.

"Oh, Selby," she said, reaching out a hand toward her—but then she seemed to think better of it, and dropped the hand back to her side. "I'm so sorry all this has happened."

She did look sorry, her eyes tired and shadowed, and Selby sucked back a wavering, unsteady breath. "It wasn't anything you did," she croaked. "You've always been so kind to me."

Morley's mouth slightly twisted, her gaze briefly lowering—and for a hurtling instant, a small, sputtering hopefulness flashed through Selby's thoughts. "And you must know," she added, breathless, "that I didn't do it. Right? That I couldn't have done it?"

Morley's eyes were grave, careful, and Selby's hand snapped out toward her, gripping her arm tight. "*Please*," she breathed, and then halted, skidded, because—

What was this? In Morley's thoughts? *Anabel*? Leaning against that wall, in the darkness, saying, *I can't do it anymore...*

"Wait," Selby gasped, and suddenly the whole world spun around, settling itself wrong and sideways. "You—did you know Anabel? Did you *see* her?!"

The look that crossed Morley's eyes was swift, unreadable—but it was *there*, an admission of something, and Selby's entire body went cold. "You knew Anabel," she said again, slower this time. "How did you know her, Morley?"

Morley blinked, and she twitched a purposeful shake of her head. "I never once met her," she replied, but she was lying, oh gods she was *lying*, oh fuck, what had Agmund said?

"You did," Selby whispered, and the world shifted again. "You did, and they found your magic on the stairwell. What's in the stairwell?"

Morley's eyes kept blinking, and her mouth slid into a smile, one that seemed oddly dissonant against the rest of her pale face. "There's nothing in the stairwell," she said, in a smooth, placating voice. "You're imagining things, Selby."

But Selby was not imagining things, she *wasn't*, and she dropped the satchel, stepped closer. "You knew Anabel," she said, her voice sounding like someone else's. "Did you bring her here? Did you lock her in that place and make her work until she *died*?"

Morley shook her head, still giving that awful smile, and Selby stepped closer. "You did!" she shouted. "Agmund was right, I should have known, you were hiding something! Was it you who framed me, too?"

Something else passed across Morley's eyes, and Selby didn't know whether to laugh, or sob. "Of course," she said, between her too-shallow breaths. "The tunnel. My things. The rock in Anabel's pocket. All things easily accomplished by a good proper earth-mage. By *you*?!"

Morley's smiling mouth opened, and closed again, but she was guilty, *guilty*, and even as Selby still couldn't fathom it, she spun and stumbled for the door. For Agmund, she needed to find Agmund, he'd known, he was such a suspicious cranky bastard and he'd *known*—

"Where are you going?" Morley demanded. "Stop!"

But Selby didn't turn around, and she swiped for the latch, about to yank the door open—when somehow, the latch *moved*. Sliding itself out of her reach entirely, while something cold slid up against her from behind. And when she whipped around to look, it was a piece of curving silver metal, scaling up her arm like an honest-to-gods snake, and then—she cried out—slamming her arm hard, strong, to her back.

"What the fuck," she breathed, but there was more metal, in Morley's hand, and now flying through the air, straight toward Selby's face. Breaking off her rising scream as the metal forced itself between her lips, reshaping into a hard ball against her tongue, while a wire-thin strap tightened itself behind her head.

"Quiet, please," Morley said, her voice high-pitched,

strained. "I can't allow you to spread these vile rumours. It's deeply unfair to me, and the work I've done here."

Selby shouted back, protesting with all her strength, but her words had turned to mush, trapped by that steel ball between her lips. And when she flailed and groped for it, her hand was suddenly snapped backwards too, by yet another string of metal, flying through the air from Morley's fingers.

"It's unfortunate that you need to be restrained," Morley's cold voice said. "But with such behaviour, I've had no choice. Now, come along quietly, and I'll deliver you to Ludwen."

Deliver her to Ludwen. Like hell she would. And even if Selby didn't have her arms or mouth, she still had her feet—so she surged forward as fast as she could, and aimed a sharp kick straight toward Morley's soft, undefended belly.

It landed with staggering force, and Morley choked and bent double, reeling backwards across the room. "How *dare* you!" she gasped, but Selby swept up her other foot, and slammed it against Morley's chest. Knocking her back against Agmund's shelf this time, hard enough to knock Scarper's skull off onto the floor.

"Stop this!" Morley ordered, breathless, clearly in pain. But Selby didn't care, and rushed forward again—until another strip of metal flew from Morley's fingers. Transforming itself into yet another wire-thin thread that snaked toward Selby's neck, and circled tight and close around it.

The pain flared sudden and shocking, drenched in dizzying panic, and Selby fought to wrench her arms free, to pull the wire off. But her hands were still clamped tight behind her back, and she gasped at the feel of the wire breaking the skin on her neck, closing tighter every time she breathed.

"Now listen," Morley said, between gasps, her hands still clutched to her belly. "You are going to cooperate, and walk downstairs with me to Ludwen. Do you understand?"

Selby's thoughts screamed their fear and their fury, trapped in Ludwen and the choking agony around her neck—but suddenly there was a single thought, swarming louder than the rest. *Downstairs*. If they went downstairs, maybe she could find Agmund. Maybe she could tell him, show him, somehow, that he'd been right.

So Selby nodded, shaky and quick, and Morley's mouth widened into that non-smile again. "Excellent," she said, in such a similar tone to how she'd always praised Selby's plant identification, and Selby's stomach curdled, and very nearly retched. She'd trusted Morley, Morley had always been so kind, and had it all been a lie? *Why*?

But there was no way to ask, and Morley gingerly picked up Agmund's satchel with two fingers, and yanked the door open. "After you," she said, so Selby went out, still with her hands clamped behind her back, the gag stuffed in her mouth, and that metal circle tight around her neck.

There was no one in the corridor, at least not here, and when Selby started for the main staircase, the metal in her mouth powerfully pulled, dragging her in the opposite direction. Toward the servants' deserted back stairs, and that complicated things, meant that Morley was taking her out the back, away from Agmund entirely...

But Selby still had her feet, still had her magic. And once they'd gone down one flight of narrow stairs, and then two, onto the second-floor landing—she spun, and ran. Pitching off as fast as possible toward the other stairs, toward that bright powerful taste of Agmund, still there, still waiting—

The metal snapped backwards, sharp, and Selby flailed, kicked, fought as it dragged her back, and back, and back. Back to Morley, who looked downright livid, her eyes glittering coals in her pale face.

"You said you were going to cooperate," she said thinly. "This isn't cooperation, Selby."

Maybe Selby's eyes gave her away, through the sputtering towering rage, and something changed, shifted, in Morley's eyes. "You were going to Agmund," she added, slow. "Weren't you?"

Selby's breath heaved, scraping out her too-constricted neck, and Morley gave that awful, thin smile again. "You *were*. After everything he and Ketill have done to you, you would go back to him? Against me?"

Against me. Like Selby owed Morley some kind of loyalty, and Morley's hands fluttered, her eyes darting downwards toward where Agmund was waiting. "You would," she hissed. "You *will*."

Yes, Selby fucking would, and maybe Morley saw that too, her hands scrabbling together, fingers twisting tight. Even as Selby could feel the taste of Agmund finally moving, striding from Ketill's office, with Ketill at his side, toward the manor's main door. To stand beside where—Selby's senses strained, caught—Ludwen was waiting. And did that mean—was Agmund *coming*? With her? To wherever they were taking her?

The hope lurched up, so strong she swayed on her feet. Because if Agmund was coming, surely she could find a way to tell him, show him, explain everything—

"*No*," Morley spat, and maybe she'd just seen the same thing Selby had, her eyes distant and furious. "Those interfering swine, gods *curse* them—"

Something almost like a laugh bubbled up from Selby's gagged mouth, and Morley whirled to face her. "No," she said again. "No. I will not allow this. I have worked far too hard for this. You are ruining *everything*, Selby!"

With that, Morley spun and spread both hands against the staircase wall beside them. Muttering something, making the magic swirl and bend strong in the air, and then—Selby tried to cry out, failed—the earth shifted, spun, settled again.

And everything went black.

36

Selby staggered sideways, her shoulder crashing into something hard and solid. A wall.

It was bare stone, old and quiet, and Selby leaned into it, twisted sideways to brush her hand against it—and then she gasped, staggered again. It was the manor's wall, down to the awful nauseating smell inside it, but how? Where?

There was no sound from Morley, though Selby could feel her in the darkness, almost close enough to touch. And the metal in Selby's mouth jerked again, dragging her sideways, and she fought desperately to follow it, to stay upright.

She was trailing behind Morley, she realized, moving through a narrow black space. A passageway, perhaps, in the walls, and she could feel the stone shifting behind her, sliding and settling into place. Yes, a passageway, deep inside the manor, and one that Morley was creating as she walked.

There was no clarity or sense to it, no way to gauge direction or location, and even Selby's ever-present awareness of Agmund's distant form seemed muddled, lost. Up somewhere, but not clear where, especially as they turned, and turned again, and again. Almost seeming to go backwards, and forwards again, and maybe Morley was trying to disorient her, or maybe this was just the way, but to *where*?

Whatever it was, it was far too close, too tight, too dark, and Selby's breath was coming faint and panicked. How were they in the walls, why was the air so stale and rotten, why was that cursed smell growing even stronger—

Her feet halted, her stomach writhing and wrenching in her gut, surging sudden bile up her throat. But it was trapped, oh gods, caught in her mouth with that damned steel ball, and she choked and gasped and silently screamed—

The ball spat out of her mouth with a sharp, painful wrench, and Selby dropped to her knees, and vomited onto the stone floor. Gods damn it, curse it, where the fuck, what the *fuck*.

"Why," she gasped, once she'd spat out the last of it, once her breath and stomach allowed her to speak again. "Why are you doing this to me? I helped you. *Trusted* you."

She could feel Morley hesitating, somewhere ahead in the blackness, and Selby shoved to her staggering feet, and followed. But she could only taste a faint trace of Morley ahead, and had she ever really known what Morley's magic even tasted like?

"I had no intention of hurting you," Morley's voice said, finally, sounding faded, and tired. "I still don't, Selby. I *like* you."

She liked her. It made no sense, and Selby struggled to keep up, to follow through the too-close, twining blackness. "Then why?" she demanded, and twitched at the feel of the stone walls folding together behind her again, closer and closer. "And where the *hell* are you taking me?"

Morley scoffed, and then barked a curt little laugh. "You really are a terrible earth-mage, Selby," she said. "You haven't figured it out by now? Not even with all the skulking around you did last night, with Fasta and Henrik, of all people?"

So Morley had known about that, then, damn it. "They

guessed," Selby shot back. "They knew there was something wrong down here. But like me, they *trusted* you, Morley!"

"As they should," Morley replied flatly. "As *you* should. Because everything I have done has been in their best interest, and yours!"

And yours. "You think this is in my best interest?" Selby demanded. "Whatever the hell you're doing right now? Trapping me in some dark pit under this hellish manor that I'll never, *ever* escape from?!"

Her voice came out shrill, frantic, because that was clearly what Morley was doing, right? And Morley didn't deny it, just kept walking, deeper and deeper, and Selby could barely even feel Agmund anymore, so muddled, so far up above, through so much solid stone.

"I'm doing you a favour, Selby," Morley's voice replied. "I'm giving you an escape. You think you would have fared any better with that scum Ludwen, after that farce of a trial they gave you? You think you'd have kept any of your magic, or your freedom?"

No, Selby didn't, and she blinked toward Morley in the blackness. "But—the only reason that farce of a trial found me guilty was because of *you*! Because you planted evidence and *framed* me!"

"Not true," Morley replied. "They'd have found you guilty either way. I just sped along the inevitable, that's all."

Selby dragged in breath, digested that. "But the rumours? The reason those assholes even suspected me in the first place? That was you too, wasn't it?"

Morley gave a laugh, short and bitter. "Marginally," she said. "I had to do next to nothing, Selby. A few hints was all it took. Especially with Agmund's swooning ex-girlfriend all too eager to believe anything she heard."

And despite everything, all the rubbish with Greta, Selby suddenly felt almost defensive of her, of the hell this must have been for her, too. "Of course she believed it," she snapped, "and so would a lot of other people in her place. That still doesn't give you any right to manipulate her into spreading horrible *lies* about me!"

"You're honestly *defending* her?" Morley's voice countered, and Selby could feel her halting in place, could taste something like anger in the air. "Have you no pride, Selby? Can you not see how thoroughly Agmund took advantage of you? Did you not *hear* what Ketill did to you and your family? Do you not know the things that spoiled-rotten girl has been saying about you?"

Selby's breath was coming too short again, the air tasting fouler with every step, but she swallowed, pulled herself straight. "Yes, I know all that," she managed. "But Agmund was good to me."

There was an instant of silence, and then another bitter laugh. "You're delusional, Selby," Morley said. "You've been under his control for so long that you're no longer seeing clearly. Agmund used you. Ketill used you. They took your freedom, your body, your very *existence*, and used it to benefit them! Just as they always do!"

The words rang through the too-tight space around them, and Selby's entire body shuddered, brushing up against the closest wall. And though the wall was so cramped and chilled and awful-tasting, it was still stone, it had been pulled from the ground by a long-ago quarryman, a muscled fellow with skin so dark it was almost black.

And something in that seemed to quiet Selby's thoughts, helping her find truth again. "I agree that Ketill used me," she said. "But not Agmund. I've been in his head, Morley. I've seen his thoughts and his dreams. He wasn't in this. Not like that."

Morley only gave that bitter laugh again, ringing through the too-small space. "So you *can* discern actual thoughts. You know, I thought you might. You could have been so *useful*, Selby."

Another hard shudder ran down Selby's back, but Morley

was walking again, the wall closing again, too close behind. "And yes, perhaps Agmund isn't as personally corrupt as Ketill is," Morley said, "but everything here—this Coven, this manor, this entire cursed *system*—is there to empower men like him. To create a toxic environment where air-mages like Agmund can walk around and spew havoc and death in their wake, and gain all the power and wealth in the world in return!"

The words echoed and rattled in Selby's head, amplified by the too-close, too-sickening walls. Because in other circumstances, she might have fully agreed with Morley, but—

"So you're using *me* to target them?" she asked, her voice small, far away. "You're trying to get rid of me, so Agmund will lose his magic for good? So you can bring down Ketill? Take away some of his funding, his influence?"

There was no reply from Morley, just more walking through this never-ending, foul-smelling maze, and now there were small pools of water under Selby's feet, seeping into her leather boots. "And you're not just using me," she said slowly. "You were using Anabel. She was working for you. Wasn't she?"

There was still no reply, but Selby's breath caught, her wet feet hesitating on the stone. Anabel had been in the dark, Anabel had been an earth-mage, Anabel had been doing that one same spell, over and over again. And Anabel had smelled like the smell, so strong like the smell, the smell that was slowly and surely becoming so powerful that Selby could barely breathe.

"Was Anabel's job to make me sick, Morley?" Selby's hollow voice asked. "Was it her job to get rid of me? To make me too sick to help Agmund?"

Morley still didn't reply, and Selby's thoughts snapped back to that awful room, those awful judging faces. *The most damning evidence of all is Mr. Agmund's magic itself*, Ludwen had said. Tainted. Contaminated. And Anabel had been there for over a year, that had been very clear, and...

Selby's feet stumbled, lurching forward, and she could feel

the blackness closing in, and slowly starting to spin. "It wasn't meant for me," she said, her voice wavering. "It was meant for Agmund. Wasn't it? *You've* been the one draining his magic all this time?!"

There was still no answer, but Morley kept moving, and up ahead—Selby blinked—there was a faint greenish light. Yes, a light, and growing stronger, and Selby staggered to catch up. To follow Morley around one more stone corner, feeling the wall close up tight and smooth and impassible behind her.

It was a room. A small, damp, square, low-ceilinged room, walled in stone, and with a single greenish lamp dangling from above. And along the wall—Selby's breath caught, broke—there were people. Five, six, no—seven people, men and women both. Standing in ankle-deep water, facing the wall, holding their hands to its stone. Casting a spell into it.

It was just one spell. One poisonous, powerful earth-spell. A spell that was very specific, very pointed. So pointed, in fact, that it felt exactly like the precise, carefully calibrated opposite of one Regin Agmund.

Selby's throat tightened and retched—it *was* opposite, it was awful, it was *wrong*—and then the comprehension flared, so appalling, so gods-damned obvious. The spell *was* targeting Agmund. And it was because Agmund felt so good to Selby that this felt so sickening. She'd been a casualty. A side effect. Because.

"You're trying to kill him," Selby's voice said, quiet, but sure of itself. "And you've been trying to, all this time. Haven't you?"

And it didn't matter if Morley didn't reply, because it was already enough, the room, the spell, the look in Morley's eyes.

It was true.

37

Regin waited, and waited, and waited.

It was like time had slowed to a crawl, and maybe it had. Even Ketill beside him was shifting, fiddling with his rings, setting the air jerking around him in annoying little twitches.

Regin opened his mouth to tell Ketill to fuck off, but then bit back the urge. Because it was only thanks to Ketill's interference that he was even here. Standing opposite Ludwen, and waiting for Seng.

He was going with her, to wherever the hell they were taking her. And he was going to shoot his mouth off, as often and as publicly as possible. He was going to wield every last scrap of his influence, and his fortune, and his fame.

He was going to fucking fix this mess.

Fuck, it was enraging. That Hendersson, of all people—they'd drunk together, eaten together, Hendersson had called him his *son*—would sign onto this. Sending Seng away, hurting her, on fucked-up trumped-up charges that had without question been set by one of the bastards in that very room.

And gods, the way Seng had looked in there. Like a wounded animal backed into a corner, still snapping and growling, like the stubborn proud wonder she was. Like she'd have eviscerated every one of them, if she'd had the means, and spat on their corpses.

And Regin had been the one to say she should confess. He'd been the coward, because he'd been so desperate to help her, to keep her. And the way she'd looked at him, gods, how she'd *looked* at him...

"Perhaps someone should go check on Ms. Seng?" Ketill said, cold and careful. "Perhaps she has suffered one of her spells?"

Regin's body twitched, already angling toward the corridor—but Ketill thrust an air-shield up in front of him, blocking him in place. While across from them Ludwen muttered something to his hanger-on, who immediately trotted off toward the staircase.

"Thank you," Ketill said loudly, with a quelling glance toward Regin. "I'm sure we are—"

But his words cut off there, because suddenly, running down the hall toward them, was *Morley*. With her skirts flapping behind her, her eyes wide and shocked, and she shoved past Ludwen's lackey without a single look.

"She's gone," Morley gasped. "Selby. She ran."

She ran. The air around Regin hollowed, and beside him Ketill stilled, while Ludwen clutched at the ridiculous-looking sword hanging off his belt. "She ran?" Ludwen demanded. "How? Where?"

"Out the window," Morley replied, through heaving breaths. "Of Agmund's room. She asked me to wait outside. I thought I was being considerate, giving her a few moments' privacy, but she must have dug into her tunnel. Run for the forest."

Ludwen gasped and shouted, yelling for more hangers-on—and in a clatter of boots, five more of them appeared from around the corner. "Go after her," Ludwen ordered. "Show them where, Morley. Now!"

They instantly ran off again, chasing after Morley, after Seng. And Regin jerked forward again, because though he didn't believe any of that shit about the tunnel, he still needed to go too. Needed to find Seng, make sure she was safe, more than anything—

But once again, there was a shield of Ketill's too-thick air blocking his way. Not strong enough that Regin couldn't get through it, but strong enough to hear all too well what Ketill was saying. *Stop. Don't. Leave it.*

Regin gritted his teeth, forced himself to follow, to think. Because yeah, if he chased Seng, he would probably find her. And was that what he wanted? She'd said she could take care of herself, survive alone in the woods. And if she was lucky, maybe she *could* still outrun these fools, after all. Maybe she could escape. Be free again. Live a good life, away from him.

Something gripped tight on Regin's chest, but he stood still beside Ketill, and waited. And waited, and waited, until one of the sweating hangers-on finally came back, huffing and puffing, and shaking his shiny head.

"No sign of her," he gasped. "We searched your room, sir"—his head inclined toward Regin—"but left everything as it was. Your window's broken, though."

Regin didn't care about the damned window, and shot a sideways glance at Ketill. "I'm going up," he snapped. "Let me know right away if you find her, or get any news."

There was none of Ketill's air blocking him this time, and Regin ran off toward the stairs. Taking them two at a time, ignoring the passing staring faces, and by the time he'd reached the second floor he was full-on sprinting, his heartbeat hammering out of his chest.

Seng had run. Taken her magic, her freedom, and run. And curse it, he should have done better last night, should have made her go then, and fucking *helped* her do it, like he'd promised. But no, instead he'd been a selfish asshole, as usual, and now he couldn't stop picturing her out there, alone, either captured, or gone forever—

He threw open the door of his room so hard it bounced off the wall, and then he hesitated, searching. Noting first the traces of other people's scents all over his room, and then the sight of the half-opened wardrobe, the broken, kicked-out window. And the shelf, still full of Seng's stuff, except for that little white dog-skull, lying askew on the floor.

Regin's hands twitched, and he went over, and frowned down at the skull. Had the searchers knocked it off? She should have taken it, right? That, and the box of ashes, too?

But she'd had no bags—he'd made her put those in storage too, curse it—and he reached for the half-open wardrobe door, yanked it all the way open.

Seng's clothes were gone. And so was his bag.

That was strange—not the bag, he didn't give a damn about the bag—but that she'd take the clothes, and not the skull. Wasn't it?

He went next for the broken window, and looked down at the sheer stone wall below it, the expanse of grounds and walls beyond. He'd seen earth-mages who could climb anything, who could all but fly, as long as there was a good-sized stone beneath their feet—but Seng couldn't do that. Could she?

The other alternative was rope, or maybe a ladder—but there'd been nothing like that in the room, and if she'd somehow still found a way out, there would be evidence of it. A ladder left behind, rope tied off to the bed, *something*. Right?

There was movement behind Regin, way too close—*fuck* his already-fading magic—and he whirled around, to where someone was standing in his still-open doorway. More than one someone. Njall, and Tomik, and fucking *Greta*.

They never came to his room anymore, for good reason, and it took an instant for the irrational rage to simmer down, for the pieces to snap together. They were here, curse it, because they knew Seng was gone. Because Greta's jackass father had made sure of it. *You're like a son to me*, he'd said, the lying piece of shit.

"What," Regin snapped, harder than he meant, and Njall shot a wary glance at Greta behind him.

"We just—heard what happened," he replied. "You all right?"

Was he all right. With Seng running alone in the woods with her clothes but without her favourite things, with Regin's magic gone forever with her—

And this was where he was supposed to spit out something empty and easy, tell them what they expected to hear. Just what he'd been making himself do, all these past weeks, even if it had taken more and more effort, felt more and more like a lie.

But as Regin stared at them now, nothing would seem to come. And instead, there was only the memory of Seng, facing off against him in this very room, her brown eyes flashing. *They don't know you, they don't care about you, they don't care that you hate it here, that you've barely been away from this hellhole in an entire fucking year...*

Gods, she'd been on fire with that, such a viper-tongued enraging compelling wench, with her unnerving way of throwing the truth in his face, even as she made it very damned clear that she still liked him, still wanted him. That there was nothing she wanted more than his dick pounding into her, holding her down spreading her open, while his mouth spewed all kinds of wild shit, *Tell me you want it, I'm your biggest fucking fantasy, witch...*

Even the memory of it set the hunger flaring up again, the grip clutching tighter around Regin's chest. She'd wanted that. She'd been in that, just as deep as he'd been. She'd seen him—all the worst, most shameful parts of him—and instead of mocking him or pitying him or judging him, she'd said—

"Do you want to come out with us?" Njall asked, with a jerk of his head toward the woods. "Have a few drinks, take your

The Mage's Match

mind off things? And hey, now that the pedlar's out of the picture for good, you're a free man again, right?"

He winked at Regin, and then shot another glance over his shoulder, toward Greta. And Regin's eyes followed his, to where Greta's head was tilting in that old familiar way, her eyelashes fluttering low...

"A free man?" Regin repeated, stupidly, as Greta glanced up at him—and gods, he knew what that look meant. Knew it all the way to his bones, and gods *fuck* him, because had this been what Hendersson had been after, in that bullshit trial? Had he thought, if Seng was well out of the way, that Regin would go crawling back to Greta again? The *hell*?

The fury whirled up in Regin's thoughts, screeching under his skin clawing away at his magic, and he couldn't do this right now, he was going to start hollering, straight in Njall's smug face. "Sorry, no," he gritted out. "I've got to go. Got some urgent shit to deal with right now."

With that, he shoved past them and strode out of the room, his hands in fists at his sides, his brain shouting at him with every step. What the fuck was he doing. Letting himself get delayed like that, when he should have already been downstairs again, keeping himself updated on what was going on. Seng wasn't invincible, no matter what she'd said. She could already be trapped. Enslaved. Lost.

There was still enough magic to feel that Ketill was in his office, so Regin sprinted straight there. Bursting in to where Ketill was already waiting, looking placidly toward him, leaning over his desk, fingers folded together.

"Has anything else happened?" Regin demanded. "Have they found any trace of her?"

Ketill's eyes kept looking at him, not blinking. "No. Not yet."

Regin let out a heavy breath, and hurled his twitchy body down into his usual chair. "Do you think they will?"

Ketill kept eyeing him, and Regin's faded magic could taste the subtle, slow burn of Ketill's familiar anger, gliding into the air around him. "Shouldn't I be asking *you* that question, Regin? Did you know about any of this?"

Regin frowned back, not following, and Ketill sighed, gave an elaborate roll of his eyes. "The tunnel. The rock. The magic-channelling. The *murder*, Regin."

Regin almost laughed in Ketill's face, but instead leapt to his feet, made an impatient circuit around the room. "I already told you, Seng didn't do any of that shit," he snapped. "She can't even lift a single rock, let alone dig an entire tunnel. Weren't you the one who was supposed to have done all that research about her?"

Ketill huffed another sigh, and looked up at Regin over his spectacles. "My research was very thorough, yes—but the evidence is before you, Regin. How else did Ms. Seng escape, if not through earth-magic?"

How did she escape. And that was the question that had been nagging in the back of Regin's head ever since he'd seen his broken window, and damn it, he still didn't have an answer. How *had* Seng escaped, without help? Yeah, he'd been the one to say, when they'd talked, that she should go out his window—but he'd meant with *his* magic, not hers. And that wall was sheer and dangerous, it was damned lucky she hadn't fallen to her death—

"I don't know," Regin replied flatly. "But she didn't murder anyone, Ketill. I swear. She was framed."

The words felt solid, true, like something Regin could finally cling to—so he let them keep going, spilling out on their own. "Somebody in that room framed her, to get to me. And I have a damn good idea of who it was, too."

Ketill's eyebrows lifted, and he leaned back in his chair. "Do you. Please, Regin, enlighten me."

Regin sucked in a breath, let it out again. "Morley," he said. "She's the best earth-mage here, she's been close to Seng, she could have planted all that evidence. And there's a suspicious as hell hidden tunnel by the back staircase, with her signature all over it!"

Ketill's mouth opened, and for an instant something sharp and hopeful flared in Regin's chest—but then it vanished, because Ketill shook his head, an ugly grimace settling across his face.

"Stop," he said. "Stop, Regin. I know there have been challenges with Morley in the past, but she is very close to several key Coven members. Dragging her into this mess will only come back to haunt all of us, I assure you."

But Regin barely heard it, because damn him, how had he been so dense? Morley had been with Seng when she'd disappeared, Morley had been the one to say Seng had run, had Morley ever explained how Seng had gotten out the window?

"Where *is* Morley?" Regin demanded. "And did anybody question her bullshit fairy tale about Seng climbing out the window?"

Ketill's eyes on him were unblinking, cold. "Morley was called away to an important meeting," he replied. "And she did not personally witness Ms. Seng's escape, so no, she was not questioned. But I assure you, Regin, if she had any involvement in this whatsoever, I would know. And so would the committee of professionals, who have done an *extremely* thorough investigation!"

Regin opened his mouth to point out that the investigation had been absolute shit, and Ketill himself had often called that committee a bumbling pack of pinheads—but Ketill raised a hand, and rose to his feet behind his desk.

"Stop this foolishness, Regin," he ordered. "I know you liked Ms. Seng, and you don't wish to believe ill of her. However, you are treading in *very* dangerous waters. You have no conception what this entire debacle has cost me, and the favours I've had to call upon to keep you out of it. You're lucky you're even still here, and still walking free, and not being charged with collusion to commit *murder*!"

The words rankled in Regin's chest, along with the godsdamned unfairness of it all, and he fought back the urge to punch the nearest wall. "*I'm* lucky?" he demanded. "Who brought Seng here in the first place, Ketill? Who fucking *blackmailed* her into this? Who didn't fucking tell me *crucial* information about her, or why she was here?!"

He was hollering by the end, but he didn't give a damn, because he was still furious about that, too. Ketill *still* hadn't owned what he'd done to Seng, hadn't even *tried* to apologize to her, and now was all too ready to believe she was a *murderer*? When all the evidence clearly said otherwise?

"Regin," Ketill said, in that infuriating patronizing voice of his, "you're low on magic. You're reacting emotionally and irrationally. I realize Ms. Seng's loss must be a blow, but if you can calm yourself, and wait until she is captured and dealt with, I will do my best to procure a replacement for her."

A replacement. The words hung there for an instant, while Regin stared—and suddenly bile surged in his throat, strong enough that he had to cover his mouth, cough it back. A *replacement*?!

"What the *fuck*," he said, his voice hoarse. "A replacement? After all that? Have you lost your fucking *mind*, Ketill?"

Ketill's face remained implacable, remote. "I have not," he coldly replied. "If anything, our experience with Ms. Seng has proven to us that this avenue is worth pursuing further. Her effect on you was highly significant. I consider our experiment with her a resounding success."

"But," Regin sputtered, "but, Ketill, you *just* said you think she drained someone—*murdered* someone—to supply me! If you believe that, you can't possibly still believe all that magic-affinity bullshit you've been spouting off to me!"

Ketill didn't even twitch, and Regin felt a slow trickle of ice, sliding down his back. Wait. Was Ketill really saying—

"You'd really do that," he said, marvelling at the words, the truth of them, as they came out his mouth. "You would bring somebody in to supply me, even if you knew they were doing it illegally. Even if you knew they were *murdering* other people to do it?!"

Ketill didn't even try to deny it, the slimy piece of *shit*, and suddenly Regin couldn't stand to look at him, or spend one more second trapped in the same room with him. But when he stalked toward the door, he ran into another one of those damned air-shields, blocking his path—and this time, Regin couldn't even begin to muster the magic to shove it aside.

He whirled around, hands in fists, but there was another shield between him and the desk, as real as any solid wall now, with no way for Regin to get through it. And what should have been a satisfying kick toward it only sent pain shooting up his foot, jangling against the chaos swirling in his head.

"Listen to me, Regin," Ketill said, his voice very measured. "You are the greatest air-mage on the continent, and a crucial element of our entire country's defensive strategy. Many people would willingly—*should* willingly—give their lives to support you. And it is petty and shortsighted of you—selfish of you—to disregard their commitment, and their bravery."

Bloody fucking hell, Regin was livid, and if he'd had his magic there would have been a deeply satisfying lightning bolt, firing down straight onto Ketill's delusional white head.

"Nobody is dying," he growled, "for my magic. *Nobody*."

Ketill just kept gazing at him, as a cool smile slipped across his mouth. "If you haven't noticed, Regin," he said, "that earth-mage peasant already has. And if you used your brain for once, you would see the latent hypocrisy—the cowardice—of being perfectly willing to accept, in the interest of national safety, the unwilling deaths of rebels and foreigners at your own hands—but not the willing deaths of your fellow countrymen, at the hands of others!"

The words felt like kicks, one after another, to Regin's already-choked throat, and for some reason his thoughts flashed back to Seng. She'd hated that too, *you shouldn't have to do it*, she'd said, *they've been using you to make their jobs easier, they don't give a damn about what you want.*

Regin couldn't speak, and he felt Ketill's air-shields around him suddenly drop. "Go," Ketill said, his voice weary, now. "Come back when you're ready to thank me for my very generous offer, and my ongoing sacrifices on your behalf. And if you tell anyone about this conversation, Regin"—he sighed—"I *will* have you incarcerated, right alongside Ms. Seng. Believe me when I say you wouldn't enjoy that."

It had been a long time since Ketill had actually threatened him with confinement, and while Regin had always seen Ketill's threats as empty garbage—spouting the usual bullshit to get his way—suddenly it felt darker, colder. *Right alongside Ms. Seng. You wouldn't enjoy that.*

But what had Seng said, just that morning? *You're going to wake up in twenty years and realize that you're alone, and you're miserable. Living in a place you hate, pleasing people who couldn't care less about you.*

And standing here, looking at Ketill looking at him, there was the sudden, sinking whisper that Seng had been right, again. She'd seen him. She'd known him. She *knew*.

"You're really threatening to *imprison* me?" Regin said, over his shoulder, as he made for the door. "Then knock yourself out, asshole. I'm done with this bullshit. And we're done talking, until you apologize to me, and to Seng."

Ketill blinked, but didn't reply, and Regin yanked the door open, hard. And because he was a petty bastard, he used the last dregs of his magic to snake out behind him, and knock over the open inkwell that had been sitting on Ketill's desk, hard enough to splatter black ink all over Ketill's pristine white robes.

"Oh, and also," Regin said, "If I can ever prove it was you who set Seng up with this, I'll fucking kill you in your sleep."

And with that, he stalked out, and slammed the door shut behind him.

38

When Regin stepped back into his room, he half-expected Seng to be there. To saunter up to him, grab his dick, and look up at him with her speaking dark eyes.

You finally told Ketill where to shove it? she'd say, maybe, once she'd brought his thoughts to the surface with sure, steady strokes of her hand. *Good for you. Finally.*

And maybe she'd drop to her knees, and suck him back like she'd been craving it all fucking day, just like he had been. And when he tangled his hands in her thick hair, and fucked her face, she'd groan around him, and he'd whisper that she was such a gorgeous, brilliant little wench, looked so good with his dick down her throat—

But Regin's bedroom was empty, and dark, and chilly now, what with the broken window. From when Seng had supposedly left, and he stalked back to the window again, and glared out of it. Was he really supposed to believe Seng had climbed down that wall? With no ropes, no magic, without Morley even noticing she was gone? It was complete bullshit, right?

But if it wasn't that, what else could it have been? What

would Morley have done with her? Or maybe it *had* actually been Ketill who'd set her up? How? *Why*?

Regin turned back to the dark, silent room, so empty without Seng in it, and his eyes again caught on her little shelf. The shelf he'd begrudged her, whinged about to other people, and he couldn't even seem to go near it, to touch the things that had been so precious to her. The things that spoke things to her, meant things. They comforted her, she'd said.

Regin sank heavily down onto his bed, and rubbed at his eyes, his mouth. Maybe—maybe Seng had left her things so he would send them back. So they would be safe with her family again. He could send things through her uncle, she'd said, and he could still remember all of that, etched clear in his thoughts. Artimus Balen, in Kaynr.

The memory of it flared too sharp, piling onto all the others swarming through his head. She'd wanted to leave, he should have let her leave. Why had he begged her to stay, promised her an adventure, said all those incriminating things. *My lover. Stay.*

Forever? she'd asked, and he hadn't denied it. Hadn't even tried.

And maybe now that Seng was gone, forever, and Regin was alone, untouched, with no magic, in this empty silent room, he could admit—to himself, at least—that he'd meant it, when he'd said forever. That the idea of Seng, there, ready and willing, a steady refreshing honest presence in the rest of his life's constant bullshit, had been like a dream. Something he'd have been more than willing to pay for, through his teeth, even if it meant more bullshit everywhere else.

Gods, it would have been good. He'd have made it good. With the fucking, yeah, but also the snarking and teasing at each other. The lazy mornings, lying in bed and talking, and maybe they'd go out to the forest, she'd touch him and suck him as he exploded trees around them.

And maybe, after that, they'd travel. Go do and see things

together, like she'd said. She could show him how she used her magic to track and hunt and hide, how she got by in the forest alone, and he could show her avalanches and hurricanes—but no, no, he couldn't think about that, not now. No, instead he'd have set her up in luxury, in beautiful apartments full of beautiful things—or, probably, as many skulls and bones and ashes as she damn well pleased—

He barked out a choked laugh, and for some reason he shoved to his feet, and went for the shelf. Finally kneeling down beside it, and he must have been drunk with the loss of his magic, or just lonely and fucked, because he actually reached out and picked up that little dog-skull, from where it was still lying sideways on the floor.

"Weird that she left you on the floor," he heard himself say, as absurd as it was. "She loved you, you know. I think more than her dead father. Can't say I see why."

The skull didn't reply, obviously, all white bone and unnerving-looking teeth, and Regin gave an unwilling shudder, and went to put it back in its place on the shelf. Strange, too, that he knew its place, and its empty eyes were looking at—

He glanced over his shoulder, reluctantly—and then blinked, because behind him, the desk drawer was ajar. Odd, because he couldn't remember when he'd last used it, so he stood, and went over, and yanked the drawer open.

Inside it was—a letter.

Regin's hand shook as he yanked it out, a single crisp white sheet, and he fumbled to light the candle, to hold the letter up to it. It was written in an unfamiliar hand, but he didn't need telling to know that it was hers. Seng. Selby.

He read it once, his eyebrows furrowing together, and then read it again. It was to Selby's mother and brother, it was her answer to why she hadn't taken her things, and it was—wrong.

It said she'd been accused of a crime. That she would be locked away, her magic lost. It told her family to keep on. It said—it said—

I hope Regin will return my things to you, it said. *And I hope you will place no blame on him for any of this, as he has been good to me. I love you both. Goodbye.*

Regin read it again, and again, and his hand was shaking now. Enough that it spread up his arm, and into his chest, and then all over him, like he was fevered or ill, because what the fuck, what the fuck, what the *fuck*. He hadn't been good to her, he'd treated her like shit, and she was supposed to have run, she was supposed to be off in the forest—

But it said she'd be locked away. Her magic lost. That had been what she'd wanted her family to know. Not that she'd escaped, and would find them, or contact them later.

And maybe that was a ruse, just to throw him off, but Seng—Selby—had always been so honest, had never shied away from the truth. And that truth would have been one her family would have wanted to hear, they'd much rather have her on the run than captured imprisoned no magic—right—right?

Regin's hand was still shaking, and he watched as his fingers put the letter back in the drawer, and pushed it shut. As they set down the candle, snuffed it out. And then reached for the door latch, pulling it open, and shutting it tight behind him.

And without at all knowing how he'd gotten there, he found himself in front of a door. Runar's door, because Selby had liked Runar, and trusted him, despite all his lying necromancing bullshit. And right now Regin couldn't trust his own head, his own bullshit, but he could trust her. He *could*. Right?

"What?" Runar's grating voice demanded, as the door snapped open. "Don't you realize that other people need to sleep?"

But Regin didn't care, and let his mouth open, say the words that were screeching in his head. "Selby's in trouble," he said. "I need your help."

39

Being trapped below Coven Manor, Selby had decided, was legions worse than being trapped inside it.

It had only been maybe a few hours, but already Selby felt sicker than she'd ever felt in her life. And more out of sorts, and out of patience, and just downright despairing.

"Are you going to cooperate?" Morley had asked, at first, and though Selby should have lied, should have said, *of course, whatever you want*, she instead stared blankly at Morley's face, and at the miserable, stinking room behind it.

"What do you mean, cooperate?" she demanded. "You want me to stay put down here in this hellhole? Or you want me to *help* you?"

She frantically nodded at the seven people leaning against the opposite wall, casting that awful spell. And not one of those people had turned around, or even glanced over their shoulders toward them. Just kept working, heads bowed, making that smell that tasted like death.

"Yes, I want you to help," Morley said, her voice cold, impatient. "Regin Agmund is a plague on this Coven, and on this entire country. Relying on him has made our military sluggish and complacent, and has placed far too much power with tyrants like Ketill. It's put millions of innocent people at risk. It needs to *stop*, Selby."

The conviction rang in Morley's voice, like she really did believe all that, but Selby couldn't stop gaping at her. "So your solution is to *murder* Agmund? When he hasn't even *done* anything?"

"Oh, he's done plenty," Morley said dryly. "He's not a blushing innocent, Selby, get the fog out of your head! Do you know how many people he's killed? How many lives he's needlessly destroyed?"

The words sounded familiar, again like something Selby might have once said herself, but she shook her head, fought to think. "Agmund doesn't want that," she said helplessly. "He never has. He wants to do the right thing. To help."

"Yes, well, he will help once he's gone," Morley snapped back, without sympathy. "Once our country learns how to function without him, and finally rids itself of short-sighted, self-absorbed blowhards like Ketill!"

"Then get rid of Ketill," Selby choked. "Go after *him*, not Agmund. *Please*, Morley."

"You don't think I will?" Morley replied. "Believe me, Selby, it's part of the plan. But Agmund needs to go first."

Selby couldn't stop shaking her head, fighting to deny the awful twitching terror of those words. Morley truly wanted to *kill* Agmund. And there was no way Selby was going to be a part of that, never.

"No," she gasped, through heaving breaths. "No. I will never help you, Morley. This is *wrong*."

She jerked her head at those poor wretched people, still casting into the wall, but Morley didn't even spare a glance toward them. Instead, she raised her hand toward the wall behind Selby, and Selby yelped as a thick coil of metal sprung out from it, and flew toward her wrists. Which had both still been bound behind her back, but she could feel the steel melding, thickening, *no*—

"These mages are being very well compensated, I assure you," Morley said flatly, as Selby yanked in vain against the cold winding steel. "And they have voluntarily submitted to a reduced sensory state, in order to better focus on their work. So any attempts on your part to distract them will be entirely futile, I assure you."

No, *no*, and Selby kept wildly wrenching against the steel, until somehow, one hand broke free—but wait, the steel clamping the other hand had transformed into a thick cuff, attached to a chain. A chain that slithered toward the stone wall, and embedded itself deep inside it. Shackling Selby there. Trapping her there.

"Stop it, Morley," she pleaded, her voice cracking. "You can't do this."

"Oh, yes, I can," Morley said grimly, as another chain flew out from the wall, and circled itself around Selby's ankle. "And you will soon discover that your choices are either to help, or to starve."

With that, Morley strode away, toward the wall where they'd come in. The wall that was already opening up to admit her, to take her away, and though Selby hollered after her, Morley didn't turn around, didn't stop. Until the stone thudded closed behind her, and Selby was left standing alone in a cold puddle of water, with her right arm and leg chained to the wall.

It was thoroughly, appallingly horrifying, and making it even worse was the smell. So powerful and pungent that it felt like she was drowning in it, and just in time she launched herself toward the closest crevice in the rocks, and vomited down into it.

Afterwards she wiped at her parched, awful-tasting mouth, which was badly in need of water—and then she realized, with a shudder, that the only water to be found was pooling foul and stagnant under her feet.

"Is there any water in here?" she called, loudly, toward the wall of silent workers—but there was no response, no heads turning, no sign that they'd even heard. "Please, could you bring me water?"

There was still no movement, no reply, and Selby put her cold trembly hands to her face, tried to choke back the sobs in her throat. She was alone. Trapped. With no food, no fresh water, and her only escape was to kill Agmund, who she could still feel upstairs, distant but still there. Agmund, who couldn't *dare* die, because Selby loved him.

The thought of that just made the sobs come harder, stronger, and Selby silently cursed herself, her own gullible weakness. Agmund didn't care about her like that, she *knew* that, had always known that. So why had she let this happen, why was the thought of Regin Agmund going cold and silent so deeply, dreadfully *wrong*.

The sobs kept coming, loud heaving strangled gasps that shook Selby all through, until they'd seemed to wring her dry. And when they finally faded, turning into lurching gulping breaths instead, there seemed to come a flattened, deadened clarity.

She did love Regin Agmund. She might not like that, or be proud of it, but it was true. And more than that, beyond that—she couldn't bear for Regin Agmund to die. Which meant—she had to do something about it. Anything.

She started by shoving herself to her shaky feet, and pulling off her wet boots and socks, and spreading them on the nearest dry rock. And then she stepped onto another rock, and proceeded to jump up and down and jog in place until her blood was pumping heat to her hands and feet.

It seemed to pump more awareness to her head as well, and she put her hands to the chains holding her, gauging the strength of them. Feeling how they were made of a particular kind of powerful alloy, crafted precisely to Morley's specifications by a distant, far-off smith. A man who hadn't asked questions, hadn't wanted to know.

Next Selby put her hands to the stone wall behind her, and

felt how the rock had come from the same quarry she'd glimpsed on the way down, mined by dark-skinned men in strange clothing. Then it had been transported and placed here by a decades-ago team of workers, efficient and distant, building the basement for one of the government's new tenders.

And that was something, because hadn't Fasta and Henrik said that the basement had been filled in? But this wasn't filled, this was the original basement, although—Selby slid her hand up, up, up—it was only part of it, and it felt a bit wrong, somehow. Like—she frowned, focused, tried to be there, in that instant, when the builder had placed this stone—it was in the wrong place. Like that builder had been *there*, and now she was—*here*.

The difference wasn't major, but it was there, and Selby flipped back and forth between them, considering it. It was a difference in geographic location, in the pull of gravity and the earth's magnetic field, and she sat on her heels, looked up at the wall. Part of the basement had been—moved. Maybe a dozen fathoms deeper than it had been originally.

It made sense, because it meant that the bulk of the manor's current basement, the ones that people like Fasta and Henrik could feel, had indeed been filled in. While this part of the real basement—the original one—had been sunk far lower. And that explained the long passageway down, and how—Selby frowned over her shoulder at the silent workers again—their work was still affecting the manor, because it was still part of it.

There had to still be spells, concealing it from prying eyes, and Selby touched the wall again, felt for Morley's distant signature in it. And yes, it was there, faint but undeniable. Feeling like—concealment, like camouflage.

That seemed important, and Selby kept feeling it, sinking into it. So deep that she almost jumped out of her skin at the sound of moving stone behind her, and she whirled around, fully expecting to see Morley standing there again. But instead, it was—

"Kal Merton?" Selby demanded, her voice coming out hollow, high-pitched. "What are you doing here?"

Kal looked distinctly uncomfortable, sidling alongside the wall away from her, and with a wave of his hand he shut the stone behind him. Which meant, of course, that he was involved in it, in all of it, the smell, the spell, the killing-Agmund plan. And he'd known, just like Morley, exactly why Selby was sick. And hadn't he been the one to feed her that rubbish, back at the very start, about Runar causing it?

Selby's anger surged, her mouth snapping open to holler at Kal for being such a lying backstabbing snake—but then she swallowed it all back, hard. She had to do something. Had to.

And right now, maybe doing something meant staying quiet. Watching as Kal circled over toward the row of silent workers, and began touching them, one by one.

It wasn't clear what he was doing—perhaps checking on them, or monitoring their work—and Selby watched intently until he touched the last in the row, and then came around again. Going back for the exit he'd made, about to leave, and Selby took a breath, pulled herself tall, and surreptitiously undid the top button of her dress.

"Hey, Kal," she called, with an attempt at a smile. "Could I ask you a favour? And do you a favour in return?"

Kal hesitated by the exit, looking warily toward her in the dim greenish light, and Selby tried for another smile, warmer this time. "I'm very thirsty," she said. "And right now, I'd do just about *anything* for a pail of clean water."

She let the *anything* hang there, too suggestive, and maybe it was working, because Kal wasn't moving. "Whatever you like," she continued, dropping her voice lower. "And I'll do it first, so you'll know I'm not baiting you. A quick fuck, maybe? Or I could suck you?"

Kal's mouth fell open, clearly appalled at the audacity of

the pedlar harlot, but he still hadn't moved, and Selby smiled again, and undid another button of her dress, slowly this time. "I won't tell anyone," she said, "even Morley. As long as you don't. Just between us."

Kal's eyes dropped to her chest, to where her shift was thankfully still covering most of it, and she saw his tongue come out briefly, wetting his lips. Thinking about it, maybe, and Selby made herself smile again. "There's nothing wrong with a simple exchange of favours," she added. "I've been doing it with Agmund for months, haven't I? And I'll tell you, Kal"—she attempted a conspiratorial wink—"he's been getting his value. Enough that he told me he wants to keep me on permanently."

And curse her, because that was what did it. Making Kal take a slow, faltering step toward her, his eyes suspicious, his mouth pursed tight. "I don't believe you," he said, but he was still coming, not stopping. "Agmund goes for skinny blonde heiresses, not chubby pedlar harlots."

Selby resented that, especially given the source, who was no specimen of slimness himself. "No, Agmund likes tits and ass," she said, the truth of that ringing in her voice. "And enthusiasm. Ask Morley, if you don't believe me. He admitted as much in the trial, even with all those old geezers listening."

She made herself laugh out loud, like it was all some amusing joke, and Kal just kept coming closer. Almost enough to touch, almost, and Selby unbuttoned one more button of her dress. "And Agmund *really* loves getting sucked," she continued, huskier. "And he'd be absolutely *furious* if he knew I did it to you. You wouldn't tell him, right? He's got the worst temper."

Kal gave a hard little grunt, a glance over his shoulder toward the row of silent, working mages. "Yeah, I'm pretty good at keeping secrets from that cocky bastard," he said. "Including the one where he's going to be laid out cold on a slab within weeks."

Within weeks. It came out vindictive, and pleased, and if

Selby even partially regretted doing this, it had entirely vanished, leaving only a cold, calculating, smiling rage behind.

"Well, we won't tell him, will we?" she said coyly, as Kal came even closer, one more step, one more. "It'll be our little secret."

Kal actually nodded, his eyes lingering on those open buttons of Selby's dress, and she reached out her unshackled hand, caressed him on the shoulder. Tasting the hunger, the pain, the self-righteousness, the loneliness, drawing him closer, he hated and envied her, he really believed she'd do this—

Her kick between his legs was straight, forceful, perfect. Making him shout and bend double, the pain blooming sharp and powerful through his thoughts, and Selby kept her hand to him, feeling his thoughts, as she knocked him off-balance, swung the chain on her arm around his neck, and yanked it as tight as she could.

Kal struggled to escape, but Selby had the distinct advantage of seeing his impulses as he thought them, and she wrenched the chain tighter on his neck, felt the fear and the pain jolt higher. Until Kal stopped struggling altogether, his thoughts now swirling with a grasping, humiliated disbelief.

"You lying *cow*," he gasped, his voice already hoarse against the chain. "You'll *pay* for this, bitch."

Selby only smiled, and jerked the chain downwards, dragging him hard to his knees on the stone. Where she wrapped the chain on her foot around his ankles, too, binding them together, trapping him there.

"Threaten me all you like," she said, breathless, smiling down into his red, gasping face. "You're still going to show me *everything*."

40

Regin was coming off like an unhinged asshole, but he didn't give a shit.

"She didn't go out this window," he growled, toward the assembled faces of Runar, Thora, Fasta, and Henrik. "I fucking *guarantee* you."

They'd all read the letter, they'd all seen where the dog-skull had been, and now they were all staring at Regin like he was a raving lunatic.

"Oh really?" Runar asked, voice cold. "And you know this how?"

"Because," Regin snarled back, "Morley's in on it, Morley's full of shit. And you two should already know that, because Thora saw something about Morley, didn't you? And you"—he shot Runar a dark look—"*lied* to us about it."

Runar didn't look in the least repentant, but beside him Thora winced, and gave an uncertain shake of her head. "Yes, um, I saw it would go badly, if you got into it with—with Morley," she stammered, "but it doesn't mean she's lying about Selby running away. And not to be contrary or anything, but don't you think Selby could have, uh, just changed her mind, after she wrote you the letter? Saw the window, and thought it was a good idea?"

Runar snorted, and put an over-familiar hand to Thora's back. "Or, more like," he said, with a smirk on his irritating mouth, "she just wrote the letter to throw you off. Make sure she'd be well rid of you for good."

The temptation to punch that look off Runar's face was very strong, but Regin sucked back a breath, made himself think about Selby. Wherever she was, whatever she was doing, she needed help. He was absolutely fucking sure of it.

"She's not like that," Regin snapped. "She doesn't do bullshit. If she wanted to cut me off, she'd either have said so, or wouldn't have left a letter at all."

None of them argued, but now it was Fasta and Henrik exchanging speaking looks. "The thing is, Agmund," Fasta said, "we already went through this entire place, and other than that back staircase, it's solid. And it sounds like multiple people saw Selby come up with Morley, and no one saw her come back down. The window is the only way out."

It was a point, an infuriating one, and Regin stalked back to the still-broken window, and glared out of it. "You really think she climbed down that wall?" he demanded. "She's not an earth-mage like you two. And without that, unless she miraculously conjured some rope from somewhere, and then made it disappear again after, she'd never have made it in one piece!"

They were all looking dubiously at Regin, like he really had lost it, and maybe he had, because a reckless, ridiculous part of him knocked out the last few bits of broken glass, and shoved one leg out the window into the open air.

"Fine," he said. "I'll try climbing down with no magic, while you watch, and then tell me you think she could have done it!"

He'd already swung his other leg out, sitting on the sash, half-ready to turn around, start lowering himself off it—but Thora made a strangled noise, and waved frantically at him.

"No, no, *stop*," she breathed. "You'll break your pelvis, it's *awful*."

And despite that unpleasant image, Regin smiled as he swung his legs back inside. "Right then," he said flatly. "Who's going to tell me Selby did this again, especially in those clothes of hers? And managed it fast enough that nobody's been able to catch her?"

Runar muttered something Regin couldn't hear, and beside him Henrik grunted, in clear agreement. "Maybe somebody helped her," Henrik said. "Or maybe she's just better at earth-magic than she let on to you."

Regin wasn't buying it—Selby didn't lie, her family was on the other side of the country, and anyone at the manor who might have helped her was standing in this damned room. "Can you track people's movements?" he demanded toward Fasta. "Either of you? Even a little bit?"

Fasta and Henrik shot each other doubtful looks, again with the *don't-tell-him-he's-losing-it* thing. "Not really," Fasta said finally. "I mean, of course, we can feel that Selby's been in here. But following where she went outdoors, hours ago, through open air? Not a chance."

A low growl hissed out of Regin's throat, and he kicked hard at the floor. That skill of Selby's had been so damned useful, if only she were here to use it...

"All right then, what if somebody got her down the back stairs," he said. "Down to that hidden tunnel we found."

His only answer was silence, with Henrik shifting on his feet, and Regin rounded on him next. "Yeah, the one you lied to me about," he snapped. "We're going down there, now, and you two are going to tell me if there's a single fucking *dust-mite* moved since last time. You hear me?"

Henrik glared back at him, but Fasta nodded, and tugged Henrik toward the door. Thora followed too, and finally so did Runar, giving an unnecessary roll of his eyes toward Regin as he went. "Listen, asshole," he said, "has it not yet occurred to you that wherever Selby is, she's better off? And maybe she doesn't *want* you to run off and rescue her?"

Regin was about to snap back a reply, but Fasta had opened the door, and jerked to a stop—because there, standing in the corridor, arms crossed, was Njall. Again. With Tomik and Greta behind him, and also Tana, because clearly she and Njall were at it again. And damn it—Regin bit back a groan—they'd probably all heard what Runar had just said, as Fasta had opened the door. *Wherever Selby is, she's better off. Maybe she doesn't want you to run off and rescue her.*

And yeah, they definitely had heard it, because Njall's eyebrows were now halfway up his forehead, and the others were gawking at Fasta and Henrik and Runar and Thora. "Uh, what's going on?" Njall asked, every word plucking at Regin's already-jolting brain. "You're not—going anywhere, are you, Regin? Or getting involved in any—illegal shit?"

Fuck. Regin rubbed hard at his eyes, because the last thing he needed right now was more messy rumours or accusations spreading around, more reasons to keep him trapped here. He needed his freedom to deal with this, needed people on his side—but beside him, Fasta was already clearing her throat, and tugging Henrik toward the door. "We'll meet you down there, then," she told Regin, curt. "Come on, Harry."

Henrik went without arguing, carefully avoiding Tana's eyes on the way by, and after a furious glare toward Regin, Runar stalked out too, with Thora close behind him. Leaving Regin standing there with his friends, the people who were supposed to be here for him, the people he'd tried so damned hard to trust. The people he'd been lying to for weeks now, maybe months, maybe forever.

They don't know you, came Selby's voice, too fierce and certain in his thoughts. *They don't care about you...*

"What's this all about?" Njall asked, his eyes searching Regin's. "You all right?"

And maybe it was the lack of magic, or the tiredness, or the panic, or Selby's voice still echoing in his head. But whatever it was, Regin sighed, and looked at his friends, and finally just—faced it. Told the truth.

"Look, the case against Seng doesn't line up," he said flatly. "So yeah, I'm pretty worried, and a few of us are looking for her. I'd appreciate you keeping quiet about it, and"—he swept his eyes back over them, mentally flicking through Njall's casting skills, Greta's gaseous manipulations, Tana and Tomik's mediocre pressurizations—"if you want to come along, we could really use the help finding her."

His voice hung there, echoing in the too-thin air—and then Njall barked out a laugh, Tomik snorted, and Tana glanced worriedly at Greta. Who had lurched back like she'd been shocked, like that time Regin had electrocuted her when she'd ignored his warning and gotten too close.

"Wait, you honestly want us to help you go *look* for her?" Njall asked, still smirking, as if this was some kind of joke. "With *them*?"

The anger punched up in Regin's thoughts, raw and overwhelming enough that he had to pinch his nose, breathe out hard through it. "Yeah, I am," he gritted out. "And what's wrong with *them*?"

But it was a waste of air even asking, he already knew, because the thing wrong with *them* was that they were outcasts. Misfits. Not as much as Selby had been, maybe, but Thora was quiet and awkward, Runar had the whole corpse-cutter thing going on, and Regin knew for a fact that Henrik had grown up just as poor as he himself had. Fasta, at least, had a titled, influential father probably even richer than Greta's—but she was still an earth-mage, who worked in construction, and therefore, in this shithole, still an outcast.

"They're not our friends," Njall said, at least dodging that point. "And I'll be honest, this doesn't make any sense. Why do you need to bother looking for her? She *killed* somebody, and then took off, and left you to clean up the mess! You can't really think *she's* the one who needs help right now?"

Njall and Tomik and Tana all snickered, like it was a hilarious joke, but Regin wasn't laughing. He could only seem to stare, first at Njall and then at the other three, and too late he realized his hands were in fists, and he was shaking.

"Yeah," he said, his voice slow, deliberate. "I do think she needs help. And if you're going to laugh at me for that, then you can all get the fuck out. *Now*."

His wavering hand jabbed toward the door, and he could see the unease filtering across their eyes. "Hey, lighten up," Njall said, raising his hands in an oh-so-innocent gesture. "It was just a joke."

And yeah, that's what they'd always said whenever Regin had brought up the way they'd treated Selby, too. And Regin had believed it, or maybe just wanted to believe it, just wanted to keep telling those damned comforting lies to himself. And gods he was such an asshole, and why the fuck had he ever sided with these pricks over her?

"Oh, it was just a *joke*," Regin heard himself say, voice flat. "My mistake. So you're all going to come help me find her, then, are you?"

But even before the words were out of his mouth, he knew what the answer would be, and watched it play out with a grim, furious certainty. The four of them glancing at each other, silently asking *is-he-fucking-serious, I'm not going off to look for a pedlar convict, are you? What if the rest of them hear about it?*

"Look, it's way too late," Njall finally replied, with a confirming glance at Tomik. "I have an early meeting in the morning."

Sure he did, and sure the other three weren't even going to justify it with excuses, and Regin was suddenly, completely just *done*. With them, with all the lies, with this stupid fucking conversation that had already wasted way too much time.

"Yeah, we all know that's bullshit," he snapped, his eyes

flicking between them. "Because none of you actually give a damn, do you? Not about my magic, my priorities, or *me*. Who *I* am, or what *I* want. You care about what I can do for *you*. And you know what? I'm *done* pretending this is fine. I'm *done* acting like we actually *matter* to each other. And I'm done"—he took a breath, let it out, waved at the lot of them—"with all of you. For good."

There were gasps all around, four pairs of wide shocked eyes, but Regin didn't care. And without waiting for a reply, he walked out, and didn't look back.

41

If being trapped under Coven Manor was a vile experience, being trapped in Kal Merton's thoughts was the next level of hell.

"You actually *think* this bile?" Selby demanded at him, as she stared down yet another nauseating wave of *lying-bitch-needs-a-knife-up-her-skirts*. "And you wonder why you're always alone in your bed?"

Kal responded with even more furious mental diarrhea, and Selby almost retched, and yanked the chain around his neck with as much force as she could muster. "Fuck off," she growled, "or I *will* vomit on your face, I swear to fuck."

It wasn't an empty threat, because Selby's stomach was heaving, already way too close. And maybe it had gotten through to Kal, or maybe it was the fact that his bloodshot eyes were almost popping out of his head, but his thoughts backed off slightly, if still simmering with a teetering snarling rage.

"I'll have you know," Selby hissed, as she tightened her hand to his meaty shoulder, "I never *once* saw that kind of filth in Regin's head. In *months* of touching him."

Kal replied with some kind of gasping verbal diatribe about Agmund being a total weakling, never actually facing real combat, blah blah blah. But speaking through the pain seemed to take up a fair portion of his mental capacity, leaving the rest for Selby to touch, feel, sift through. Searching.

It was something she'd only ever really done that one time with Agmund, when they'd been fighting in his room, though maybe she'd known for a while now that she could do it, if she tried. But the idea of searching through someone's thoughts had always felt like a violation, an unalterable cruelty—at least, until she'd encountered the cesspool that was Kal Merton's brain.

"Come on, asshole," she murmured. "Make yourself useful. Starting with, how did you get down here."

She could feel Kal's thoughts fighting her, trying to conceal their secrets—but even the attempt seemed to bring the memories here, to the surface. Visions of the same maze-like, ever-deepening tunnel Selby had come down through, but this time with the awareness that the stone walls moved, and that the path forward was marked by a subtle, barely perceptible spell, traced into the maze's smooth stone floor.

It took an incredible amount of skill and power to navigate through it, Selby could see that, and it was a source of pride for Kal that Morley had selected him to be her confidante, rather than that undeserving lout Henrik, or that frigid bitch Fasta. Who'd actually refused Kal's generous expressions of interest more than once, claiming coldly to Kal's face that Henrik was twice the mage he'd ever be, and Kal was still going to get her back for that, someday—

"Gods, you are *vile*," Selby gasped, as she gave another hard yank on that chain. "Fasta is way too good for you. And she's right, Henrik *is* twice the earth-mage you are."

Selby didn't quite know if that was true, based on her own limited experience of proper earth-magic, but it was enough to set Kal's thoughts frothing again, more seething swill about how Henrik was a dirt-poor uneducated bumpkin degenerate, who was only here because Fasta wanted him, and it was sweet justice that Henrik had reportedly fucked almost every other girl in the place but her—

Selby took the opportunity to sift through Kal's thoughts again, this time around the memories and visions of the maze. Searching for hints of another way in, or out—but as far as Kal seemed to know, this was the only way down.

Damn it. Selby leaned back again, gulping for breaths of the foul air, and she reached for the reassuring feel of Agmund again, distant but steady above. And for an instant there was the brief, hurtling wish that she'd tried doing this with Agmund, in his thoughts. Circling, exploring, plucking out images and memories. *What was your favourite day like, what's the most ridiculous spell you know, what's made you laugh the hardest, what's made you cry.*

There was a lump forming in Selby's throat, her eyes angling over to that row of earth-mages, and she swallowed hard, forced her focus back into Kal's thoughts. "How do you make them do this?" she said aloud, her voice wavering. "Why don't they do anything else?"

She could feel Kal trying to suppress the answer, but again it was entirely too obvious, and Selby swiftly searched the memories. That had been one of Morley's biggest challenges, keeping the team sedated and working properly—Anabel, in particular, had repeatedly tried to escape—and there was a healer who came once a month, at exorbitant cost, to renew the spells. And at this point, they were so heavily sedated that if their hands were on the wall, they were working, and if not, they were sleeping.

Maybe there was something there, if Selby could just interrupt the workers, stop them casting, somehow—but now, oh gods, there was the image of the healer doing something new, a month or so back, at Morley's request. *I've fixed the issue*, Morley had told Kal afterwards, her eyes grim and satisfied. *As per their contracts, if they stop casting for more than eight hours, their magic will begin to drain.*

The change hadn't been just about prevention, Kal had understood very clearly—but also about secrecy, security. So if one of the workers did escape, their magic would drain, and before they could tell anyone, they—

They would die.

The horror surged up in Selby's thoughts, in her throat, and she clamped her mouth shut, breathing hard. So that was what had happened to Anabel. It hadn't just been the endless casting, the exhaustion. It had been Morley. And Kal had *known*.

It was abhorrent, impossible, absolutely disgusting that someone could actually do that to someone else, and Selby tightened her grip on that chain around Kal's neck. "So, you murdering swine," she demanded, "if there's only one way down here, is there a way to at least communicate with someone above, while you're here?"

Kal's thoughts immediately dredged up the answer, willingly this time. "Of course not, bitch," his mouth said, strained and hoarse. "Because then people like you and Fasta and Henrik might figure it out. Morley's not *that* stupid."

His tone suggested that he thought Morley was a little bit stupid, however, and that was an interesting lead, so Selby followed that, too. Going back to the source of that statement, a memory of Kal asking Morley, *do you really think this exit is secure, just sitting here in an open staircase?*

It was a fair point, Selby could admit, but Morley's reply to Kal had been distracted, dismissive. *I know what I'm doing*, she'd said, without a single glance toward him. *I created the concealment spells myself. There isn't another earth-mage in existence who knows what they are.*

But. Kal knew what those concealment spells were. And that was another promising lead, so Selby followed it, to the creeping memory of a furious Kal trailing Morley one day, soon after she'd foolishly brushed him off with that comment. And he'd followed Morley all the way down here, using his own spells to hide, while he watched her cast that concealment, felt it through the walls, until it could have been his.

Selby's heart pounded faster, and she reviewed the images again and again. Kal knew the concealment spells. He could cast them. And, presumably, that meant...

He could break them.

"So here's the deal, Kal," Selby said. "You're going to take the concealment spell off these walls. Now."

Kal's body beneath her had slowly gone slack under the chain, but he jerked up again, panting hard. "I'm not going to do shit for you," he said, his voice cracking. "Morley's going to be back here any minute, and you're going to be *fucked*."

That was true, Selby realized with horror, because not only did Kal's thoughts confirm that Morley would soon return, but he also knew that she'd called in that healer again. And it would only be hours before Selby was slogging on the wall with the rest of them, and maybe afterwards, when no one was looking, Kal would come down, and teach her a few well-deserved lessons—

Selby's skin was crawling, the disgust pounding through her skull, and if she'd had any hesitation before, she certainly didn't now. She didn't get a choice? Well, then he didn't, either.

She plunged deep back into Kal's thoughts, deeper than she'd ever imagined she could possibly go. Straight back to Kal's knowledge of that spell, sinking into his ability, his skill, his awareness, his consciousness...

Kal's body bent and contorted under her, his thoughts desperately resisting, screaming *what is she doing, stop, stop*—but Selby didn't stop, and she had it now, thrusting Kal's hand to the wall—

And with a burst of magic, a scream from his mouth, the spell erupted from his fingers—and the concealment collapsed.

42

When Regin finally got down to the back stairwell, he was greeted by four sets of eyes, staring at him.

"What," he growled, frowning at the lot of them in the dim lamplight. "Did you find anything?"

They collectively looked at each other, and finally Fasta spoke. "We haven't. There's no sign of this wall being moved since we did it ourselves."

Shit, fuck, *damnation*. "You're sure?" Regin demanded. "Keeping in mind that Morley is better than you are?"

Fasta and Henrik exchanged glances again, and Regin didn't miss that stubborn, *he's-lost-it* look on Henrik's face. "We're quite certain, yes," Fasta said, stiffly. "As far as we can tell, it's only our magic on it, with nothing out of place. It's exactly as we left it."

Regin was about to start yelling, and he clenched his hands tight, tried to think past the bubbling rage. "Well, look again. There's got to be another way down. Or you've missed something. She *has* to be here."

Fasta's hand was on Henrik's arm now, clearly trying to hold him there, but he brushed it off and strode over, leaning too close in Regin's space. "Look, you hot-air jackass," he snapped.

"We're not your fucking *servants*. I know you think you rule the realm, but you need to back the hell off. And maybe try facing the truth that not every girl in the world wants you!"

He shot a furtive look over his shoulder toward Fasta as he said it, as if to confirm that she wasn't one of them, and Regin almost barked out a laugh. As if he was stupid enough to tangle himself up with yet another high-maintenance spoiled heiress, after what he'd dealt with these past months?

"Yeah, well, Selby wanted me," Regin snapped, though he knew he should shut his mouth, even as the words kept spilling out of it. "She *loved* me."

They were all staring at him now, and the silence was broken by Runar, letting out an obnoxious, too-loud snort. "You actually do believe that," he drawled, shaking his head. "Let's all be honest here. Selby was *paid* to fuck you. She was doing her *job*. And in return, you mocked her behind her back, wouldn't even be *seen* with her, and treated her like trash. And you honestly can't understand why she wouldn't jump at the chance to run away from you? Wake *up*, asshole."

The fury surged hard in Regin's chest, the retort rising in his throat—when he realized, with a curdling jolt of fear, that they were actually going to *leave*. Henrik tugging at Fasta's arm, Runar already stepping away, gods *damn* it—

"Wait," Regin gasped. "Wait. Please."

They hesitated, but just barely, and Regin could hear his heartbeat, could taste the empty air around him. Gods, what he wouldn't give for his magic right now, it always helped, made everything easier—

"Look, I know I fucked up with Selby," his voice said, sounding strange to his ears. "Especially at first. I was an asshole. I did treat her like shit. I didn't deserve her."

The four pairs of eyes were on him, waiting, but they hadn't left yet, and fine, if this was what it took, Regin could do this. "But then I got to know her," he heard himself say. "And it was—good. Really, really good. For both of us."

There wasn't any change in their eyes, yet, and Regin's heartbeat thudded louder, faster. "She was always honest with me. Always generous with me. And her magic is fucking brilliant, she's gorgeous, she's a total firecracker in bed, always up for anything. And she's brave, she takes care of the people she loves, she does what needs to be done. And she knows me, actually *me*, and I can actually *trust* her, and"—he swallowed hard, still couldn't say it—"I care about her. A lot. Enough that I asked her to stay. For—for good."

Gods, it sounded pathetic, as if him asking a girl to stay—for pay—was the height of his life's achievement, but Runar's head was tilted, his mouth pursed. Judging him, Regin realized, and weighing the truth of his words.

"So what did Selby say," Runar snapped. "When you told her that."

Gods, Runar was an infuriating dick, but under Regin's anger was something too strong, too close. "She told me she would, for free," his voice said, unsteady, hoarse. "But only if I left here, forever. And then, just today"—he had to take a breath—"she told me she *loved* me."

All four sets of eyebrows went up, and Runar's mouth opened again to speak—when suddenly, out of nowhere, Fasta and Henrik both startled, and stared at each other.

"What the—" Fasta said, while Henrik let out a low, muttered string of curses. And then he shot straight for the staircase wall, putting both hands to it, with Fasta close behind him.

"What?" Regin demanded, and his heartbeat was pummelling his chest, trying to break free. "What is it?"

Henrik shook his head, eyes closed, like he was concentrating, while Fasta fished out paper and charcoal from her pocket, thrust the paper flat to the wall, and began scribbling letters and numbers on it. And none of this made any sense, and Regin was rapidly losing the last of his patience, and thank the gods, here was Thora, putting her hand to Fasta's back, while understanding filtered across her wide eyes.

"They've found something," she said, breathless. "Part of the basement. Sunk far below. It must have had some kind of concealment spell on it."

Which meant that it didn't now, somehow, and Regin's chest constricted tighter, his breaths coming short and shallow. "Wait. Does that mean Selby's down there? Right now?"

It had to be true, it had to be, Selby was still here, still alive—and it was like the world tipped over when Thora nodded at him, confusion and disbelief all over her pale face.

"I think so," she said. "But not—not for long. Morley's on her way."

How Thora could see that, Regin couldn't fathom, but suddenly there was only sheer, silent terror, screaming through his head. "Can you find a way down?" he demanded at Henrik, at Fasta, at the world. "As fast as fucking possible?!"

Fasta kept scribbling, but Henrik leaned back, took a breath. "Maybe," he replied. "It won't be the right way, but it'll be a way. If we can keep the place from collapsing on our heads."

Fasta nodded beside him, still scribbling. "It could work," she added. "But it's going to take both of us in the passageway, to just hold the manor up. And there's no way to guarantee we'll get you back."

But it didn't matter. Nothing mattered, but Selby, and Regin getting to her, this fucking instant.

"Then I'm going down," he said. "Now."

43

The concealment spell was gone for only minutes, if that.

Selby had known it would be fleeting, but it felt like no time at all before she felt it shudder back into place around her, now reeking of Morley's magic. And when Selby dove back into Kal's thoughts, intending to cast the spell again, she couldn't seem to find the right place. It was like she'd broken the memory, somehow. Broken him.

Kal was still scrabbling against her, weakly, his face a horrific shade of purple, and suddenly Selby couldn't bear to keep touching him, and she shoved him away. Leaving him coughing and retching, his shaky fingers grasping tight against his bruised, reddened neck.

"Morley knows, you bitch," he croaked. "She's coming."

Selby didn't bother to answer, and squeezed her eyes shut, reached again for Agmund. She felt clouded, somehow, contaminated from all that time in Kal's brain, and Agmund up above was a distant twinge of clarity, perhaps brighter than before. And maybe he would have noticed the concealment spell vanishing, somehow, maybe Fasta or Henrik would catch it and tell him, please gods, please...

The sudden sound of crunching rock snapped Selby's head up—and there, of course, was Morley. Stalking from the entrance toward them, and looking ready to kill.

"What the *hell* did you just do," she spat at Selby. "And how the *hell* did you do it!"

Selby didn't reply, but beneath her Kal pulled himself up, his tunic drenched with sweat, his ankles still caught in Selby's chain. "She made me," he gasped, his voice ragged. "She went into my head and *made me*."

Morley stared at him, at them—and suddenly a new length of chain flew from her fingers, and wrapped itself around the wrist of Selby's free hand. "How," Morley growled, as the chain jerked Selby backwards, embedded itself into the solid stone wall behind her. "*How* did you learn to do that?"

Selby wasn't telling Morley anything, and she yanked uselessly at where both hands were now chained to the wall behind her. "How did *you* become such a coldhearted monster?" she shot back. "You're going to *enslave* me, and you're raging at me for undoing a single spell?"

Morley's breath was coming very fast, the whites of her eyes too visible in the dim greenish light. "Because you're risking *everything*!" she shouted. "You're risking the entire plan I have worked *years* for! I have been *kind* to you, Selby, and *this* is how you repay me?"

"You haven't been kind to me!" Selby countered. "And how have I risked anything? It was only one spell, and I can already feel that you've put it back, no one will even notice!"

She hoped it wasn't true, please gods, and Morley opened her mouth again—but then, suddenly, there was something terrible on her face. Something that made her entire body go still, her eyes staring wide at the ceiling above.

"*Damn*," she breathed. "It's Fasta and Henrik. Kal, you ward them off. Keep them out!"

Under different circumstances, Selby might have almost enjoyed the look of pure horror that crossed Kal's eyes—but he staggered off, still coughing, and Morley stepped closer to Selby, as another thick chain snapped up into her fingers.

"I *was* kind to you, Selby," Morley said again, her voice hollow. "I was *generous* to you."

Selby wrenched desperately against the chains binding her to the wall, but they only pulled her back harder. While the chain in Morley's hand floated up, and—*no*—snaked itself cold and close around Selby's *neck*.

"Do you know how many times I could have killed you by now?" Morley's empty voice continued, as the chain circled tighter. "Dozens of times, Selby, and no one would have even noticed, or cared. *No one*."

The panic surged, screeching in Selby's head, her eyes desperately darting to the blackness above them. Were Fasta and Henrik really coming, would Kal keep them away, did they know she was down here, was she imagining the feeling of Agmund, tasting stronger, coming closer, please gods *please*—

"If you hold still, there will be less pain," Morley said, her eyes just as cold and empty as her voice. "See, Selby, how I am still giving you far more than you deserve."

The thunder in Selby's chest flared up, hard—and suddenly her whole body was kicking, squirming, desperate. Fighting to touch Morley, fighting to do anything, her mouth screaming shrill, ringing through the thick vile air—

But stars were flashing behind Selby's eyes, the air vanishing, the pain in her throat spiking as the chain tightened still further. Not long now, her vision was failing, she kept screaming and screaming and nothing was coming out—

"Goodbye, Selby," Morley said, and the world faded to black.

44

Regin hated being underground.

"Come *on*," he hissed at Fasta, who kept pausing to scribble on her paper, lit only by the light of a strange glowing rock she'd scrounged up from somewhere. "We have no *time*."

Fasta didn't even look at him, just kept scribbling, her body pressed close up against Henrik's. While Henrik seemed to be digging and carving and hauling and holding up the stone around them, all at the same time, in a show of skill that might have been impressive if Regin wasn't so damned terrified.

"It's fucking Merton," Henrik growled, breathless, the sweat a slick sheen on his face. "Trying to block us off. We'll get through, motherfucker."

Regin didn't doubt that—they'd actually come a decently long way through this claustrophobic stone hellscape—but Selby was down there, he needed to get there, panic shouting and punching in his skull—

"Keep going that way," came Thora's voice from behind Fasta, one hand still tight to Fasta's shoulder, the other clasped in Runar's, pulling him close and silent behind her. "Almost there. Whatever you're doing. Almost there."

Fasta nodded, kept writing, and Henrik grunted, leaned his whole body against the wall in front of them. Which collapsed spectacularly into dust, filling the already-shitty stale air around them, but with a distracted wave of Fasta's hand the dust dropped, settling to the stone beneath their feet.

"Almost there," Thora said again, like a chant, and Regin bobbed on the balls of his feet, his hands in fists. His whole body shouting for it, needing it, come on, come *on*...

And then, faint but undeniable, there was—her voice. Selby's voice. Shouting, in fear or pain, or maybe both, and it was like someone had stabbed Regin in the chest. Sheer panicked rage, screaming everywhere, he had to get out, had to get there, why the *fuck* was he still trapped in this godsforsaken *nightmare*—

"Please," his voice rasped. "You've got to get me there. *Please*."

Nobody replied, but Henrik hurled his body at the next wall of stone, and Fasta was there now too, both hands flat to it. Selby's screams scraping in Regin's head, flaring, so strong he could feel it, taste it, *please*, gods—

And suddenly the wall was gone, collapsing into rubble before them. Showing something greenish behind it, something open, and Selby's screams were here, in his head, alive.

Regin leapt over the rubble without thinking, without looking, because his eyes were only on the source of those screams. On his girl, tied up against a wall, with fucking *Morley* standing in front of her, and tightening a fucking *chain* around her neck.

"Stop!" he shouted, loose stones kicking up under his feet, and maybe—somehow—impossibly—there was the tiniest sliver of awareness, of response, in the air around him. And he focused it, compressed it, split-second reflex, shot it across the room, his beautiful brave girl alive almost dead, air hurling at Morley's face, into her eyes, please—

And Morley staggered. Only slightly, but maybe just

enough, because the chain around Selby's neck sagged, and Morley whirled around, her hands in fists.

"What the—" Morley began, but Regin was already here. On her, against her, shoving her bodily away, and Selby's terrified brown eyes were staring at him like he was a vision, something not real.

"Selby," he croaked, as he clutched uselessly for the chain still around her neck—but her eyes snapped up, catching on something past him. And Regin spun around, just in time to see Morley swinging another chain toward his head, this one with a fucking steel *ball* on the end of it, and his frantic ducking dodge barely escaped it, pain instead blooming shrill through his shoulder.

"Oh fuck no, you don't," he growled, scrabbling and grabbing for the chain, and luckily he was bigger than Morley, stronger, with longer reach. Enough that he could wrench the steel ball away, and hurl it across the room, one less earth-mage thing to deal with—

But then his eyes caught on people, a strange-looking row of people. And fuck, he'd barely missed one of them with the ball, but it hardly registered because now Morley had a *knife*, the witch, and was madly swinging it—not at him, but at Selby?

"Fuck *off!*" Regin shouted, giving a well-aimed kick at Morley's torso, but she jumped back just in time. At least giving him space, and he whirled around to Selby again, her trapped body shaking against the wall, how the *fuck* did he get those chains off...

"I've got it!" came a voice from across the room, and a quick glance over Regin's shoulder showed Fasta's pale form, standing just inside the wall, her arm outstretched. Henrik and Runar and Thora were nowhere to be seen, maybe holding up the tunnel, or maybe they'd run for good—

But the chains holding Selby to the wall suddenly dropped, clattering to the floor. And she was free, rubbing at her bruised neck and blinking at him, her eyes wide, bright, incredulous.

"Regin," she gasped, and then, oh gods, she was here. All up against him, all soft warm close relief. Like someone had blasted open this awful miserable room, and let the sun beam down into it.

"Selby," he said back, into her hair, his arms gripping as tight around her as they possibly could. "Are you all right. What the *fuck*."

She gave that laugh of hers, hoarser than it should have been, but then it broke off, suddenly, her body gone tense against his. Because Morley was still doing this, of course she fucking was, and Regin could feel the first boulder, flying straight for his head, and he tackled Selby to the earth just before it smashed against the wall behind them.

"What the fuck!" he said again, leaping up and whirling around, making sure to keep Selby behind him—and here was Morley, halfway across the room, out of his reach, with a pile of huge, rough-looking boulders beside her. They were weapons, Regin's thoughts shouted, too late, as another boulder rose up, and hurled itself straight toward his head.

There was no time to move, to even breathe—but suddenly Selby's arms gripped around Regin's waist, her warm body taut and close behind his. And he was going to die, would have died, except—

Where Selby was, there was air.

The air-shield formed just in time, not even a handsbreadth from his face, and the boulder bounced off sideways, smashing uselessly against the ground. Making Morley start and stare, and Regin laughed aloud, his body almost shaking in the twitching wide relief.

"You got more of that?" he called, widening his stance, feeling Selby's arms go even tighter. While his own hand gripped hard over hers, saying *thank you, gods I've missed you, don't stop.*

The next boulder lifted with only a flick of Morley's hand, and hurled itself toward them—but the air was already closer, easier. Still weak, still thin, but *there*, and Regin's shield was stronger this time, blessed solid air around him, his girl his magic, *here*.

"Keep touching me," he breathed over his shoulder, and in reply Selby's hands immediately moved, fingers spread. Doing it willingly, eagerly, exploring his chest his arse and even his crotch, and he almost laughed at the ridiculousness of it, of his girl feeling him up making him hard, putting on a show, while this maniac tried to kill them.

But it was working, like it always did. Almost like it was relaxing Regin, unspooling him, letting down his guard. And he'd wondered, more than once, if that was why the touching and fucking had always worked so well with this. No bullshit about Selby illegally feeding him magic, but just making him calm enough, open enough, to feel it again.

Another boulder shot through the air, and this time the air-shield was bigger, better. Driving the offending boulder straight back toward Morley, who had to use both arms to shove it away, her pale face contorted with hatred.

"You are an entitled, disgusting *pig*," she called, her voice carrying across the room. "Selby, can't you see he's *using* you?"

She hurled another giant boulder, but Regin easily blocked it this time, and behind him Selby gave a hard laugh. "*He's* using me?" she called back. "You were the one who wanted to *enslave* me, and force me to help you drain Regin's magic, and *kill* him!"

Drain his magic. Kill him? The confusion must have been there, rising in Regin's thoughts, and that always saved so much tedious explaining bullshit, because behind him Selby took a breath, and explained.

"Those mages," she breathed, and she meant the weird row of people across the room, "have been here for over a year.

Casting a spell into the building itself. A spell meant to drain your magic, and ultimately kill you."

The fuck?! But suddenly it made perfect sense, all snapping into place at once, and Regin whirled around to look at Selby. Knocking her hands off him in the process, but he impatiently put them back, searched her eyes.

"That's what it's been, this whole time?" he said, but it wasn't even a question. "As long as I stayed here. And damn it"—a hard laugh barked out of his mouth—"the worse my magic got, the less I went out, the more I stayed here. Fucking *hell*."

The truth was there, in Selby's eyes, and in a breath Regin's fury was here, too. Screeching up sharp and powerful, and when Selby's eyes darted back behind him, following another boulder toward his head, a fierce wave of his hand sent it flying, smashing against the opposite wall.

"Who else was part of it?" he demanded, searching her face, because with her skills, she had to know. "The Coven? That fool Committee?"

"As far as I know, just Merton," Selby replied, glancing briefly over Regin's shoulder, maybe looking for the slimy little snake. "And those mages. Though I'm not sure if they even knew, Morley had them sedated, they had to sign awful contracts. And Anabel was one of them, but she escaped, but part of the deal was that if they left, their magic would start to drain, and they would *die*."

She was talking too fast, the way she did when she was upset, and Regin put both hands to her face, held her eyes, knocked aside the next flying boulder without even looking. "And the target was just me? Or you, too?"

His rage flared again, because he was thinking of Selby's sickness, of how awful she'd felt these past months, and she took a little gulping breath. "I think I was—collateral damage, at first," she said. "Since anything that affects you would also affect me, because of our affinity being so strong. But then

Morley saw how much I was helping you, and how this was affecting me, and so she started trying to target me, too. It's why I felt so much better too, when we were—"

She flapped her hand toward him, or rather toward his still half-hard dick in his trousers, and suddenly there was an awful, appalling understanding in Regin's head, dragging him down into the earth. Right. Right.

"So you really were fucking me for the magic that whole time, too," he said, trying to sound like it didn't matter. "Or for your health, I guess. That makes sense. I should have realized."

Selby's brown eyes were looking at him, not even twitching at the feel of another flying boulder, bouncing off Regin's airshield. And gods, what the fuck was wrong with him, why did he feel like the world was suddenly choking him, strangling him, he hated being underground, this fucking *room*—

"No, you asshole," Selby snapped, as that familiar stubbornness glinted in her eyes. "Sure, feeling less sick was a lovely side effect—but I've already told you, I liked you. I wanted you. I *love* you."

Oh. The pressure eased off all at once—gods, Regin had missed her—and he couldn't help a sudden flash of a smile, a moment of unguarded, perhaps dangerous truth. "Yeah," he said. "Same."

Selby's eyes widened, maybe following that where it led, where not even Regin was sure he'd gone—but suddenly the earth under their feet rumbled, and slid sideways, and—cracked in two.

"The fuck!" Regin shouted, whirling around, because that witch Morley was still there, *still* fucking doing this. Looking at them with a smug sneer on her mouth, did she think she could bury them, or some shit, what the *fuck*—

"Oh hell no," Regin growled, but when he leapt aside, dragging Selby with him, the earth just slid again. Like he was on ice floes, or quicksand, his feet staggering, sliding helplessly off-balance.

Selby behind him was no better, as she wasn't that kind of earth-mage, and Regin's eyes swept the room, toward where Fasta had been. But there was no sign of her now, and how had Regin missed that, where the fuck were they?

Morley across the room was standing on solid earth, her hands sweeping sideways and back again, like she thought she was some kind of god. But there was only one god in this room, and he was drawing the heat and the static through the air, letting it linger on his fingers.

"Don't let go," he said, to where Selby was clinging at him again, and he breathed the air in, let it fill his lungs—and then let it snap. Soaring down a shearing white fork of lightning, straight toward Morley's head.

Selby gasped behind him, whether of shock or pleasure he couldn't quite tell, but Morley blocked the lightning bolt, just barely, heaving a smooth flat rock up over her head. Sending the fork's path sideways, where it diffused into the earth, but Regin had more of that, Selby was still touching him, fisting his dick, *fuck* yes.

Morley had to scramble to escape the next fork, letting off on waving the earth beneath their feet, and Regin dragged against the shitty air down here, whipping it up faster, stronger. Making a gods-damned massive underground storm, because he fucking *could*, and why the fuck not. Morley was done fucking with him and his girl, fucking *done*.

The next fork actually did catch, making contact with Morley's upraised arm, but she somehow grounded herself without taking the brunt of it. A clever move, sure, but she couldn't last much longer, and Regin whipped the storm harder, higher, wind blowing in his face, whistling against the stone.

The fear streaked through Morley's eyes, and without warning, she bolted. Not toward where the exit was, on that wall, but toward where there looked to be a round metal grate, embedded in the middle of the stone floor.

And with a wave of Morley's hand, the world—changed. The room's middle—the part where Regin and Selby were—sank. The edges, holding the exit and those mages, rose up. And the grate flew into the air, because behind it, under it, there was a rushing, billowing, furious blast of water, surging straight up into the air like a massive dam had broken.

Morley was flooding the room.

45

Regin stared at the water, his thoughts his body gone entirely still. The cold inky wetness was already pooling around his feet, his ankles, how could there be so much, Morley must have kept a reserve, just for this. For him.

He could feel Selby tugging at him, dragging at his arm, saying something. But the words didn't land, there was no way to escape water, the walls were too high, this room way too small...

"Regin!" Selby's voice shouted, and something was trying to wrench his arm from its socket. "Come *on! Run!*"

Regin blinked toward her, at her familiar face, at her wide, panicked brown eyes. His girl, afraid, and he gave a hard shake of his head, fought for focus.

"Come *on*," she said again, pleading—and this time, Regin's legs moved. Following toward where she was half-dragging him to the edge of this sunken, rapidly filling pool, it was already to his knees, all liquid rising *death*.

"Can you climb," Selby gasped, shoving him toward the sheer wall, and Regin looked up at it, reached out an arm—but his first uneasy hand-hold on the stone suddenly shot out, like the stone was punching him off, and he wheeled backwards hard, almost fell over into the rushing water below.

"*No*," he choked back, because standing high up above them was Morley, looking down to where she'd sunk them so deep that the water would be over their heads in minutes. And where was Fasta, where the fuck was Henrik, if Regin didn't get out, the lightning, the water, he would—

Regin's storm was still there, still whipping above their heads, but he couldn't seem to change it or break it, not now, not with water up to his thighs. Couldn't even manage a proper air-shield to pull them upwards, because the clouds were flashing above them, loaded already to strike, and it was taking all his strength to hold it off. And he was in *water*, even one bolt in this could kill them both, *no*.

"You try," he gasped, shoving Selby toward the wall instead. "Go. *Please*."

But the stubborn wench wasn't going, was just here, still clinging to him. "*No*. I'm not leaving you, I can swim."

"Well I can't," Regin shot back, his arms trying and failing to thrust her away, when had he gotten so weak? "And I'll drown you, or electrocute you, you can't, you *can't*."

The pain of it was choking him, he'd come so close to saving her, making her safe. Paying her back, for everything she'd done for him, she didn't deserve this, she didn't, hold the strike back, *hold*—

"You don't owe me *anything*," Selby's voice hissed, so close. "You don't have to pay me back. I make my own decisions, asshole."

Regin almost smiled, because that was his girl, such a stubborn little witch, not even bothering with a basic fucking *thank you*. And she was going to die, he was going to kill her, the strike was screaming in the air now, fighting to get out—

"No," he rasped, and the water sloshed at his thighs, ice-cold prickling at his skin. "Go, Selby! Please, get away, *please*!"

He didn't care how it sounded, how it looked, his hands swatting shoving desperate toward her, because it was taking everything to hold the lightning off, so close now. It was the only answer, it was inevitable, and the more he tried to thrust it away, the stronger it surged—

"Can't stop it," he gasped, because it was here, part of him, his body flailing against this awful enclosing slippery death. "Can't, I can't."

But here were Selby's brown eyes, suddenly, in front of his, her hands gripping tight on his waist. "You can," she ordered. "Deep breaths, Regin. You can do this. Hold it off. *Breathe.*"

He fought to obey, to pull in air, but it was so close, here. Morley looming above, smiling as they drowned, not looking up, so easy, just one single hit—

"No," Selby hissed again. "That's what she wants. Don't you fucking *dare*, Regin."

The panic kept shouting, water at his waist his ribs, and he shook his head hard, his storm circling wild above to match. Whipping higher and stronger, it was coming, sharp white release so close, bubbling up and up...

"Need it, have to, can't!" he babbled, his head still shaking, lost beyond his control now. His arm reaching up, feeling it, and Selby's hands dragging on him felt negligible, meaningless. "Go, get away from me, run, *please!*"

Morley was laughing above, the sound carrying down over the rushing looming horror. Enclosing him, trapping him, rising to his neck, and Regin heard himself cry out as the lightning finally took form, crackling above them in the air.

"No!" Selby's voice yelled, over the rest of it, her eyes wide and frantic in his, her hands clutching hard at him. But it was too late, he was casting, couldn't stop.

And here, distant in his head, were all the memories of her, the regrets. So many times he should have touched her, kissed her, told her the truth. That time in the forest, when he'd almost lost her, begged her to come back, should have let her go...

"NO!" she shouted again, still alive, in this instant, before he killed her. Before the horror became truth, became irreversible, how could he have done this, killed the one girl he trusted, the girl he *loved*.

Until—he didn't.

The spell had still crackled through his fingers, still truth, the water here, at his chin, the air churning above—but somehow, impossibly, the spell had gone—sideways. Taking life not as a lightning bolt, not as electricity that would stop both their hearts—but instead, as an air-shield.

It made no sense, the lightning was *there*, waiting, it *had* to come, and Regin's body, Regin's magic, reached again. Drew for the lightning, let out the lightning—but again, somehow, it was a shield. Bigger, stronger, circling around his head, around Selby's. Keeping the water away.

His body tried again, on its own, while the sky swirled and crackled overhead, because in all the ways his magic had fucked up this past year, it had never cast the wrong spell entirely. And if he was dying, wasn't he dying, the *hell*—

There was a strange noise from Selby's body in his arms, and he'd killed her, or had he? Her eyes were distant, dazed, but her hands were still clinging around his back, and here was the taste of her magic, deep and warm. She was—casting?

Yes, casting. Using more magic in this instant than he had ever, ever felt on her, and Regin stared at her, felt the magic as it worked, sank home, *changed*.

She was in Regin's *head*. It was his storm, his air-shield, his spells—but Selby had cast them. *Changed* them.

"What the fuck," he croaked at her, and he felt the magic pull back, twining away from his thoughts. Saw Selby's eyes seeing him again, and then flicking upwards, to where the water was now surging over their heads. But the shield was like a huge bubble, extending from Regin's chest up around both their heads, and while there wasn't much air, they were still breathing. For now.

And beyond the bubble, and the water above it, Regin could feel the storm. Still cracking, still swirling, still waiting. But—holding. Just enough. *Somehow.*

"Sorry," Selby said, breathless, while the water churned behind her head, held off by his invisible shield. "I just—"

Regin grasped for her face with wet shaking hands, dragged her close. "Thank you," he said, and it came out raw, reverent. "*Gods.* I *love* you."

She gave a choked laugh, her eyes blinking, and she put her hands to his face, too. Just looking at him, holding him, while the water whirled behind, the world sounding muddled and thick around them, going so dark it was almost black.

"What next," Selby said, with another little laugh, and Regin almost laughed, too. They were alive, he hadn't killed her, they would get out of this, they *would*—

But then Selby's eyes snapped to something behind him, jolting wide and horrified. And when Regin whirled around, he found a massive wall of stone, hurtling flat and deadly toward them.

Regin couldn't swim, didn't know how to move in this shit, but Selby clearly did, yanked him away—but here was another wall, closing in, punching past the edge of his air-shield. And then another, coming closer all the way around, Morley was going to crush them, his air-shields wouldn't hold against that, Selby would be *dead*—

A voice was shouting, maybe his. Magic swirling, maybe his. An air-shield firing away from him, expanding to encompass Selby's entire body, suspending her in it, so not a single finger touched the edge.

"Regin!" her mouth screamed, but there was no sound beyond the rush of water in his ears, and he hurled her up, away, his magic pooling and exploding wide. Rising and meeting the still-swirling storm above, with Morley standing beneath it.

And with one final breath, Regin let the spell fly. Felt it connect with Morley, with him, lightning finding earth, home, water, and stopping every beating heart in its path.

It was done.

46

Selby could feel Regin cast the spell. Could smell it, taste it, hear it echo in her bones.

"NO!" she screamed, while her body kicked, thrashed, fought to escape this cursed air-bubble he'd snapped her into. Keeping her out of the water, keeping her safe—while he was in it, in the water, making lightning, drowning.

Selby barely noticed the flash and boom up above, barely felt it making impact. Because everything was here, in this godsforsaken flood, where Regin Agmund was dying.

"No!" she shouted again, but her face was suddenly flooded with water, as the air-shield around her collapsed. Regin's magic, collapsing, and Selby dragged in a mouthful of water in a shouting silent scream.

She kicked herself upwards, flailing and frantic, and somehow, oh gods, found air. Coughing and sputtering, gasping for it, gulping it in—and then hurling herself back downwards again, into the wet blackness, because Regin was still there, still there, still *there*.

She couldn't feel him, suddenly, oh gods, but she kicked toward where he'd last been—and her first touch at his slowly sinking body made her recoil, her breath fighting to explode in her lungs. He felt wrong, *was* wrong, like the images of him in her head were only echoes. Like there was nothing there, nothing inside.

She grasped at him anyway, pulling at the dead weight of him, trying to kick off, push up. But he was so big, so heavy, the echoes of water of magic of death so loud, screeching in her head. What was she going to do, oh gods, please, *please*...

It felt impossible to keep from choking, from sucking in another lungful of water, and another helpless kick up did nothing, nothing. And neither did putting her arms around Regin, trying to give him magic, because there was still nothing, only those fading memories, and the gulping sobs were swallowing her, the water finally filling her mouth, he loved her, she was going to *die*—

When suddenly, somehow, the water vanished. Running off, pooling away, coughing itself out of Selby's lungs. And was the ground rising, or the water draining, she couldn't tell, couldn't care.

"Don't be dead," she choked, clinging frantic to Regin's body, her ear pressed to his silent, solid chest. "You can't be dead, you *can't*."

There were people here, suddenly, moving and shouting around them, but Selby didn't look up. Just kept clutching desperately to Regin, because her touch was supposed to bring the magic back. *Don't stop touching me*, he'd said. *Keep touching me.*

And touching him still meant there were those faded images, of Regin dying, through his own eyes. And as horrifying as it was, it was still *him*, still his thoughts, his memories, Selby still holding on, never letting go.

The sobs ripped out her throat, strangling her, because now there was the vision of him, minutes or a lifetime ago, looking at her under the water, in the near-blackness. *Thank you*, he'd said. *I love you.*

It couldn't be true, it couldn't, but then he'd saved Selby's life, at the expense of his own. Regin fucking Agmund, sacrificing himself for a pedlar. For her.

And now he was gone.

There were hands pulling at her, tugging her away, and Selby shoved back at them, clung harder. Couldn't let go. No. *No.*

"Please, Selby," came a voice, Thora's voice. "Runar's cleared his lungs, now he needs to get at his heart. It's his only chance."

His only chance. The words hurtled through Selby's head, and she snapped back to look at the face, Thora's face. "A chance?" she repeated, hollow, and Thora fervently nodded, one hand to Regin's shoulder, the other to Runar. Who was leaning over Regin's body, one hand now pressing flat against Regin's chest.

The magic jolted electric between them, making Regin's body jolt too, and Selby flinched as Runar did it again, and again. Making Regin's heart work again, there was no way it could work, none—

But Thora kept desperately nodding, her hand still to Runar's, and Runar kept going. Jolting Regin's limp body again and again beneath him, like he was a rag doll, empty, *gone*.

"It's not working," Selby gasped, the water running freely down her cheeks, the sobs breaking her voice. "It's not, it won't, he's gone, he's *gone*."

Runar didn't look up, but his mouth twisted, his fingers spreading wider. "Shut up," he snapped. "Touch him. And if you can get in his head, fucking *do* it."

Get in his head. Selby stared, startled—but then put her hands back to Regin, to his cold still face. Searching past those lingering images for thoughts, there was nothing, there would never be anything again, he was *dead*, but she would keep trying, keep going, until the end, please gods, please.

"You can't be dead," she whispered, the tears dripping from her eyes. "You can't. You're Regin fucking Agmund."

And here was the memory of her calling him that, him saying *stop calling me that*. And she touched it into him, half-smiling half-sobbing, because she'd liked setting him off, winding him up, and he'd liked it too, the bastard.

Next was the memory of them doing it on that rock, in the forest, out in the open. Regin striking down lightning onto that tree, flashing her that warm, insolent smile. *Come for me, witch*, he'd ordered her. *Prove to me just how good my dick is, how it fucking owns you...*

And beyond that, so many times in his bedroom, him on top her on top, that one glorious time with him behind her. Her sucking him off, he'd felt so good, tasted so good, there was so much more they could have done, would never get a chance to do again...

"You wanted it too," she murmured at him, letting her hands slide downwards, over him, going wherever they pleased, because maybe this was the last time she'd ever get to do this. "You lying bastard. You should have *seen* what I would have done to you."

She pressed the images deeper into him, just like she'd done when he'd had his nightmares. Letting them linger, twine into his, feel them become his own...

His own. Touching back.

Selby gasped, cried out, stared—heard Thora laugh—heard Runar mutter a relieved curse. And watched, felt, saw, the thoughts spin, turn, come alive. Regin's thoughts. Alive?

Regin's chest heaved, suddenly, on its own, and there was the thump-thump of his heartbeat inside it. Alive.

Selby's laugh came out high-pitched, hysterical, because Regin's mouth was coughing, and his eyes were blinking open, and she was on top of him, leaning over him. Meeting his blue eyes, alive, *alive*.

"You asshole," she gasped, and she could see him, taste him, could feel the thoughts twisting louder, stronger in his head. *What the fuck, where am I, where's Morley, you're here.*

Regin's body under hers was shivering, his breaths still raspy and shallow, but his hands were on her now, and she could feel him drinking in the magic, making it his. Even using it, somehow, to pull more air into his chest, to draw the oxygen to his blood.

"How," he croaked—his voice, he was *alive*—and Selby blinked down at him through her wet eyes, and tried to smile.

"Runar," she said, waving toward his blurry form beside them. "Started your heart up again. Gods, I could *kill* you for doing that."

Regin's mouth twitched up, the lightness flickering in his thoughts—but then it skittered into darkness as his head twisted, looking up over toward the side. Toward where Morley had been.

"Yeah, you got her," came Runar's grim voice beside them. "Thank fuck, because she was going to kill us all, and them, too, with that fucked-up death-spell she had them on."

Them? Death-spell? Selby's eyes snapped up, followed Runar's—and found a row of blinking, shaky-looking mages, staggering toward them on unsteady feet. Morley's mages, awake and seemingly coherent again, and that had to mean she truly was gone.

"Good," Regin said, briefly closing his eyes—but then one eye opened again, finding Selby's. "Did you really mean that?" he said, his voice still thick, slurry. "Shit we're gon' do?"

He meant the images Selby had put into his head, and she twitched as he touched them back. Things like her tying him to a tree, her riding him in an open field, taunting him with her body, her words, his cock pounding her throat until she gagged, and then yanking out to spray off all over her breasts...

"Of course that's what you're thinking about, you self-absorbed *troll*," Selby murmured, but her hands were on his face, stroking him, adoring him. "Not even a thank-you to Runar? Or a sorry for almost *dying* on me? Or for taking way too damned long to get down here in the first place?"

Regin groaned aloud, but one of his hands had come up to her face too, fingers spreading wide. "Ungrateful wench," he murmured. "I don't owe you *shit*, I saved your fucking *life*."

Selby couldn't help a slow smile, warm and genuine, even as her eyes kept blinking away the wetness still streaking down her cheeks. Regin Agmund was alive, Regin Agmund was here, Regin Agmund was *hers*.

"Oh, I'll pay you back, asshole," she replied. "You just wait and see."

47

It didn't take long until what felt like half of Coven Manor's population was down in this too-tiny room, talking and gossiping and milling about all at once.

There were the water-mages, cleaning up the mess Morley's flood had made, and the fire-mages, chatting and casting warming spells over Morley's still-dazed-looking workers. There were several of the Directors, murmuring and shaking their heads over Morley's sheet-covered body, and there was a large group of air-mages—notably lacking Greta, Njall, and the other usual suspects—all circled around a kneeling, angry-eyed Merton. Who, it turned out, had been hiding in the wall this entire time, like the cowardly scum he was.

"Don't let him out of your sight," Regin had ordered them. "He's got to answer for what he's done. Lying piece of *shit*."

The air-mages had actually cooperated, some of them even smiling and nodding at Selby, as though she was somehow suddenly legitimate. And though she wanted to believe that was due to her helping to rescue Morley's trapped mages, and almost being *killed*, she had a strong suspicion that it was more due to the fact that Regin was still here, sitting so close beside her on a rock, with his long arm slung over her shoulder, pulling her close.

"Uh, where are your friends?" Selby ventured, finally, after what felt like hours of this, answering questions and making statements, telling the same story again and again. "Shouldn't they be down here, what with you almost dying and all?"

The glance Regin gave her was odd, inscrutable. "Nah," he said, too casually. "I'm done with the lot of them. You were right, they were shit friends."

Really? Selby opened her mouth to demand how the hell that had happened, but was headed off by the infuriating sight of Captain Ludwen. Who, along with that truth-seeing swine Bekkan, had somehow found his way down here, too, and was asking, his voice booming through the too-small space, how on earth Regin had discovered the true culprit, and exposed a long-standing slave-trafficking ring.

Regin told it all again, curtly this time, and more than once he deferred questions to Selby, and to Runar and Thora and Fasta and Henrik, who had all hung around too, corroborating the story. While Runar kept hovering his hands over Regin and Selby, muttering unintelligible comments about magic availability and blood sugar levels and utter adrenal exhaustion.

"You two really need to get out of here," Runar said to them, once Ludwen and Bekkan had finally wandered off. "Leave this manor entirely, get some fresh air, and *sleep*."

"Really?" Selby replied, blinking incredulous toward him, and then at Regin, and then at the hubbub all around. "You think we can just—*leave*?"

Runar gave an exasperated roll of his eyes. "Yes. You can. I've addressed your shock and sleep deprivation for the time being—so use it, and get a few hours' distance from here, and *rest*."

Selby was still blinking at the thought, but beside her Regin seemed to fully accept it, rising unsteady to his feet. "Good by me. This stinking hellhole is probably still draining both of us."

He glanced down at Selby, raising an eyebrow, holding out a hand. And after an instant's hesitation she took it, let him pull her up—but then stopped, and turned to look at Runar and Thora. They'd saved Regin's life, they were ridiculously brilliant, and yet—

"Will you tell me why, first?" Selby asked. "Why you're both even here, when you hate it so much? And what's with the soldier guy? The, uh, reactivating?"

Thora blinked, glancing intently away, while Runar swallowed, a cool smile coming to his mouth. "Just doing our jobs, sweetheart," he said. "Just like you."

But Selby knew how Runar felt about this place, about why people did their jobs around here. *I've been there*, he'd said, *it's not fun.*

"I could search your thoughts, you know," she told Runar. "Find it all out for myself."

Runar's replying smile looked almost genuine, his head shaking. "Well, thank you for sparing us that deeply violating experience," he said, voice light. "And keep your mouths shut, please, for the love of the gods. But stay in touch, why don't you? Maybe we'll work something out at some point."

Thora nodded beside him, and reached out to give Selby a warm, fervent hug. "I'm so happy for you," she whispered. "You two will be so good for each other."

Her thoughts seemed to surge with her certainty of that, and Selby smiled and wiped at her eyes as she stepped back. And then found herself briefly pulled into Henrik's rough embrace, and then Fasta's more graceful one, both silently whispering of exhausted relief. Though Henrik's thoughts were also oddly caught on the sight of Fasta, whose hair had come out of her usual braid, and was hanging loose and messy around her lovely face.

"Thanks, all of you," Regin said, with a curt nod toward the four of them. "If any of you ever need to call in any favours, let me know. We'll be around."

With that, he grasped Selby's hand, and pulled her off toward the exit. Which Fasta and Henrik had finally been able to excavate, now that Morley was well out of the way, and Selby readily followed Regin through the awful dark passageway, up and up and up. Until they finally came out into fresh, wonderful, clean-smelling air, and the faint orange light of the slowly rising sun.

Selby briefly hesitated in place, drinking in the sight and the smell of it, but Regin kept moving, pulling her behind him. "Can you bring all Selby's things up from storage, please?" he said, to the first maid they saw in the corridor. "And a week's worth of packed food from the kitchens? We'll get it all at the front door."

The flustered-looking maid babbled her agreement and scurried away, while Regin kept walking, keeping Selby's hand in his. Until they were back in his old familiar room, which, oddly enough, now featured a broken-out window.

"Here," Regin said, tossing over his half-full satchel Selby had previously packed, which they'd found downstairs. "Pack up the rest of your stuff, we're leaving for good."

Oh? Selby blinked at him, but then silently, obediently wrapped up her precious things in her clothes, and slipped them into the bag. Her mother's hair, Simon's whistle, her father's box, Scarper's skull. Her thoughts whirling, but not thinking, not daring to think. They were leaving.

"All right?" Regin asked, once his own things were packed, and Selby nodded, and willingly clasped his hand again. And his thoughts behind his hand were all purpose, all *just-get-the-fuck-out-of-here*, and she let him draw her downstairs, through the corridors, toward the manor's front entrance. Almost, almost—

"What's this, Regin?" interrupted a frosty voice, and when Selby spun to look, there was Ketill. Standing directly before Regin, his arms crossed, his eyes narrow with suspicion. "Where are you going?"

"We're leaving," Regin replied, voice clipped. "I'm done."

The surprise flicked across Ketill's eyes, but was swiftly followed by grim disapproval, tightening the lines around his mouth. "Simply *leaving* is not an option, Regin," he said coldly. "You have obligations. *Extensive* obligations."

Regin barked out a hoarse, bitter-sounding laugh. "Nice try, old man," he said. "I have no contract. I've spent the last twelve years serving this Coven and my country. And I lost my magic for over a year, almost permanently, no thanks to you. I'm fucking *done*, Ketill."

Ketill blinked, looking genuinely taken aback—but then he seemed to collect himself, looking down his nose toward Selby. "You are not, in fact, *done*, Regin," he said smoothly. "Ms. Seng's trial under the Committee is not yet complete. She is still accused of murder. And *she* still has a contract, and is not permitted to leave the premises."

"Oh, don't feed me that bullshit, Ketill," Regin snapped back. "You showed me her contract, and it says her main obligation is to serve *me*, whatever I'm doing, above everything else. So if I'm not staying here, she's coming with me. And also"—he released Selby's hand, took a step closer to Ketill—"if you'd bother to take five minutes, and go down into the fucking *dungeon* that your fucking *colleague* tried to *kill* us in, you'll find out that even that asshole Ludwen agreed that Selby is innocent, and he's cleared her of all charges!"

Ketill blinked again, and Regin stepped even closer, looming over Ketill's suddenly small-looking form. "Also," he said, "you treated Selby like shit, you treated her family like shit, you were going to let her be imprisoned and *enslaved*, and you never even apologized *once*. We're fucking *done!*"

Ketill visibly spluttered, his mouth opening and closing uselessly, and Regin grasped Selby's hand again, and pulled her around Ketill, toward the door. But then he abruptly jerked to a halt, for no discernible reason, though his body felt taut all over, his thoughts behind his hand tilting at impatience and rage.

"Fuck *off*," Regin said, without turning around, but Ketill only strode closer, his robes swaying placidly around his ankles.

"Your attitude is unbecoming, Regin," Ketill said, and Selby could feel his magic now, cold and rigid, a flat solid wall under Regin's fingers, blocking him in. "After all I've done for you, this is how you repay me? I brought you out of squalor, I nurtured your skill, I gave you fame and fortune and purpose. I even brought you Ms. Seng. And now you spurn my kindness, and abandon your obligations, and callously reject the people and country who so desperately need you?"

Regin flinched, almost curling in on himself, and Selby could see the mess of images Ketill's words were stirring up in his thoughts. His responsibilities, his obligations, his privilege, his fame, everything Ketill had given him. All of it twisting in Selby's own chest, stoking her skittering fear, what if Regin listened, backed down, what if he did what he'd done every other time, until now...

But Regin's fingers on hers were still tight, still sure, and there was a new, quiet determination in his thoughts. He'd *died*. Selby had almost died. They were *leaving*.

"No, Ketill," Regin said, sounding weary, but steady. "I'm taking my life back. I'm doing what I need to do, what I should have done years ago. And if you don't take down this wall, I will."

Ketill gave an awful, thin smile, and Selby could feel his magic in the air, thickening under Regin's fingers. And it occurred to her, suddenly, that maybe Ketill was the one mage in the world who could stop Regin Agmund. The one mage who could trap him here, against his will, like a pet in a cage.

"I don't think so, Regin," Ketill said calmly. "You have obligations. Your country needs you. You're staying."

There was an instant's hanging, jolting silence—and then a

sudden, screeching, hurricane-force wind. Blasting down the corridor, and against Ketill's wall, all furious whirling power, enough to send Selby staggering sideways, against Regin's solid form.

But he was here, holding her close and safe, because it was his wind, of course. Blaring against Ketill's wall, fighting to break through it, but Ketill kept giving that thin, cold smile.

"Excellent, Regin," he said, as his robes whipped around his legs, his body stiff and unmoved. "It's gratifying to see your magic so improved."

The wind suddenly stopped, as abrupt as it had begun, leaving Selby clinging breathless and shaky against Regin's steady weight. But still grasping as tight as she could, needing to give him as much magic as humanly possible, and she felt it bloom out of him again, this time in the now-familiar spell of his air-shield.

The shield unfurled around them, an invisible beautiful bubble of solidness, pushing against Ketill's wall. Fighting to stretch it, bulge it, break it—but the wall remained solid, implacable, unmoving.

"Stop this nonsense, Regin," Ketill said. "We can have a rational discussion, work out some alternatives. Perhaps a vacation is in order."

A vacation. So *now* that was an option, after Regin had barely left this stinking hellhole in a *year*, and Selby couldn't help a harsh, grating laugh. Making both Regin and Ketill turn to look at her, Regin with something she couldn't read, Ketill with that smug soulless condescension written all over his face.

"Ms. Seng, your amusement is misplaced," Ketill said coldly. "I have also brought you out of poverty, out of a disreputable profession, and into the most prestigious magical facility in the land. I have given you meaningful work, with unlimited access to the most powerful air-mage on the continent. An opportunity many women would willingly *die* for."

Poverty? *Disreputable*? Selby could barely breathe through

the sudden towering rage, and she clenched her teeth so tight it hurt. "How *dare* you, asshole," she spat. "You almost *destroyed* my *family*. And Regin's not a pet, he's not a weapon, he's not yours to offer up on a platter! And neither am I, and we are fucking *done*!"

She strode toward the exit, stupidly, because she immediately, painfully, bounced off that damned air-wall. And now Ketill was the one laughing, the sound carrying loud through the empty entry hall, and Selby suddenly realized how odd it was, with half the manor's occupants milling about out of bed, that no one had yet interrupted them. And maybe that meant Ketill was using that same people-repelling spell Regin had used, and maybe no one would come, or care.

"You're going to stay here, Regin," Ketill continued, in that calm, remote voice. "And you're going to cooperate. Or else."

Or else? The threat sent a shudder down Selby's back, her eyes snapped to Regin's—when suddenly, somehow, her breath—vanished.

Selby retched, fought to drag in air—but there was nothing. Empty. Like the air around her had completely evaporated, sucked away, leaving only emptiness behind.

Her throat choked, frantic and desperate, while Regin whirled around to look at her, his eyes wide and suddenly terrified. "Stop, Ketill!" he shouted, and through their still-joined hands Selby could feel Regin's magic, his spells, fighting back. Firing one after another toward her, around her, trying and failing to break this, whatever Ketill had done.

"I will only stop," Ketill said, his voice barely perceptible over the roaring in Selby's ears, "once you agree to a rational compromise."

Selby's body was already thrashing, her lungs fighting and failing to gasp in air, the panic screaming through her head. She was finally going to die, Regin's magic wasn't enough, he was still weak from being *dead*, he couldn't do anything, they'd been so close to getting away for good, Ketill was going to kill her—

And suddenly she felt Regin considering it, even as his spells kept casting, trying, failing. If he agreed to Ketill's compromise, maybe they could live off-site, maybe he could take a leave, work something out, where he didn't have to see Ketill every day, wouldn't have to keep fighting this insatiable urge to tear his fucking head off—

No, Selby's thoughts shouted at Regin, into Regin, and she was distantly relieved when he stopped his casting, and blinked at her. Like he'd actually heard that, and she forced herself to think, through the wheeling shrieking panic.

Don't you dare agree, her thoughts gasped toward him. *He'll just keep doing it to you. Every single time you step out of line.*

Regin gaped at her, even as his own panic clanged through Selby's hand, his fingers trembling against hers. "I have to," he said. "I can't lose you. Not *again*. Not like this."

His voice cracked, and Selby could see, suddenly, in his head, what losing her would do to him. The guilt, the rage, the loneliness, the old darkness rising and rising, he'd just found this, he needed this so much, please...

Gods damn it. Selby's thoughts were fading, slipping in and out, Regin opening his mouth again. He was looking at Ketill, he was going to say yes—

Touch him, she managed, into Regin's thoughts. *Any way you can. And don't let go of me.*

Regin looked at her, her breath her body about to explode, terror screeching everywhere. *Please*, she choked, silent. *Now!*

And in a breath, Regin thrust himself forward, toward Ketill. Gripping one hand in Selby's still, but extending his other one out, urgently. As if to say, *all right, I agree, let's shake on it—*

There. Regin's hand closed around Ketill's, and suddenly Selby could feel it. Ketill's hand, Ketill's arm, Ketill's body, Ketill's brain.

Ketill's thoughts.

They were cool and distant, just like the rest of him, but Selby could see them now, could touch them. Could feel the all-powerful, all-consuming need to keep Regin here, because Regin was safety, status, power. Regin was *his*.

And that—that certainty, that astounding arrogance—was where Selby's grasping, frenzied touch went. Not subtle, not kind, but just ripping, tearing, pulling apart. *No, Regin's not yours, no, you didn't save him, and no, he doesn't owe you anything.*

The world had begun to darken around her, her legs starting to give way, the only saving grace those too-tight fingers on hers. *No, no, Regin's not yours, he never was, he's his—*

When suddenly, oh gods, there was air again.

Selby gasped and heaved for it, dragging in blessed fresh lungfuls of it, and Regin was here, his arms close and fierce around her. His thoughts shouting *please-be-here* and *don't-stop-breathing* and *what-the-fuck-did-you-just-do.*

Selby wasn't quite sure herself, still, but when she looked past Regin, Ketill was just standing there, blinking. Looking down at his hands, and blinking again, and again.

"Mr. Agmund, correct?" he said, carefully, like the words were strange on his tongue. "What are you doing here?"

Selby could taste the shocked disbelief swirling through Regin's form—*what the fuck*, his thoughts shouted—but he squared his shoulders, met Ketill's eyes.

"I'm leaving," he said. "For good."

Ketill's white head nodded politely. "Ah, yes, of course," he replied. "Best wishes for safe travels."

Regin's whole body twitched, his astonishment flashing visceral through Selby's fingers, but he nodded back. And when he turned to leave, pulling Selby behind him, there was nothing stopping them this time, no walls, no magic, nothing.

A glance over Selby's shoulder showed a bemused-looking Ketill still standing there, watching them go. But Regin didn't even look, just kept going, until they reached the pile of bags waiting by the door. Their clothes, Selby's things from storage, and what looked like a good month's worth of food, gods bless that kitchen.

"Ready?" Regin asked, once they'd both loaded up with bags, and he'd shouldered the door open, raising his eyebrows, waiting. "Now that we've got all your shit to lug with us?"

Selby rolled her eyes at him, but walked past him, outside, into the cool, clean, fresh air. Into freedom.

"Yes," she said. "Let's go."

48

Selby and Regin walked for a long time without speaking, hand in hand, moving deep into the trees, toward the rising sun. Not on a road, not following any kind of defined path, but Selby could feel that it was a route Regin had used many times before.

And despite that comment of his about the lugging, it seemed that travelling with Regin Agmund was astonishingly simple, because the bags just bobbed along behind them, floating in midair. Held up on whispery currents of Regin's magic, which felt stronger and brighter with every step they took.

Regin kept glancing over at Selby, as if expecting her to protest or complain, but there was absolutely no reason to, out in the cool air and the trees. Finally free of that cursed manor, of Morley and Ketill and all the rest of them, forever.

But Regin still hadn't said, and his thoughts behind his fingers were very purposely on moving, on keeping course, getting to a specific place he knew where they could sleep for a while. Not on Selby, or what this was, or what it might mean.

"Where are we going?" Selby asked, finally, and Regin glanced toward her again, his eyes very distant, very careful.

"Well," he began, hesitant, "I thought—maybe we could go east. Back to find your family. And then"—she could taste the rising trepidation in his thoughts—"if you wanted, you could come along up north. See my dad's old place."

Selby's steps faltered, and Regin halted too, looking at her with that unease in his eyes. Waiting to hear her answer, whether she wanted to stay with her family, or go with him. Giving her the choice.

And suddenly the rising warmth surged up, so powerful that the world around Selby tilted, and she flung herself toward Regin's stiff form, curling close into the safe strong heat of his arms.

"Of course I'd like to come north with you," she said, into his chest, against the too-rapid beat of his heartbeat. "Thank you."

She could feel him relaxing, his thoughts unspooling, letting their guard down. But not quite all the way, and she pulled back, enough to meet his still-uneasy eyes.

"And after that?" she asked, because that was the last, most important question—and she felt Regin's chest rise and fall against her, his hands clenching on her back.

"Well," he replied, and there was a glimpse of genuine fear, hurtling behind his thoughts. "I thought—maybe—if you still wanted—we could do some of that shit you said, before. Travelling. Thinking. And stuff."

Something constricted in Selby's throat, sudden and close, but Regin swallowed, kept speaking. "And look, I know what I said to Ketill about that contract, but you don't have to keep to it, all right? You can do whatever the hell you want."

He truly meant that, Selby could feel it, and she took a long, fortifying breath. "Well, what if I wanted to forget that damned contract," she said. "But still come with you."

There was a sharp twitch all down Regin's body, his eyes intent on hers. "You'd still do it for free, then?" he asked, quiet. "You really meant that?"

Selby tried for a smile, but it felt shaky, and she had to blink back the sudden wetness pooling behind her eyes. "Hell, yes," she replied. "Though maybe you'll change your mind, once your magic's back to normal again. Once you don't actually need me anymore."

Regin stared down at her, like that thought hadn't even occurred to him, and he barked out a hoarse laugh. "'Course I still need you," he said, even quieter than before. "It was never just the magic. You know that. Don't you?"

Selby nodded back up at him, though a twinge of uncertainty might have still been there, whispering, betraying her. And maybe Regin caught it, his throat convulsing as he looked at her—and then he made a strange choking sound, and yanked her close again. His hands skittering on her back, his face buried in her hair.

"You've been—*everything*, Selby," he croaked. "You—you *saved* me. You've been so damned generous, so damned good to me, all this time, when I didn't at all deserve it. I just—I'm so sorry. So fucking sorry."

Oh. *Oh.* Selby's body seemed to melt into his, into those impossible words, into the fervent stroking of his strong hands against her, the shaky drag of his breath against her hair. "You deserved so much better," he gasped. "Gods, I wish I could go back and do it all over again. I would have—should have—"

His voice choked, broke, and suddenly there were just visions, flashing from his churning thoughts into hers. Visions of Regin Agmund meeting Selby at Coven Manor's gate, feeling nervous but determined, wearing his finest clothes, and his best smile. Visions of him welcoming her, introducing himself, offering her his hand, escorting her inside. And then making introductions, showing her around, taking her to a spectacular dinner. And throughout it all, making sure his protection and his favour toward her was very publicly clear. Making sure every last person in Coven Manor knew not to fuck with Regin Agmund's honoured guest, with the gifted earth-mage who bore such a rare, powerful affinity with his magic.

And with that all settled, he'd have shown Selby up to his room. He'd have offered to make it comfortable, to arrange for whatever she'd wanted. And when he'd caught sight of her full bags, and realized how important they were to her, he'd have gone and demanded that a new shelf be brought up for her at once. And then he'd have waited while she'd unpacked, asking her about each of her prized possessions as she'd set them out, listening to all her memories and tales, learning about the people she loved. And then he'd have offered up any of his own possessions for her to touch and learn from, too. Freely welcoming her knowledge of him, doing his best to answer her questions, to make her feel at home.

And then, finally, once he'd again made her choice clear—*you can still walk out of here, forever, no questions asked*—he'd have taken her to bed. Kissing her, breathing in the scent of her, stroking and cherishing her stunning, untouched body with gentleness and care. Worshipping her like the impossible gift she was, the beautiful, brilliant goddess who hadn't come only to share his bed, but to bring back his priceless lost magic, his calling, his hope. To give him the air again, to help him breathe again, to make his entire world fresh and bright and new again.

And in the days and weeks afterwards, as they'd gotten to know each other, he'd have kept his commitment to total honesty, too. He'd have let her see all the shameful, secret thoughts he'd still tried so hard to hide. How often he'd watched her. How deeply he'd admired her. How he'd brought himself off again and again to memories of her. How he'd seethed with jealousy over Runar, and sometimes even Kal and Henrik, too. How empty he'd felt when she was gone. How he'd repeated all her pointed, powerful words, over and over again. How damned much he'd needed her frankness, her openness, her consistent dismissal of his fame. How she'd seen him at his lowest, at his absolute worst, and still—somehow—found him worthy.

I'm so fucking sorry, vision-Regin whispered again, stroking it through his hands into Selby's back, kissing it into her hair. *I don't deserve you. Still don't even know why you're still here. Why you'd want to keep putting up with my shit.*

But somehow, Selby was shivering against his chest, and she pressed back her own visions, too. Visions of Regin Agmund smiling, touching her, teasing her, meeting her. Regin Agmund listening, learning, defending her, offering her choices, wielding all his stubbornness and his power on her behalf. Regin Agmund not once doubting her amidst all those accusations, Regin Agmund giving her an adventure, Regin Agmund fighting the whole world to save her. And finally, just today, Regin Agmund freely offering up his entire life—his work, his magic, his fame, his future—in exchange for hers.

Regin huffed out a sharp, shaky breath, and then wrenched Selby even closer, pressed his lips tight to her hair. "Was the least I could do," he rasped, out loud. "Was already dead, before you."

Selby swallowed down the lump in her throat, shook her head. And she couldn't find a way to say it, couldn't explain it, could only press the raw surging truth of it back into him, so hard it almost hurt. *No. No. Hell, no. You need to stay alive, you need to stay here with me, you need to never die again, ever. And also, gods help me, you are damn well going to learn how to swim.*

"Fuck, really?" Regin croaked, the dismay too strong in his fingers—and suddenly Selby was laughing, shrill and helpless into his chest, and he was chuckling, too. The sound so warm, so easy and relieved, like she'd never heard it before—and it distantly occurred to her that she'd so rarely seen him apart from that constant, miserable drag on his magic. And what would his magic even be like, without it? What would *he* be like?

But perhaps she'd thought that too loudly, or she was still

too raw, too open to him, because Regin gave another low chuckle, touched a twinge of genuine-feeling regret into her back. "Don't get your hopes up," he murmured, soft. "Pretty sure I've always been an asshole, and that's probably not going to change much. But my magic..."

Something quivered in his voice, in his hands, and Selby waited as he exhaled, his breath fluttering her hair. "Look, I'll be honest, 'cause you'll see it anyway, but I think—I know—my magic's always going to be better with you around. Stronger. Like that day out on the rock. But I don't want you to think— you know it's not—"

His voice broke, the frustration shuddering through his hands, and now it was his thoughts again, his truth, opening wide toward her. Showing her what it meant, how he felt, what he couldn't find the words to say. *I want my magic, I want how this feels, what it gives me—but I want you more. Would still want you without it. Would never want you to feel trapped, or obligated, or—*

But Selby was already nodding against him, and pressing back her own acknowledgement, her understanding. "Look, it's not just you," she replied thickly. "The things I've been able to do these past weeks, after all this time with you, it's—"

She couldn't finish, wincing, but Regin had stilled for a breath, his surprised thoughts shifting, reorienting around that awareness—and then shuddering into a warm, bright relief. "Yeah, your magic's been brilliant," he said lightly, with a short chuckle. "And fucking terrifying, wench. You can cast through my *head*, for fuck's sakes."

With the words, there was his memory of Selby doing that, down in that cold watery darkness. Taking his spell, his knowledge, his power, and—channelling it. Changing it. Something he'd never once imagined someone else could possibly do.

"Well, I'm pretty sure that's really, *really* illegal magic," Selby said, muffled into his tunic. "Especially the permanently-fucking-around-in-people's-brains part."

She was thinking of what she'd done to Ketill, and she was still a little appalled by that—but against her Regin laughed again, the sound vibrating through his chest. "Yeah, like I said, terrifying. Shoulda known you had something like that up your sleeve. Vicious little witch."

He didn't seem disturbed, though—quite the contrary—and when Selby pulled back to glare at him, he was grinning down at her, his blue eyes dancing with warmth, with approval, with affection. With the same affection that kept whispering behind his hands, shimmering with impossible things like *I love it* and *It's so fucking hot* and *I can't wait to see what you do with it next*.

Selby's breath caught, her cheeks damnably heating, and Regin's grin pulled higher, into something sharp and hungry. "Speaking of which," he murmured, "I remember somebody promising me some stuff, if I came back from the dead."

Selby attempted another glare toward him, but he only kept grinning back, and let his hand trail down her front, brushing against her hard nipple through her dress. "You weren't putting me on, were you?" he said, husky. "At the very least, you could suck off the guy who went and *died* for you."

Selby's mouth twitched up, and her hands were already slipping down his back, finding his gorgeous hard arse. "Yes, well," she murmured back, "I already sucked off that guy, what, five times in the last three days?"

Regin scoffed, rolled his eyes. "And you think that somehow makes you *exempt*?" he demanded. "Fair warning, wench, if I'm giving up my *life* to travel the world with you, sucking me off is a once-a-day *requirement*."

Giving up his life to travel the world with her. It still felt too new, too impossible, like it couldn't be real—but Regin Agmund was still here, still touching her, still grinning at her, still holding his thoughts and his truth wide open for her to see. *You know you don't have to, but fuck yeah I want it, want all of it, want your perfect little mouth on me whenever you'll give it, please.*

A hard, thrilling shudder jolted up Selby's back, pooled deep into her groin, and she couldn't stop smiling, squeezing his arse through his trousers. "Well, if that's the case," she said, as lightly as she could, "do I at least get some more rewards out of the deal?"

"Maybe," Regin replied, his hand cupping brazen and protective over her breast now, his other hand giving a proprietary squeeze to her arse. "If you're good."

Selby couldn't even try to be offended, couldn't stop beaming at him. "But I'm always good. Aren't I?"

He laughed at that, his eyes crinkling at the corners, warm, wicked, here, *hers*. "You, good?" he asked, and he pulled her closer, pressed a soft, sweet kiss to her mouth. "Always, witch. Now get on your knees, will you?"

Selby did.

EPILOGUE

The pub was crammed and bustling, filled with the sounds of talking voices and clanking cups. The wooden bar under Selby's hands was sticky and well-used, and murmured its memories of past drunken shenanigans so loudly that Selby could barely hear the muscled, dark-haired man speaking beside her.

"Are you from around here, honey?" the man asked, his eyes dropping to the admittedly low neckline of Selby's dress, which was currently missing its top button. "I don't remember seeing you here before."

"No, just in town for a few days," Selby replied, and smiled at the barmaid as she brought over a mugful of ale. "Though I've been hearing a lot about all the thieving around here lately. Sounds pretty intense."

The man's eyes flitted up to Selby's face, briefly, and then back down to the neckline of her dress. "Oh, yeah," he said. "Real unusual."

It sounded like another dead end, but just in case, Selby surreptitiously brushed her elbow up against his through his tunic. And sure enough, it was all *look-at-that-rack*, *how-do-I-get-her-upstairs*, and nothing useful whatsoever about where the thieves were hiding, or how they'd managed to steal huge amounts of coin from almost everyone in town.

Selby sighed, and opened her mouth to tell the man to get lost—but now here was Regin, leaning his tall form back against the bar between them, and eyeing the man with deep dislike.

"Get lost, asshole," he said. "And keep your eyes to yourself."

The man glanced darkly up and down Regin's form—he was shorter than Regin, but definitely bulkier—and curled his lip. "And why should I listen to you?"

"Because I'm Regin Agmund," Regin said, coolly, and it was almost comical to see the man's eyes go wide—first in disbelief, and then recognition, and then downright horror.

"*You're* Regin Agmund?" he squeaked, backing away sideways, raising his hands in apology. "Damn. Sorry, sir, sorry."

Regin didn't reply, just glowered at the man as he went, and Selby gave him a little nudge, a kick of her boot at his trousers. "You are such an asshole," she informed him, lightly. "I had it completely under control."

Regin reached around and grabbed Selby's mug, took a long gulp of her ale. "Yeah, yeah," he said, and with his other hand he spun Selby sideways toward him on her stool, and stepped closer between her legs. "Still didn't like how he was looking at you. Although"—he reached down, caught a long finger on her too-low neckline—"you could cover up, for fuck's sakes."

Selby rolled her eyes at him, even as her hands came up to slide against his tunic, her boot hooking around his leg. "*You* did that, asshole."

Regin smirked at her, and took another drink of her ale. "I'm not the one who suggested we go at it in that shop's broom closet," he said. "Greedy little wench."

Selby kicked at the back of his leg, though her face was already warming at the memory of it. Regin pinning her up between the brooms and mops, pulling her breasts out of her dress, plunging deep between her legs while she screamed.

"Did I see you complaining?" Selby replied, as levelly as she could. "No. Quite the opposite."

With the words, she flicked a memory into him, and the responding flare in Regin's eyes said that he'd seen it. Himself, with his engorged cock jutting out of his trousers, saying, *If you don't please me, witch, I'm going to throw open this door, show this whole place how hard your tits bounce when you take my dick—*

"But I was doing all that for you, love," Regin said lazily, and his audacious fingers came up, tweaked her hard nipple through her dress. "I know how much you like a good public fucking."

Selby couldn't help a darting glance at the people talking and drinking all around them, but thankfully no one had seemed to notice. They usually didn't, ever since Regin had started growing out his hair and his beard, and together with his bulkier form—he ate constantly these days—he looked more and more like a scruffy northern woodsman than the Regin Agmund of portrait fame.

"I do not," Selby replied, belatedly, but Regin laughed, and now here was a swift series of memories, parading straight from his still-playing fingers into her hard nipple. Her moaning in an open hayfield, her pressed to a stone wall in an alley, her buck-naked in the back of a moving wagon, her screaming Regin Agmund's name while he held her out an upstairs window, his dick buried deep inside her—

Selby was already breathing hard, her tongue coming out to brush her lips, and Regin chuckled, low and triumphant. "Is there anywhere you wouldn't do it?" he asked, raising his eyebrows at her. "A morgue, maybe?"

Selby swallowed, and gave a surreptitious glance down to that telltale bulge in his trousers. "What better place," she managed. "Celebrate life, and all."

Regin made a face, leaned in a little closer. "Yeah, you'd

probably get off on that," he murmured. "Or let the dead bodies kill us. Fine, a latrine."

Selby inhaled the delicious smell of him, looked up at him under her fluttering eyelashes. "Fine, you've got me," she said. "No latrine."

And so it was that several minutes later, Selby and Regin were crammed into one of the pub's tiny public stalls, with the sounds of people all around, talking and slamming doors and doing their latrine business. At least the little stall didn't smell, thanks to one of Regin's many useful air-spells, but it was probably still filthy, and Selby was deeply grateful when Regin took one revolted look, and threw up a protective air-shield all against the walls, along with his usual sound-spell.

"Now, you little witch," he breathed now, rounding toward her, his fingers crushing hard against her breasts as he tugged them out of her dress, spilling them over that too-low neckline. "Since you're the one who's making me fuck you in a filthy crowded latrine"—his long fingers pinched her jutting nipples, hard—"I get to pick which one of your tight little holes I'm fucking. Deal?"

Selby couldn't seem to reply, already arching into the touch of those fingers, and she pulled his shaggy head down for a kiss, his mouth hot against hers, his teeth nipping on her lips. "Why the hell do you get to decide?" she countered, breathless. "You were the one who picked this job, with its complete lack of clues, I have questioned like forty-five people in this town so far and *nothing*—"

"Oh shut your whining mouth," Regin snapped, with another sharp nip at her lips, and a stinging slap to her arse. "I've got another good lead, we're meeting them in the morning, and you're going to fucking *deliver*, witch."

Selby gasped, her hand gone down to find his familiar hard cock, and squeezing it perhaps too tight. "*I'm* going to deliver?" she demanded. "When you're the one who hasn't even perfected that stun-spell yet?"

The stun-spell was one of Regin's newer ones, one that allowed him to strike someone with lightning, without quite killing them. It was deeply difficult, requiring easily four times as much magic as a regular lightning strike, but it was also highly useful, especially in the line of work they'd somehow fallen into this past year. Solving problems, catching thieves and murderers, getting information, even throwing their weight around with the government and the Coven. Because when one half of you was Regin Agmund, and the other half was a thought-stealing pedlar, you could get into a hell of a lot of places, and accomplish a lot of things, that most people couldn't.

And over the past year, they'd accomplished more than Selby would have ever imagined. Not only had they caught multiple thieves and murderers, but they'd also shut down several laws targeting pedlars and peasants. They'd secretly undermined at least three unjust military strikes. They'd publicly advocated for fair wages and working conditions. And at least once every month or two, Regin would shave and dress in his finest clothes, and go stand before committees and councils and crowds. Speaking with all his usual directness and force, defending people who needed it—and then he would finish it all off with a spectacular lightning show, to shouts and stomps and applause. Using his magic to make a difference, to do work that mattered, just like he'd wanted all along.

Of course, afterwards he would always be approached by various politicians, military personnel, and Coven members, begging for him to return, and offering everything from coin to titles to threats. But thankfully, none of it had come from Ketill—he'd retired from the Coven altogether, last they'd heard—and Regin had roundly refused every offer, every attempt. And Selby knew, all the way to her bones, that he would never, ever go back.

"Like hell I haven't perfected that stun-spell," Regin growled now, and with a gust of sudden wind he blew up

Selby's skirts, his hand gripping at her bare arse. "I haven't killed anybody in what, four months?"

"Oh, four *months*," Selby replied, rolling her eyes back at him, the derision clear on her voice. "Like you deserve some kind of *prize* for not *murdering* people."

"That guy was *scum*," Regin snapped back, "and you know it. Hell, you were the one who put his foul memories in my head, what the fuck did you expect me to do with that? Pat him on the back and send him on his way?"

His hands were pinching harder, one on her breast one on her arse, and Selby leaned deeper into them, slid her own hands around to grip at his own glorious round arse. And she didn't point out, though perhaps she could have, that she knew Regin had actually enjoyed killing that vile murderer, that he still liked the thrill of a good clean hit now and then—and thankfully Regin didn't point out, though he could have too, that Selby had been touching him at the time, could have easily stopped him casting that spell, and hadn't. And instead, she'd fucked him afterwards, frantic and desperate on the forest floor, the images of that lightning bolt ricocheting back and forth between them.

"Such an ungrateful wench," Regin said, as he spread her legs wider apart, propped her up on an invisible bubble of air. "When I used that entire damn payout on you, buying you expensive shit. Just like keeping a fucking *mistress*."

His eyes were insolent, challenging on hers, as if daring her to refute him, while his hand slid up between her legs, lingering into her already-clenching wetness. And Selby moaned, grinding up against him, searching for a reply, because he was right, he did buy her a lot of things. Lovely, custom-made, single-sourced things, dresses and shoes and art and jewelry, even that beautiful ring he'd made entirely by himself, under the goldsmith's careful direction. And every time Selby's fingers brushed against it, there was the memory of Regin blinking, putting it on, his fingers whispering, *Is it all right, does it feel good, please say you like it...*

"I'm way better than a mistress, asshole," Selby gasped, as one of those clever fingers slipped up deep into her, oh gods. "I keep you rolling in lucrative work, I *earn* half that coin, I make your magic better and stronger than it's ever been. And"—she shot him a smug smile—"I suck you off for breakfast almost every morning, and also, I'm the best fuck you've ever had in your *life*."

None of it could be argued, as Regin well knew, since Selby had exclusive access to all the memories that proved it. And over the past year, she'd continued to wield Regin's thoughts and longings in bed to her full advantage, pinning down even his most fleeting desires, and turning them into bared, blistering truth between them. No matter how secretive or shameful, no matter how it looked or sounded, because Regin Agmund was *hers*. Hers to know, hers to enjoy, hers to taste and taunt and tease and torment—even if it was in a filthy public latrine.

"Well, you know that's all just the bare minimum, witch," Regin replied now, his voice cool, his eyes alight. "Because if I'm binding myself to one girl for the rest of my life, she'd damn well better suck me every day, and more. And right now"—there was a flurry of motion, hands, air, as he spun Selby around, bent her over double—"she's going to beg me to pound her up the ass in this filthy public latrine."

Fuck. Selby had known he was going there, of course he was. And though they'd been dabbling in that particular activity for a few months now, she fully knew how much Regin still craved it, how it was still a forbidden secret thrill. Having his own virgin goddess any way he wanted, anywhere he wanted, made all the better because she always knew, always made it part of the game, always—

"*Wait*," Selby protested, as Regin bent her over further,

kicked her legs apart. "Slow down, you great *prick*, it still hurts from last time—"

Regin gave a husky laugh, blowing Selby's skirt up higher with another gust of air, exposing her entire lower half to his eyes. Except her tight knee-high leather boots, of course, but those were his too, worn just because he liked the look of them, like this.

"Yeah, and it's going to hurt even more this time," he murmured, as his strong hands tilted her hips up even further, pulling her arse-cheeks a little apart. "You won't be able to sit for a *week* once I'm done with this."

It wasn't an empty promise, Selby knew from experience, and she tried for a glare over her shoulder, even as her thoughts shouted back into him, pleading at him, *oh gods, yes, please, don't stop.* "You asshole," she hissed, out loud. "Don't you even *think* about putting that giant overblown dick anywhere near there yet, you—"

She broke off at the sudden, shocking feel of it, that smooth hard head pushing right *there*, oh gods. Without any kind of oil or lubrication whatsoever, and Selby cried out as Regin gave that husky laugh again, pushed a little harder.

"Yeah, that shut you up," he breathed. "Now beg me, witch. Or else you'll be taking it dry, with no warmup, just like this."

Gods curse him, and *bless* him, and Selby cried out again, even as those strong hands pulled her apart further, and that huge, demanding cock drove harder against her tight resisting heat. About to punch its way through, break its way in, and while they had done that before, and it had been shocking and painful and delicious, she did have this damned meeting tomorrow, had to deliver...

"Fine, fine," she gasped. "Do what you want, asshole, and get it over with. There. You happy?"

Regin gave a low growl of disapproval, and there was the thrilling feel of his hand, slapping hard to her bare, exposed arse-cheek. "Disrespectful little wench," he said. "I said, you're going to beg me to pound your ass. And the more lip you give me, the more you'll have to beg for. Or else."

He pushed in again, his hands stretching her open, hinting now at tightness and pain. Making Selby's breath come shorter, her body clenching back at him, her thoughts still silently pleading, *yes, hell yes, keep going*. "How about I'll beg you to put that thing away," she managed. "Get yourself off for once in your life."

Regin's slap to her arse was harder this time, echoing slightly against the sound-spell around them. "I don't get myself off," he growled. "That's what you're for, witch. Last chance, or else."

As he spoke the pain fired again, that smooth hard tip just squeezing its way inside, oh gods, oh gods. Leaving Selby gasping, panting, hands scraping at the air-shield in front of her, Regin's huge, dry dick was going to pound her ass, oh gods, oh fuck—

"Fine!" she half-shouted, half-groaned. "Fine. Pound my ass. Please."

He eased off the pressure, just a bit, but he was still there, just inside her, invading her, stretching her open, pinning her there. "Not good enough," he said, though his breath sounded short, too, the hunger blazing beneath his gripping fingers, his smooth prodding head. "Say, *please, Regin, please pound my ass in this filthy latrine until I scream.*"

Selby's entire body convulsed, tightening on his still-invading cock, making him laugh out loud, the bastard. "Also," he murmured, "say, *please, Regin, pump my ass full of your spunk, until I'm gaping wide open, and leaking it all over this filthy latrine floor.*"

Selby moaned aloud, betraying far too much of her own hunger, and Regin laughed again, gave her arse-cheek another hard slap. "And," he breathed, "tell me you're my own greedy wench, my own personal fucktoy, a foul-mouthed little *hellion* who'll do *anything* to get my cock up her ass."

Fuck, he was such an asshole, and he was so damn good, and Selby's entire body was shaking for him, craving for him, and she took a hard breath, let it out. "Please, Regin," she gulped. "Please, pound my ass until I scream. In this filthy latrine."

There was another low chuckle, an approving grip of his hand on her arse-cheek, and thank the gods he eased off the pressure, pulled that hard head out of her resisting heat with an obscene-sounding pop. "Better," he whispered. "And?"

And. Selby dragged in another breath, trying to think, as those hands pulled her up more, apart more, showing him everything between her legs, how it throbbed for him, pleaded for him. "Please," she gasped, "please, Regin, please. Take me, fuck me, fill my ass full of your spunk."

There was another approving grip of that hand, and then the delectable feel of that hard cock again, now sliding down lower, against her spread-open wetness. Not sinking inside where she craved it, because that would be far too kind—but instead rubbing himself against it, slicking himself up with her juices.

"Look at you, dripping wet for this," he murmured. "Wouldn't you just love to have my dick up your hungry little cunt right now, witch?"

Selby groaned helplessly, her body grasping wet against that hard sliding cock, betraying her. "Yes," she whispered. "Yes, Regin, oh gods, *please*."

His replying laugh was husky, triumphant, that slick shaft now sliding further up her crease, spreading out the wetness. "Nice try," he breathed. "You're only getting this one way right now. And only if you keep begging me. Properly."

He still felt so good, impossibly good, that hardness going down to soak up even more of her wetness, so close, oh gods. And suddenly Selby just needed it, so desperately she couldn't think, couldn't pretend to resist, couldn't even try.

"Please, Regin," she pleaded. "Please, fuck my ass. Fill me

until I'm gaping wide open for you, until I'm leaking your spunk all over this filthy latrine floor."

The wetness was everywhere now, his hard slick cock sliding long and purposeful against her resisting tightness, coating her with it. "And," Selby gasped, "I'm your own filthy fucktoy, your own depraved little wench, I'll do anything to get your cock inside me, any way you can. So please, please, shove it up my ass, *now*."

Regin's groan behind her was guttural, thrilling, and finally that slippery silken hardness was right there, pointing against her, jabbing itself against her tight heat. But it was soaking wet now, slick and dripping, and Selby took deep breaths, tried to relax, to take this, to welcome it.

"Open up," he whispered behind her, and here was the clear, vivid image of it, in her thoughts, through his eyes. Herself bent double, with her skirts up, her legs spread, her entire crease wide open to him, showing him everything that was his. And his cock was so hard it was almost painful, just nudging into that tight little hole, looked so good, felt so fucking good, should he go slow, be sweet, or should he just take it—

"Take it," Selby gasped. "Please, Regin, *fuck me*."

There was another harsh, guttural groan, his hands pulling her wider, more open, apart—and then—

Selby screamed as he smashed inside, breaking through all her body's resistance, burying himself to the hilt. Her ass invaded, pinned, stretched open on his huge dick, oh fuck, oh *fuck*.

It burned, impossibly taut and tight and full inside, and even more when he ground himself deeper, settling her close and tight against his hips. While his heavy bollocks pressed below, bulged in just the right place, and Selby cried out again, breached, trapped, completely at his mercy, oh gods.

"You like that, witch?" he demanded behind her, grinding a

deep circle inside, and Selby desperately nodded, her breath coming out in rasping, choking gasps.

"Yes," she breathed. "Yes, I love it, I love you, Regin, fuck me, pump me full of your spunk, *please*."

There was a strangled sound behind her—a brief, desperate image of how fucking good she was, his thoughts wild and screeching for her—and then he pulled out, and slammed back inside. So hard and so perfect that Selby scrabbled against him, on him, struggling to escape, to stay, but he had her pinned, no escape, no relief from that massive invading cock.

He drove inside again, merciless, powerful, everywhere, and Selby screamed again, her body grasping and struggling, pushing and pulling. Trying to impale itself deeper on that cock, even as the rest of her flailed, floundered, nowhere to go, nothing else but this—

"No getting away now, witch," Regin gasped, as he plunged in again, and again. "You begged for it, this is what you fucking get."

Yes, gods, yes, Selby's entire body was trembling, her mouth crying out with every thrust, every deep, shocking gouge of that huge prick inside her. "But it's so much," she whimpered. "Too much, you're so fucking *huge*, Regin—"

"Hell yeah, I am," he breathed behind her, pounding in so hard the world spun. "But you wanted this, wench, your ass is *mine*, I get to do whatever the hell I want with it—"

He was everything, his slamming invading cock was everything. Ravaging painful impossibly intimate pleasure, taking her, making her his, and Selby's breath was coming in sobs now, lost, desperate, glorious. "Yes," she gasped. "I'm yours. Please, Regin. *Please*."

There was one more driving slam of that cock, his hands digging painfully into her hips—and there it was, oh gods, his voice shouting as he pumped out inside her, in pulse after shuddering pulse. Filling her, making her his, giving her that deep essence of him that was only hers, always hers, always.

"Fuck," Regin whispered, shaky, and his gripping hands on her hips finally slackened, his cock softening a little inside. "Gods *damn* it, wench."

Selby's mouth gave a trembly laugh, or maybe another sob, and one of Regin's hands slid smooth and reassuring up her bare flank. While his thoughts behind it whispered their hazy contentment, their undeniable affection, all *so good, love, so fucking good.*

And then his hands came to her arse, which was still jammed full of his now-softening cock, and she could see it, through his eyes, as he slowly pulled himself out. Could feel the suction pulling, could hear the obscene sound it made as he popped out—and now here was the sight of it, just as obscene, just as thrilling. Her body stretched and used, gaping wide open where his cock had been, and leaking out copious amounts of his thick, viscous white spunk.

"Look at you," he breathed. "Dripping all this spunk out onto the floor. Such a greedy little wench, making a filthy mess."

Selby gave another helpless moan, and in reply Regin laughed, the sound husky, warm, affectionate. "My little wench," he murmured, and now there was the feel of a rag, sliding against her, gently mopping her up. "*So* good, love."

Selby waited until he finished, her legs shaking dangerously now, and finally he dropped her skirts, tossed the rag down the latrine, and gave that telltale pat to her arse. *Up*, it said, and with effort Selby finally stood up again, staggering slightly on her feet. But Regin instantly caught her, turned her around, bent down to press a light little kiss to her forehead. *So good*, he said again, pressing it through his lips. *The best.*

Selby shot an almost-shy smile up toward him, and slipped up her tingling hand to stroke his hot, reddened cheek. "You mean that?" she asked. "Good enough that I might get a reward?"

Regin's replying grin was warm and breathtaking, his blue eyes saucy on hers. "Hell, yeah," he replied. "You'll be screaming my name, wench. But"—he made a face, cast a brief glance around them—"not in here, for fuck's sakes. This is fucking disgusting."

"It was *your* idea!" Selby retorted, and Regin raised his eyebrows at her, all infuriating disbelieving *innocence*. "I was *joking*," he said coolly. "Only a greedy wench like you would actually bend over and beg to have her ass pounded in a filthy public *latrine*."

"You are such a hypocritical *dick*," Selby hissed, but Regin only smirked back, and dropped his air-spells with a flick of his fingers. And then took her hand, leading her out of the stall, straight past several blinking observers, but Regin didn't pay any attention, and neither did Selby. Because that *had* been so damn good, *so* worth it—and she well knew that Regin always delivered on his promised rewards afterwards, too. He'd spread her out under the stars and take his damned good time with her, until she was indeed screaming his name.

"So you really think this meeting tomorrow will do it, then?" Selby asked, once they were back out in the cool, quiet night air. "Is it with that suspicious guy you told me about this afternoon?"

"Yep, that's the one," Regin said, as they turned off the main road, and headed toward their camp in the nearby forest. "He's definitely hiding something. So now it's all on you to save the day, love."

He shot her a sideways half-smile in the moonlight, and Selby smiled back, bumped her elbow against his. "Have you given any thought to afterwards, then?" she asked. "Do you want to take on another job, or take a break for a while?"

"Nah, I could go for another one, if you're good," Regin

replied, giving her another sidelong look. "We could go check in with your ma, at least."

They'd been relying on the pedlar network as a source for much of their work these past months, since pedlars were more informed than almost anyone on all the gossip and political goings-on, and could easily pass on information. It also gave Selby plenty of opportunity to see her family, something Regin was always very conscious of, and she shot a swift, genuine grin up toward his watching eyes.

"I'd love that," she told him. "Thanks."

Regin shrugged, giving that familiar self-conscious rub on the back of his neck—and with it, nudging from his elbow into hers, was a twinge of something else, too. Something Selby had felt from him a few times lately, but something he'd seemed... protective of.

Selby hadn't wanted to push at it, because she did still want to allow Regin his secrets—but maybe he'd caught her awareness anyway, his eyes angling again toward her, his breath coming out in a slow, shaky exhale.

"You ever think about us maybe building a place out east?" he asked, a little too quickly. "Nothing too fancy, nothing we'd need to stay at all the time. But just something nearer your ma, in case you ever wanted to..."

His voice trailed off, his eyes darting toward the treeline up ahead, and Selby faltered, blinking uncertainly up at his guarded face in the moonlight. "In case... what?" she echoed. "What would I want to do?"

Her voice had gone too thin, her heart suddenly thundering against her ribs, because he couldn't mean—they should stop travelling? Quit their work? Or... or break up?!

Regin winced, flinched, shook his head—and then he snapped out his hand toward Selby's, gripping tightly at her fingers. But not pushing anything, not showing her anything, just... waiting. Offering.

So after a careful breath, Selby nudged her awareness

forward, slowly seeking into his thoughts. This was still something they were cautious about, something that had the potential to be truly dangerous, or deeply violating—but she knew Regin trusted her, and she wanted to honour that trust. To only gently follow that twinge, that whisper, that hidden truth of whatever he was struggling to say.

And the first vision she found was—his father. Regin's blond, barrel-chested father, looking so impossibly large, and—laughing. Laughing as he tossed Regin's small, squealing body into the air—and then whooping aloud as Regin held himself there, keeping himself aloft in the wind, beaming gleefully down at his father's flushed smiling face.

And then—his father teaching Regin how to make fire, how to stoke it with only the air from his hand. His father holding Regin tight in a storm he couldn't stop. His father showing Regin how to hunt, how to set up camp, how to predict tomorrow's weather from the sky, and heartily chuckling when Regin would change it, just to be contrary, just to make him laugh.

But then, in a dizzying jolt—Ketill. Always there when Regin needed him, yes, always waiting with food, help, answers—but also always discontented, disapproving, demanding more. *Again, Regin, again. Cleaner this time. Stronger. Watch your temper, watch your control. Yes, you need to read the book, you need to take care, you need to be responsible for once. I hope to gods you don't ever have children of your own, Regin.*

And breaking into that last bit, bright and vivid, the image of Selby's own face, frowning down at Regin in his bed at Coven Manor, and looking supremely irritated, her bottom lip jutting out. *Oh bullshit. You'd be a passable father, there's loads worse.*

And how those words had... echoed, in Regin's thoughts that day. How they'd lingered, festered, in the days and weeks afterwards. How they'd turned into something—something almost like longing. *Well, I wouldn't stop you from having kids,* he'd told Selby, that night they'd fought in the forest. *If that's what you wanted.*

And now—now it occurred to Selby, for the very first time, that Regin *had* wanted that. He'd wanted her to want it, and thereby to take the decision, the guilt, the potential waiting catastrophe, out of his hands. *I hope to gods you don't ever have children of your own, Regin.*

Selby swallowed hard, carefully drew backwards out of Regin's thoughts, felt those painful memories, those miserable longings, folding away safely behind her. Until it was only Regin's uncertainty, Regin's bitterness and guilt, pulsing through his fingers into hers.

"Look, you don't have to," he said now, in a rush. "I mean that, Selby. You've already given me enough, more than enough, and you don't deserve to put yourself at risk again, or give up what *you* want at the altar of Regin fucking Agmund. Especially if I might just fuck it up anyway, dragging an innocent kid into my shit—"

Oh gods, oh curse Ketill for this, and Selby whipped her head back and forth, squeezed Regin's hand as tightly as she could. "No, Regin, *stop*," she choked. "You're finished listening to Ketill's rubbish, remember? He probably just wanted to scare you off the idea of a family, so he wouldn't ever risk losing you to them! Of *course* you'll be a good father, and of course you should have kids if you want them!"

Regin blinked at her, his brow deeply furrowing. "But—" he began, and then hesitated, drew in breath. "But—do *you* want them, though? I mean, I know how much you like what we're doing now, I love it too, I love doing something important, making a difference. And I don't want to give it up, but—"

His voice broke, and the misery pulsed through his fingers, glinted in his eyes. Enough that Selby had to drag in a long breath, sift through her own whirling thoughts. Total honesty.

"I—I do love what we're doing," she said slowly. "And I'd love to keep doing it too, as much as we can. But"—she let him see the bare hopeful truth in her words, in her touch—"that doesn't mean we can't have kids, does it? I mean, both of us travelled all throughout our childhoods, why would this need to be any different? And you're right, having a regular place nearer to Ma to stay for a while afterwards, or whenever we needed to, that would make it—easier, wouldn't it?"

Regin stared back at her for a long, frozen moment, as something like disbelief flashed across his thoughts. "You—you would actually *want* to?" he asked, too sharp. "But you—you've never—said. Or even thought it to me. *Never*."

Selby grimaced, shook her head, because—no. She hadn't. Because she'd never forgotten Regin's memories of those women who'd almost had his children, and the sheer raw bitterness of his rage toward them. And at the time, she'd thought—she hadn't realized—

"It's just—you were so angry about those times it almost happened," she whispered, to his unblinking eyes. "I thought it was because you—didn't want it. I didn't realize it was because—you *did*."

Regin's throat convulsed, his shoulder jerking a shrug, and curse it, the more Selby looked at him, felt him, the more it occurred to her that she'd avoided this, too. She'd kept steering clear of his thoughts and memories of it, all of them tainted with such bitterness, such sadness. Maybe because she hadn't wanted to hear him say—*no*.

"All right, well, this is obviously a much-needed lesson," Selby finally said, her voice not quite steady, "that we still need to talk about these things! Out loud! Leave it to you to be secretly wanting *kids* all your life, asshole, and not even *trying* to tell me about it!"

Regin's mouth twitched, huffed a sound almost like a laugh. "I *am* trying to tell you, wench," he replied, husky. "And it's not that I've wanted them all my life. Just want them—now. With someone I know I can trust. With—*you*."

With you. It swooped in Selby's belly, choking in her throat, prickling behind her eyes. And before she could stop it, she hurled herself forward into him, clamping her arms tightly around his waist. "Me, too," she choked, into his chest. "With you."

Regin's arms folded around her too, drawing her closer, as his shaky exhale shuddered his chest against her. And it took an instant to realize that he was—*weeping*, his breath gasping like that into her hair, his thoughts wrenching again and again with a deep, juddering relief.

Selby kept clutching him tight, the water squeezing from her own eyes onto his tunic, until she could feel his twitching discomfort, his whispering shame. But she quietly guided it away, replaced it with those familiar visions of exploding trees, even stronger now that she'd so often seen them firsthand.

Regin seemed to willingly welcome it, sinking heavier into it, until he was pressing his own tree-exploding memories back, his visions twining and tangling with hers. And then somehow it became a competition, each of them shoving louder and louder explosions at each other, until they were both laughing too hard to continue, and Regin finally drew back from her, surreptitiously wiping his arm at his eyes.

"Vicious little wench," he murmured, though his smile was so warm, almost painfully fond. "You do realize any kids of ours are going to be holy terrors, right?"

Selby laughed again, a little shaky this time, and tried for a shrug. "It'll be fun," she said lightly. "An adventure. Right?"

Regin blinked, but then his grin pulled even higher, his eyes shimmering with gratitude, with appreciation. Seeing her, knowing her, understanding her. The great Regin Agmund, her lover, her partner, her best friend. Hers.

"Right as always, my brilliant little witch," he replied, clasping his hand in hers, drawing her toward the trees. "It'll be an adventure."

BONUS EPILOGUE

Regin Agmund's magic was, apparently, fucked.

"It's not hard, Daddy," four-year-old Eldry informed him, wrinkling her little brown nose. "You only reach"—she thrust out her chubby arm toward the pinecone—"and *squish!*"

The pinecone snapped, crumpled itself together into a small, perfect little ball, hovering in midair. While Eldry beamed at Regin, and then opened her fingers, allowing her pinecone-ball to fall and splinter, scattering in dusty pieces to the mossy ground beneath it. "Easy! See?"

Regin laughed and shook his head, and forced his concentration back to his own floating pinecone. Reach, hold it, feel it, find the air around it, and...

"Squish!" Eldry ordered, and Regin obeyed, snapping the air tight—but the pinecone only splattered apart, pelting them both in the face, and smelling distinctly of something burning.

"Not like that!" Eldry protested, with a disapproving pout toward Regin. "Why do you always burn?"

Regin laughed again, sitting back on his heels beside her, and tossing off a quick wind-spell to sweep the pinecone bits out of her dark wavy hair. "Can't do it, kiddo," he said wryly.

"You'd think I'd be able to handle a little squish, right? Supposed to be the best air-mage in the world, you know."

Eldry rolled her eyes at him with her typical derision, and then patted him on the head before wandering off to collect more pinecones. While Regin sat there smiling, watching her, feeling something swoop and sway in his chest.

Gods, parenting was fucked. And it had been fucked ever since that very first night it began, when Selby had snapped upright in their tent, gripping painfully at Regin's arm. Firing his sleep-drunk thoughts full of panic, and excitement, and—this. This life, this tiny impossible human, their *daughter*, sparking alive inside her.

They'd often talked and guessed how being pregnant might feel for Selby, sure—but that fateful night, Regin had instantly discovered that he hadn't been slightly prepared for the surreal, shocking truth of it. They'd made this child, it was alive, it was theirs, *theirs*. And in Selby's sweeping scattering thoughts, Regin had seen—he'd felt—just how much *theirs* it was. How it already felt so familiar to Selby, so right, like something she desperately needed to protect and nurture and cherish.

Regin had felt it too, and they'd sat up together all that night, just holding each other, feeling it together, marvelling at it. And it had become a constant refrain for him in the weeks and months after, just touching Selby throughout the day, seeking that loop, that sight, that certainty of their new life inside her. Their daughter.

Selby had known it was a girl very early on, but the rest of it had taken longer, had gradually revealed itself with Eldry's slowly growing brain, her small waking thoughts. And Regin would never forget that bright morning in the forest when Selby had yelped mid-step, and groped at the nearest tree for balance. "Air-magic?!" she'd demanded, down at her belly. "Really?"

Regin had startled and stared, staggered over to feel it—and then he'd laughed, too loud and giddy, grinning too wide at Selby's disgruntled but rueful face. His daughter was trying to cast air-magic, her tiny but stubborn attention fully focused on Selby's lungs, trying to catch the air, to keep it close.

Of course, her teeny baby efforts were far too weak for Selby to even feel, but it was there, his daughter was an air-mage, she was, she *was*. And while Regin had tried not to gloat too much, he'd felt a bizarre, exuberant joy at the truth of it, at the impossible awareness that not only had he made a daughter, but he'd given her his magic, his power, his calling. An *air-mage*.

And maybe it had meant so much because of Regin's father, who'd carried a bit of air-magic, just like his own father and grandfather before him—and now Regin was passing that legacy on, carrying on his father's name, his gift. Or maybe, more selfishly, it was just because Regin could feel his daughter's magic, could feel her casting, and it just felt so damned familiar. So instinctive. So much... like his.

It had been an inexplicable comfort, and it had helped to carry Regin through those last awful few months of Selby's pregnancy. When their daughter's voice had become so strong Selby felt frantic with it, fighting and failing to keep the constant stream of invading thoughts out of her head. By the end of it, Selby hadn't been able to sleep or fuck when Eldry was awake, and she'd sometimes even started speaking aloud what Eldry was saying, what Eldry kept silently shouting at her. Until Runar—who'd attended Selby all through her pregnancy—had finally made the call to induce Eldry early, for the sake of Selby's mental wellbeing. And while Eldry's birth had been its own horrifying level of hell, easily rivalling Regin's worst experiences in battles and in death, afterwards Selby had finally been free again—and their secret speaking daughter had miraculously emerged into her own small, self-contained form. With Selby's brown skin and eyes and hair, and yes—still—Regin's magic.

They'd named her Eldry Agmund, Eldry because Regin

had wanted to give her a name like her mother's, and Agmund because of the way Selby's thoughts had stuttered when they'd first spoken of it. When she'd silently said, far too casually, *Well, if we were married, that would be her name anyway, wouldn't it?*

The family-taking-the-father's-name thing was a stupid government rule, a thing that was pushed on women and kids after conventional marriage, a thing Regin hadn't once thought Selby would actually care about. But as he'd stared at his brilliant, still-bleeding girl, who'd just birthed him a beautiful daughter, and willingly borne all the pain and misery that had come with that—it had felt like she'd stabbed him straight in the chest.

"You don't—want my name, love," he'd croaked at her, fighting not to let her see the truth of his shock, his disbelief. "I mean, it's fucking *Agmund*—right?"

Selby had grimaced, twitched a shrug, fixed her blinking eyes on their perfect nursing daughter, and far too late, Agmund's horrified brain had realized that this had been something else they should have actually talked about. Out fucking loud. He'd thought it was settled, he'd given Selby a ring, they'd agreed to have a family, they'd made a whole *life* together. And she hated the government and registrations and stupid fucking rules that made no sense—right?

But his poor weakened girl had been too damned exhausted to hide it, her thoughts wavering, as a betraying drop of water had streaked down her cheek. And Regin had desperately clutched her hand, hurled her full of all the furious truth of his affection, and his regret.

"Marry me, Selby," he'd gasped. "Let me make you my wife. Please."

Selby had startled, choked, stared at him with huge, brimming brown eyes, while across the room Runar had loudly snorted, giving Regin a much-needed release for his pent-up rawness. "Oh, fuck off, you smug necromancing *snake*," he'd snarled, spinning around, crackling a bit of threatening air around Runar's head for good measure. "I'd have asked her ages ago if I'd known she wanted it!"

But Runar had only snorted again, and maybe Regin even deserved it, because yeah, he should have damn well known she'd wanted it—right? But Selby had already been touching back at him, pressing him her own fervent regret, her own rising uneasy awareness throughout her pregnancy that she'd just wanted—more.

"I didn't even think about it, when we first got together," she'd told him, out loud, the truth glimmering in her eyes and her touch. "But you've just been—so good, in all this. So generous, and supportive, with me throughout every minute of it, and I shouldn't be suddenly wanting even more from you, Regin, I—"

But Regin had shushed her with an urgent kiss, with more blaring truth from his hands. She was his, his girl, the perfect mother of his perfect daughter, and fuck yes, he was going to marry her, she was going to carry his name, and be Selby fucking Agmund, if she could really bear it, gods damn it.

But Selby had laughed, light and easy like he hadn't heard from her in months, as she'd hurled back *yes, yes, yes*. So later that summer, once they'd all recovered a bit, they'd had a lovely little wedding under the sky, with all their friends and Selby's family. And when they'd kissed the lightning had crashed all around them, and made the entire audience gasp and shout, while Regin and Selby had grinned at each other.

Selby Agmund had still taken some getting used to, afterwards, but a selfish, possessive part of Regin could admit he quite liked it, and would be extremely displeased if it ever changed. And maybe to soften the blow, or just return the favour, he'd sometimes started giving his name as *Regin Seng*, especially on jobs, and with strangers, and at questionable establishments. And it had turned out to be pretty damned useful having a second name, too—a way to get more of his anonymity back, and also a way to get Selby to give him that speaking little smile of hers whenever she heard him use it.

It usually led to more fucking—as so many things still did—though if Regin had one complaint about parenthood, and the past four years, it was the impact it had had on his preferred fucking schedule. He still wanted it at least every day, and he knew Selby still did too, thank fuck—but Eldry had always been a shit sleeper, and was likely to pop up nearby whenever they least wanted her. And Selby's sleep had been shit lately too, and Regin had taken Eldry out hunting this morning just so Selby could get some rest—though he'd had to fight the temptation to trap Eldry in a sensory-blocking air-bubble instead, so he could gently fuck his exhausted wife to sleep.

But even despite that, Regin still wouldn't trade it. Would never give this up. Eldry had been such a gift, such a revelation, and even at four years old she already seemed to instinctively understand him, and his magic, in a way that only Selby ever had. But even Selby would laugh and wryly shake her head as Regin and Eldry jabbered and argued with each other over it, using their own terms and explanations that were incomprehensible to anyone else. Not just the squishing, but the *skeeting*, and the *squattering*, and the *steeving*, and so many more—and it had challenged Regin's magic in ways he'd never even considered before. In ways that sometimes left him entirely defeated, and fully convinced that his own magic was fucked.

It's your fault, love, he'd irritably complained at Selby, more than once. *She's got the earth-magic in there somehow, just enough to make it fucking impossible.*

But Selby would just grin at him, let him see that familiar glint in her eyes. *What, can't handle a challenge, asshole?* she'd purr back at him. *Are you really telling me the world's greatest air-mage can't keep up with a four-year-old?*

It had always spurred Regin on more, kept him fighting to keep up, to do better, to learn more. But today—he sighed as he watched his brilliant little daughter wandering around the clearing, adding more and more pinecones to the floating mass of them now bobbing behind her—today, his magic just wasn't good enough. Maybe because of how tired they all were, or how damn much he missed his wife in his arms and on his cock, but—

"Squeaker!" Eldry exclaimed, whirling around toward the house, letting all her pinecones fall at once. "What do you want?"

Regin had only now felt it, too, and he half-laughed, half-groaned as he turned to where their shaggy sheepdog—named Squeaker, by you-know-who—was barrelling across the clearing toward them, his long pink tongue lolling out, his gleeful brown eyes fixed on Regin's face. And Regin belatedly braced himself for the inevitable impact of paws and fur and slobber, fending off Squeaker's wriggling, yelping body with firm pets and slaps of his hands.

"Yeah, yeah, I see you, buddy," he said, but he was chuckling again, more warmth bubbling inside his chest. He'd never once imagined having a dog as part of his life, or his family—or at least, so he'd thought. But Selby had somehow plucked something out at some point, maybe that memory of him watching a soldier playing with a puppy—and then, for his birthday a few years back, he'd come home and found this. This excitable, insatiable bundle of frantic doggy energy, all too eager to accompany them on the road, to help Regin hunt and track, and to keep an eye on his girls when he couldn't. And just like his girls, his dog didn't give a shit if he was Regin fucking Agmund, and only wanted his treats and attention and praise.

So Regin showered Squeaker with pets and enthusiasm, and then instructed him to go greet Eldry without knocking her over—something they were still working on—before frowning in the direction of the house. He'd left Squeaker with

Selby on purpose, so this meant either something was going on, or she wanted him back.

"C'mon, you two," he said, striding over to sweep Eldry up onto his hip, and waving Squeaker forward. "Mama needs us, all right?"

Thankfully, it didn't take long to reach the grounds of their little stone house, at the end of the familiar path. The house was a warm, cozy, solid place, and Fasta and Henrik had come out to help build it, letting Selby personally choose every last piece of wood and stone. Afterwards they'd helped Selby with furnishings and decorations, too, and Henrik had custom-built gods knew how many shelves, chests, and display cases for Selby's favourite things. And once it had all been done, Selby had clasped both hands to her chest, and told them all, with tears streaking down her face, that it was the most wondrous place she'd ever felt in all her life.

After that, Regin—who'd mostly tried to stay out of the proceedings—had also demanded that they build a huge solid wall around it, one that would naturally support his own air-shields. And now—he grimaced and walked faster—his wall-fortified shield was now keeping out three new guests, standing together with Selby outside it. Runar and Thora, and their small, serious, dark-haired son Kian.

And damn it, Regin should have felt this, should have at least felt Selby and Squeaker passing out through his shield, and he instantly dropped the shield, raised his hand in a rueful wave toward their guests. "Hey, all," he said. "Sorry. You can get in now."

Runar loudly huffed, rolling his eyes, but Thora gave Regin her usual patient, understanding smile. "No, we're the ones who stopped by uninvited," she replied. "We just thought maybe you could use a break today. And a check-up, too."

Thora's future-seeing would never cease to be uncanny, even when it was in their favour—but today, Regin was too damned relieved to care. "That's really good of you, thanks," he said, and he meant it. "And Eldry will love having the company too, right, kiddo?"

Eldry was currently half-hiding behind Regin, and eyeing Kian with uncharacteristic shyness, but Regin knew it would be a matter of minutes before they were running around shrieking, and he gave a reassuring pat to her head before striding straight for Selby. Who was still looking way too damned tired, and Regin hooked his arm around her, drew her close, slipped his hand down against her belly. Against... their son.

And gods, why they'd done this again, Regin couldn't fathom. Why they'd willingly waded into yet another pregnancy, with this constant drain on his wife's body and mind, a drain that already seemed so much worse this time. Even as their son—their *son*—still felt somehow softer, gentler, not nearly as stubborn and fierce as Eldry had. And Regin already loved their boy so much it hurt, couldn't stop seeking that awareness of him, growing and swimming in Selby's belly. Even as he still hated how tired this was making her, and how desperate she was to pretend it didn't matter, because she needed their sweet tiny boy so much, too. He was theirs. *Theirs*.

Regin only vaguely heard Runar huffing again, and now there was a pointed nudge of magic at his shoulder. "Why don't you two go in, and do your... thing," Runar snapped. "We'll wait out here, and watch the kids, and then we'll talk after. All right?"

Gods, yes, and Regin didn't even hesitate, just jerked a nod, and dragged Selby off toward the house. Leaving her to handle the social niceties, calling back a laughing thank-you over her shoulder, and imploring Eldry to try to be good, while Regin hauled her inside, threw up his sound-spell, and slammed the door shut.

"Fucking *finally*," he growled, spinning toward his girl, grabbing at her plump little ass, burying his face in her neck. "Gods, wife, how do we *live* like this."

Selby was already gasping, half-laughing, but clinging back at him, too. Grabbing his own ass, his back, his chest, his dick. And fuck, she was so good, such a brilliant perfect girl, shoving down his trousers like that, brazenly pulling him out, taking him in hand. Pumping him with deft, certain strokes, swelling him up to full and instant hardness, scattering out furious flares of pleasure with every breath. While her own hunger flooded back into him, shuddering with how much she wanted this, how much she'd missed him, how she fully believed he had the world's fattest, most gorgeous, most obliging cock—

"Fuuuck, yes, I do," he groaned, tilting his head back, bucking into her hand. And not hiding any of his own streaming thoughts in return, how damned good she felt, how much he'd been craving her, how much he needed to feel her, how unbelievably shitty his magic had felt all fucking morning—

But wait, wait, she'd caught that, damn him—and that was hesitation, *guilt*, skidding through her pleasure. And Regin winced, balked, shook his head, shoved back more of his own thoughts, too fast. *It's fine, love, I don't care, don't you dare feel guilty, you're growing our fucking son.*

But that was his stubborn little wench, shoving right back at him, pouting up into his face, squeezing his cock just a little too tight. *And don't you dare hide these things from me, Regin*, she shot back. *I'm an adult, I'm your wife, I want to know. I want you to feel good. I want to take care of you, just like you take care of me.*

Regin's dismissal rose on its own—that was his job, Selby was his wife—but again she was there, here, slapping it away. *None of that martyr rubbish with me*, Regin, she snapped. *We're in this together. We're a team. A family. So you're going to suck it up, and fuck my mouth like you mean it. Just like you damn well want to.*

Oh, gods, she didn't mean that, but yes she did, yes his vicious pregnant firecracker was going to fall on her knees for him, right here in the middle of their damned kitchen. And she was going to look at him like that, plead with him with big brown eyes, as she tilted her head back, and opened up her plump, perfect little mouth. Waiting for him to fill it, to fuck it, *yes*.

"Fine, you stubborn little cocktease," Regin gasped, groping his tingling hands at her hair, even as his fingers still skittered, saying, *are you sure, are you sure*. "You really think your pretty little mouth can handle getting pounded by this dick right now?"

But fuck, Selby's own hunger was already surging back, her eyes damnably greedy on his bobbing, aching cock—so Regin fought for control, fought for breath, as he shifted forward, let his leaking cockhead nudge and prod at her lips. At where she instantly kissed and sucked him, such a good little wife, *fuck*.

"Well, I suppose you can fucking try, wench," Regin breathed, prodding in deeper, shuddering even fuller as she opened, deepened the suction. "You can try to handle this stretching you out, shutting you up. Fucking your tight little throat until you *choke* on it."

As always, he kept his hands on her, kept some distant part of his thoughts focused on her mental responses to this, on whether he was ever taking it too far—but it was only her sheer furious hunger, feeding straight back into it, *give me more, Regin, more*.

"Yeah, you keep begging me, wench," he growled, as he shoved himself in deeper, harder, felt the bliss blast and burn, *fuck*. "You keep begging me for this cock. Beg me to use you, to make a mess of you, to let you suck out its spunk—"

Please, Regin, Selby silently gasped back, as she moaned around him, her lips and tongue consuming him, sucking so hard at him, gouging him into her throat. *Please, Regin, use me, make a mess of me, let me have your spunk, please—*

Regin didn't even see it coming, and he shouted aloud as he bent double, as his captured straining cock locked, sprayed, obeyed. Surging out wild and helpless and desperate into his begging wife's hot waiting mouth, and bless her, she was still sucking, still stroking, her hands clamping his arse, drawing him closer. Until she did actually choke on him, gods damn it, and Regin hissed as he drew back, eased off, let her suck out the rest, swallowing it all down like a good little wench, fuck.

She took it slow releasing him, running her tongue over his too-sensitive head, finding every last drop, before letting him fall from between her sweet plump lips. And gods, he was still half-hard, and a dark, selfish part of him thrust his cock back at her again, watching it kissing and smearing at her lips, until he'd swelled back to full hardness again.

"You're not getting off that easy, witch," Regin breathed now, low and hot in his throat. "You're gonna be a good little wife, and offer up another tight little hole to your husband, aren't you?"

Selby's moan wasn't even slightly feigned, shuddering through her breath and her thoughts—*please, Regin, please*—and he couldn't catch it, couldn't stop it, could only grab at her, yank her up, prop her on a bubble of air, so he could unbutton her dress with his greedy shaking fingers, and hurl the fabric away. Exposing his girl's smooth brown curves for his sight-starved eyes, drinking up her full breasts, her slightly swelled belly, her thick thighs, with that cunt hiding between...

"Open up, wife," he hissed, bending down to suck at one peaked brown nipple, and then the other. "Show me what's on offer."

Selby instantly obeyed, shamelessly spreading wide, and oh, Regin liked that, loved that, loved that he could feast on her with his eyes, could trace his hand against her, could coolly slide his fingers up into her tight, clenching heat, feel her gasp and squirm. Because yeah, this cunt was always and forever his, he was going to do whatever the fuck he wanted with it, and right now that meant jamming it full of cock, fucking it full of him until she screamed.

He wasn't even saying it aloud, now, the craving

screeching swallowing his breath, but Selby could still hear every word of it, was still moaning and gasping and silently begging him for it. And he should have dragged it out more, but fuck, her cunt was already wide open and dripping wet for him, and he needed to fill it, needed to fuck it. Needed to settle his cockhead just into those waiting kissing lips, and then watch, breathless, as he breached them, spread them apart, impaled that slick softness full and deep on his rock-hard cock.

"That's it, wench," he gasped, his eyes fluttering on the sight, as that hot sweet tightness swallowed him, consumed him, ravaged him whole. "You take this good dick like a good little wife. You suck it all the way in, swallow it whole, beg it to pound you, to fucking *own* you—"

Selby was nodding, shuddering all over, hurling her sharp screaming craving through her clinging scraping fingers on his back. "Please, Regin," she gasped. "Please, give it to me. Please, fill your wife with your cock, please pound me, own me, be with me, take care of me like this, *please*."

Regin groaned and nodded, hissing as he plunged all the way, buried himself deep—but amidst the sheer shattering need, his shaking body and trembling hands, his thoughts had again—caught. Held. *Be with me. Take care of me like this.*

As if—oh. As if this wasn't just about—about what he wanted. Wasn't just about Selby pleasing him, giving him what she knew he liked best. No, she wanted it too, she needed it too, and Regin damn well knew that, didn't he? But maybe—maybe some shameful, stupid little part of him still didn't fully believe it. Of course Regin Agmund's weak pregnant wife didn't want him spewing selfish shit and demanding she please him, but she was, she needed it, needed him—

"Yeah, I'll take care of you, wife," he breathed now, hoarse, but he was, he was holding her desperate eyes as he slowly eased out, and then sank back in, smooth and deep. "I'm gonna fuck this little cunt so hard, gonna pound it until you're screaming for me. Gonna remind you who you fucking *belong* to, witch."

Selby gasped, nodded, clung to him, streamed him full of *yes* and *please* and *more*, and Regin's hands were stroking her now, drinking up the feel of her, trembling at the loop of how good it felt for her too, his hands so warm and strong and reassuring across her shivering skin.

"Good, wife," he rasped, as he kept driving in, touching her, pressing back his own hunger, his own longing. "Look at you, being so good, taking your husband's cock like the perfect little wife you are—"

And yes, the way his wife moaned, the way she felt, squeezing and shuddering like this on his dick, please, fuck, more—

When something—knocked. At the kitchen door. It was Runar, gods damn it, and Regin loudly cursed as he cast his scattering thoughts outward. And found Eldry and Kian running around safely in the yard with Squeaker, so what the fuck—

"What," he gritted out, over his shoulder, even as he kept going, swiping Selby's awareness of Runar away. *You let me deal with this, wife, you only think about me when I'm fucking you.*

But damn Runar, the bastard actually opened the kitchen door, and stepped inside. And while it wasn't the first time Runar had seen this, it was probably the most obscene, what with Selby lying buck-naked and spread-eagled in midair, her full breasts blatantly bouncing with every ongoing slam of Regin's driving cock, even as her unease and alarm studded through her thoughts, her gaze darting to Runar's wide-eyed face.

No, wife. Regin shot back, because he was not letting fucking Runar ruin this, not when he was finally taking care of his girl, just the way she needed. *Forget him,* he ordered her. *You look at me. You worry about being good for me, and taking my dick like I told you.*

"What, asshole," Regin snapped at Runar, as he maybe made more of a show than necessary of palming his wife's full bouncing breasts, while his slick cock kept pumping in and out of her tight wet cunt. "We're busy, so get the fuck on with it."

Runar twitched, wrinkled his nose, shook his head. "To start, Eldry and Kian somehow made up a spell that unlocked your root cellar," he said, "and they've already eaten a whole jar of jelly between them, and now they're throwing all your carrots at each other. And also—"

Regin cut him off with a sharp growl, though he didn't let up on his rhythm, on his caressing of his wife's perfect breasts. "You think I give a shit?" he demanded toward Runar. "You said you'd watch them, didn't you? You can come whinge at me when they start throwing knives."

Runar huffed, but still wasn't actually leaving, so Regin took the opportunity to slowly draw himself out, hissing as his slick straining cock bobbed free of his wife's hot cunt—and then he tilted her thighs up, slipping himself down lower. Yeah, she was just as slippery there as he'd hoped, such a good little wife, getting so wet for him like this, opening up her tight little ass for him like this. And he let Selby see the strength of his approval, his satisfaction, as he gave an experimental little nudge in, felt for any discomfort or reluctance—but yes, yes, she wanted it as much as he did, wanted him using all her holes, just as she should.

"Good, wife," he breathed, as he slowly, carefully eased forward, into that sweet, sweet ring of heat. "Look how good you are, opening your tight little ass so wide for your husband's fat cock—"

He was jolted back again by Runar's snort at the door, and this time Regin full-on spun and snarled at him, and flashed down a menacing little bolt of lightning onto the floor beside him. "Did I say you could watch?" he demanded. "Out, asshole!"

Runar finally rolled his eyes and went, thank fuck, and

Regin snapped his full attention back to his perfect little wife, who was half-smiling up toward him, as yet more craving jolted through her fingers. So Regin smiled back, silently told her how beautiful she was, how tight, how perfect, as he buried himself deep inside her hot, spasming hole.

"So good, wife," he breathed, out loud, as his hips finally met skin, his cock shoved as deep as it could go. "Look how pretty you are, with your husband's cock all the way up your ass. So proud of you for being so good for me. Being so brave for me."

Selby gasped, shook her head, the sheer staggering craving again catching, too tight and too close, but Regin was here, he was touching her, one hand now sliding fingers up into her slick empty cunt, the other one cradling at her hot, sweaty face. "So good, Selby Agmund," he whispered, holding her eyes as he touched her, caressed her, fucked her, felt her fear and her longing and her truth all rising to him, meeting him, showing him everything she'd maybe still tried to hide, too. How she still wanted more, felt guilty that she wanted more, Regin couldn't actually still want all this, he couldn't, not now...

But Regin laughed, low and fond as he shook his head, as he curled her up to kiss her, now fucking her with his fingers his cock his tongue. "Nice try, wife," he drawled at her. "But I'm right here with you on this, all right? And you're not getting the fuck away from me, not ever. So now you're gonna suck it up, and take me however the hell I want, and fucking *thank* me for it, like a good little wife should. *Now*."

Selby's laughing relief choked into the longing, her affection shuddering so strong he almost couldn't withstand it, but then, oh, she was nodding. Nodding. "Gods, yes, Regin," she gasped, her eyes glimmering on his face. "Thank you, Regin. Thank you for taking me, for being here for me, taking such good care of me—"

And hell yes, this was it, Regin caught in it now too, hitching himself into her, fingers plunging and stroking, his teeth and tongue scraping at her straining throat. *Keep talking*, he ordered, through his hands. *Keep begging me, wife, thanking me, wanting me, needing me—*

"Please, Regin," she gulped, and he was full-on rutting now, maybe slamming too hard, but he didn't care, she didn't care. "Please, keep fucking me, Regin. Keep filling me, keep taking care of me, keep being here for me. I want you so much I need you so much I can't stand it without you, you're mine, mine, *please—*"

It was like she was wringing him out, pumping him tighter with every perfect word—and Regin almost crumpled as he shot out into her, blowing out as hard as he ever had in his life, his relief shouting out his mouth, skidding through his fingers. And fuck, Selby was catching it, flashing it back, drowning in it, her full consciousness dipping away for a breath as the ecstasy trampled through her, convulsing her again and again on his fingers and his spraying spasming cock.

Regin held her through it, kissed her again and again, until he felt her awareness slipping back again, curling quiet and close up against him. Whispering of such deep, shaky contentment, such soft sprawling gratitude, and oh, gods, she was even weeping, wetness streaking down her flushed cheeks.

"Shhh, love," Regin murmured, easing himself out of her so he could better kiss it away, so he could lie down beside her on his air-bubble, fold her close into his arms. "It's all good. You're so good. Such a good brave wife, Selby Agmund."

She shuddered and curled tighter against him, her thoughts still so close, so raw. Still showing, so strong, how much she'd missed him, how she'd been trying so desperately to push through it too, to ignore the exhaustion and the slowly creeping loneliness, to not break down or beg.

"Fuck, love," Regin murmured, stroking her again and again, fighting back his own rising guilt, because she didn't want his guilt either, he wanted to be here, wanted to offer what she needed. "We're going to learn from this, and work out a plan to get through it, and get the time together we need, all right? Even if I need to start locking Eldry in that air-bubble after all."

Selby choked a laugh, shook her head. "She'll just—escape," she replied, her voice too hoarse. "Pop up in our damned bedroom."

Regin's own chuckle scraped out his throat, because yeah, Selby wasn't wrong, damn it. "Right," he said. "Well, then, we'll—"

But then, gods curse it, another knock at the door. And even as Regin groaned, and pulled back to cast a highly impenetrable air-shield, Runar had already stalked inside, and yanked over a chair. "You can blame Thora for this," he snapped, without preamble. "But what I was *trying* to say earlier, was that we have a proposal that might help. Thora's been wanting to get out of the city, and I've been wanting a quiet place to work on a few things. So we'll build a little place near here, and stay until your son is born. I'll keep an eye on Selby's pregnancy, and we can trade off on the kid-watching."

What? Regin's mouth dropped open, but he couldn't deny that sharp, quivering flare of hope, flaring from his fingers into Selby. And oh, she was flaring back at him, speaking briefly of genuine longing—and then all the reasons why it wouldn't work, or it wasn't fair. Wasn't fair to trap Runar and Thora here, when they could be travelling, when Selby and Regin would rather be travelling, but it was just too tiring with the pregnancy like this, too tiring to even follow Selby's ma in the shop wagon. But Selby's ma would come babysit again soon, she always made time every fortnight, and...

"You're sure you'd really want to?" Regin demanded at Runar, too sharp. "Wouldn't you rather be out doing something interesting, rather than being stuck here for months on end?"

But Runar rolled his eyes, as if he thought Regin was even more dense than usual. "Not everyone feels the perpetual need to be gallivanting all over the country like you two," he snapped. "We *like* staying put, so we can focus on our work. And this place... isn't bad."

He'd given an irritated wave around them, meaning maybe the house, or the land—and damn right they weren't bad, Regin had bought leagues of this old-growth eastern forest, and it had plenty of room for roaming, spellcasting, and game hunting. And their perfect little walled house was also perfectly placed within the woods, not too far from the nearest town, but still too far for any stray autograph-seekers or Coven representatives to show up. But...

"Look, Runar, you know you don't owe us anything, right?" Regin said, quieter, searching his eyes. "If that's what this is about?"

He was referring to the fact that he was personally bankrolling most of Runar's research these days, on the loudly stated understanding that it was in his own self-interest. Runar's knowledge and research had helped them on multiple projects now—a few of which they were still working on from here—and Runar and Thora had helped Regin develop some useful new air-spells, too. But maybe most important of all, Runar's healing skills had been a true godsend during Selby's last pregnancy, and Regin was therefore highly reluctant to let him go.

"Of course I don't owe you anything," Runar retorted. "I've given you five times your money's worth, asshole. But this will be good for us, and for Kian, and for all of you. And you know Thora wouldn't advise it without being convinced of that first, so I suggest you stop complaining and say yes, and then cover up, and go fucking *thank* her."

Well. Regin couldn't quite choke back the strange sound from his throat, and beside him Selby was full-on shivering, and fervently nodding. "We—we will," she gulped. "Thank you, Runar. Thank you both."

Runar waved it away and stood again, darting a narrow-eyed glance toward where Thora's blonde head had poked in the door to beam at them. "It's our pleasure," she said brightly. "And Fasta and Henrik will be here tomorrow to start working on our new house, too."

Regin huffed a laugh, shaking his head, feeling Selby instantly brightening beside him—because yeah, it had been a while since they'd seen Fasta and Henrik, and watching them build was always a good show. While Runar barked an irritated growl, and swept over toward Thora at the door, clapping his hand over her eyes. "I told you two to cover up, for fuck's sakes!" he snapped toward Regin and Selby. "We are not here for your tawdry little show! Now, or at any point in the future!"

Regin would usually have told Runar to fuck off, but he was suddenly in too good a mood to bother, grinning at Selby as he waved her discarded dress up through the air. And Selby was beaming back up at him, even as water streaked from the corners of her bright, blinking eyes.

Thora gave a polite cough at the doorway, pulling Runar out after her, and quietly closing the door behind them—which meant that Regin didn't need to bother covering up his girl after all. And instead he could kiss her, and wipe that wetness away from her eyes, and show her his own hope, his own relief. His own raw, devastating love for her, burned too deep to ever waver, no matter how tired or sex-deprived or low on magic they were, no matter what tried to come between them.

"I love you, Selby Agmund," he told her, out loud, maybe just to make her hear it, to see that look in her eyes. "And you really aren't ever getting away from me, you know."

His voice cracked a little, because in truth, it had probably gone well beyond normal or healthy at this point, how damned dependent he was. How he'd never be able to look twice at someone else, how he couldn't even imagine anymore what it was like to fuck without seeing each other's thoughts. And with someone else, how he'd never know, still never really, *really* know, how much it had to do with Regin fucking Agmund, rather than just... *him*.

But like always, his perfect wife saw it, and knew it, and just twined her arms around him, and kissed him back. Tasting of sweetness, and wonder, and hope. Of home.

Just you, Regin Agmund, she whispered. *Always, always, just you.*

∼

THE END

∼

THANKS FOR READING!

Thank you so much for joining me for Selby and Regin's story! I loved getting to explore how a downtrodden heroine and an arrogant celebrity might come together, and find a way to fall in love despite all their differences.

And if you're wondering what happened to Greta, I wrote a free story about that! She's been up to no good all this time, and she's about to get the correction she deserves... find out how in *The Mage's Groom*. It's free for subscribers on my mailing list at finleyfenn.com... I'd love to stay in touch with you!

And for even more Mages, the next book in this series is *The Mage's Master*. It tells the tale of how Fasta and Henrik make a dark, dangerous deal, in which Henrik becomes Fasta's master...

Finally, I'd love to hear your thoughts about this book! Come share your feedback on my Facebook group, Discord server, or Patreon (which also has some delicious artwork from this book!). You can find them all linked on my website at finleyfenn.com.

Thank you again for joining me on this adventure! Hugs!

ACKNOWLEDGMENTS

As always, I've been so grateful for all the readers and friends who have so generously shared their enthusiasm and support for this series. Thank you so much!

I also want to thank my generous beta readers who have offered me their thoughtful insights on this book: Anne-Marie, Ari, Jo Henny Wolf, Lauren Mauchley, and Mary Lynne Nielsen. And special thanks to my Right Hand Marykate, and my incredible author friends Lillian Lark and Lizzy Bequin.

I'm also forever grateful to my amazing Patreon supporters, my generous beta reading team, and my advance reviewers.

And of course, I need to thank my own magical partner, who has given so much fierce support to his obsessive writer wife. Thank you, my love.

ALSO BY FINLEY FENN

THE MAGE'S MASTER
The Mages: Book 2

She's determined to have her way with him. And he's going to make her pay...

Fasta Valgeirr always gets what she wants. She's rich, poised, and beautiful, and one of the top earth-mages in the realm.

But she can't have the one thing she wants most: Henrik Hallen. Her poor, working-class employee.

Henrik is big, burly, and commanding, crushing rocks and hurling boulders with dizzying power. And though Fasta's often caught his yearning glances toward her, he's always kept their relationship friendly. Respectful. Professional.

Until Henrik lands in deep trouble. And Fasta is waiting and ready to help, with one condition...

Henrik finally gives her what she wants. And in return, he can indulge his own forbidden fantasies, too...

But Henrik's longings are even darker than Fasta imagined. And he won't stand for a casual, throwaway affair with his spoiled, entitled boss.

Instead, he wants to put Fasta in her place in the dirt. Teach her who's really in charge. And give her a humbling she'll never forget...

Can Fasta bend the knee to her rough, dangerous new ruler, and learn her lesson? Or will she end up forever crushed?

ALSO BY FINLEY FENN

THE MAGE'S GROOM
The Mages: Bonus Story
with Email Signup

When a brilliant mage gives up and goes home, she finds her master waiting...

Greta Hendersson was supposed to do great things in life. Build a career, rack up accolades, make a perfect marriage.

But when her two-year relationship with the world's most famous air-mage blows up in her face, everything else falls apart, too. And all that's left is to go home...

To where her head groom has been patiently waiting. With a collar and whip in his hand...

FREE download!
www.finleyfenn.com

ALSO BY FINLEY FENN

THE MAGE'S MAID
The Mages: A Prequel

He's a perfect, upright lord. Except when he likes to kneel for his housemaid...

Mik Mastersson has it all together. He's handsome, titled, accomplished, and a top-tier air-mage—and now, all he needs is a proper lord's wife.

The only problem is, he can't keep his hands off his housemaid...

Miss Kay Courser has loved Mik for years, and revels in all the secret, filthy ways she can bring her lord to his knees.

But she knows she'll never be wife material—and when Mik makes that truth painfully, appallingly clear, Kay decides she's had enough. Enough of being a plaything, a toy, a convenient escape for a lord who doesn't really care.

Or does he? And when Mik comes home to find Kay gone, how far will he humble himself to bring his brilliant mistress back again?

ALSO BY FINLEY FENN

THE LADY AND THE ORC

He's the most feared monster in the realm. And she's what he needs to win his war...

In a world of warring orcs and men, Lady Norr is condemned to a childless marriage, a cruel lord husband, and a life of genteel poverty—until the day her home is ransacked by a horde. And leading the charge is their hulking, deadly orc captain: the infamous Grimarr.

And Grimarr has a wicked plan for Lady Norr, and for ending this war once and for all. She's going to become his captive—and the perfect snare for Lord Norr.

There's no possible escape, and soon Lady Norr is dragged off toward Orc Mountain in the powerful arms of her greatest enemy. A ruthless, commanding warlord, with a velvet voice and mouthwatering scent, who awakens every forbidden hunger she never knew she had...

But Grimarr refuses to accept half measures—in war, or in pleasure. And before he'll conquer Lady Norr's deepest, darkest desires, she needs to surrender *everything*.

Her allegiance.

Her wedding ring.

Her future...

And with her husband's forces giving chase, Lady Norr can't afford to play such a dangerous game—or can she? **Even if this deadly orc's plans might be the only way to save them all?**

ALSO BY FINLEY FENN

THE HEIRESS AND THE ORC

Once, he was her dearest friend... but now he's a monster.

In a world of recently warring orcs and men, Ella Riddell is determined to ignore it all. She's the wealthiest heiress in the realm—and soon, she's to wed a lord, and become a real lady.

Until the night her engagement-party ends in utter *disaster*, and Ella runs for the forest—**and straight into the powerful arms of a hulking, deadly orc.**

And it's not just any orc. It's *Natt*. The orc Ella made a secret, foolish pledge to, many years past...

He's huge and shameless and vicious, not at all the gangly, laughing daredevil Ella remembers. **And he's here with one shocking, scandalous aim: to wreak vengeance on Ella's betrothed. With *her*.**

With her hunger.

Her surrender.

Her undoing.

Ella knows she should run, even if this deadly enemy was once a friend. Even if his scent drags up a dark, forbidden longing. Even if his kisses are the sweetest, filthiest thing she's ever tasted in her life...

But will Ella truly risk her perfect future, for an orc? Will she face the bitter truths of the past, and brave the terrifying Orc Mountain, before more war rises to destroy them all?

ABOUT THE AUTHOR

Finley Fenn is "the queen of dark orc romance" (Virgo Reader), and her ongoing Orc Sworn series has been praised as "sexy, romantic, angsty, and captivating ... utter brilliance" (Romantically Inclined Reviews).

When she's not obsessing over her stories, Finley loves reading, drooling over delicious orc artwork, and spending time with her incredible readers on Patreon, Discord, and Facebook. She lives in Canada with her beloved family, including her very own grumpy, gorgeous orc husband.

For free bonus stories and epilogues, special offers, and exclusive Orc Sworn artwork, sign up at www.finleyfenn.com.

www.ingramcontent.com/pod-product-compliance
Lightning Source LLC
LaVergne TN
LVHW040035080526
838202LV00045B/3348